NO STONE UNTURNED

PAM LECKY

Storm

Ebook ISBN: 978-1-80508-693-2
Paperback ISBN: 978-1-80508-694-9

Cover design: Ghost
Cover images: Adobe Stock, Shutterstock

Published by Storm Publishing.
For further information, visit:
www.stormpublishing.co

ALSO BY PAM LECKY

The Lucy Lawrence Mysteries

Footprints in the Sand

The Art of Deception

Dedicated to my children,
Stephen, Hazel & Adam

PART 1

The Trouble with Charlie

ONE

St John's Wood, London, October 1886

Lucy Lawrence looked up from her book with a start. Something had struck the windowpane, shattering the silence of the room. For a moment she wondered if she had imagined it, but Horace, her ginger cat, was staring at the window, his eyes wide and his ears laid back.

'What is it, Horace?' Lucy asked. But the cat simply settled down with a yawn and resumed his nap. Lucy laughed. 'What a useful fellow you are!'

She went to the window, her curiosity too niggling to ignore. There was nothing obvious to account for the sound she'd heard but as she turned away, something caught her eye. A blackbird was hopping towards the undergrowth near the wall, one of its wings half-open and held awkwardly. The poor thing must have flown into the window. Wasn't there a superstition about that? For several minutes Lucy stood watching the bird's hiding place. Perhaps she should send her maid Mary out to see if the bird could be helped? But minutes later, to her relief, the bird emerged and flew up in to the bare branches of the cherry tree.

The afternoon was drawing in. To continue reading the lamps needed to be lit, but Lucy remained standing at the window. It wasn't just that the abandoned book no longer held any interest: the real problem was boredom. It was half past four on a cold, grey afternoon and another evening alone was all she had to look forward to. As Charlie's trips away had become more frequent, so too for Lucy had the melancholy contemplation of the four walls around her. After ten years of marriage perhaps this was how every couple ended up, but it wasn't what she had envisaged the day she agreed to elope.

She sighed and considered the mirror image of her own home across the road: highly respectable, pretentious and bland —much like its inhabitants, she thought with a wry smile. Despite her family connections, Lucy had been ostracised from the beginning, the ladies of Abbey Gardens making it clear what they thought of her elopement and the subsequent scandal for the house of Somerville. At first, she didn't care, too wrapped up in her own happiness and relief that she had escaped Yorkshire, but gradually the exclusion had its effect. And now it was magnified by being trapped in an increasingly lonely marital home.

It was all right for Charlie: he had his clubs and business interests and was rarely at home. One morning at breakfast, Lucy had broached the subject of her loneliness with him. He had suggested she do charity work. Wasn't that what most of the ladies did, Charlie said, before burying his nose in his newspaper. Now the highlights of her week were the days she spent visiting patients at the Royal Free on Gray's Inn Road. There, at least, the other ladies accepted her at face value and she had formed new friendships. But it wasn't enough. Other days she prowled the galleries and museums, eager for knowledge, desperate to find an interest. But at the end of every day she still had to return to Abbey Gardens to eat alone or endure silence if

Charlie was in one of his moods. She had given up so much to be with him, but he had changed. Gone was the fun-loving man-about-town: he had been replaced by a surlier version, particularly when they were alone.

Shortage of money and no heir were the predominant themes of their arguments in the early days. At first, Lucy had stood her ground. Charlie had known well the risk of no dowry if they eloped. A letter from her father's solicitor soon after they settled in London had confirmed it. As for her childless state, she had seen several doctors but none could give her a reason. Encouraged by his parents, Charlie had insisted the blame had to lie with her. After several miscarriages, it was easier to agree. If she still daydreamed of being a mother, she kept it to herself.

Over time, they had fallen into a routine of avoidance. Love had flown long ago and with no money of her own and estranged from her family, Lucy had no choice but to stay. Burnt bridges and all of that, she could almost hear her mother sneer. Her only hope was Charlie would turn back to their marriage and they might salvage something. In the meantime, the future stretched out before her as bleak as a Yorkshire moor in midwinter.

But it wasn't in Lucy's nature to mope. She would speak to Charlie on his return from Scotland and try to explain how she felt. If only they could afford a little holiday; she was convinced some time spent together might re-ignite the spark. They had honeymooned in Italy and she had adored the country and the climate. Not that it had to be somewhere foreign; she'd happily settle for Brighton or Lyme Regis. But she couldn't help herself. Soon she was daydreaming of the piazze of Rome, Siena and Florence. She could almost feel the warmth of the sun on her skin.

The sight of a police constable walking down the road brought Lucy back to everyday life. As he drew closer, she realised the policeman was looking for a particular house. Could scandal lurk behind one of her neighbours' doors? How intriguing! But to her astonishment, he stopped at her gate, consulted a card he pulled from the pocket of his greatcoat and turned in. Lucy scooted back to her seat. What could he possibly want?

Seconds later the sound of the bell echoed through the house and she heard the maid's distinctive step in the hallway. The door opened and Mary's head peeped in. Her colour was high and her blond curls were escaping her cap. Lucy recognised the warning signs: a domestic situation was developing. Only that morning she heard cook complaining to Mary she was run off her feet. Matters below stairs weren't happy and she couldn't blame the servants for being aggrieved. Mary had been hired as her lady's maid but now had to combine those duties with parlour maid too. The constant lack of money meant they were often short-staffed, but the consequences were always hers to deal with. Like most men, Charlie had a talent for avoiding any hint of domestic trouble.

'Are you at home, at all, ma'am?' the maid asked, her Dublin accent more pronounced than usual.

'No. Send whoever it is away, there's a good girl.'

Picking up her book, Lucy tried to concentrate but found her attention focused on the murmur of voices out in the hallway. Mary came in again, this time her face as white as her apron.

'Well?'

'I'm fierce sorry, ma'am, but it's the polis and he says it's urgent.' She took a step closer and lowered her voice. 'There's no budging 'im. Awful serious, he is! Insists on seeing you, ma'am.'

'*Policeman*, Mary, please!' The maid blushed and Lucy regretted the reprimand. 'Did he tell you what he wants?' she asked in a gentler tone.

'Yes, it's about the master, ma'am. I... I think you need to speak to him.'

Lucy frowned. She could think of no reason for Charlie to be involved with the police. It must be serious, for Mary was usually robust in disposing of unwanted visitors. 'Very well, Mary—show him in.'

Moments later, Mary ushered a burly policeman into the room. 'Constable Enright, ma'am.'

'Come in, Constable, what can I do for you?' Lucy asked, looking up at the figure whose tall form now dominated her drawing room.

Much to her surprise Mary lingered at the door, her fingers twitching at her apron. But Lucy didn't have time to question the maid's odd behaviour or admonish her. The constable took a step towards her, removing his helmet and tucking it under his arm. By his solemn expression she knew it wasn't good news.

He cleared his throat. 'I'm sorry to disturb you, madam. I'm from Vine Street Station.'

'Vine Street—aren't you a little off your beat?'

'Yes, ma'am. I've been sent by my inspector. Would you mind confirming if this is the residence of Mr Charles Lawrence?'

'Yes, it is and I'm his wife. Is Mr Lawrence in some kind of trouble?'

'Possibly, ma'am. There was an unfortunate accident on Regent Street earlier this afternoon. We believe your husband was involved.'

Relieved, Lucy shook her head. 'That can't be, Constable. My husband left for Edinburgh four days ago to visit his parents.'

'Oh!' he said, his brow furrowed. 'That's strange.' From his pocket he drew out a card and handed it to her. 'Would you mind taking a look at this? It was found on... uh, the deceased.'

Deceased? Lucy's mind was spinning as she glanced at the

visiting card. It was Charlie's. 'My husband is a man of business, Constable,' she said. 'Perhaps this unfortunate person was a professional acquaintance and had Mr Lawrence's card on his person.'

'We don't believe so, ma'am. The card was one of many and came from a case found in the inside pocket of the dead gentleman's jacket.'

Mary gasped and crossed herself. Lucy glanced at her and shook her head. There had to be a logical explanation for this mix-up. Charlie was in Scotland.

'I do not know why a stranger would have my husband's card case, if indeed it is; however, as I said, he is away. This can't have anything to do with him.'

The constable cast her a glance laced with sympathy, which was disconcerting. 'Please ma'am, my inspector—Inspector McQuillan—has asked for a family member to attend Dufour Place Mortuary to make a formal identification. For the sake of the gentleman's next of kin, it is important we confirm his identity as quickly as possible. Our only lead is the card case and its contents, ma'am. So even if it's just to eliminate your husband... Perhaps there's someone available?'

Lucy sighed. 'No, constable, there's only me.'

The constable shifted on his feet. 'I hate to ask, ma'am, but it would be of great help to us...'

'Very well, I'll come and assist you if I can.' Of course, it couldn't be Charlie, Lucy reasoned, but the policeman wasn't going to take no for an answer. Someone had to go. Besides, it would relieve the tedium of another evening with only Horace the cat for company.

Soho, London

Lucy alighted from the hansom cab on Broad Street and waited while Constable Enright tossed a coin up to the cabbie. Despite her warm coat, she shivered as a gust sent the last of the autumn leaves scurrying along the pavement.

'This way, ma'am,' the constable said, turning down a narrow street. Halfway down, he slowed and they entered a cobbled courtyard. Even at the entrance gate the odour of disinfectant hung in the air. Inside was worse, and it was all Lucy could do not to gag. She wondered how the people who worked here could stand it. That and being in close proximity to death all day. Was it something you could get used to?

Constable Enright led the way down a long featureless corridor. Several rooms branched off the hallway but Lucy kept her eyes on the broad shoulders of the police officer ahead of her. None of this had anything to do with Charlie, of course. Boredom and curiosity had driven her here, but now she was regretting the impulse. Death made her uncomfortable and she was about to view the body of a stranger. What had possessed her to agree to this? She really would have to find more hobbies.

The police constable stopped at a door with the sign: 'Mortuary Superintendent'. Inside, a middle-aged man sat behind a desk. He glanced up, his expression one of pique.

'This is Mrs Charles Lawrence, Superintendent Hendrick,' Enright said.

The superintendent stood and waved Lucy to a seat beside his desk. 'Thank you, Constable, I'll take things from here.' The constable closed over the door and Hendrick turned to Lucy. 'Thank you for coming, Mrs Lawrence. I know this must be upsetting for you.'

'It isn't upsetting in the least, but it is certainly inconvenient. I had no desire to visit this place, but the constable was insistent I accompany him.' Mr Hendrick gave her a startled look. 'I should explain, Superintendent. As I told the policeman, it can't be my husband in your mortuary as Mr Lawrence is visiting his family in Scotland and isn't due to return to London until the end of the week.'

'I see.' Hendrick said, rubbing his chin. 'That complicates matters.' He frowned down at the papers on his desk before looking across at her again. 'Perhaps it might be best if we show you the deceased's belongings first. That way we can avoid... any unnecessary unpleasantness.'

The idea of looking at any of the deceased souls lying in the rooms she had passed made her shudder. 'I would appreciate that, sir.'

Hendrick left the room and Lucy heard him call for one of his colleagues. 'Angus, bring me the personal items of the gentleman the Vine Street officers brought in earlier.'

On his return, the superintendent smiled awkwardly, sat down behind his desk and began to fidget with his pen. Lucy looked about the office, happy to avoid conversation. The silence was uncomfortable but there didn't seem to be anything appropriate to say in the circumstances. Slowly her sense of unease grew. *What if?* was lurking at the back of her mind. No; she couldn't think along those lines. She focused her attention on the clock above Hendrick's head, wishing she was back in her own drawing room.

A few minutes later there was a tap at the door and a tall gentleman appeared in the doorway. Well-dressed, in a perfectly tailored Ulster coat of superfine black wool, glossy topper and finely crafted leather gloves, the man had a distinguished air and she wondered if he had foreign blood in his veins as his skin tone suggested. Striking, more than handsome, was her assessment of him. Surely he was someone you were more likely to see at Ascot than a mortuary, she thought. But then mortuaries were not her usual choice of places to visit either. Perhaps he was here to identify someone too.

Much to her consternation, he flicked a glance at her before greeting the superintendent by name. In that moment, she had been assessed and dismissed. It was an uncomfortable sensation and for the first time since she arrived Lucy suspected she was out of her depth. The newcomer stepped further in to the office.

'Mr Stone, you didn't waste much time,' Hendrick said, sitting back in his chair.

'Vine Street notified me about Lawrence. Has there been a formal identification of the body yet? The police indicated it would happen today.'

Lucy smarted at his words, now well disposed to dislike this stranger who dared to use such disparaging terms about Charlie.

Hendrick stood up, glancing apologetically at her. 'No, not yet. This is *Mrs* Lawrence; she only arrived a short time ago.' He turned to Lucy. 'Mrs Lawrence, may I present Mr Stone? He's an insurance investigator.' By his tone, she guessed he did not hold Mr Stone or his occupation in high esteem.

The newcomer approached her, taking off his hat to reveal slightly curling ebony hair. Mr Stone gave her a nod of acknowledgement, but there was no hint of apology for his previous discourtesy. Instead, he subjected her to another scrutiny that verged on rude. There was something extremely arrogant about the man, she decided. And a tiny bit scary.

With a curt nod, she looked away. But she was curious to know why an insurance company would be interested in her Charlie. Of course, the only explanation for all of it was that there was another Charles Lawrence running around London up to no good. That must be it. However, Lucy's heart began to pound. Letting out a slow breath, she returned to her survey of Mr Hendrick's document filing cabinets, determined to ignore this Mr Stone with his unsettling gaze.

'Mrs Lawrence believes her husband is in Scotland, so I thought it best she examines the personal effects first, rather than the remains,' Hendrick said to Mr Stone.

'He's *definitely* in Edinburgh,' Lucy piped up. 'There has been a mistake.'

Mr Stone exchanged a doubtful glance with the superintendent. 'I'm happy to await the outcome, in any case,' Mr Stone
remarked.

Then he took the seat opposite her. Now fuming, Lucy just
knew he assumed she was lying. She clasped her hands in her
lap and prayed the nightmare would end soon. What had
seemed a bit of an adventure was now taking on a different tone.
And she was all too aware of being under the watchful eye of
the insurance man who seemed to be perfectly at his ease,
resting his gloved hands on the top of his cane.

'Ah, Angus,' Hendrick said as a small dark-haired fellow
entered the office carrying a box. 'Leave it on the desk.' He
turned to Lucy. 'Mrs Lawrence, would you care to inspect these
items for me?'

Lucy took a deep breath to steady her nerves as she rose
from her chair. This was merely a formality; soon she would be
on her way home. Mr Stone stood too, but somehow she sensed
it wasn't merely manners but curiosity. He stepped closer to the
desk, his gaze moving between her and the box. She willed
herself not to react no matter what was in it. Did they not
realise Somerville blood coursed through her veins?

The cardboard box contained a monogrammed handkerchief stained with blood, a card case and a hunter watch. Lucy
couldn't look away as numbness suddenly shrouded her senses.
Each and every item in the box was familiar to her.

'Please, Mrs Lawrence,' Hendrick said, gesturing towards
the items. 'Could these be your husband's?'

But it can't be, she told herself over and over as she took off
her gloves. Slowly, she reached out and picked up the card case.
She ran her fingers over the delicate filigree decoration—she had
been with Charlie the day he bought it. She slipped open the
lid. Charlie's cards. Swallowing hard, she placed the case back
in the box and took up the watch. Flipping it open, she saw the

crack in the glass. The watch had stopped at one thirty-five. She turned it over and gasped even though she knew what she would find. There was a dent in the metal plate, but the inscription was perfectly legible.

To Dearest Charlie on our Wedding Day, Love Lucy.

TWO

For several moments, Lucy stared at the watch in her hand; the implication of its existence in this dreadful place slowly seeping into her consciousness. If his things were here, could he be too? Could Charlie be... *dead*? She placed the watch back in the box but couldn't tear her eyes away from it.

'Mrs Lawrence, are these your husband's possessions?' Hendrick asked, his voice more insistent now.

'Yes.' She drew herself up. 'These are my husband's.'

'I'm sorry to hear that, Mrs Lawrence. Unfortunately, this isn't sufficient for identification purposes. There will have to be a formal identification of the body as well. Shall we?' Hendrick asked, for all the world as if he were escorting her to a box at the opera. Lucy hesitated, unable to think clearly. The room was collapsing in on itself, splintering into tiny slivers of light. She grasped the handle of her umbrella until her fingers hurt. It helped. A little.

Hendrick frowned at her. 'I must insist, Mrs Lawrence. The sooner the better.' He moved towards the door. An over-whelming urge to weep came upon Lucy. How she regretted not bringing Mary. To face this alone... to face whatever lay in the room beyond was unthinkable. And yet she had to do it.

Hendrick led the way down the corridor. To her surprise, her limbs co-operated, but she might as well have been wading through molasses. She was vaguely aware of Mr Stone two steps behind her.

A wall-mounted gaslight threw grotesque shadows onto the walls of the large white-tiled room they entered. Several bodies lay on marble slabs, anonymous beneath linen sheets. One form was so small it had to be a child. Finding the notion of it distressing, Lucy had to look away. It was the most appalling place she had ever been in.

From just inside the door, Hendrick called across to the attendant. 'Angus, please show this lady the body from Regent Street.'

The attendant had an emaciated appearance, so common in those who had known childhood poverty, with his enormous leather apron almost swamping his body. His eyes swept over her before he acknowledged Mr Stone. He gestured towards the nearest slab. Lucy had to force herself to move. Mr Stone also stepped forward, taking up a position at her side. The outline of the body beneath the sheet *couldn't* be her Charlie. This was surreal.

'Are you ready?' Angus asked, his voice tinged with sympathy.

Lucy swallowed a shaky breath and licked her lips. 'Yes.'

The attendant slowly pulled away the sheet. Beside her, Mr Stone sucked in his breath. It was worse than she could have imagined. There wasn't much left of the man's facial features; the injuries were so bad Lucy wasn't even sure it *was* Charlie. Horrified, she stood transfixed.

'An unpleasant end for anyone,' Hendrick remarked from the doorway.

Mr Stone turned to him. 'How can you expect anyone to make an identification with the body in this state?'

'There isn't much I can do about it, Mr Stone. I'm only doing my job. Mrs Lawrence? Is there anything, any feature you recognise about this man?' Hendrick asked.

'I'm... I'm not sure,' she said, acutely aware of the thumping of her heart and the dryness of her mouth. Perhaps if she took shallow breaths, the nausea would abate.

'Indeed! I'm not surprised. This is cruel, Hendrick,' Mr Stone said, a sharp edge to his voice.

For the first time she was in accord with the gentleman, but she knew to escape the room she would have to make the identification. Gathering her courage, she looked down at the mangled remains once more. The fair hair was matted with blood, but it was possible it was Charlie's. The tweed of the man's jacket was familiar. She glanced up at Mr Stone. 'It may be my husband. He's the right build.'

She thought she saw a glimmer of understanding in his eyes. 'Does he have any distinguishing marks?' he asked gently.

'He has a birthmark on his right shoulder...'

'Angus, please check, there's a good fellow,' Mr Stone said. Behind them, Hendrick muttered under his breath then coughed, but he remained at the door.

Angus carefully pulled down the shoulder of the jacket, then the shirt. A large brown birthmark was visible. There could be no doubt. Her stomach twisted, but she reached out to rest her palm on Charlie's shoulder. He was ice cold. She swayed slightly, and Mr Stone cupped her elbow as if to steady her. Lucy shook him off.

'Yes—it's Charlie... my husband.'

'Very well,' Hendrick said briskly. 'I'm happy to proceed on this basis. Do you agree, Mr Stone?'

'You're certain?' Mr Stone asked, his eyes boring into her, almost as if he wished she was in error.

'As I can be!' She turned to Hendrick. 'May I leave?'

'There are a few formalities, Mrs Lawrence, but as soon as they are done, I'll arrange for you to be escorted home. My condolences. I'm sorry it's your husband.' His kindly words nearly undid her.

'I need a moment... please,' she said, brushing past Stone, then Hendrick and out into the hallway.

'There's a bathroom down on your right, Mrs Lawrence,' Hendrick called after her.

Lucy walked a little way down the corridor but had to stop when a wave of dizziness overcame her. Leaning against the wall, she pulled a handkerchief from her bag and clutched it to her mouth, willing her stomach to settle. Her head ached and she couldn't stop shivering, Charlie's smashed face to the forefront of her mind.

She was a widow; a fact as cold as her husband, lying on that awful slab like a bloodied and broken doll. Why had he lied about going to Edinburgh? *Nothing* made sense. Her throat constricted in panic. She didn't know what to feel, what to do. From inside the mortuary room, the men's voices intruded into her jumbled thoughts.

'Are you satisfied there can be no doubt?' she heard Mr Stone ask.

'The birthmark and his belongings clinch it, don't you think? Thank goodness for the card case. We would never have found out who he was without it,' Hendrick said.

'Yes, it was extremely lucky. When Vine Street found it, McQuillan sent me a telegram, as he knew of my interest in this man.'

'And what would that be?'

'That's confidential information I'm not at liberty to divulge, Hendrick. Just make sure Mrs Lawrence signs all the paperwork before she leaves,' Stone said.

'Don't tell me how to do my job! Inspector McQuillan

would have my guts for garters if I made a mistake. I'll send you a copy of my report. Everything will be done properly, as usual.'

'I'm delighted to hear it!'

There was a pause, then Hendrick said in an icy tone, 'Do you wish to examine the personal effects before I release them to the widow? As it's a case of accidental death, the police have no more interest.'

'An accident? Are you sure? Were there any witnesses?' Stone sounded surprised.

'You'll have to ask Inspector McQuillan. We're not police officers,' Hendrick snapped as he came out into the hallway. He didn't notice her, but marched down to his office, his shoulders stiff.

Lucy remained outside the mortuary room, trying to decide what to do. Should she go back in? Say a final farewell? But she recoiled at the idea of seeing or touching Charlie's body again, then instantly was ashamed. It was her Charlie; she owed it to him. But Stone and the attendant were still in the room. She decided to wait. When they left, she would say goodbye in private.

'Nothing changes around here,' she heard Stone remark.

'No, sir, it don't,' Angus replied. 'After all these years, 'endrick's still afraid of the bodies. Never seen 'im touch one, ever.'

'Not everyone is comfortable around the dead, Angus,' Stone said.

Angus chuckled. 'These poor buggers can't hurt no one no more.'

'Very true. Anything useful you can tell me about Lawrence?'

'The constables that brought 'im in said his nibs 'ere slipped and went under a dray cart. Broad daylight on Regent Street, so there must have been someone abou' to see it 'appen.'

'Let us hope so. Is there anything unusual about the body?' Mr Stone asked.

'No, sir. Much as you'd expect having been trampled to death. Head all but smashed in. Poor blighter didn't stand a chance with them massive hooves. And as for the wheels... At least it would have been quick. That poor woman—not right her 'aving to see 'im like that.'

'I agree, but it has to be done,' Mr Stone said.

Lucy caught her breath, as unwanted images flooded her mind. It must have been a horrible death, but almost instantaneous—that was something to cling to. Then she wondered why Mr Stone was so interested in how Charlie died. It had to have been an accident; what other explanation could there be? Yet he appeared to be surprised.

'Was he a naughty boy, then?' Angus asked.

'Unfortunately for his family, I believe he was. But I was hoping for mistaken identity, to tell the truth. Lawrence was my best and only lead.' Stunned by his comment, Lucy moved closer to the door. He was investigating Charlie?

'One of your big cases, sir?'

'You know better than to ask, Angus... Here, thanks for your help.'

'Oh, thank you very much, sir. I'll drink to your good 'ealth with this. Always a pleasure doing business with you. Are you done with 'im, then?' Angus asked.

'Most definitely. Sadly, he's of no use to me now.'

Mr Stone came out into the hallway and stopped dead when he spotted Lucy standing there. 'Oh!' he exclaimed, his gaze flicking back to the mortuary room. The colour rose in his face.

At that moment, Mr Hendrick's head popped out of his office door. 'There you are, Mrs Lawrence, would you mind? It won't take too long.'

She nodded but kept her eyes fixed on Mr Stone, doing her

best to convey her repugnance. But to her surprise, his expression softened and he took her arm, guiding her towards Hendrick's office. He pulled out a chair for her. 'Fetch a glass of water, Hendrick,' he snapped.

Hendrick scowled at him before quitting the room. She understood why Hendrick disliked him so much. The man was overbearing.

Mr Stone looked down at her, his expression indecipherable. 'My condolences, Mrs Lawrence. This is a distressing business; however, I need to ask you some questions about your husband. May I call on you in a few days? Here is my card.'

Lucy glanced down at the card he handed her. The audacity of the man! When she glanced up, there was no hint of compassion in his eyes. Again, her overwhelming impression was that he was analysing her every word, her very demeanour. 'Please do not, sir. I have nothing to discuss with you.'

Lucy caught the flicker of annoyance as his eyes hardened. It was quickly masked. 'You're upset, as is only natural in these tragic circumstances,' he said smoothly. 'Unfortunately, I must insist. I'll contact you next week.'

Before Lucy could respond, he bowed, turned on his heel and left.

THREE

Somerville Hall, Yorkshire, December 1886

The fifty-minute carriage journey from York station had been uneventful, but Lucy was in a state of nervous anxiety. Eventually, they turned off the main road and drew up alongside a high boundary wall. She peeped out of the window. The gates of Somerville Hall were closed. Not very welcoming, Lucy reflected, but she wasn't surprised. As they waited for the gate-keeper to appear, she eyed the family motto displayed in gold lettering across the top arch of the gateway. *Hic Sunt Dracones*. Beneath, a fire-breathing dragon and a white rabbit confronted each other for eternity. Back in the mists of time, someone in the family had exhibited a sense of humour. Just as well, for the present owner was a very dull dog, in her opinion.

No welcoming light spilled out on to the snow from the gate lodge. In fact, the entire place had a deserted aspect and Lucy's stomach twisted once more in anxiety. But a return to London was neither feasible nor appealing. Besides, it was getting late and darkness would soon descend. As the wind rose, the ancient trees standing guard at the entrance creaked and groaned from the weight of the snow on their boughs. Wasn't it strange how she'd forgotten how bleak Yorkshire could be in winter? But then there were many things about Somerville Hall and its inhabitants she had managed to suppress over the years.

'McNee! Open the gates, man!' the coachman roared, making her jump.

A few minutes later, a man appeared in the doorway of the lodge and regarded them with a quizzical expression. Muffled up in a greatcoat, he shuffled towards the gate, muttering under his breath. Lucy tried not to stare as his gnarled fingers struggled with the lock and key, but soon the gates juddered open with a squeal of protest. The gatekeeper stood back and motioned for the carriage to enter. As soon as they passed through, he slammed and locked the gate behind them. With a jerk, the carriage bowled forward, but the snow was thick on the ground and progress was slow. The coachman cursed and laid his whip to the horse's back.

Lucy couldn't resist pulling down the window to look towards her final destination and was immediately struck by the deep silence of the snowy dusk. The square mansion stood at the end of the long carriageway; its granite façade absorbed the dying rays of the sun and smothered them mercilessly. All her doubts and fears crystallised in that moment as she contemplated the days ahead within its walls. There were few happy memories connected with the house in which she had grown up. Distant parents and a brother destined for great things took little interest in the life of a mere girl. What had possessed her to come here? All of a sudden, she longed for the noisy and malodorous streets of her beloved London.

As the carriage rattled along, the parkland gradually revealed itself, radiating out in undulating lawn with woodland beyond, in deep shadow. Unseen ravens took flight and croaked in reproach at the disturbance of their roost. Lucy, slightly spooked, closed the window and drew the sheepskin throw more tightly around her knees.

When the carriage drew up at the imposing portico of Somerville Hall, the coachman clambered down, rocking the carriage. 'Wait here a moment, ma'am,' he called to her, before taking the steps two at a time and tugging the bell pull. Somewhere within, a cacophony of barking erupted. The door swung open. A smartly-dressed gentleman stood framed in the doorway.

''Tis Mrs Lawrence, Mr Jameson,' the coachman explained as he descended again. 'Just fetched her from the train.'

It was with mixed feelings that Lucy crossed the threshold. So much had happened since last she had seen the inside of Somerville Hall. She had forgotten how beautiful the entrance hall was, with its buttermilk walls and ornate plasterwork. In the centre, a staircase swept upwards, then split and curved away with an arched stained-glass window gracing the return. Set to one side of the stairs was a Christmas tree, at least twelve feet high. Its lingering pine scent was delightful, bringing to mind Christmases of the past.

'May I, madam?' the butler asked, interrupting her observations. His hand was outstretched for her coat and bonnet. 'If you care to wait a moment, Mrs Lawrence, I'll inform the master you have arrived,' he said, passing her things to a footman who had appeared silently from the nether regions. Jameson didn't quite grimace, but Lucy knew he had already judged her by the quality of her attire and the lack of an accompanying maid.

The butler melted away, and she was conscious of the footman's curious stare. She attempted an air of unruffled calm, but then caught a glimpse of herself in a mirror. With dismay, she noticed her auburn hair—her one nod to pride—appeared dull and bedraggled and her eyes stood out impossibly blue against the pallor of her face. A succession of sleepless nights had taken

their toll. With urgent fingers, she pinched her cheeks and tried
to fix her wayward hair.

'Sir, Mrs Lawrence has arrived,' the butler announced from
the doorway of a room halfway down the hall.

'Excellent, Jameson, show her in.'

The pleasant aroma of cigars greeted Lucy as she entered the
library. It instantly triggered thoughts of her late father, who
had a great fondness for them.

Richard Somerville, her brother, was seated behind a desk
at one end of the enormous room. Even though their last
encounter in London six weeks before had been a fiasco, she
was relieved to see a familiar face. They had never been close,
the age gap making them virtual strangers. She knew him to be
only thirty-nine, but his bearing and expression suggested a
much older man with sleep-depriving concerns. Richard's
pallor and thinning blond hair added to his washed-out appearance. Fleetingly, she wondered what possible worries *he* could
have. To be master of Somerville had its responsibilities, but
they were hardly onerous.

Her brother rose from behind the desk to greet her. With a
wave of his hand, he directed her to sit down. 'Lucy, you're in
good health, I trust? It is good to see you here at last. I was
surprised to receive your telegram… delighted, of course, as are
the rest of the family, but what changed your mind?'

'You must forgive my foolishness when last we met,
Richard. I was struggling to come to terms with Charlie's death.
At the time, I did not fully perceive how bad my situation was,
or just how quiet the house would be without him. I soon
realised how intolerable it would be to spend Christmas alone.'
Richard grunted, his brows puckered. She was happy for him to
believe loneliness and financial hardship had driven her to Yorkshire—not fear for her life.

'Indeed, and it would have appeared so odd for you to stay in London under such circumstances,' he said.

Appearances meant everything in the Somerville family, she was well aware, but his tone held censure and her hackles rose. 'To whom?' she asked.

Richard frowned. 'To society in general, of course. Which reminds me. Did you not receive my letter? I was happy to send a maid to accompany you on your journey from York. It is most improper to travel unaccompanied.'

The rebuke stung. Deliberately alluding to her lack of servants, and the poverty it implied, was unkind. Her final act before leaving London had been to dismiss her remaining domestic staff. It was not a pleasant memory. Letting go of Mary, her lady's maid, had been particularly difficult.

'Do not concern yourself. I am well used to fending for myself,' she said, with more conviction than she felt.

Richard looked shocked, which pleased her enormously. With a huff, he sat back in his chair. 'Most irregular!'

'Yes, isn't it? But times are changing, Richard. In London, a married woman has a lot more freedom now.' Lucy beamed at him, determined not to appear weak.

Richard picked up a letter opener, and ran his finger along the edge. A muscle twitched in his cheek as a sour expression settled on his features.

'Perhaps, but you're a young widow, and a Somerville, and therefore need to be circumspect.'

Afraid of letting fly, Lucy had to bite back a retort and instead took the opportunity to survey the library. Above the fireplace was an ancient stag's head, made uglier by the reflection of dancing flames licking about its neck. Reputedly, her grandfather had shot the animal, one of the largest ever found on the estate. However, she considered it a visual insult to the Louis XIV chairs situated on either side of the fireplace below. She had always detested it.

Pools of light around the oil lamps threw the rest of the room into shadow. But she could make out shelf after shelf of books and hoped there would be something interesting to read. It was her passion, and she was afraid there wouldn't be much else to do in this house. Reading had been her refuge from loneliness while growing up, with escape possible within the pages of the books she had read. It was extraordinary. Sitting in the room again, that long-forgotten comfort enveloped her.

'Well, you are here now,' Richard said at last. 'What are your immediate plans? I'm happy to renew my offer of a home here. Indeed, I believe it would be the best solution to your present difficulties.'

'Thank you for the offer, but I'm undecided as yet. You must remember I have lived in London society for some time. I'm not sure how country life would suit me.'

Her brother shook his head. 'You do not have the funds for that style of living any more.'

'Richard, I imagine it is too soon to decide on anything. Until probate is through and I know what my final financial position will be, it is all speculation.'

'Hardly! I have been privy to Charlie's papers, don't forget, and it did not make pleasant reading. Did that solicitor chappie not explain it to you?'

Lucy tensed. 'I'd rather not discuss it now. I'm tired after the journey.'

'I understand. No doubt you wish to rest before we dine. I'll have the housekeeper show you to your room. The family will meet you in the blue salon before dinner. We dine at eight sharp.'

'Is that a dismissal?' she asked, half-joking.

'Lucy, you have come to stay—'

'Temporarily,' she interjected.

'Temporarily, but I would like to see you attempt to be civil to the family, in spite of what occurred in the past. You can't deny that your behaviour was far from fitting for a Somerville and caused a great deal of distress to our parents. Even I experienced the repercussions of your... actions.' Richard drew breath. 'However, we are happy to draw a veil over it though I would add mourning is no excuse for bad manners.'

It took a good deal of self-control for Lucy not to lash out. How pompous he was. And any mention of Charlie's death was still distressing, as it brought to mind that awful afternoon in the mortuary. His passing had set her adrift in bewilderment and, unfortunately, poverty.

'I'm here on sufferance, then?' Lucy asked, her throat tight.

'You're here because the family decided it would be a kindness to offer an olive branch, particularly as it is Christmas. When your husband died, I knew it was my duty as head of the family to take you on.'

'Forgive me, but I do not wish to be *taken on* by you or anyone else.'

His cheeks reddened. 'Did you not realise how bad your affairs were?' Only recently, Lucy had discovered the unpleasant reality, but she remained silent. 'Once your husband's debts are cleared, and there are many, trust me, there will be virtually nothing left for you to live on. The house in St John's Wood will have to be sold. It was mortgaged to the hilt.'

'I beg your pardon! What do you mean?' Lucy cried. 'I had no idea there was a mortgage. The house was an inheritance from Charlie's uncle.' She clenched her fists in anger and dismay. 'Charlie should have told me... but then he never discussed money matters with me.'

'As is only proper, Lucy. However, you can't stay there much longer. I'm sorry to be so blunt, but you must face the facts. That's why I made my offer of a home here at Somerville. Most people in your position would be delighted to be rescued from the jaws of the workhouse.' Richard laughed, rather unkindly she thought.

'Oh yes, I'm grateful,' Lucy answered, seething at his patronising tone and her late husband's appalling mismanagement of their affairs. How had it come to this?

'For whatever reason,' Richard continued, 'your husband named me executor. I assume it was his way of trying to mend bridges and ensuring you would be cared for in the bosom of your family. The solicitor gave you a copy of the will. There can be no doubt. I have a responsibility towards you until such time—'

'I do not know why Charlie made such a will,' Lucy blurted out. 'I'm sure the solicitor could have handled the estate perfectly well. There was no need to involve you, especially after all this time.' Richard's stare turned icy. 'None of this makes sense to me,' she said, trying to be conciliatory. Antagonising him wasn't a clever course of action no matter what the provocation.

'No one could have foreseen what has happened,' Richard said. 'It is most unfortunate Charles has died so young and so tragically.' This was addressed to the blotter on his desk. Then he glanced up and she thought she saw a spark of sympathy. 'I'm sorry, Lucy, but things may turn out for the best in the long run. It's time to forget the past.'

It was too much. Promptly, and to her eternal embarrassment, she began to weep before her brother.

FOUR

To Lucy's astonishment, Mrs Hughes, the housekeeper, took her to her old bedroom on the second floor. Assailed by memories, she halted unsure in the doorway. She struggled to remember how it had looked before, for it had been transformed. Flocked wallpaper adorned the walls now and beautiful rugs on the polished wooden floor gave the room a welcoming atmosphere.

From the little she had seen since her arrival, the new mistress of Somerville, her sister-in-law Sibylla, had left her mark on the house. The Metcalf dowry, courtesy of Sibylla's father, had brought life back to Somerville: one of the many benefits of marrying a rich industrialist's daughter. It appeared Richard had made a far more successful marriage than she. But the strange thing was she hadn't met one servant she recognised from old. It was almost as if Sibylla was trying to obliterate the past. The changes must have upset her mother, and Lucy wondered how she was coping with not being in charge.

Exile from Somerville had meant Lucy had never met Richard's wife or been included in any of the family occasions. Two years after her marriage, she learned of her father's demise in the newspaper and wept bitter tears. Grief-stricken, she pleaded with Charlie to write to Richard so they could attend the funeral, but he refused saying he would not crawl to the Somervilles. A year later, sight of Richard's betrothal and marriage announcements in *The Times* were the final seal on her exile. Within days, Charlie produced a diamond bracelet as if it would compensate. Disgusted, she never wore it, but shoved it to the back of a drawer. Over the years she learned not to read too much into Charlie's more extravagant gestures, or, at least, to read them correctly. When the reality of her changed financial position had become apparent after Charlie's death, she had sent Mary directly to the pawnbroker with the bracelet.

'Why don't you rest, ma'am?' the housekeeper said, with a look of concern as she beckoned her in.

'Yes, I will, thank you, Mrs Hughes,' Lucy said as she stepped inside.

'I'll send a maid to help you dress in a wee while,' the housekeeper said, before taking a turn about the room, twitching the curtains and smoothing down the cover at the corner of the bed, until, eventually, she appeared satisfied. 'A nice cup of tea will set you to rights. Drink it while it's hot, ma'am.' She pointed to a tea tray on a little table beside a fireside chair.

The scent of freshly made biscuits wafted towards Lucy and her stomach growled. As the door clicked shut behind the housekeeper, she sagged with relief. She still couldn't believe she was back in Somerville Hall. In her wildest dreams she never thought she would see this room again, or her family for that matter.

Munching on a piece of shortbread, she pulled open the heavy drapes, but it was now pitch-dark outside. Memories of long summers spent out in the parkland came flooding back and she longed to explore her old haunts once more. After breakfast, she decided, she would do just that. Then she stiffened. Would it be safe to venture out? The hasty departure from London couldn't have gone unnoticed, and she suspected a certain gentleman would easily locate her if so inclined. But would he dare enter the grounds of Somerville? Lucy suspected he was capable of anything, and it would be foolish not to take precautions. She drew the curtains closed with a snap.

Sitting down at the dressing table, Lucy smiled sadly at her reflection. So much had happened since she had last sat here on the morning of her departure for her London Season. Eager for escape, she had promised herself she would never return to Somerville, and meeting Charles Lawrence had set her plan in motion. Foolishly, she had ignored her parents' concerns and threats. She had believed they would come round. Charlie had shared her belief. Too late, Lucy realised it was the lure of the Somerville money that had drawn Charlie to her.

She trailed her fingers across the polished wood before resting her hand on her travel escritoire. Rummaging in the pocket of her jacket, she found the key. Turning the lock, she pushed the trigger for the secret compartment. Her wedding photograph in its silver frame was at the top. She pulled it out and locked the box before placing the photograph on the mantelpiece. It was an act of defiance in the face of her family's disapproval.

Charlie. Despite their unhappiness, she still missed him. A multitude of 'what ifs' had haunted her since his death. With his boyish good looks and easy manner, he had won her over in one afternoon. Not long in London, she had persuaded her mother to visit the National Gallery instead of a proposed picnic with a group of young ladies, who chattered endlessly about the earl of this or the duke of that. Having recently met many of these *paragons* of the male sex, Lucy was convinced the city was full of the most empty-headed men in England. How was she to find her soulmate amongst their number?

Never one to miss an opportunity, Mother had dragged along someone she considered *suitable*. Thomas Hardwicke was a verbose, exceedingly well-heeled man of forty. Unfortunately, he was also the dullest man Lucy had ever met. He was, undoubtedly, something of an art expert and for the first half hour Lucy had listened to his monologues, delivered at the top of his voice as they stood before each painting. Encouraged by Mrs Somerville, Thomas looked as if he might keep it up for the entire afternoon. As a particularly tedious tale emerged of a lucrative purchase he had made recently, Lucy spotted a young fair-haired man standing a little apart, listening intently. As she looked away from him, she caught a glimpse of a roguish smile and eyes brimming with mirth. The handsome stranger understood her predicament precisely.

To this day, Lucy wasn't quite sure how he managed it, but within minutes he had cheerfully called to Thomas by his name and joined their party. The young man chatted away as if he and Thomas were old friends, despite the look of confusion on Thomas's face. Far too polite to admit he didn't know him, Thomas nodded and smiled and made the fatal introductions. Ten minutes later, Lucy was on the newcomer's arm. Twenty minutes afterwards they were in the next room—alone. Relieved to be free of her mother's dreary choice, she was also intrigued by Charlie Lawrence's sleight of hand. Before she knew it, they had arranged to meet the following afternoon in Regent's Park.

For the next two weeks, Charlie turned up almost everywhere the Somervilles went. Initially, her mother was watchful but content to let the budding romance blossom. Full of charm, Charlie won Mother over easily enough. Lucy, ripe for adventure after the constraints of her Yorkshire life, fell heavily and found herself searching for him whenever she entered a ballroom, drawing room or concert. Invariably, she found him.

Handsome and romantic, he was everything Lucy dreamed of, but on her mother finding out the state of the Lawrence family coffers, everything changed. Threatening to send her back to Yorkshire, her mother demanded she give him up and her father was summoned to London to intervene. Thomas Hardwicke was soon in their midst again and Lucy fell into despair. She had become used to the stolen kisses, warm embraces and snatched conversations. Who at eighteen could resist words of love spoken in hushed tones? She could not and would not forsake him. Encouraged by her faithfulness, Charlie made plans. Lucy rode along on the wave of romance and, weeks' later, found herself on her wedding night wrapped in the arms of her choice.

But Charlie was gone now, and the future stretched out before her, fuzzy and unformed, leaving her anxious. Weary, she sat down by the fire to gather her thoughts. In a couple of hours she would have to face her mother, her sister-in-law and her brother. Would it be unpleasant, much like the scene with her father in London all those years ago, when he had threatened to marry her off to one of his cronies? At twenty-eight years of age, Lucy hoped she was more than capable of standing up for herself.

Lucy fell to reminiscing about her childhood. But the overriding memory of growing up in Somerville Hall was of feeling insignificant, standing in the shadow of her *darling* brother. Unbidden, a distressing recollection crept into her mind. It was her eighth birthday. Her mother had made her a promise the week before. Sitting in her best dress, Lucy waited for hours for her parents to appear for nursery tea—a very special treat. But they never came. In the end, her governess had put her to bed, unable to console her. Subsequently, she discovered they had travelled that day to Richard's school to watch him captain the rugby team.

And so a pattern was laid down for the rest of her childhood. Disappointment followed disappointment until her expectations were set to nought. Trying to gain her parents' attention, she had been driven to pranks and outrageous behaviour. The result had been the opposite of what she had intended: they gave her up as a lost cause. And, as her star had tumbled still further, Richard had basked in their parents' admiration. The heir who could do no wrong. Lucy laughed. Even on his infrequent visits home, he had been overbearing and full of self-importance. Lucy learnt to avoid him.

But now she was blue-devilled. Hearing from Richard she was about to lose her home had shaken her. It would mean a loss of independence. To live at Somerville again would be intolerable. What possible life would she have as a widowed aunt in Richard's home? There *had* to be an alternative. If only she could persuade him to secure the house for her or to agree to her becoming his life tenant. Anything would be better than being buried alive in the country.

An hour later, the entrance of a maid woke her. Lucy straightened up in the chair and regarded the girl standing at the door. She carried a steaming jug.

'I'm Edith, ma'am. Mrs Hughes sent me. I do for Mrs Somerville,' she said with a smile, before placing the jug on the washstand and turning to Lucy with an expectant look.

Lucy stared at her as her sleepy brain tried to catch up. 'Yes, of course. Thank you.'

The maid crossed to the armoire and stood for a few moments surveying the contents. Lucy almost squirmed with embarrassment. All her beautiful clothes were gone. What remained were mourning clothes, most of which had been hastily and inexpertly dyed black by Mary or bought in the second-hand market. Her two evening dresses must have been a pathetic sight compared to what the young girl was used to handling for her mistress.

'What would you like to wear this evening, ma'am?' the girl asked, a slight quiver in her voice.

'Whatever has survived the journey best,' Lucy said. The

maid appeared to accept this without a change in facial expression. But Lucy knew she would be the talk of the servants' hall within the hour, assuming the footman or butler hadn't embarked on an assassination of her character already. By now they would all know her lamentable history and treat her accordingly. It was the way of country houses. If only she could have kept Mary with her. Despite her youth, Mary had been fiercely loyal and would have been a welcome ally in the servants' hall.

Pushing aside these pointless longings, Lucy turned her attention to the evening ahead. It was vital she came across as self-possessed to her family. Any hint of weakness and they would try to take control. Sibylla was an unknown quantity, but she knew well how manipulating her mother was, and Richard had already shown this afternoon that his pomposity had no limit.

After a quick wash, she felt better and Edith helped her into a dress of black velvet. It had once been a prized possession; a glorious sleeveless cornflower-blue gown with a low square neckline. It had been a gift from Charlie. Stripping it of its lace and watching Mary sink the lovely fabric into the bucket of dye had been a painful moment. She had baulked at trimming it with crepe, but had observed the tradition, more to honour Charlie's memory than to appease her judgemental family. Her only consolation was it fitted her form perfectly.

She sat still at the dressing table while Edith brushed out her hair to begin the torturous process of twisting, pulling and pinning. The maid maintained a steady chatter, but Lucy did not listen. A tight knot of anxiety had formed in her stomach. All too soon, the first bell sounded for dinner and Edith was congratulating her on her looks and placing a black cashmere shawl around her shoulders. With a last glance in the mirror, Lucy wished she could replace the ugly dress with a suit of armour.

.   .   .

The murmur of voices grew louder as Lucy neared the blue salon. The pretentious designation made her smile for it had always been just the drawing room when she lived here. Her curiosity about her sister-in-law was increasing by the minute. Could she be a sensible woman? Tonight would give her the answer.

The door stood ajar.

'Have you taken leave of your senses, Richard? It's the only possible explanation for taking her in to our home.' The strident female voice halted Lucy in her tracks, and she stood motionless with her hand on the fingerplate of the door.

'Sibylla, please! There's no need to discuss this again, I have an obligation—'

'Pooh! What has changed? And I thought she wanted nothing to do with us. I tell you, Richard, you have been taken in. You're far too soft. Before we know it every waif and stray of the county will be presenting themselves.'

'My *daughter* belongs here with us,' a gentler lady's voice interrupted. But Lucy could detect the familiar steely undertone in her mother's voice. It brought to mind the last time they had spoken. And that wasn't a pleasant memory.

'With all due respect—' Sibylla said.

'How I detest those words,' Lucy's mother cut in. 'Somehow they are always a precursor to the most *disrespectful* comments imaginable.' There was a pause, then she continued in a firmer tone. 'With the death of Charles Lawrence, Lucy is alone in the world so it is only right she return here to her family home.'

'I knew it! This is your doing,' Sibylla exclaimed, her voice trembling. 'We will entertain a house full of guests in a few days, and Mrs Hughes has given her one of the best rooms on your instructions. I do not understand why my wishes were ignored.'

'Do you not, Sibylla?' Lucy's mother asked, her voice silky smooth. Lucy's ears pricked up; all was not well at Somerville, it seemed.

'Mother and I discussed it at length. Lucy must be treated properly for I'll not have it said I shirked my responsibilities to my sister,' Richard said.

'What right has she to expect anything from us now?' Sibylla asked. 'Her behaviour has brought nothing but shame to the family. What are we to *do* with her? Indeed, Richard, I must ask if she's to live off us indefinitely.'

'That's enough! Lucy is recently widowed. Have you no compassion?' Richard demanded.

'Yes, Sibylla, how can you be so hard-hearted towards your sister-in-law?' exclaimed Lucy's mother. 'To err is human.'

'Oh, for goodness' sake!' Sibylla exclaimed.

Someone cleared their throat and silence reigned for several moments. Sibylla's crass comments hung in the air, and Lucy's face began to burn. At that moment she wanted to return to her room and pack her bag.

'Richard, who are we waiting for?' A voice Lucy did not recognise piped up.

'My sister Lucy, Uncle Giles. I explained it all to you earlier,' Richard answered.

'Do I have a niece, Charlotte?' Uncle Giles asked. Lucy's mind was whirring, trying to place him. She had a vague memory of hearing of a Giles Bradshaw, her mother's youngest brother, but she had never met him.

'Yes, Giles, you do,' she heard her mother answer.

'Are you sure, Charlotte? I don't remember her.'

The conversation was taking a bizarre turn, and Lucy couldn't risk loitering outside any longer in case a servant appeared. Feeling far from confident, she entered the salon as the clock struck the hour.

At one end of the room, which was indeed very blue, sofas

and chairs were arranged around the marble fireplace. Two
women sat facing each other. Both heads swung around on her
entrance and stared as she advanced. Her mother had aged;
now silver-haired, a trifle gaunt about the face and in widow's
weeds, her pale blue eyes held little promise of affection.
Nothing had changed there. Across from her, a younger woman
with red hair regarded her with open hostility. Elegantly
dressed in green silk with a delicate fringed shawl draped
around her slender shoulders, she was certainly fashionable but
not particularly happy, her mouth forming a thin line of
disapproval.

A little outside the group at the fireplace, in a wingback
chair, an elderly gentleman with white hair and beard sat apart.
As Lucy advanced, he struggled to his feet.

Richard came forward to greet her at once. 'Good evening,
Lucy. I hope you're rested?' he asked, taking her arm and
bringing her towards the ladies.

Her mother rose stiffly to her feet and stepped forward,
arms wide. 'My dear Lucy,' she said, smiling broadly, 'You're
very welcome.' To Lucy's surprise she sounded sincere and
embraced her, the scent of violets almost overwhelming. Lucy
was at a loss for words for Mother had never been demonstra-
tive. Instantly, she was on her guard.

'It is wonderful to have you home. I do hope you will
consider staying with us longer than a few weeks?' her mother
said, tucking a possessive arm through hers. Lucy did not miss
the significant glance towards the younger woman.

'Thank you, Mother,' Lucy said, fighting hard to control her
disappointment. Clearly, she had strayed on to a battlefield.

'And this is my wife, Sibylla,' Richard said.

'Delighted,' the woman said, sounding anything but, as her
critical gaze swept over her. A limp handshake was offered. The
woman's comments moments before still rang in Lucy's ears,
and she was determined to dislike her.

As Sibylla's eyes lowered to take in her unfortunate dress, Lucy pasted a smile on her lips. 'It is lovely to meet you at last, Sibylla. Thank you for inviting me into your home for Christmas. So kind and so *generous* of you.'

Sibylla stiffened and glanced at her sharply.

'Would you do the honours, Richard?' the bearded gentleman asked, as he moved towards them. 'Who is this pretty wee thing?'

'Lucy, this is Captain Giles Bradshaw, your uncle,' Richard explained. 'I don't believe you have ever met.'

'No, we have not,' Lucy said.

'Royal Navy, my dear, since I was a lad,' Uncle Giles explained. 'HMS... oh, what was it again?' he asked, looking towards her mother.

'*Gallant*, dear.'

'Ah yes. What a beauty!' he said, his eyes taking on a dreamy quality. 'They don't build them like that any more. It was an honour to be her captain.'

'Retired Navy Captain,' Richard said with a hint of exasperation. 'You must forgive Uncle for his memory is a trifle unreliable. He will probably demand to know your name at breakfast every morning for the next week.'

Soon her hand was enveloped in a crushing handshake as she made her how-do-you-do.

'Nonsense, Richard, nothing wrong with being a little forgetful at my age, eh, my dear?' Uncle Giles asked, smiling warmly at her.

'No indeed, sir,' she said. 'One of the privileges, I dare say.'

This appeared to please him. 'What a clever young lady you are! I shall take you into dinner. I think you and I will become staunch friends.'

When the second bell sounded, Richard offered his arm to his mother and, much to Lucy's delight, Sibylla was left alone to trail behind them to the dining room.

FIVE

As the remnants of Lucy's nightmare slipped away, she lay rigid, her heart thumping as if it would burst. The bedroom was in darkness but she could make out a slit of light at the window. She pulled back the bedclothes and tiptoed across the room. Through the chink in the curtains, she peeped out. There was a pale hint of dawn on the horizon, but as the light increased, the vast expanse of lawn lay footprint-free under a fresh fall of snow. Nathaniel Marsh, the tormentor of her dreams, was not there. Gradually, her breathing slowed. She was being irrational, for he couldn't have found her so soon. He may not even be looking for her at all, she reasoned. Feeling braver, she opened the curtains and stood for some time mulling over her situation. If only there was someone she could confide in.

Lucy checked her watch but it was only a quarter past seven. The family would still be in their rooms. Relieved, she returned to bed even though she knew sleep would not return. Pulling the covers up to her chin, she waited for the warmth to seep back into her bones. The last time she was so bone-achingly cold was the day Charlie died.

And the shocks and unpleasantness had continued. A few

days later, she was amazed to come face to face with Richard at the solicitor's office. After her initial annoyance at what she assumed was interference in her affairs, she was left in a state of disbelief once the will was read. It was not the will she had seen a few years before, but dated only two months previously. Charlie had left her in the hands of her estranged brother by naming him as his executor. Feeling betrayed, she did not hold back, making it clear to both Richard and the solicitor what she thought of the arrangement. Lucy returned home delighted she had put Richard to the rout, but as it turned out, her victory was to be short-lived.

True to his word, the tiresome Mr Stone had arrived at the house demanding to speak to her. Forewarned, she had told Mary under no circumstances was he to be admitted. Days later, a letter arrived from him, requesting an interview. Although she admired his tenacity, she had torn it up and thrown it on the fire. Each follow-up letter met the same fate. After several weeks the letters ceased and she believed she had seen the last of him and put him from her mind.

Then, a few weeks' later, Nathaniel Marsh appeared one morning at Abbey Gardens. He was a respectable-looking man in his mid-fifties, tall and well-dressed and she recognised him as a mourner from Charlie's funeral. He had not made himself known to her at the graveside, but stood with several other gentlemen behind the next row of headstones.

'Mrs Lawrence, I'm so sorry to disturb you at this sad time,' he said, once Mary had closed the drawing room door. 'A dreadful business, dear lady. Your husband was a fine fellow. We were business associates these last few months.'

'I'm happy to meet you,' Lucy said, waving him to an armchair. Charlie had never mentioned him, she was sure, and she was curious why he had come. He refused her offer of tea. After removing his hat, Mr Marsh sat down, his smile revealing a gold incisor. For some reason, it put Lucy in mind of a pirate.

'I won't intrude, Mrs Lawrence. Let me be brief. If you could give me your husband's papers and effects, I'll be on my way.'

Startled, she sat staring at him. What on earth could he mean? 'Those are private, sir.'

The benevolent look vanished from Marsh's face, and he moved to the edge of his seat. 'Your husband and I were part-ners. I urgently require certain items he had in his possession. Speed is of the essence. My clients do not care about his demise, you must understand. They expect business as usual.'

'Sir, I have no knowledge of my husband's business affairs, and he did not keep any of his papers here. I suggest you talk to Mr Faulkner, his solicitor,' she said, trying to keep her temper in check. She retrieved the solicitor's card from her purse and handed it over. 'I'm sure he can help you with whatever you need.'

Mr Marsh stared at the card, then slipped it in to his pocket. 'You don't understand how urgent this is,' he said, scowling at her. 'Your husband owed me money, a great deal of money. The business will collapse if I don't get the—' He paused and ran a handkerchief over his forehead.

'Where is his study?' he demanded suddenly, jumping up. He towered above her, his eyes wild. Lunging towards her, he placed his hands on the armrests on either side of her. Terri-fied, Lucy shrank back and could only stare up at him. With a roar of rage, he stepped away before charging out of the room. Baffled by his behaviour, she trailed behind and saw him disappear into Charlie's study. The commotion drew the cook and Mary up from the kitchen. They stood in the hallway, wide-eyed. She signalled to them to stay put. With trepidation she approached the study, then hesitated in the doorway as Mr Marsh began to pull out the drawers of Charlie's desk and rifle through them. Horrified, Lucy protested, but he continued to ransack the room, ignoring her completely. She did not know what he was looking for and was too afraid to ask.

At last, he appeared satisfied she was telling the truth. But he advanced on her, breathing heavily, his face twisted in anger and frustration. Lucy recoiled against the doorframe, the edge digging into her shoulder.

'You haven't heard the last of this,' Marsh hissed. 'I want what belongs to me.' With a snarl, he brushed past her. At the front door, he turned and fixed her with a stare. 'I will find them, you know. I hope you have not been foolish enough to try and sell 'em. The *accident* which befell your husband was unfortunate. I would advise you to be most careful, Mrs Lawrence. Two tragedies in the one family would be considered very... unlucky.'

The door slammed shut, and the women stared at each other in disbelief.

'No more visitors, Mary, please,' Lucy said, her voice shaking. 'No matter who they say they are.'

'Yes, of course, Mrs Lawrence.' Mary twisted her hands, her eyes darting between Lucy and the cook. 'We'd best see to this,' Mary said eventually, turning to Mrs Trevor and jerking her head towards the study. The maid gently closed the study door after them. As Lucy walked away, she could hear their frantic whispering.

Standing in the centre of the drawing room, Lucy tried to calm her breathing. Should she go to the police? The man had threatened her in her own home and in front of her servants. But how could she explain any of it? If Charlie had been up to mischief would she be answerable for his actions? It was clear Mr Marsh was no businessman. What had Charlie really been up to? The suspicions she had suppressed came tumbling back. The late callers; the hurried departures and messages arriving late at night. Why had she not questioned Charlie more closely? But she knew why: the rebuffs were too painful to bear. She recalled Mr Stone's questions at the mortuary—it appeared he thought Charlie was involved in something. Hadn't he referred to Charlie as his best lead in a case? Whatever was going on, she didn't want to be involved. But now what was she to do? Mr Marsh wanted something from her and appeared convinced she knew what it was. *Damn you, Charlie*, she thought and slumped into a chair, despondent and afraid.

Her eyes fell to the fireplace. With disgust, she had thrown Richard's invitation to spend Christmas at Somerville into the fire only an hour before. It had flared up and died quickly in a burst of flame before falling on to the hearth where it now lay as an ash skeleton of rebuke. Distasteful as it was, it presented an option. Putting distance between herself and Mr Marsh was an appealing idea. She decided to take refuge in Yorkshire.

The east-facing suite on the second floor of Somerville Hall was traditionally the boudoir of the lady of the house. A large apartment, it had its own sitting and dressing rooms and commanded a view over the lake and parkland. Much to her surprise, Lucy discovered her mother still occupied it. As she entered the room, she was amazed to see it remained exactly as she remembered. Sibylla's hand was notably absent. She had to admit a grudging respect for her mother's tenacity, for it was almost as if she did not recognise Sibylla's rights at all. No wonder the two women were at loggerheads.

Her mother was sitting up in bed, sipping her hot chocolate, dressed in a white lace nightdress and cap with a paisley shawl around her shoulders. Weak morning sunshine threw her face into relief, and Lucy was struck by how beautiful she was, despite her years. With a queenly wave, Mother beckoned her towards the enormous four-poster bed.

'Good morning, Mother.' Lucy kissed her cheek and breathed in the sweet violet perfume.

'Good morning, my dear. What a welcome sight you are. I'm enjoying a quiet day today as I need to be well rested for when the guests arrive on Friday. Bring the chair over and we can chat. Have you eaten?'

'Yes. I have just escaped from the breakfast table... and Sibylla.'

'How did you get on?'

'The silence was instructive,' Lucy said.

'Oh dear, *that* bad!' Her mother's eyes were alight.

'I imagine I'll survive the experience. Is my elopement the reason for her hostility or is she generally unpleasant to visitors?'

Her mother chuckled. 'You know what these nouveau riche are like. They are so strait-laced when it comes to other people's morals. Richard should never have married someone so middle-class, but he fell heavily and would not listen to my objections. Her family are ghastly, but thankfully we see little of them.'

Lucy chuckled. 'What possessed you to stay here when Richard married? Why did you not remove to the townhouse in London? Surely it can't be easy taking second place.'

'Trust me, I don't,' Mother said with a smug smile. 'As it happened, Richard needed to put all his resources into the estate. The roof in the east wing cost a small fortune to repair and drainage works, or some such, were required on the home farm. Then Sibylla insisted on redecorating and buying new furniture. The London house wasn't fit to live in, as it was rented out for years. I couldn't impose the cost of refurbishment on him.'

'Has the Metcalf money run out?'

'Do you have to be so crude, my dear? Richard has every-thing of that nature under control. Frankly, Sibylla is little more than an ornament on his arm. But be on your guard, my dear. She has a nasty temper. As you may have guessed, we barely tolerate each other.

'What did you do to her?' Lucy asked, amused.

'The assumption does you no credit, Lucy,' her mother said, haughtily. 'As it happens, soon after the marriage I discovered she was inept. At first, she was grateful for my help as she did not know how to run a house like this. Then the boys arrived, one after the other, though she takes little interest in them. The poor little mites have been shipped off to school. Poor Richard didn't know what to do. So it was easier for everyone if I stayed.'

And convenient for you, Lucy thought.

Her mother bent towards her and lowered her voice. 'Then there was the *incident*.'

'Pray tell,' Lucy encouraged her, surprised her mother was confiding in her of all people. There was something strange about this intimacy. Was her mother softening up with age or looking for an ally?

Mother wrinkled her nose in distaste. 'There was an assignation, and I was unfortunate enough to stumble upon it. In the stables—can you credit it? And with a jumped-up solicitor from Harrogate, if you please.'

So the frosty Sibylla had blood, not ice, running through her veins. Somehow it made her seem more human. 'Did you inform Richard of this tryst?'

'Good heavens, no! He worshipped the ground she walked on in those early days. It would have destroyed him. However, I made sure she knew I knew. That's why she's afraid to challenge my position in the house.'

'I see.' Lucy was not at all surprised Mother had used Sibylla's indiscretion to gain the upper hand. It had always been her way.

'Never mind that silly woman. I want to hear all of your news,' her mother said.

'Why the sudden interest, Mother? The silence from Yorkshire for the past decade has been rather marked.'

'You harbour resentment. It isn't an attractive quality in a young lady.'

'Being excluded from my father's funeral, my brother's wedding and every other family occasion for the last ten years may have nurtured it. I defy anyone in my position not to feel some bitterness.'

Mrs Somerville sniffed. 'Honestly, you brought it on yourself. Your father was clear what the consequences would be if you went off with that young scoundrel.'

'Charlie was a good husband,' she lied. Lucy had no desire to hand her mother ammunition.

'Is that so?' One delicate eyebrow shot up. 'Nevertheless, now he's gone you must decide on your future.'

'Charlie is barely cold in the ground. I need time to grieve.'

Again the mocking look. But how could Mother possibly know their marriage had been floundering? Lucy began to feel uneasy.

'In the meantime, stay with me here at Somerville,' her mother said. 'At least until your mourning is over. I long for female company.'

Lucy smiled despite the alarming picture her mother's words conjured up. 'You have managed perfectly well without me up to now. Besides, you have Sibylla.'

'I can't deal with her, Lucy,' her mother said with a frown. 'The truth is *that* woman has no respect for my advancing years.'

'She doesn't *always* submit to your will, you mean.'

Her mother gave her a sharp glance. 'As I've said, we have had our differences. Now, as for your interesting situation, what are your plans? Has remarriage entered your head at all?'

'Mother!'

'It makes perfect sense after a decent period of mourning. Please avoid another scandal. One in a lifetime is enough, even for you.' Her mother stared off into the distance. 'I can think of several suitable local gentlemen. In fact, one or two, who will be here over Christmas, would probably be prepared to overlook your past. At least, you have kept your looks.'

'Thank you, but I find the idea of marrying again repugnant.'

'But how silly, my dear! You're far too young to remain a widow. You should trust my judgement next time. Yours proved singularly inadequate first time round. Can you deny that Charles Lawrence was the worst possible choice?'

Lucy smarted but was determined not to give her mother any leeway. 'I do not wish you to matchmake for me.'

'You may feel differently in a few months, you know, when your grief has eventually... evaporated.'

'If I do, I shall run straight to you, do not fear,' Lucy retorted.

Mother huffed and treated her to a doubtful look.

A swift change of subject was called for. Lucy did not wish to discuss her private affairs any further. 'How is Richard? He has the look of a man under considerable strain.'

'Nonsense! He's perfectly fine. He's such a good son, and I have wanted for nothing over the years. Why even this morning he came and sat with me before he left for London. He offered to drop my pearls into the jewellers to be cleaned while he's in town. As you may recall, I always wear them on Christmas Eve. But there was no need as Edith takes excellent care of my jewellery.'

'Gracious, you still have them? Should they not have gone to Sibylla on her marriage?'

'Oh no, she could never do them justice. Heirloom or not, I refused to part with them. That grasping madam will never have them. I'll ensure they go elsewhere when I'm gone.' She plucked at the bedcover with angry fingers.

Lucy smiled. 'They are too ostentatious for my taste.'

'I wasn't going to leave them to *you*.' Her mother's eyes

narrowed. 'However, if you were to decide to return to the fold...'

'I'm not sure they would be enough of a temptation,' Lucy said.

'How heartless you have become! London has made you hard, Lucy.'

'Hmm, and still I remain unmoved.'

'You always were a strange one!' her mother exclaimed.

'Thank you, Mother. It is such a comfort to know how much I'm cherished.'

SIX

Two days later, before dawn, the house burst into life. With a large party of guests expected for the Christmas celebrations, the servants wore harried expressions as they went about their duties. The maids swarmed about, antlike in their black uniforms, with Mrs Hughes barking out orders. Any footman found loitering or fraternising was dealt with swiftly by Jameson, who appeared to take great pleasure in chastising his underlings. All the while, Sibylla stalked the rooms and hallways with a grim and critical eye, striking terror in the hearts of the younger servants. Once Lucy had eaten her breakfast, she crept upstairs to her room, determined to keep well out of harm's way.

Later, while partaking of a solitary luncheon in the dining room, she heard Richard's voice out in the hallway. He had returned from London. Keen to speak to him about her situation before the house was swamped with guests, Lucy sought him out as soon as her meal was over. But Jameson informed her the master was with his steward and did not wish to be disturbed. Eager to avoid both her mother and Sibylla, Lucy made straight for the sanctuary of the library.

It had always been her favourite room. With floor to ceiling bookshelves, it even had a ladder on wheels to access the books on the upper shelves. As a child, her father had tolerated her presence only because he recognised a fellow bookworm. Sadly, it was the only time she had felt close to him, and now, standing inside the door, she recalled one dreadful afternoon when she was only six or seven. A large picture book of botanical drawings was a firm favourite, and she would often spend hours lying under his desk poring over the pictures. This particular day, however, the book was almost out of reach on a shelf and as her tiny fingers grappled with it, it had moved suddenly. The priceless tome slid to the floor and landed with a sickening thud. As the binding split, some pages had slipped out. With a roar, Father had banished her, and it was several weeks' later before he allowed her back in. She had a sudden longing to see that book again.

As Lucy made her way along the shelves examining the spines, she soon discovered much of her father's renowned collection had been replaced by newer and more fashionable works. Most of the books appeared to be unread, the spines crease-free and the pages shiny and unblemished. Disgusted, she concluded Richard must have sold off the collection and substituted it with cheaper volumes to fund his wife's desire for all things sparkly and new. However, she was hardly in a position to criticise for she had used the pawnbrokers in her time of need. But why then the lavish Christmas party if his finances were shaky? It didn't make sense.

If Richard employed a cataloguing system it soon defeated her, and she resorted to strolling up and down, choosing books at random. The collection was impressive if you judged it by quantity, but it was not to her taste. Most distressing of all, Elizabeth Blackwell's *A Curious Herbal,* the childhood botanical favourite, was not to be found. Almost on the point of giving up, she spotted a shelf of more modern-looking books. To her

delight, she found *The Portrait of a Lady*, a book she had over-
heard some ladies discussing in a tea room and had vowed to
read.

Book in hand, she made her way to the window at the far
end of the room where some chairs were arranged to make the
most of the light. She drew up short. Unbeknownst to her,
Uncle Giles had been in the library all the time; however, he
was fast asleep. It seemed a pity to disturb him so she turned on
her heel, but a creaking floor board gave her away. He sat bolt
upright.

'Who are you, young lady?' he demanded.

'I'm Lucy, your niece. I'm sorry to have disturbed you.' His
face remained blank as he stared up at her. Flummoxed, she
scrambled for something to say that might spark a memory. 'I'm
Charlotte's daughter, Lucy. Do you recall we met before dinner
the other evening? I have come from London and will be staying
here for Christmas.'

A slow smile spread across his face. 'Well, why didn't you
say? That rings a bell and now I think on it, you have a look of
your late father,' he said.

Relieved, she sat down opposite him. 'How long have you
lived at Somerville, sir?'

'Must be all of three years now. When I left the navy,
Richard offered me a home here. My navy pension wasn't up to
much. It was Charlotte's doing, of course. But he's a good
fellow.'

'Yes, sir, I believe he is. Tell me, do you miss your life at sea?'
Lucy asked.

Uncle Giles's face transformed. 'Ah my dear, it is the best
life a man can have. My ship, the *Gallant,* was the pride of the
navy, you know. I have travelled the world and seen things,
some of which would put you to the blush.'

'I'm sure you could share some of your more sedate adventures,' she said with a smile.

'I'd be delighted—' he said, breaking off at the sound of the door opening.

Richard walked in and came towards them. 'There you are, Lucy. Jameson said I'd find you in here. I believe you were looking for me?'

'Yes. I wished to consult with you,' she said.

'Would now be convenient?'

She gave her uncle an apologetic glance. 'Yes, please.'

To Lucy's surprise, Uncle Giles winked at her as she stood.

'Fetch your coat and we can take a walk down to the lake. The snow is melting at last,' Richard said.

Richard was waiting for her at the bottom of the front steps with two excited spaniels at his feet raring to go. Taking her arm, they fell into step and the dogs took off. Lucy stole a glance at her brother's face. As she barely knew him, she was unsure how to broach her problem. She opted for acquiescence.

'Richard, I would like to apologise for my hasty words the other afternoon. I can't imagine what came over me.'

He held up his hand, his austere expression softening. 'There's no need to apologise. Grief can have a strange effect, and you have been through a lot. Women are ruled by their emotions, I have always found. But, of course, they can't help it.'

Not trusting herself to reply, Lucy let him steer her along the path towards the lake which shimmered in the distance. The dogs were mere specks now as they raced ahead full of enthusiasm.

'I admit the last couple of months have been difficult,' she said after a while. 'The uncertainty surrounding Charlie's financial position is a concern. Mr Faulkner hasn't been forthcoming. All my enquiries have been met with excuses and if I hear 'Don't worry your head about it,' one more time...'

'Don't distress yourself, for it is all under control,' Richard replied.

The temptation to thump him was strong but Lucy's instincts told her he had to be handled with care. 'But I must know what I am to live on,' she insisted. 'I can't make firm plans until I do, and I have no wish to be a burden on anyone.'

'If the need arises, we will discuss it in due course. Besides, if you're living here, there will be no need to worry about such things.'

Lucy gave up, exasperated. Richard was ridiculously old-fashioned. They continued on in silence for several minutes. Lucy was delighted to see Sibylla had left the parkland untouched. As a child she had spent her happiest hours out on the land, away from the restrictions of the schoolroom and the whines of her unhappy governess. Her parents had not cared enough to curb her outdoor adventures.

'The park is looking well,' she commented. 'If the weather stays dry, I look forward to exploring during my stay.'

'Naturally, it isn't at its best this time of year. Surely you remember how well the park looks in spring?'

'I do, but it is pretty now, all the same, blanketed in snow. In London, the snow becomes a horrible mess within hours and the streets become most unpleasant. This is glorious in comparison.' Lucy sucked the cold air into her lungs and was at peace, the only sound the crunch of the snow and gravel beneath their boots and the happy yelps of the dogs in the distance.

'We will make a country girl of you again,' Richard said, chuckling. 'Of course, everything will seem strange to you at first, but I hope you can settle into our way of life. Do you know, we have a wide circle of friends and there's always something going on. Far from dull, I think you will agree.'

Not wanting to contradict him, Lucy smiled, but she was beginning to feel trapped. She was determined to return to London as soon as she had come to some agreement with him about the house in St John's Wood. It was obvious he wanted her to stay at Somerville, which struck her as peculiar considering their history. But she already knew she couldn't bear it, with the two women of the house at war and the days promising to be an endless round of at-homes, afternoon teas and embroidery. It would be incredibly tedious compared to what she was used to, and even though she knew she would be financially restricted, it was still preferable to being bored to death.

'If the weather holds, we will have a few days' shooting when the guests arrive,' Richard remarked, looking skyward. Then he looked down at her and frowned. 'Of course, most of the ladies prefer to stay indoors.'

'You remember?' she asked.

'Yes! How could I forget? You were nearly shot by Myles Chancellor.'

'You exaggerate, Richard; he hit the tree. Besides, it was only a bit of fun.'

'I never saw Father so shocked,' Richard said. 'I feared he'd have a heart seizure.'

'But it was so unreasonable. I only wanted to be a beater for the day and what higher calling could there be when you're nine years old?'

'Lucy, you were wayward, even then.' He scowled down at her.

'So, tell me, who is coming tomorrow?' she said, anxious he did not rake up all her past transgressions.

'The usual set, of course,' Richard replied. The Christmas gathering was a long tradition at Somerville when friends and family descended for the festivities. Coming to a halt, he laid a hand on her arm. 'As it happens, I was wondering if you would be willing to help Sibylla. I'm sure your assistance would be invaluable.' He gave her a searching look. 'It would be an excellent opportunity for you to get to know each other.'

'Yes, it would,' Lucy replied with a sinking heart. She could never imagine wanting to know Sibylla any better, but knew she would have to make some effort during her stay.

'Splendid.' They walked on. 'After Christmas I have to leave for town again. Your husband's will is proving troublesome, and I need to visit the solicitor. I can't make head nor tail of his accounts. But do not worry, I'm sure Mr—'

'Faulkner?'

'Yes, that's the chap. He must know more about it.'

'I'm sorry if it is proving an inconvenience.'

'No, not at all. A diversion, if I'm honest,' Richard said. 'Would you know who Charles's business associates were? It might be best if I were to consult with them directly.'

'No, I don't know anything about them,' Lucy said, with a flash of panic. She didn't want Charlie's reputation sullied any further or to drag her brother into whatever trouble Mr Marsh represented.

'I see. Not to worry.' To her surprise, he sounded dismayed. She hadn't expected him to be taking his executor duties so seriously. They continued on in silence for several minutes.

'Did he, by any chance, leave any papers at the house in St John's Wood? Anything relating to his finances that might be helpful?' he asked.

She froze momentarily as the image of Nathaniel Marsh ransacking their belongings sprang to mind. 'No. Mr Faulkner has everything of importance.'

'Jolly good.' Again, his words belied the look on his face. Could Charlie's affairs be in a worse state than she had suspected?

'I'm sorry if he didn't keep adequate records, Richard. He was never organised, and he didn't stick with anything for very long. My offers of help were rejected, so in the end it never seemed worth my while taking an interest. Of course, I could always tell when a particular scheme was coming to an end by his mood. Then days or weeks later he would come through the door with a spring in his step and a smile on his face, and I knew things were looking up.'

'A great one for schemes, was he?' Richard gave a mirthless laugh. 'A precarious way to live and support one's wife.'

'Yes, but he did his best,' Lucy said firmly.

'Of course.'

By now they had reached the water's edge where a small wooden jetty stretched out into the water. It looked treacherous, with the glitter of frost on the boards where the winter sun did not reach. A small rowing boat bobbed in the water, tied up near the end of the jetty. The wind was rising and the water was lapping the side of the boat.

'Now, tell me, can you still row a boat?' Richard asked.

Amused, she studied the rowing boat for a moment. 'Of course I can, but that's hardly *HMS Gallant*, is it? I expected something much grander the way Uncle Giles keeps mentioning it.'

Richard roared with laughter and looked years younger. It's a shame he doesn't laugh more often, Lucy thought. But then she remembered how frightful his wife was and she understood.

Later in the afternoon, Lucy was summoned to Sibylla's sitting room. Completely ignoring her, Sibylla sat at her desk, her pen moving swiftly across scented paper. An obvious tactic to put her on the back foot, Lucy knew, so she sat down and waited patiently for her to finish. She observed her sister-in-law closely, admiring her fashion sense, for she was always immaculately turned out. Today, her gown was a deep blue moiré silk, embroidered with tiny white roses at the cuffs and hem.

Sibylla put the note in an envelope, addressed it and placed it face down on the desk, a gesture which did not escape Lucy's notice. At last Sibylla looked across at her, unsmiling. 'Richard suggested you might help with the preparations. Am I to understand you have experience in entertaining?' she asked, one delicate eyebrow arched.

'Charlie and I often hosted parties in town,' Lucy replied, unruffled by Sibylla's snide tone. 'And, of course, I always helped Mother here before I married.'

Sibylla gave her a long searching look. 'I'm at a loss as to what you could do for me so late in the day. All the arrangements were made weeks ago.' This sounded like a rebuke, and Lucy had to suppress a smile. 'I suppose you could do the flowers for the blue salon. I assume you know one flower from another?'

'I believe I do.' Lucy wondered how many weeds she could surreptitiously include.

'Good. Speak to Matthews, the head gardener. He will show you what is available in the forcing houses.'

'If you think of anything else, please let me know,' Lucy said, starting to rise, with escape to the forefront of her mind.

'I haven't finished,' Sibylla said, with a belligerent look. 'Please stay where you are.'

Lucy braced herself as she settled down in the chair once more.

'I won't pretend I'm overly delighted at your arrival in my house. However, Richard has always been gullible and led by his mother. As you're here, I expect you to behave with decorum. Family and friends arrive tomorrow. A more refined and cultured group of people would be hard to find in all of·Yorkshire. Due to your state of mourning, I hope you will stay in the background. I'm sure I do not need to remind you that only the severest black will be tolerated in your attire. Anything else would offend our guests' sensibilities. I was most surprised to notice the dark grey cuffs on your dress yesterday. An oversight, I assume? You may join us for dinner, but other than that, you should keep to your room.'

'I understand,' Lucy said. The woman was truly a horror.

Sibylla's chin jutted out towards her. 'There will be several young gentlemen in the party, including my younger brother. Under no circumstances are you to put yourself forward. Let me tell you, anything of that sort and you will find yourself on the first train to London.'

It was on the tip of Lucy's tongue to say she couldn't think of anything more to her liking than fleeing to town, when a maid entered looking scared to death. Sibylla was told in halting accents there was an emergency in the kitchen and she was wanted by cook.

'She expects me to go down to the kitchen! Has she lost the use of her legs?' Sibylla demanded.

The young maid's lip trembled in response. Sibylla muttered something under her breath. 'Yes, yes,' she said to her, 'I'll be there directly.' At the door, she paused and turned to Lucy. 'Have I made myself clear, sister?'

'Perfectly, Sibylla.'

Sibylla sniffed and followed the maid out of the room.

On her way out Lucy's curiosity got the better of her and she flipped over the envelope on Sibylla's desk. The letter was addressed to John Ashby, a solicitor in Harrogate. Now, why was Sibylla writing to him, she wondered.

SEVEN

Christmas Eve, Somerville Hall

The arrival of the guests commenced early in the afternoon, heralded by the continuous crunch of wheels on gravel. Mildly curious, Lucy watched them alight from their carriages, noting with interest who had been worthy of an invitation from Sibylla. She had no great desire to be one of the welcoming committee down in the hallway, even if Sibylla had asked it of her, and had stayed in her bedroom. Her presence would have resulted in curious stares or impertinent questions and she did not wish to be an object of interest: a black sheep returned. Most of those same family members had shunned her whenever their paths had crossed in London in the intervening years. She was still too fragile to run that particular gauntlet.

Later in the evening when she entered the blue salon, she was overcome by the unfamiliar sensation of standing alone on the edge of such an event. An unexpected pang of grief caught her off guard. It was possible life without Charlie, notwithstanding his faults, might prove challenging. But her sombre attire would make it easy to blend into the background, so she skirted the perimeter of the room and found a chair, half hidden in a window bay. From here, she could observe the forty or more guests while maintaining a distance. Some, she knew, were staying in the house for a few days, while others were local families invited only for the famous Christmas Eve banquet.

It was as if the salon had been invaded by a flock of exotic birds, each displaying their plumage in a kaleidoscope of colour. Every conceivable shade of silk, satin and velvet was on display, and it appeared likely the jewellery boxes of Yorkshire had been emptied for the occasion. It almost hurt to look upon so much glitter and sparkle in such a confined space. Thankfully, the gentlemen in full black evening dress were perfect foils for their more vibrant companions.

Through a gap in the crowd, Lucy spotted her mother. Charlotte Somerville looked magnificent. Standing next to Uncle Giles, she was in a dark grey silk dress, piped in black and around her neck were the famous Somerville pearls. Two long loops of lustrous pearls were clasped together with a large emerald which caught the light and shimmered softly in the lamplight. Lucy could understand why Sibylla might be jealous. The set was showy, but Lucy had to admit the effect was breathtaking.

'Hello, Lucy, do you remember me?' a tentative voice asked. Lucy looked up to see a young woman, soberly dressed in a dark green gown. Her brown hair was scraped back in an unflattering style, but Lucy recognised her immediately. They had been close friends growing up, as Judith Chancellor's father's estate, Blackheath Manor, ran next to Somerville. Lucy and the Chancellor daughters had run riot between the two.

'Judith! Of course I do,' Lucy exclaimed, jumping up and shaking her warmly by the hand. 'How lovely to see you. You're well, I trust?'

'Thank you, I'm very well. I was so glad to learn you would be here.'

'And I am delighted to see a friendly face. Please, won't you join me?' Lucy asked.

Judith sat down, smoothing her skirts, then turned towards her with sympathy in her large grey eyes. 'I was so sorry to hear about your husband.'

Here was genuine sympathy and the first of its kind since entering Somerville. Lucy had to take a moment, fearing her voice would break. 'Yes, poor Charlie. It was a terrible accident, Judith. But I'm slowly coming to terms with it, and thank you for your letter of condolence. I took great comfort from it.'

'It was the least I could do, but I'm glad to have the opportunity to say it in person.'

'You are a dear. I have to admit being here at Somerville feels strange for I never expected them to be the least supportive or to invite me. Richard has been... surprisingly agreeable, though more affected than I remembered. And Mother has been suspiciously welcoming.' Judith raised a brow, but passed no comment. 'I'm not sure what I was expecting, but the undercurrents in the house are peculiar. This isn't a happy home. Richard is under stress but tries to hide it. My mother is acting as though I'm the prodigal daughter when we both know how she really feels and Sibylla is an utter nightmare. Mind you, my mother has contributed to that, there can be no doubt.'

Judith leaned closer. 'I know I shouldn't say it, being a guest, but your sister-in-law isn't well-liked.'

Lucy laughed. 'I wonder why.'

'She... oh, I see, that's a rhetorical question.'

'Dear Judith!'

'Still, it is only right they welcome you home again after all this time. They treated you abominably.'

'Don't waste your sympathy on me, Judith. I was a headstrong and impulsive fool. I should have heeded Vicar Quake's sermons on reaping and sowing, and I might have saved myself a lot of heartache.'

Frowning, Judith shook her head. 'But to cut you off completely was positively medieval. My parents were horrified at the time. I recall my mother looking up Debrett's—your husband's family had impeccable lineage. She couldn't understand what objection there could be.'

'Empty coffers, my dear,' Lucy said with a smile. 'Then I made things worse. I refused my mother's choice in London even when I was told the alternative would be to return in disgrace and marry old Grimshaw. Even if I hadn't met Charlie, that would have caused ructions in due course. No doubt I would have ended up running away with a footman on the morning of the wedding. I was always destined to cause a scandal.'

Judith gasped. 'I never knew about Grimshaw. Was it your father's idea?'

'Yes, he was very keen; however, I get goosebumps just thinking about it, even after all this time.'

'You'd be a rich widow now!' Judith said. 'Oh, I beg your pardon, that was an insensitive thing to say.'

Lucy smiled. 'Not at all, you're probably right. However, would it have been worth it to live with him? I doubt it. Remember how his corset used to creak?'

'I do! Every Sunday at church I could see your shoulders shaking whenever he moved. I had to focus on sad things to avoid bursting out laughing,' Judith said with a giggle. 'Lord, you haven't changed one bit!'

'No, I haven't. I'm still as irreverent as ever. But enough about me. How are your family, Judith? Is your father here this evening? I would dearly love to see him again.'

'Unfortunately, he wasn't well enough to make even such a short journey. He was upset, for this is the first year he's missed Christmas Eve at Somerville, and he particularly wished to meet you again. You will come and visit him, won't you?'

'Of course I will.'

Judith squeezed her hand. 'He will be delighted, thank you. He persuaded me to come on my own this evening. Quite daring of me, don't you agree?'

'Nonsense! Why should you not?' Lucy said, dismayed at her friend's timidity, though understanding it only too well. Spinsters were condemned to be invisible. That or drudges.

'We lead a very quiet life at Blackheath. Father has been ill the last few years and has been steadily getting worse. I have been looking after him since Mama passed away.'

This explained a lot, Lucy thought. Poor Judith had been left behind while her sisters escaped. 'What about Helen and Emily? Do they visit and help out?'

'They come when they can, but they have their own families now and the distance is too great,' Judith said, looking uncomfortable.

'I understand. But you must come and stay with me in London for a little holiday. I'm sure you could be spared for a few days.'

Judith became flustered. 'It is kind of you, indeed... I would like to very much, but—'

Lucy patted her arm. 'Don't distress yourself. We can talk about it before I return to town.'

'Oh! I thought you were back at Somerville permanently. Richard implied as much when I spoke to him earlier.'

'Did he indeed! I could never fit in here,' Lucy said.

'There have been a lot of changes, certainly.' Judith's voice was tinged with sadness.

'Yes, and not for the better, as far as I can see,' Lucy said.

Sibylla's former lover, if her mother was to be believed, turned out to be Lucy's neighbour at dinner. John Ashby was a robust and red-faced young man, who spoke endlessly of the local hunt throughout the meal. Lucy's initial fascination soon evaporated.

She couldn't fathom why her sister-in-law would have chosen such a dreary man for a dalliance. In fact, she doubted it so much she began to wonder if Mother had made it up. Sibylla was at the other end of the table seemingly preoccupied with the gentlemen on either side of her. But Lucy did catch a few surreptitious glances in Mr Ashby's direction and wondered if the affair could still be alive. Why else would she have been writing to him?

Lucy's other dinner companion was the local vicar, Mr Thorn. A stern-faced middle-aged man, he spoke little to her, despite several attempts she made to engage him in conversation. His expression when he did look at her held something akin to disapproval. Lucy could only assume he knew of her history and was taking a dim view of it. Suspecting her sister-in-law had deliberately placed her between the two most tedious gentlemen in the room, she spent most of the meal trying to come up with suitable retaliation.

Once the dessert dishes had been removed, Sibylla rose and all the ladies followed her to the salon. But it was Lucy's mother who held court, leaving Sibylla sour-faced and struggling to control her temper. Lucy almost felt sorry for her. But there were few women who could compete with her mother in full flow before a captive audience.

Lucy soon realised most of the women present seemed reluctant to engage in conversation with her. It was plain Sibylla had carried out a discrediting campaign prior to her arrival from London. Why her sister-in-law saw her as a threat she couldn't imagine, but it only strengthened Lucy's resolve to return to town as soon as possible.

Seeing Judith was trapped with a group of matrons holding forth on the decline of England's morals, she decided to come to her rescue and coaxed her away. 'Let's find a quiet corner and have a proper talk.' Judith jumped up eagerly.

They were barely seated when the gentlemen rejoined

them and soon the tall and forbidding form of Mr Thorn appeared before them.

'Good evening, Miss Chancellor,' he said, completely ignoring Lucy and staring at her friend in a manner which made Lucy uneasy.

Judith stiffened, then slowly looked up. 'Mr Thorn.' Her tone was such most would take the hint and rapidly disappear, but Thorn regarded the vacant spot on the sofa as if waiting for an invitation to join them. Lucy was trying to find a suitable off-putting remark when Richard rushed up to them.

'There you are, Thorn. We are ready for you now,' he said.

Mr Thorn gave Judith an oily smile and walked off.

Richard took up position at the door and cleared his throat. 'Dear friends, could I ask you all to follow me down to the hall? The village children have arrived to sing carols for us.' There were delighted comments as everyone filed out and down the stairs. This was always the highlight of Christmas Eve at Somerville.

Feeling nostalgic, Lucy linked Judith's arm and they descended together. The children were grouped at the bottom of the staircase beside the Christmas tree. Mr Thorn was keeping a peremptory eye on the carollers who were casting anxious glances in his direction. Lucy heard Judith sigh and perceived a slight flush to her cheeks, her eyes fixed on the cleric. But Lucy had seen enough to realise it was annoyance not longing that afflicted her friend.

Once all the guests were down in the hall and standing in quiet anticipation, Thorn gave a nod and the children commenced their recital. It brought some happy memories flooding back for Lucy. Her father had loved to hear the children sing, and she had often seen him surreptitiously wipe away a tear.

'Aren't they wonderful?' she whispered to Judith.

But her friend was staring hard at Mr Thorn and appeared not to hear her.

Just before midnight, her mother beckoned and asked Lucy to accompany her to her room. With a promise to call at Blackheath in a couple of days, she took her leave of Judith. Jameson escorted them up the stairs, lighting the way with a lantern. Mother leaned heavily on her arm as they ascended, and they had to stop several times for her to catch her breath.

Lucy was alarmed. When she lived at home, she had never seen her mother abandon a party early. 'You are unwell?' she asked as soon as Jameson had left them alone.

'Yes, my dear. I have the most fearful headache. Would you be so good as to ring for Edith?'

'Of course.' Lucy crossed the room and pulled the bell at the side of the fireplace. Her mother sat down at her dressing table with a weary sigh. 'Is there anything else I can do for you?' Lucy asked, growing concerned as her mother's face had a grey tinge.

'Could you undo the clasp on these?' Mother indicated the pearls. 'The weight around my neck is unbearable.'

Lucy undid the clasp and laid the pearls down on the dressing table. The emerald caught the light as she did so. 'The emerald is so beautiful,' she remarked.

Her mother's smile, reflected in the mirror, was strained. 'Yes, it is, but I thought you didn't like the set.' Slowly she took out the pearl and emerald earrings and placed them beside the necklace.

'True, but it doesn't mean I can't admire the quality of it, Mother. I would not wear such a large piece. Where is the case? You shouldn't leave them out like that. They might be damaged and those earrings could easily be lost if they fall to the floor.'

'Don't worry. Edith will look after them and give them to Richard to put in the safe.'

At that moment, Edith bustled in the door, took one look at her mistress and began to fuss. 'Lord, ma'am, you're done in!'

'Don't plague me, Edith,' her mother said, but Lucy could see she was relieved to see her maid.

'It's one of your bad headaches, isn't it?' Edith asked.

'Yes,' Mrs Somerville admitted. 'Would you make up some laudanum for me?'

'I'll stay with her, while you do it,' Lucy offered.

'Thank you, ma'am. I'll be as quick as I can,' Edith replied and disappeared out the door.

'Let me help you out of your dress,' Lucy said.

'Edith will do it,' Mother said. 'Don't fuss, Loo!'

A lump formed in Lucy's throat. No one had used that particular endearment for many years. 'I don't mind, Mother, I'd like to help. Please?'

'Oh, very well.'

By the time Edith came back, she had her mother in her nightgown resting against the pillows on the bed with a damp handkerchief applied to her forehead.

'Bless you, ma'am,' Edith said. 'I'll see to her now.'

'Good night,' Lucy said, as she watched Mother down the glass of cloudy yellow liquid.

With a grimace, Mrs Somerville gave the glass to Edith and turned to Lucy. 'Thank you, my dear, your help has been invaluable.'

EIGHT

Christmas morning broke sunny and clear and Lucy was looking forward to the day ahead. Regardless of Sibylla's command she stay out of sight, she had no intention of complying. There was something she wanted to do. For years her absence at her father's funeral had troubled her. Dick Somerville was buried in the family plot in the local churchyard which was reached by a pleasant stroll through the park. The previous evening over dinner, the house guests had discussed going to Harrogate for Christmas Morning service, so Lucy knew she could slip away to the graveyard and have the privacy she yearned.

She crept out early, taking a slight detour to the forcing houses. There she collected a wreath Matthews had prepared for her by prior agreement. The beautiful arrangement of holly, yew and ivy almost made her resolve fail as emotions overpowered her. Her father's rejection had been the hardest to accept. She still couldn't fully understand why he had acted so brutally, even though with hindsight Lucy realised his fears concerning Charlie had probably been well-founded.

Half an hour later, she was relieved to find the churchyard deserted. Anxiously looking about in case the unpleasant Mr Thorn was around, she followed the gravel path through the headstones to the far side of the tiny chapel. The family plot was located under the bell tower and was sheltered by a stand of ancient yew trees. The lichen-covered headstone towered above the grave. Staring at it, she could almost hear the soil hitting the coffin lid and the drone of old Vicar Quake's reedy voice.

'Oh Papa!' she whispered, 'I have missed you so.'

Moving closer, she realised her father's inscription was not the newest. *Annabel Somerville, died 8ᵗʰ May 1880, age 2 months* was carved directly beneath her father's name, *Richard Anthony Somerville*. Overwhelmed, Lucy cried, both for her father and the little niece no one had bothered to tell her about. Poor Sibylla and Richard. Losing a child must have been dreadful. Could it explain why Sibylla was so prickly? Perhaps she should make more of an effort to befriend her.

She dried her eyes and laid the wreath down on the grave. A sudden screech made her jump, but it was only a magpie squabbling with its neighbour. *Horrid birds*, she thought and turned away. Taking a shaky breath, for she knew she would not visit here again, she made her way to the gate.

Lucy took advantage of the fair weather and strolled around the park for an hour. She found it easier to reflect on her circumstances away from the distractions and politics of the house. Resolved to return to town by New Year, she knew she needed a strategy to deal with Marsh. How was she to protect herself? Confiding in Richard was out of the question: he was far too moralistic. If he found out about Marsh, he would likely throw her off. But the notion of returning to Abbey Gardens with no servants in situ was nerve-racking. There would be no Mary to thwart unwanted visitors. Perhaps she could take up her friend

Lady Sarah Strawbridge's invitation and stay with her until the danger had passed but she had no idea how long that would be. Or perhaps she should swallow her pride and go to the police?

And then there was the difficulty regarding where she was to live. While Somerville was full of guests, any opportunity to pin Richard down on an amicable solution regarding St John's Wood was unlikely to arise. If the house had to be sold, could she afford to stay in London? Answers remained elusive. Resigned to waiting it out, she made her way back to the house.

But as she stood in the hallway removing her hat and coat, Edith came out of the library and rushed down the hall towards her.

'Please, ma'am, Mr Somerville would like to see you, straight away,' she said, indicating the library with a nod.

Lucy noticed the maid's eyes were red-rimmed. 'Are you well, Edith? Have you been crying?' she asked before turning and handing her things to the footman.

Edith swallowed hard. 'Ma'am, you'd best hurry.' The maid continued to regard her with a nervous expression, her eyes flicking between her and the retreating footman.

Lucy clutched her arm, suddenly recalling her mother's fragile state the night before. 'Is it my mother? Is she still unwell?'

Edith wouldn't meet her eye. 'You could say that, ma'am.' With a stifled sob, Edith wrenched away and skirted around her towards the green baize door to the servants' quarters. What a strange thing to say, Lucy mused, staring after the maid. With a churning stomach, she wondered what could be going on and headed for the library.

They were waiting for her. Sibylla was sitting in an armchair, ramrod straight with a smug expression, while Richard was leaning against his desk, looking grim. The hairs on the back of Lucy's neck prickled. Something *was* wrong.

'Sit down, Lucy,' Richard said, his formal tone making her

wary. He rounded the desk and sat down. Whatever could have happened?

'Is something the matter? I met Mother's maid out in the hallway and she was distressed. I hope Mother isn't unwell?'

'In the circumstances, she is as well as can be expected,' Richard said.

Lucy's stomach flipped. 'I don't understand; Edith said something similar,' she said, looking between the two.

'The Somerville pearls are missing. Stolen, in fact,' Sibylla announced. Richard glanced at her sharply as if to reprimand, but Sibylla merely raised a brow at him.

'Good heavens! How extraordinary!' Lucy exclaimed. 'Surely you don't suspect Edith? Why, she's utterly devoted to Mother.'

'Agreed. And furthermore, Edith has been in service in this house for six years. I do not suspect *her*,' Richard snapped.

Lucy's mind raced. With the house full of guests it would be difficult to find the culprit and there were so many places you could hide stolen pearls in the rambling wings of the mansion. Then she noticed the way they were looking at her.

Flabbergasted, she straightened up. 'Are you accusing *me*? I had nothing to do with this,' she said, half laughing in disbelief. 'Why would I do such a thing? I know how much she loves those pearls.'

'Edith has told us you were the last person to touch them last night and you knew Mother had taken laudanum. You could have entered the room at any time during the night knowing she would not wake,' Richard said.

'Anyone could have done so, not just me. Besides, Mother said Edith would give the pearls to you to lock away in the safe. I had no reason to believe otherwise.'

'Edith neglected to give them to me as she was more concerned about Mother's state of health than her jewellery.

She claims the pearls were left on the dressing table. When she went in to wake Mother this morning, she realised she had forgotten to bring them to me. Mother's room was thoroughly searched, but the pearls were gone. Straightaway, she came to see if I had them. She was certainly at fault leaving them unattended; however, I do not believe she stole them.'

'And that leaves only... you,' Sibylla said.

'And a house full of guests,' Lucy insisted.

Sibylla laughed. 'You can't be serious. No one would abuse our hospitality in such a way.'

Lucy rose to her feet, shaking. 'But you dare to accuse me? Search my room if you must. I have nothing to hide.'

'That is being done, as we speak,' Sibylla said with a smirk.

Appalled, Lucy glared back at her. 'Good. Then you will see that I could not have done it. You will not find the pearls amongst my possessions.'

'Unless, of course, you have hidden them somewhere in the house or the grounds until it is safe to move them,' Sibylla said. 'And you were out early this morning. Don't deny it, for I saw you cross the lawn at an unearthly hour. I was much struck by that. Such an odd thing to do.'

'If you must know, I was going to the churchyard to visit Father's grave,' Lucy replied looking at Richard, who dropped his gaze. 'But this is pointless. It would appear you have found me guilty already.'

Sibylla's face was now white with rage. 'Every one of our guests is well known to us, and let me assure you, none of them are thieves. However, you're a virtual stranger in this house. No doubt the temptation was too much, and I can almost understand why you did it.'

Richard looked down at his desk and hissed, 'Yes, Sibylla, thank you.' Then he gave Lucy a look tinged with pity. 'I, too, can understand it. You're in reduced circumstances and must resent being reliant on me for your future security. The pearls would provide you with a substantial sum of money to start over. Though I do not comprehend how you thought you would get away with it.'

Sibylla sniffed. 'It is sad to see a Somerville reduced to such an act of betrayal.'

Lucy fumed but remained silent, her mind churning as all the implications of the situation stretched out before her. No one could vouch for her whereabouts during the night. Her only hope was that most of the other guests were in the same situation and Richard would eventually see how ludicrous the accusation was. Any of the guests or servants could be guilty.

Richard cleared his throat. 'If you would be good enough to fetch the pearls, we can agree to overlook the incident and I'll not have to involve the police. There will be no scandal.'

'Yes! Please spare us that,' Sibylla chimed in.

'I have nothing to hide as I did not take them,' Lucy ground out.

Richard's eyes hardened. 'Then you leave me no choice but to inform the police in Harrogate.'

'Good!' Lucy said. 'I hope they will get to the truth of the matter as quickly as possible.'

'Please go back to your room and remain there. The servants will bring you your meals,' Sibylla said, with a dismissive wave of her hand.

Richard stood up. 'Please do not speak to any of the guests about this. Mother is distraught and has taken to her bed. The guests have been informed she's taken ill to explain her absence from the festivities today.'

Sibylla looked up at Richard. 'I warned you she was trouble, but would you listen? No. Now see where we are.'

Lucy glared at her. Richard sat down and stared down at his desk.

Stiff with rage, Lucy left the library, barely foregoing the pleasure of slamming the door. A rising panic flooded her veins as she made her way to her room and she could feel the horrible clamminess of perspiration on her skin. What was really going on? Who had taken the blasted pearls?

Determined to find answers, she went straight to her mother's room. Edith answered the door and immediately tried to close it. Lucy wedged her foot against it.

'Please, Edith, I must speak to my mother immediately.'

Edith flicked a glance back into the room. 'Mrs Somerville is resting and she doesn't want to see you.'

'Edith, I have been accused in the wrong, and I know you didn't do it either. Please let me speak to her and hopefully this stupid muddle can be sorted out as soon as possible.'

Edith mulled this over for a few seconds then stood aside.

'Please don't upset her,' Edith said. The maid crossed the room and went into the sitting room, leaving the door ajar.

The bedroom was in semi-darkness and it took several moments for Lucy's eyes to adjust. Her mother was resting against the pillows on the bed, a handkerchief pressed to her mouth. She stared at Lucy as if she were a stranger.

'Mother?' she asked softly. 'It's Lucy.'

'Why are you here?' Mother asked, her voice cracking with emotion.

'Richard and Sibylla have accused me of stealing your pearls. You know that's ridiculous. I would never steal from you.'

No response.

'Mother?'

'I don't wish to see or speak to you. After all I have done for you! I felt sorry for you and persuaded Richard to invite you here. How could you? You have betrayed my trust.'

'No!' Lucy cried, stepping closer. 'It's not true! You must believe me.'

Edith came back into the room. 'I think you should leave,

ma'am. Mrs Somerville has had an awful shock. The doctor has been called. He will be here soon.'

Lucy, bewildered and hurt, turned to her mother. 'On my honour, I did not steal from you and I'll do my utmost to find out who did.'

But Mother turned away on a sob.

NINE

Two Days Later

During the morning, a steady stream of guests took their leave of the family on the front steps. Lucy stood at her bedroom window and watched yet another carriage pull away. The police had not appeared, but slowly it had dawned on her Richard didn't want his guests to know about the theft, happy to believe her guilty. They were closing ranks to avoid a scandal. But it meant precious time had been wasted. The real culprit was undoubtedly congratulating themselves on their success and halfway to London or wherever they hailed from. Unless it had been a servant who had taken the pearls. That was another strong possibility, but she doubted Richard had even considered it.

A sudden rush of anger left her breathless and shaking. This limbo was intolerable; her room had become a prison cell. Deeply troubled, Lucy turned away and sank down on the bed. She picked up *The Portrait of a Lady* which she had abandoned earlier but Henry James's words swam before her eyes and she let the book fall on to the green silk counterpane. Concentration was impossible. How on earth was she going to escape the inevitable? It appeared the necklace was still missing. Every time Edith had come with her meals, she had questioned her. But the maid would only shrug. Suspecting Sibylla had warned Edith to tell her nothing, Lucy eventually stopped asking.

No doubt the police would arrive now the guests were out of the way. They would believe the accusations levelled against her, and she would be carted off to the station in Harrogate. She knew, because she had checked, there was a footman standing outside her door. Escape was impossible and, besides, she was innocent. Fleeing would only make things worse.

If only she hadn't been so impulsive. Why hadn't she stayed in London, informed the police of Marsh's threat and moved to lodgings in a different part of town? It would have been so easy to become invisible and start a new life, allowing the city to swallow her up. With a shiver, she pulled her legs up under her, burrowing into the soft folds of her shawl. *I won't give way to tears*, she thought. *I'm stronger than this.*

Across the room, the broken lid of her escritoire lay on the dressing table, its hinges twisted. Two footmen had ransacked her bedroom on Christmas Day, urged on by Sibylla. With great reluctance she had handed over the key, and had stood by help-less as they had tipped out the contents onto the bed. Not happy with that, Sibylla had urged them to take it apart, which had been done none too gently. Lucy's fear someone might have planted the necklace in her room while she had been out had caused her to break out in a cold sweat. But they had found nothing. Sibylla didn't even try to hide her disappointment, slamming the door as she left.

It was almost five o'clock when Mrs Hughes came for her. Lucy was surprised when she was brought down to the servants' quarters and shown into a basement room, where two police officers were conducting their interviews. It was the first sign of danger: she was being interviewed as though she were a servant, not one of the family. Defences up, she bristled with nerves.

The more senior man, red-faced and loose-jowled, regarded her with open hostility as she sat down. His companion was a lanky young man with a pock-marked face and watery eyes.

'I'm Sergeant Wilson and this is Constable Carter. Take a seat, Mrs Lawrence, please.' He glanced down at a list in front of him and made a tick against it with a pencil. 'You know why we are here?' he asked.

'Someone has stolen my mother's pearls,' Lucy said.

'Someone? A serious charge has been made against *you* by your brother,' the sergeant said.

'A false charge, I can assure you,' Lucy snapped. 'I'm innocent. I did not steal my mother's necklace.'

'I'll thank you to remember it is my job to determine who is guilty or not,' Wilson said.

'Forgive me, but I was under the impression it was for a court of law to decide such things,' she retorted.

Wilson gave her a withering look and grunted.

'Do you not realise the real culprit is long gone? Why did you not come when the theft was discovered on Christmas Day?' Lucy asked. Wilson smarted but made no comment. 'It had to be one of the guests.'

'Well, you would say that, wouldn't you,' he responded, quick as a flash.

Lucy stiffened. How on earth was she to convince him of her innocence? 'For some reason my brother will not contemplate the idea one of them could have done it. Indeed, a servant could also be responsible. Have *their* rooms been searched?' Wilson shifted in his seat but continued to smirk. Lucy took a steadying breath. 'Anyone could have entered my mother's room and taken the pearls during the night.'

The sergeant flicked a glance at the constable who was

scribbling in his notebook. 'I have spoken to all the servants and to the family. Other than her maid, no one knew she had taken something to help her sleep, but you.'

'And most of the guests are regular visitors and would know the rooms are never locked. The thief was only waiting for the right opportunity,' Lucy replied.

'Why not last year or the year before? The only difference is your presence in the house. And, most importantly, how would they know the pearls were still in the room?'

'An opportune theft, perhaps?' she snapped.

Sergeant Wilson rolled his eyes. 'However, *you* knew for certain. Your mother told me you undid the clasp and put them on her dressing table,' he replied with a self-satisfied look.

'She asked me to,' Lucy pointed out, her anger finally igniting.

'Like the feel of those pearls, did you?' he asked, leaning towards her. 'Or was it the emerald that caught your eye?'

'No!'

'Bitter you were thrown off when you eloped, you hoped to get your revenge on these good people,' he continued. 'No doubt, you planned it all along, eh? Your brother told us you changed your mind at the last minute about coming here for Christmas. Had your recent change in circumstances anything to do with it? According to Mr Somerville, you're virtually penniless, which gives you a motive.'

'What? That's utter nonsense,' she said, her stomach turning over. She could guess who had poisoned him against her.

'I don't know. Seems plausible to me.'

Lucy clenched her teeth. 'My brother and sister-in-law are mistaken. I have no grudge against my family. On the contrary, I'm recently widowed, and I was grateful to them for welcoming me into their home. Why would I betray their trust so? It is ridiculous.'

The sergeant's eyebrows shot up. 'Is that so?'

'Yes!'

'Well, you have a strange way of showing your gratitude.' The constable snorted and the sergeant rested his rather large chin on his steepled fingers. 'It all boils down to this, Mrs Lawrence. Your family believe you did it. *I* believe you did it. You had the perfect opportunity, and you knew you could go back into her room and she would not wake.'

'The pearls were on the table when I left. It was the maid's job to give them to my brother to put in the safe. I had no reason to believe she would not do so.'

'We only have your word for it. Now, Mrs Lawrence, please be good enough to give my constable a full statement.'

'Certainly,' she said, 'though it hardly seems to matter what my version of events is.'

The sergeant smiled and sat back in his chair, 'Your problem, as I see it, Mrs Lawrence, is the evidence points to you and only you.'

'What evidence would that be?'

He held out his hand. A solitary pearl nestled in his palm. 'Can you explain why this was found under your bed?'

Lucy could think of nothing to say.

Harrogate Police Station, the Next Day

Much to Lucy's surprise the cell in Harrogate Police Station was larger than she had anticipated. However, all her other expectations were fully met: the building was old, cold and rat-infested and the food left a lot to be desired. For most of the morning she was left in her cell with only the constable stopping by with her breakfast. Lucy was sure it was a deliberate ploy by the sergeant to make her feel vulnerable.

Around midday, she was taken out to be questioned. The interview room looked suspiciously like a store room which had been hastily set up with a table and a couple of chairs. Boxes and crates were stacked up against the wall and the window was so obscured by grime, it was impossible to tell if it was day or night in the outside world. A smoking oil lamp sat on the table, its fumes making her empty stomach queasy.

Sergeant Wilson sat glowering at her. Not in a co-operative mood, she folded her arms, set her expression to indignant and stared right back at him.

'When is this farce going to end?' she asked after several minutes of a silent war of wills. 'You can't keep me here indefinitely.' She had no idea if this was true, but she had to try something.

'Can't I, now?' he said, rubbing his chin.

'Surely I'm entitled to a solicitor? What proof do you have?'

Wilson chuckled. 'Proof, is it? Are you a police officer now? You still haven't explained the pearl found in your room.'

The man was a clown. Unfortunately, he was a clown with a lot of power over her. 'My bedroom was searched on Christmas Day. There was no sign of any pearl then.'

'Your brother says differently.'

'Then he's lying! Did you question the footmen who searched my room or indeed my sister-in-law who was present? They could verify what I have just told you. My brother is trying to put the blame on me,' she said.

'Come now, Mrs Lawrence, you know that's highly unlikely. Why would he do such an unspeakable thing to his own sister?'

'I do not know. You would have to ask him.'

He shook his head. 'It would be in everyone's interests if you were to confess at this stage.'

'I can see how it would be in *your* interest,' she said. 'However, as I didn't do it, I have no intention of confessing. You had much better spend your time finding the real culprit. One of the guests or servants could easily be involved.' Her exasperation was growing by the second. 'How many times do I have to tell you I'm innocent?'

Wilson gave her a pitying look. 'I understand how someone in your position could be tempted into a temporary... moral lapse. Those pearls are worth a small fortune according to your brother. If you could tell me where you've hidden them, I'm sure I could persuade the Somervilles to reconsider and welcome you back. Mr Somerville is a gentleman, he'll forgive you.'

Lucy sighed in frustration. 'I have no wish to return to Somerville Hall, thank you.'

The sergeant shook his head. 'This can't end well for you.'

'And it will not end well for you either. If this goes to court, it will make you a laughing stock. With evidence which must have been put in my room by some malicious individual, and no witnesses, your case against me is ludicrous. My sister-in-law has coveted those pearls for some time. Maybe you should ask her about them.'

'What an ungrateful woman you are,' Wilson spluttered. 'How can you say such things after all they have tried to do for you in your present circumstances? It's a shame it is, you turning up again after all you put your family through and betraying their trust in such a fashion.'

They were interrupted by a knock on the door. The constable stuck his head in.

'Sergeant, you're wanted at the desk.'

'Not now, Constable Carter. Can't you see I'm in the middle of an important interrogation?'

Carter glanced at Lucy then back to the sergeant. 'You'd best come, sir.' He lowered his voice. 'Looks like trouble.'

Sergeant Wilson grunted as he stood. 'I'll be back,' he said to her as he made for the door.

'I can't wait,' she snapped.

Minutes later, she was surprised to hear raised male voices

outside. Then the door opened. But it wasn't the sergeant. A tall, expensively attired gentleman entered the room. She recognised him immediately and gasped. 'You!'

Standing just inside the door, leaning on his cane, Mr Stone regarded her with a steady look which held a great deal of amusement. 'We meet again, Mrs Lawrence,' he said at last.

'What are *you* doing here?' she demanded.

Stone's expression hardened as his gaze raked over her. There was little she could do but endure his scrutiny. After a few moments, he removed his silk top hat and placed it, along with his cane, on the table and took the sergeant's seat. His eyes continued to bore into her, causing her stomach to tighten in anxiety. Here was a far more formidable man than the sergeant to deal with.

'Now that isn't particularly friendly, Mrs Lawrence,' he remarked, 'considering I'm about to secure your release.'

TEN

Lucy stared at Stone in disbelief. 'My release? Forgive me if I sound ungrateful, sir, but I don't understand. Why do you want to help *me*?' she asked.

Mr Stone sat back in his chair, regarding her much like a butterfly pinned to a page. 'You're the widow of Charles Lawrence.'

'Yes, but you already know this. What has it to do wi—?'

'It has everything to do with my presence here, Mrs Lawrence.'

She recalled his remarks at the mortuary. Clearly, he had believed Charlie was involved in something nefarious, but why would he turn up here in Harrogate? Now? What connection could there be?

'Would you care to explain?' she asked.

'We have unfinished business, Mrs Lawrence,' he replied with the ghost of a smile.

Lucy frowned. 'Do we? I wasn't aware of it.'

Mr Stone shook his head. 'Or *choose* not to be.'

Lucy narrowed her eyes and glared at him. 'Why were you at the mortuary that day? You never explained your presence or your interest in my husband. Did you know him in some capacity?'

'Unfortunately, yes, after a fashion,' Stone answered. 'And I could have explained it all, if you had granted me admission to your home on the numerous occasions I called.'

The heat of embarrassment rose in her face. 'I was not receiving anyone. I was... I *am* in mourning. If it were that urgent, why did you not contact my solicitor?'

Stone raised a brow and pursed his lips. 'No matter. I believe we can help each other now and I can make this foolery go away.' He waved vaguely towards the station front desk. 'In return for some information.'

Suddenly wary, Lucy gave him a cool look. 'What kind of information, Mr Stone?'

'Please don't be concerned, for we need not discuss it here, Mrs Lawrence. If you are agreeable, I'll sort out this little misunderstanding with the sergeant and we can adjourn to the private parlour of the Red Fox Inn across the road.'

'Wait!' she said, as he stood up. 'I have no intention of going anywhere with you. I do not know you.'

'You'd rather rot away in this godforsaken place?'

'Mr Stone, I'm here because my so-called family, for some reason I can't comprehend, want to put the blame on me for the theft of a family heirloom. It isn't personal, but my faith in human nature has deserted me somewhat,' she said. 'Why should I trust *you*?'

With an exasperated sigh, the man sat down again. 'Mrs Lawrence, I understand you have had a difficult time.'

'Truly, I doubt you have any idea at all,' she replied.

A flicker of impatience crossed his face. 'Let me assure you, you can trust me. In fact, I have your best interests at heart. The reason I'm here is to find the Somerville pearls and have the culprit brought to justice.'

Not quite able to believe her ears, Lucy smiled tentatively. 'You're here about the pearls?'

'Yes, your brother's insurance company has engaged me in the matter. When your brother gave me a list of his Christmas guests this morning, I spotted your name. Upon enquiring of your whereabouts, I was informed you were here and why.'

'And you don't believe I was responsible?'

This was incredible. Was her luck changing?

'I'm fairly certain you were not,' he replied, 'and I'm usually right in these matters.'

'It would appear you're to be congratulated on your superior understanding, but who are you really, Mr Stone?'

He smiled properly for the first time, and it wasn't unpleasant to behold, making him less threatening and austere. 'I'm a specialist investigator. I scrutinise claims and probe suspected fraud where high-value items are involved.'

'Such as the Somerville pearls?' Mr Stone bowed his head. 'Do you think this might be a case of fraud?' Lucy asked. While she knew for certain Richard had framed her, it was incredible this man shared that view. But it had never occurred to her that Richard was making a false claim: she had suspected it was expediency that had prompted his actions. Scandal was to be avoided at all costs.

'Far too early to say, Mrs Lawrence, as I only arrived yesterday evening.'

Deflated a little, she mulled this over. 'But you have been to Somerville Hall? You have spoken to my brother Richard?'

'Yes, I have and it is why I'm here,' he said. 'I didn't believe a single word he said.'

On entering the Red Fox Inn, Lucy was shown upstairs to a private room to freshen up. Having splashed her face and tidied

her hair, she returned downstairs. Despite its overpowering
aroma of beer and strong tobacco, the Red Fox private parlour
was warm and welcoming. Stone was in the doorway ordering
food from the landlord, so she settled down beside the fire and
observed him closely. He had not struck her as the knight in
shining armour type when they had met before. And could it
really be a coincidence that he should pop up again? She was
indebted to him but suspected he was only helping her to
further his own ends. However, at this moment, she was without
a friend in the world; whatever information he wanted from her
she would try to provide if it meant her freedom. She couldn't
fathom what she could impart that he would want to know, but
Lucy was certain it had to relate to Charlie's business affairs.
And that was a problem as she knew nothing about them.

Seeing Stone in action at the police station, she had been
impressed. Her release had been so easily achieved. The
sergeant had been obstructive at first, but eventually produced
his prized piece of evidence. Stone took one look at the pearl
and started to chuckle and shake his head, pulling out a loupe
from his inside pocket. Briefly, he examined the pearl lying in
the palm of his hand. The sergeant, red-faced, had blustered.
Stone responded by scratching the surface of the pearl with his
fingernail. Lucy had exclaimed as a flimsy flake had peeled
away. The pearl was a fake. Stone had lost no time in informing
the sergeant what he thought of his powers of detection. With
what appeared to be a great deal of satisfaction, he had left
Sergeant Wilson a quivering wreck in his wake through sheer
force of will and a barrage of legalese.

A young servant girl entered the room and prepared a table
near the window. Lucy sat gazing into the fire, her palms flat on
the settle on either side of her. All of a sudden she was weary
and the brave front she had maintained was starting to crumble.
Richard had thrown her into this situation, God only knows
why, and without the slightest concern for her well-being. Her

mother and sister-in-law had been all too ready to believe her a thief. How was she to retrieve the situation? She sighed heavily; she was everybody's pawn, and she didn't even know the rules of the game.

'That sounds defeatist,' Stone remarked as he came towards her.

'No, sir, I'm contemplating possibilities,' she said, still staring into the flames.

'Might I enquire what troubles you?'

She leaned against the high back of the settle and began to tick off her fingers. 'Let me see. I appear to be under suspicion of criminal activity. I have been shunned yet again by my family and my belongings are in a house in which I am no longer welcome. Added to this my beloved brother is executor of my husband's estate and wants to sell my home. Mere trifles, I know, sir, but for me the idea of returning to Somerville Hall is abhorrent. However, the difficulty is, how else am I to retrieve my money and belongings? I require funds to purchase my fare to York and train fare to London. You find all of this amusing, Mr Stone?'

'No, not at all, but you're taking a very bleak view of the situation and obviously haven't counted on my intervention.'

'Again? What have I done to merit such charity?'

'As I tried to explain earlier—' They were interrupted by the young servant entering the room carrying a tray laden with food. Stone gestured towards the table. 'Please, Mrs Lawrence, won't you join me?'

He pulled out a chair for her. 'The soup smells wonderful. I'm hungry, I must admit,' she said, sitting down. With a wry smile, she looked out the window in the direction of the station. 'The food provided across the road was inedible. Even the mice turned their noses up at it.'

'You should never have been arrested. I hope the experience wasn't too distressing?'

Lucy couldn't help but smile. 'I'm relieved not to have to spend another night at Her Majesty's pleasure. Thank you.'

'Not at all,' he said. 'I'm glad to have been of assistance.'

'But why have you helped me? Everyone else assumes I'm guilty.'

'I could not allow such an obvious miscarriage of justice. Unfortunately for the real culprit, I'm under no illusion regarding the case against you. It is far too convenient, and I was immediately suspicious. The local constabulary did not strike me as being competent when I called upon them late yesterday evening. Once I learned your brother was the local magistrate, I suspected they were happy to do whatever he told them to do.'

'Yes! It was sickening to see them kowtow to him. They would not listen to anything I said. It was ridiculous. Richard waited until all the guests had left before calling them in. And another thing. Only my room was searched and by the servants, not the police.'

He tutted and shook his head. 'Very remiss.'

'Yes, and all the while one of the guests could have left with the pearls in their bag,' Lucy said.

Stone snapped to attention. 'Do you believe the culprit was a guest? Have you any proof?' he asked.

'No, how could I? I was virtually a prisoner in my room. Don't you see, it had to be one of them or perhaps one of the servants. But why was my brother so eager to accuse me?'

He put down his spoon. 'Because it was convenient to do so. My dear Mrs Lawrence, you need to look at all of this objectively. It will make perfect sense when I reveal to you one important fact of which I'm certain you're unaware.'

'Which is?'

'According to my sources, your brother is in serious financial difficulty.'

'Good Lord!' Lucy exclaimed. 'Funnily enough, I did wonder when I discovered my father's library collection had been disposed of, but I saw no other sign of financial distress. No, no, you must be mistaken. Look at the house, the expensive furniture... this Christmas they have entertained a house full of guests at enormous cost. Richard spoke of settling an allowance on me as my husband's affairs were not left as they should have been.'

He sniffed. 'All for show, Mrs Lawrence. No doubt he hasn't revealed the truth to his wife or your mother. When a case such as this comes my way, the first thing I check is the financial position of the claimant. I'm in the lucky position of having connections where most others do not. It was a simple matter to put the enquiry out in the clubs. It is common knowledge your brother is struggling to meet his commitments and his bank is less than pleased with him. It is rumoured he lost a substantial amount of money during the summer.'

'Good heavens!'

'Do eat up, your soup will go cold.'

Lucy picked up her spoon, but continued to stare at him. 'And you believe my brother, finding himself in serious difficulty, faked the theft to claim—'

'You see, I knew you'd work it out. Some bread?' He offered her the basket.

She took a piece without taking her eyes off Stone. 'And he was happy to sacrifice me?'

'I imagine, once the insurance company paid up, he would have had the whole thing hushed up and you would have been sent on your way,' he said.

'With my character in tatters! But it was sheer chance I agreed to come to Yorkshire.'

'It is likely he would have set up a servant instead, but he had to do it when the house was full of guests to make it difficult for anyone to investigate. Your present financial situation was the perfect motive for the police, and he encouraged them to believe it.'

'Hence the fabricated story of the pearl being found in my room.' Mr Stone nodded his head in agreement. 'I feel ill,' Lucy said. 'How could he?'

'Not particularly gentlemanly, I would agree,' Stone replied. 'It speaks of desperation.'

'How can you prove your theory? What will you do?'

'News of your release has most likely been sent to Somerville. I shall return there after luncheon and inform Mr Somerville there was insufficient evidence against you and I suspect one of his guests was the culprit. The real blow will be when I tell him I'll advise the company not to pay out at this time. He will not like it. He will bluster and threaten me, but I'm well used to it. Your belongings will be retrieved, and we will catch the late train to London together. Tomorrow morning I'll report my findings to the insurance company. They trust my judgement and will not pay out. Your brother will panic. But he can't risk showing his hand and will have to wait. In time he will become desperate and, if I'm right, he will, after a sufficient interval of time, attempt to sell the necklace. I may intervene by having a quiet word with his bank. If they threaten to foreclose, he will have no choice but to act.'

'At which point, you will catch him?'

'Undoubtedly! Now, you look done in. Would you care for a glass of wine?' Mr Stone enquired.

ELEVEN

Overwhelmed by Mr Stone's revelations, Lucy stared down at her untasted wine, her fingers twisting the stem of the glass. He sounded confident, but until she was away from Harrogate, she couldn't feel safe. If Stone was right about Richard, and she grudgingly had to admit it sounded plausible, she had no doubt her brother would try to salvage the situation by convincing the sergeant to re-arrest her. She wouldn't put it past him to produce more 'evidence' to avoid suspicion falling on him. She was powerless. Her only hope was to trust Stone to keep his word and get her back to London.

Lucy took a sip of her wine and tried to relax. 'What a strange choice of career, Mr Stone, if you don't mind me saying. I have never heard of an insurance investigator before. Was it something you always wanted to do?'

His eyes crinkled as he smiled. 'No, indeed. There are few choices open to younger sons, as I'm sure you're aware. I was not particularly enamoured by the prospect of the church or a soldier's life. Much to my family's delight, I chose to leave Kent and took up the law.'

'A noble choice.'

'Yes. However, I found I became bored with it. A chance meeting with an old friend who wished for advice on a tricky case of insurance fraud cemented my belief that my future lay elsewhere. To my father's everlasting dismay, I appear to have a talent for investigation and have prospered. Naturally, he does not like the idea of me mingling with what he considers the criminal classes, despite the fact that many of those I deal with are aristocracy, and not just the underbelly of cities such as London.'

'It can be dangerous?' Lucy asked.

'Sometimes. Desperation can bring out the worst in people, but luckily it is verbal abuse I receive the most. Though I have received a few scars and bruises courtesy of some unhappy fraudsters.'

'No wonder your family disapprove. But it must be fascinating work.'

'I have no regrets, Mrs Lawrence. Every case is a challenge.'

'Except for this one. You appear to have solved this with little effort.'

'It is too early to claim a victory. Until your brother tries to sell the necklace, it can only be speculation. In all likelihood, the necklace is hidden at Somerville but I do not have the right to search the property. But do not worry, I believe I'll be proved correct in time.'

From the corner of her eye, Lucy spotted a gig drawing up outside the police station. 'I don't believe it! Look, it's him!' She watched as Richard jumped down, handing the reins to his groom. Taking the steps two at a time, he looked about uneasily, then disappeared through the doorway of the station. Lucy was delighted to see him so rattled but knew it meant trouble. 'Why is he going in there? Will he try to have me arrested again? I'll not spend another night in that place,' she said half rising from her seat. 'I should have left Harrogate immediately after you secured my release.'

'Calm yourself, you will not be taken into custody again. I'll make sure of it. Somehow I do not think the sergeant will co-operate with your brother this time. He's been made to look a fool for detaining you already on the flimsiest of evidence.'

'How dare Richard do this! We were never close growing up but this...' She trailed off, exhaling deeply. She was determined she wasn't setting foot in that police station again. 'I fear he's capable of anything. How do I protect myself, Mr Stone?'

'Do as I suggest and you will be fine.'

'I hardly know you, but it seems I have little choice but to have faith in you. I'll consider whatever you advise.'

Moments later, Richard emerged with Sergeant Wilson close at his heels. A heated exchange ensued on the top step, with the sergeant looking as though he was coming off the worse. Eventually, he pointed over to the Red Fox Inn and stomped back into the station.

'I believe your brother is about to pay us a visit,' Stone remarked. 'Might I suggest you go upstairs? There's no need for you to meet him. It will only distress you.'

'Not in the least! I should like to have it out with him.'

'But you may jeopardise my position, and it will not serve any useful purpose,' Mr Stone pointed out.

'It would give me great satisfaction—is that not purpose enough?'

'Undeniably, but I would advise against it.'

'If someone had treated you this way, Mr Stone, would you stand by and say nothing?'

'No one would dare, Mrs Lawrence,' he said, shooting his cuffs. Then his expression softened. 'Do consider. As executor of your husband's estate, he still has power over your finances, temporarily, at least. It would be wise not to engage with him at this point. In due course, his greed will deliver his downfall in a far more satisfying way than you calling him out in the front parlour of a public house. I'll deal with him as I outlined earlier. Quickly now, he's almost at the door.'

Annoyed by his condescending tone, Lucy was tempted to refuse. He drummed his long fingers on the table, holding her gaze, a challenge in his dark eyes.

'Oh, very well,' she said, doing her best to ignore his satisfied twitch of a smile. At the door which led to the stairs, she hesitated and turned towards him. He shook his head and mouthed 'go'. With seconds to spare, she slipped out. But there was no way she was going to miss this. She didn't completely close over the door, leaving a crack through which she could see into the room.

'Good afternoon, sir,' Stone said, rising to greet Richard. 'What can I do for you?'

'Good afternoon, Stone. I want to know what progress you have made since this morning.' Richard was looking towards the remains of their meal on the table. 'And perhaps you can explain what possessed you to have my sister released?'

'I'm sure you will be relieved to hear she's innocent and a potential miscarriage of justice has been averted.'

Richard glared at him. 'Explain!'

'The only evidence against your sister was a pearl reputedly found under her bed. As Mrs Lawrence was absent for several hours on Christmas morning, anyone could have put it there in the hope of casting suspicion on her.'

'No! It had to be Lucy. She knew the pearls were in the room and Mother would not wake. It pains me to say, but you do not know my sister's lamentable history. She was always wild and eloped at eighteen, causing scandal and uproar. As you would expect, my father cut her off without a dowry. Then that blighter of a husband of hers dies a few months ago and leaves her penniless. Of course, I stepped in and offered her a home, holding out the olive branch and all that. Only for my mother's sake, you understand. Let me tell you, she wasn't having any of it until she realised just how bad things were. Then she came running to Yorkshire, contrite as be damned. If I'd known what she was planning, I would have had her turned away.'

Lucy had to smother the urge to rush in and confront him. She could hardly believe her own brother would speak about her in such a way. From behind the door, she willed Stone to hit him, but he didn't oblige.

'Thank you for sharing this with me, sir, but it is irrelevant,' Stone said, calm as you please. 'The whereabouts of the Somerville pearls is all I'm interested in. There's no evidence to connect her with the crime. The pearl the sergeant produced for me was a cheap imitation and therefore *not* from your mother's necklace.'

'What?' Richard spluttered. 'Don't be ridiculous, Stone! It came from Mother's necklace—I'm sure of it.'

Stone remained silent. Lucy almost laughed for Richard's assertion was tantamount to admission. Richard paced up and down. After a few moments, he came to a stop. 'It must be—' Lucy couldn't believe it: he still didn't realise his mistake.

'A case brought against your sister would be demolished by any defence barrister worth his salt, and rightly so, with only circumstantial evidence against her and the fact the police had no opportunity to question the other guests, the servants or search their rooms.'

Richard shook his head. 'Dash it, I didn't want my guests inconvenienced!'

'A crime was committed in your house, sir.'

Lucy crept closer to the door.

'Bah!' Richard twisted the wedding band on his finger. 'I knew it had to be Lucy, so there was no need—'

'Certainly someone wishes us all to believe Mrs Lawrence guilty.'

Richard smarted. 'It was with great reluctance I confided my suspicion to the police. One does not want to believe one's own sister is involved. Damn it, I had no choice.' Lucy had to squeeze her eyes shut and count to ten. When she opened them again, Stone was staring at her brother with a look of disgust, and Lucy sensed he was barely holding onto his temper.

'Did she not deserve the right of every accused? As a magistrate, sir, you know the law: innocent until proven guilty. Any misunderstanding could have been avoided if the police had been informed immediately the discovery of the theft was made. Precious time and possible evidence have been lost,' Stone continued, his tone brisk, cutting off Richard who had started to object. 'Sir, you must understand I can do nothing further at this point. The real culprit was one of your guests or servants, and I'm satisfied Mrs Lawrence is innocent. The case is now in the hands of the police, and I return to London this evening. I'll be recommending to Sanderson & Irvine they do not pay out at this time. Hopefully, in due course, the police will solve this. Now each of your guests will have to be tracked down and interviewed, all of which will take a considerable amount of time and effort.'

Richard glared, his hands clenched. 'Is that necessary, Stone? Any hint of scandal must be avoided. I had hoped to keep this affair private; besides which, I do not for a moment suspect any of my guests, no matter what you say. They are all important people.' He gripped the back of the settle. 'I don't want this to reach the newspapers. My mother is elderly and frail—'

'The claim will not be settled without a proper investigation being carried out,' Stone said firmly.

'Yes... of course, but have some compassion. This is all distressing for my mother and my wife.'

'Indeed it is, sir. *And* for your sister.' Lucy almost cheered.

'That's as may be,' Richard replied with a grimace, glancing again at the table. 'Where is she, anyway?' Lucy stepped away from the door, suddenly afraid her hiding place might be discovered.

'Mrs Lawrence is resting upstairs. She's badly shaken, sir, and I understand her accommodation across the road was not to her liking.'

'Eh? Oh, I see. Yes, well... it's her own fault.'

'In the circumstances, Mrs Lawrence wishes to return to town. This would be best, I think you will agree? Perhaps her things could be sent here? We hope to catch the quarter past four train from York.'

Unable to resist, Lucy edged up to the door again. From the look on Richard's face, she knew he would not object. Stone was making it clear she was now under his protection. Richard looked worried, which pleased her very much.

'Yes, I will arrange it,' he muttered.

'Thank you, sir. I'm sure she'll be most grateful.'

Richard turned away with a scowl and sat down on the settle. 'I don't know what I'll tell my mother. Those pearls meant the world to her. Of course, I want them found, but it looks unlikely now *if* what you say is true. I shall have to replace them, and I can tell you it will cost me a pretty penny. The emerald alone would buy a small country. What do you think they will do with it?' he asked. 'Sell it?'

Lucy stifled a chuckle. It was almost as if Richard was asking Stone how to dispose of the necklace.

'There are several difficulties faced by the thief, as I see it, sir,' Stone replied. 'The piece is famous and easily recognised. Word has been sent out to all the reputable jewellers in the country to be on the lookout for it, particularly the emerald, as it is so distinctive. So whoever has stolen it will have to find an establishment which will not ask too many questions. This will require a foray into the criminal underworld which isn't without its risks and will be highly dangerous for anyone not versed in how those particular gentlemen carry on their trade.

The easiest option for the thief would be to break up the necklace into its individual pieces and sell them off. But then the full value will not be attained.'

Lucy could have sworn she heard a groan from Richard, which was quickly covered by a cough.

'An unsavoury world you work in, Stone.'

'Yes, sir, indeed it is,' Stone said, fixing him with a stern gaze.

'But if it never turns up at any of these premises, or what have you, the claim will be settled?'

'No doubt. However, these things can take years, particularly if the item is of high value. Your insurance company will want to be sure there's no possibility of the item being recovered.'

'Years?' Richard exclaimed.

'Yes.'

Richard stood abruptly and moved towards Stone. 'Look, old man, we are both men of the world. I would like this whole sorry affair sorted out as quickly as possible. The pearls could be anywhere in the country by now, even abroad. We can hardly expect them to be found at this stage. Would it not be easier to have the claim settled and not waste police time? I'm sure I have paid a small fortune in premiums to Sanderson & Irvine over the years, as did my father and grandfather.'

Lucy clenched her fists in anger. Richard really was a slimy toad.

'They will not pay out until I'm satisfied a full and proper investigation has been carried out... sir,' Stone stated, his expression stern.

Hurrah, that's put him in his place, Lucy thought, and to her great satisfaction she saw her brother turn away from Stone in defeat.

TWELVE

King's Cross Station, London

Until darkness had fallen, Lucy had checked off the stations southwards out of habit. Little sleep for many days had left her exhausted but anxiety gnawed at her, making rest of any kind sporadic at best.

What a day it had been. She could hardly believe that Stone, of all people, had come to her rescue. For the latter part of the journey, he had slept, and Lucy had taken the opportunity to study him. It was obvious from his grooming he was a fastidious man and his build and colouring hinted at a love of outdoor pursuits. He was taller than Charlie had been and although they had travelled first-class with more than enough leg-room for the average man, he had appeared uncomfortable and, even in his sleep, had moved around as if to find a better position. Although her assessment of him that day in the mortuary still appeared to be accurate, she had to admit he was a gentleman. And one with expensive taste to judge by his clothes.

Lucy wondered if there was a Mrs Stone waiting for his

return. He did not wear a wedding band, but that was no guarantee of the single state. She couldn't deny he was an attractive man, though a little cold for her taste. But there was something intriguing about him. A commanding manner and an analytical turn of mind were useful attributes in a rescuer and, no matter what his motives were, he had acted in her best interests. It struck her how different he was to Charlie in every way, then felt a pang of guilt.

Stone still hadn't brought up the subject of Charlie but she knew it was only a matter of time. He had said he wanted information but she couldn't think what she could know that would be of interest. And she didn't doubt he would call at Abbey Gardens soon. Tenacity, Lucy suspected, was one of his traits and a prerequisite in his line of business.

'Mr Stone, wake up! We have arrived at last,' Lucy said as the train came to a stop. Stone's eyes popped open. Outside, weary travellers started to make their way along the platform. Lucy was sure, like her, they were longing for their beds. But only an empty house awaited her. It was all very well running back to London, but what about tomorrow and the days to follow—what was she to do? Her circumstances had changed, certainly, but not in the way she had hoped on setting out for Yorkshire.

The locomotive threw out one final gurgle of steam and the figures outside the window were swallowed by a white cloud.

'I do apologise,' Stone said, straightening up. 'How long was I asleep? I hope I didn't... disturb you.'

'Don't mention it,' she replied, 'a few gentle snores don't bother me.' He gave her a sheepish look, and she smiled. 'Charlie, my husband, always slept on the train. I admit *I* may have dozed a while too.'

Lucy picked up her wooden writing box and tried to secure the lid. Then sighed. 'It was broken when my room was searched. Such a pity, for I'm extremely fond of it. It was a gift from my father on my sixteenth birthday. I hope it isn't beyond repair.'

'That's a shame. Let me see, Mrs Lawrence. It may not be as bad as you think.'

Stone examined the escritoire. 'I know someone who can fix this for you. My man George is clever with tricky items such as this. Will you entrust it to me?'

'It is kind of you to offer. I would appreciate it. Thank you.' Lucy removed her belongings from the box and handed it over before picking up her carpet bag.

'It has been a long day,' Stone said, consulting his watch. 'It is almost midnight. Let me see you home, Mrs Lawrence.'

Lucy froze. 'There's absolutely no need, Mr Stone. You have done more than enough for me today.'

'No, I insist. It is far too late for you to travel alone.'

A peasouper, sulphurous and choking, hung over the city and with so many late trains arriving at the same time, a long wait for a cab seemed inevitable. The other passengers, looking miserable and chilled, were crowded around the entrance. Porters were running about as they came under increasing pressure to procure cabs. However, Stone soon secured a porter and sent him scurrying off to hail a hansom.

'How on earth did you manage that?' Lucy asked, aware of some envious glances from other travellers.

Stone smiled. 'I'm acquainted with his brother.'

Lucy raised a brow but made no comment, taking his proferred arm as they walked towards the throng of people at the entrance.

'You must be looking forward to the comfort of your own home, Mrs Lawrence.'

'Yes, though I didn't expect to be back here quite so soon.' A hansom pulled up in front of them and Stone handed her up.

'Abbey Gardens,' she called to the cabbie, as Stone clambered in beside her.

With the final bag secured, the porter thumped the side of the hansom, and they set off into the night. The cab lurched over a hole, making her bump up against Stone in the confined interior. Being so close, she was aware of his bergamot scent, warm and spicy. Glancing up at his profile, she wondered what he was thinking. Was he too envisaging how intimate the journey would be? Heat suddenly suffused her face. She needed to direct her thoughts elsewhere.

If she didn't know her way to St John's Wood so well, it would have been almost impossible to determine where they were with the fog so dense. She could make out islands of yellow suspended in the air where the street lights glowed. In between was the swirling darkness and, all the while, the rank aroma of the city assailed her. Lucy had heard stories of what lurked out there under the cover of darkness and the echo of the horse's hooves on the cobbles set her nerves on edge. The city was no place for a woman alone at this time of night. She hated being indebted to Stone but at this point she was beyond ever repaying him.

After several minutes she half turned to him. 'Where do you live, Mr Stone?'

'Kensington. I have rooms in Westbourne Grove.'

'My! Do all insurance investigators live so well?'

'Only the successful ones.'

She laughed softly and guessed success in his chosen career accounted for his self-assured manner. Whatever the reason, it was appealing. She couldn't remember ever meeting any of his family but then her Season had been cut short. Lucy knew exactly who to ask to discover more about him. Lady Sarah Strawbridge knew everyone and usually their darkest secrets too. On her next visit to the Royal Free, she'd pin her down and find out as much as she could. It wasn't fair he knew so much about her.

'My brother painted a black picture of my character to you this afternoon. I'm surprised you're willing to be seen with me,' Lucy remarked.

'Mrs Lawrence, I'm shocked! You were listening at the door the whole time.' He raised a brow but smiled.

'Of course I was! How else was I to know what Richard was up to? I daresay you find my behaviour shocking but I have too much to lose, Mr Stone. My husband's death changed everything. I can't make decisions for myself until the estate is probated. It is frustrating. And to be at the mercy of my brother is intolerable.'

'And even more so since he's tried to implicate you in a theft,' Stone commented. 'I'm not judging you, Mrs Lawrence. If anything I admire your courage.'

'I don't feel brave, only weary.'

'But you must have friends here in London who will support you?'

'A handful have stayed true. In other cases, there were letters of condolence which appeared to be sincere, but not a word since. It's as if I have become invisible. One lady cut me on the street, and I've known her this five years or more. Widows aren't popular, it would appear.'

'It is a common problem, I believe,' Stone said. 'Most wives deem young attractive widows a threat to even the most happily married of men.'

His use of 'attractive' wasn't lost on her and cheered her up. 'How odd! I have never considered myself in a predatory light. Do you consider me dangerous, Mr Stone?' she asked and immediately regretted it. It sounded far too flirtatious.

His eyes glittered in the darkness. Lucy held her breath. 'You have the potential to be whatever you wish, Mrs Lawrence.

Once your period of mourning is over, I imagine you will spread your wings.'

To her surprise, his answer disappointed her, its formality cutting through her self-esteem. But her pride would not let her show it. 'What a romantic image you conjure up. Unfortunately, by the time the solicitor winds up Charlie's affairs, I'll be more likely to have had my wings clipped forever.'

'Mr Somerville indicated there were difficulties. Your husband's financial position was precarious, some unfortunate investments being the cause, I believe?'

'It would appear so, but I wasn't privy to his business affairs and have seen none of his papers. The solicitor and Richard are dealing with the estate.' She sighed. 'Whatever hope I had was vested in Richard, but he will hardly wish to help me now, and if what you say is true about *his* finances, there's no prospect of a good outcome at all. I may lose my home. I may lose everything.'

'What will you do?' he asked softly.

She turned away from him and looked out into the night. 'I have no idea.'

As the hansom turned into Abbey Gardens, Lucy became despondent. Hopefully, Stone wouldn't notice anything amiss and would leave as soon as she was dropped off. It was embarrassing to be in such difficult circumstances with no servants but it was unlikely he would expect an invitation to come into the house at this late hour. His questioning could wait for another day.

'Will your servants still be up?' he asked, looking out at the house, almost as if he had read her mind. Luckily, the fog obscured the upper storeys with their telltale shuttered windows.

'No. I'm not expected. With all the fuss, I forgot to send on a telegram.'

'That's unfortunate,' he said with a frown. 'Let me help you with your bags.' Before she had a chance to object he had hopped down. 'Wait for me, please' he called up to the cabbie.

'Right you are, guv.'

Lucy walked up the path, and Stone followed with her bags. When she reached the steps, she turned around with a bright smile. 'Just leave them there, please, Mr Stone. I can manage.'

'How will you get in? Do you have a key? I'll wait until you're safely inside,' he said.

How gentlemanly but also inconvenient, she thought. She rummaged in her bag and drew out a set of keys before stepping up to the front door.

'Oh!' she exclaimed, swinging around. 'This can't be right.'

The door was ajar. Stone stepped up beside her, then halted. 'Go down the path and stay there,' he commanded in a fierce whisper.

Lucy didn't argue, her heart pounding. He drew a sword stick out of his cane and used it to push the door wide open. Lucy tried to see past him but the hallway was in darkness. Stone stood still, his head tilted. He took another step towards the door and halted again. Lucy couldn't bear the suspense and climbed up the steps as he crossed over the threshold. For a few seconds, she hesitated but her curiosity won out. However, as she entered the hallway behind him she was almost overcome by a foul odour. Stone swung around and gestured for her to leave but she shook her head. Lucy heard Stone mutter something under his breath but she stood her ground.

'What's in there?' he snapped, pointing with his sword stick.

'Charlie's study,' she whispered.

As he pushed the door open the smell intensified. Stone recoiled and grimaced momentarily before entering the room.

Lucy followed him in. The streetlight threw a weak yellow light into the room. As her eyes adjusted, she could see the study was in disarray. The foul smell was emanating from the desk area.

'Turn on the lights, please, Mrs Lawrence,' Stone demanded.

Squinting into the darkness, she found the box of matches on the sideboard. Her hands shaking, she lit a taper and opened the valve on the nearest wall light. Seconds later the gas light popped and spluttered into life.

In the middle of the desk, crawling with maggots, was a dead cat.

'Oh no!' she cried. Not Horace!

THIRTEEN

Lucy stood transfixed. The sight and smell of the scene made her stomach heave and her skin crawl. She knew right away who was responsible. It had to be Marsh.

'This is your cat?' Stone asked, spinning around. Swallowing hard, desperately trying not to cry, she could only nod. 'There's malevolence at work here,' Stone said. 'This is a personal threat and no ordinary burglary. Where are your servants?' he demanded.

There was no point in keeping up the pretence any longer. The handkerchief she held to her mouth muffled her words. 'Gone, Mr Stone.'

'But—'

'Yes, I lied to you because I was embarrassed. The house is empty and has been since I left. There was no money to pay their wages, and I dismissed them all before I travelled to Yorkshire,' she said. 'I couldn't afford to leave them here nothing to do, eating their heads off.'

Stone slid the sword into his cane and twisted it to lock. He looked back at the horror lying on the desk and sighed. 'I understand. Let me deal with this unfortunate animal. Would you fetch some old newspapers? I'll wrap him in them, and then perhaps you would be so good as to boil a kettle of water.'

'Certainly, but shouldn't we check to see if there's anyone in the house who shouldn't be?' she asked, not relishing going down to the kitchen on her own; not that she'd ever admit it.

Pointing to the cat with his cane, Stone said, 'This looks at least a week old. It is safe to assume the perpetrators are long gone. I'll ask the cabbie to fetch the police.' He crossed the room, skirting around the desk and flung open the window.

'No! Please don't do that,' she protested, advancing further into the room. 'You mustn't involve the police.'

He swung around. 'Good Lord, Mrs Lawrence, why ever not? This dead animal has been left as some kind of warning. I believe you're in serious danger from the worst type of blackguards.'

'I'm sorry, but I must insist. I may know who is responsible,' she said with a sheepish look.

From the front door, Lucy watched as Stone retrieved his bag, before paying and dismissing the cabbie. She was relieved he was going to stay awhile even though she would not have blamed him for leaving her to sort the mess out alone. As he walked up the path, he gave her a wry smile.

'I'll dispose of the dead animal first,' he said.

'Thank you. I've left some newspaper for you.'

She made her way down to the kitchen and, after several futile attempts, managed to light the range. Minutes later, Stone came through, carrying Horace's remains wrapped in the newspaper. She unlocked the garden door and told him where the bin was kept. Once Stone was safely outside, she let her tears fall. Horace had been a comforting presence in her life, her only company sometimes for days on end.

When Lucy heard the door close as Stone re-entered, she

quickly dried her tears. 'Thank you, that was an unpleasant task. It was so kind of you to help,' she said as he approached.

'Don't mention it. Now, with your permission, I'd like to check the rest of the house. It is only to put your mind at ease, Mrs Lawrence.'

Lucy nodded. He came up to the range, holding out his hands to the heat, then rubbed them together. 'It's starting to freeze out there.'

'I'm sorry, it's not very warm in here either. The range will take some time to heat up.'

'It's no matter. I'll make a start upstairs now,' he said.

'Thank you—I'd feel much safer if you wouldn't mind checking.'

'Try not to worry,' he said.

Easy for him to say, she thought, it wasn't his home that had been violated.

'It is highly unlikely there's anyone here,' he remarked, heading out the door but she heard him activate his sword stick and drew her own conclusion.

For a moment, she stood before the range, trying to muster some courage. He was right, of course, whoever had invaded her home had done what they had set out to do—to scare her to death—and left. Lucy set the kettle down on the range. She would not be found wanting; she'd investigate the downstairs rooms herself.

Lucy started in the dining room but to her dismay, every room she entered had been searched and the contents strewn. From the floor above, she could hear Stone moving about. With a sense of foreboding, she followed him upstairs. Nothing had been sacred. Lucy faced a trail of destruction, with the contents of drawers, wardrobes and shelves scattered all over the floors.

The devastation showed an increasing level of frustration as she climbed higher up the house.

To her consternation, whoever had carried out the search had even ripped open the parcel marked 'Effects of Charles Lawrence' and stamped 'Dufour Place Mortuary'. The blood-stained clothes lay on the floor. With a shudder, Lucy bundled them up and tied the parcel as best she could before shoving it into the wardrobe. Despondent, she couldn't bear to see any more. She went back downstairs to the kitchen to wait for Stone.

She made tea but couldn't drink it as another wave of depression and fatigue hit her. When Stone came in and sat down opposite, she struggled to pull herself together.

'Would you like some tea or there may be brandy up in Charlie's study?' she asked.

'No, thank you, Mrs Lawrence. I'd prefer if you would explain what is going on. Every room in the house has been thoroughly searched. What were the intruders looking for?'

'I don't know for sure, Mr Stone.'

'But you said you knew who might be responsible,' he replied.

'It is a guess, but it is a man I do not wish to see again. He frightened me.'

'You had best tell me all,' Stone said with a sigh.

Could she trust him? It seemed she had little choice. 'A stranger called here one morning, shortly after Charlie's funeral. He claimed he was Charlie's business associate. At first, he was pleasant enough but turned antagonistic when I refused to hand over Charlie's effects. He searched Charlie's desk right in front of me, ignoring my protests. Then he threatened me as he left, in the presence of my servants too. It was a terrifying experience. If he knew the house was empty he may have decided to return and look again. It's too much of a coincidence. I fear it must be his doing.'

'Who was this man?'

'He introduced himself as Nathaniel Marsh.'

Stone's eyebrows shot up. 'Describe him, please.' Stone sat back and listened as Lucy described Marsh in detail, right down to the gold tooth.

'Unfortunately, I know of this man,' he said with a grimace. 'He has many aliases. However, he doesn't crawl out from beneath his rock very often. What did you do to anger him?'

'Nothing! At least, I didn't set out to, but I believe my husband must have. How do you know of him?'

'We have crossed paths before. What happened when he visited you? Every detail, please,' Stone demanded.

'Initially, I was sure it was a visit of condolence, but he had hardly sat down when he demanded Charlie's personal property, just like that. I was astonished. He claimed Charlie had something which belonged to him and owed him a lot of money.'

'Did he give you any details about their business partnership?'

'No, but I didn't ask. I was too shocked by his demands. All he said was that his business was in jeopardy. He was desperate to find whatever it was Charlie had in his possession at the time of his death.' Lucy took a deep breath. 'He's the reason I went to Somerville for Christmas. I assumed I would be safe there.' She gave a strained little laugh. 'How wrong could I be? I hadn't reckoned on my brother's duplicity.'

'Why would you, indeed?' Stone replied. 'A most unfortunate turn of events.'

Lucy shrugged. 'The truth is I hoped by the time I returned to London, Mr Marsh would have forgotten all about me. I believed he was the kind of scoundrel that preys on vulnerable women, trying to trick them to hand over money, and when he hadn't succeeded, he would move on to some other poor soul.'

Stone shook his head. 'Have you any idea how dangerous it is to cross a man like Marsh?'

'Obviously not,' Lucy said, indicating upwards towards the study, 'but I'm sure you're about to tell me.'

Mr Stone treated her to one of his challenging stares before he continued. 'It is best you know what sort of man you're dealing with.'

Lucy dipped her head and took a deep breath.

'Very well, Mrs Lawrence, I won't sugarcoat it.' Stone leaned towards her, his expression grave. 'Marsh's organisation, and I don't use the term lightly, is involved in practically every criminal venture in this city from opium dens to racketeering and worse. The police and I have dealt with some of his underlings, but he's proven to be untouchable *and* invisible. The fact he showed up here could mean he's frantic to find whatever was in your husband's possession.'

'I can confirm how desperate he was, for he scared me and my servants and paid no heed to my protests.'

Stone sighed and sat back. 'If your husband was involved in any of his schemes, he was a fool of the first order.'

'How would I know? Mr Marsh was not forthcoming and Charlie never spoke about any of his business schemes,' Lucy said.

'But surely you must have some notion? Did Marsh not say what he was looking for?'

Lucy glared across at him. 'No, he did not, and I was too afraid to ask.' She paused to calm herself. 'There was one thing which struck me as odd, though. He said he hoped I hadn't sold them. But why would I sell Charlie's papers? It made no sense to me. I have no idea what he meant by that.'

'I believe I do,' Stone said, his eyes alight.

She glowered at him. 'If you have known all along what this is about, why all of these questions? Why keep me in suspense?'

'To confirm my suspicions,' he replied.

'What suspicions, sir?' Lucy couldn't take much more of this.

'Your husband had come to my notice. Both the police and I were investigating him in the weeks leading up to his death.'

'So that's how you knew of him... But Charlie wasn't a criminal.'

He remained silent.

'Oh!' Her shoulders sagged a little. 'What did he do?' Lucy placed both hands around her cup of tea. They were shaking.

'You may not like what you will hear.'

'Mr Stone, there has been no joy in my life since last October. Trust me, one more piece of bad news will not crush me.'

'You're a very unusual young woman,' he said.

'And you, sir, are procrastinating. Tell me!'

Stone laced his fingers where they lay on the table. 'Do you know anything about Kashmir?'

Lucy shook her head in bewilderment at his question. 'In northern India, is it not? Famous for its beautiful shawls. My mother has a particularly fine example.'

'Yes, they are treasured the world over, but it isn't shawls I'm interested in. There's a region in the north of the country known as Padar, but I doubt you have ever heard of it.' She shook her head. 'Recently, it has become famous as a rich source of sapphires. The area where the sapphires were found is remote. It is high up in the mountains and unpopulated. Some say there was a landslide and the gems were spotted and picked up by passing traders. Others say they were found by hunters who traded them for food and shelter. Whatever the case, they turned up in Calcutta and when the maharajah learned of this, he immediately sent his men to retrieve the precious stones and return them to Kashmir.'

'Why was he so anxious to retrieve them?'

'Because they are the finest quality sapphires ever discovered and are priceless,' Stone said. 'They are most prized for their hue and brilliancy with a texture like velvet. The maharajah, realising their worth, now controls the only mine, and it is heavily guarded.'

'They sound magnificent. I would love to see one of those sapphires.'

'Have you not?' he asked.

'No, I'm sure I'd remember seeing something so wonderful.'

'Hmm,' he murmured.

Lucy stared across the table, her anger and frustration building. 'I'm under the impression you believe I have seen these jewels. But I have never been to India. I do not see what any of this has to do with me or Charlie.'

Stone hesitated, regarding her with a strange expression. She knew he was taking her measure yet again. 'Last year, the maharajah sent his most trusted courtier, Neeraj Khan, to London with ten of the uncut gemstones. He wished to have them set in various pieces of jewellery. One night, three of the stones were stolen from one of the commissioned jewellers in Hatton Garden and have never been found. I was called in by Bradford's, the insurance company, the day after the theft. I spent months investigating and was on the verge of finding out who was involved when your husband died. The trail went cold upon his death.'

It was ridiculous. He seemed to be implying Charlie had been involved in a robbery. At worst, Lucy had suspected shady business transactions, but he had never done anything to her knowledge to come under the beady eye of the law. Clearly, she had been mistaken. 'And you're searching for these missing sapphires?'

'Many people are looking for them. Our friend Mr Marsh is most *definitely* looking for them, as evidenced by his visit before Christmas and sending his men here while you were away.'

'I don't understand. Why would he believe my husband had the maharajah's sapphires?'

'My dear Mrs Lawrence, they were seen in your husband's possession on more than one occasion.'

'No, that's ridiculous!' she exclaimed. 'Charlie would have had nothing to do with stolen gems.'

'He may not have realised they were stolen at first, but I believe he did in the end. I think he was going to the police the day he died.'

'But he never reached them,' she said.

'No, his partner made sure of it.'

'Mr Marsh?' she asked.

'Yes. Logic would suggest he was responsible.'

Stunned, Lucy cried: 'But that means Charlie was murdered!'

FOURTEEN

Stone placed a glass of brandy on the table. 'Please drink this, Mrs Lawrence.' Lucy's hand shook as she picked up the glass. Charlie's death, gruesome as it had been, had been bearable as a traffic incident, but to contemplate the notion he was deliberately dispatched was difficult to comprehend. And terrifying. Marsh's parting words on the day of his visit rang in her ears with greater significance.

'I can't believe it! Murdered!' Lucy glanced up, hoping Stone would contradict her. 'But the police told me it was an accident and that he slipped on the cobbles. They never voiced any doubt.'

'It was certainly made to look like an accident and virtually impossible to prove otherwise,' he answered. 'Drink, please.'

As she swallowed a mouthful, her eyes filled with tears. What could he have done to deserve such a terrible end? 'Poor Charlie!'

Offering her a clean handkerchief, Stone returned to his seat. 'I'm sorry, I shouldn't have been so blunt.'

Lucy blew her nose. 'No, Mr Stone. It's far better I know

the truth. But I... I don't know what to think. Could you be mistaken?'

'Unfortunately, I do not think so. The street was busy and most of the witnesses swore he slipped on the cobbles as he crossed over. But it is too much of a coincidence particularly as he was entangled with Marsh and his gang. He would not be the first man to meet such an end. In a moving crowd it would be easy to shove someone unnoticed. It wouldn't take much with the roads always so greasy under foot.'

'Would Marsh have done it? He looked capable of it.'

'No, he would not risk being implicated. One of his associates would have carried out his orders. Mr Lawrence most likely would not have realised he was being followed or recognised who it was. Marsh's network across the city is vast.'

'Tell me the worst, Mr Stone. What was my Charlie involved in?'

'Are you sure you want to hear this? Why not get a night's rest and we can talk about it tomorrow?' he said.

'Yes, I'm sure!'

Stone looked at her with concern. 'Very well. From the outset, the police suspected Marsh was behind the theft of the sapphires, but no one knew what he did next. It was even speculated he had taken them abroad to sell. I spent weeks on the Continent making enquiries but to no avail. But Marsh was clever and bided his time. Then he set up an ingenious scheme to defraud. Slowly his syndicate began to work the scheme. How your husband first became involved no one knows. Perhaps he was one of the first men approached to buy shares.'

'I don't understand, Mr Stone. Shares in what?'

'They used the stolen sapphires to convince investors they had a working mine in Padar. Most people aren't aware there's only one mine and it is controlled by the maharajah. Before long, your husband was the frontman. A gentleman of charm, I understand, with good connections, so they had him approach his acquaintances in the clubs. If it's any consolation, I'm of the opinion he considered it was all above board in the beginning. The funds he invested in the scheme were substantial.'

'So that's where our money went!' she exclaimed. 'He mortgaged the house. I only discovered it a few days ago. It must have been to raise extra money to invest.'

'More than likely, Mrs Lawrence. Your husband must not have realised the scheme was fraudulent at that stage.'

'How could he have been so foolish?' She sighed. 'My husband could be gullible, Mr Stone. He would have been easy to recruit. His impetuous character had drawn him into many a dubious undertaking, though, to my knowledge, nothing of a criminal nature. This I have found out from mutual acquaintances since his death for he never admitted it to me. If told the scheme was a quick way to get rich, he would have been hooked straight away. No doubt he was a wonderful ambassador for the criminals without even realising what he was doing... until it was too late.'

'Yes, and he was successful. The investors numbered over fifty. Two days before your husband died, a meeting had been arranged in a small hotel in Soho where all the investors were to meet. For some reason, your husband failed to appear.'

'And you think it was because he had found out about the trick... the scheme?'

'Maybe, or perhaps he threatened Marsh he would reveal it all to the police or demanded his money be returned.'

Lucy's heart sank. 'Which signed his death warrant.'

'Yes. Marsh is utterly ruthless. He would not stand for betrayal. The investors were concerned when no one turned up at the hotel that day. A great deal of money had already changed hands and some of them even had share certificates for the new mining company. Suspecting the worst, two of them went to the police. They only knew one person connected to the scheme and that was your husband. They had never met any of the others involved.'

'And the police informed you,' she asked.

'Correct. They suspected the gems the men had seen were the stolen ones, and they knew I was working for the jeweller's insurance company. I tried to track your husband down and even called here and at his club, but was told he was away on business. There was no trace of him.'

'And I thought he was in Edinburgh visiting his parents.'

'I doubt it. More likely he was hiding out somewhere in London, scared for his life.'

'Why didn't he confide in me?' she asked.

'Perhaps he was honourable enough not to put you in danger.'

'But he has!' Lucy exclaimed.

'To be fair to your late husband, he must not have realised the danger he was in or he believed he knew how to handle Marsh. However, it would take someone far more experienced and clever to outwit London's most wanted man.'

Lucy gulped. 'He is that notorious?' Stone nodded. 'And untouchable?'

'So far, he's proved difficult to link to any of his criminal activities. I hoped to get to him through your husband. But when Mr Lawrence had his accident on Regent Street, all hope of implicating Marsh died with him. When the police suspected the accident victim was your husband, they contacted me as they knew of my interest in him. I went straight to Dufour Place.'

She took another sip of brandy. 'Where we first met.'

'Yes. I'm sorry you had to be the one to identify him. An unpleasant duty for anyone.'

She shrugged. 'It was appalling and still gives me night-mares. But most of his family are in Scotland, so there was no one else. Do you believe Charlie still had those gems when he died?'

'Yes.'

'Could they have been on him when he was killed?' she asked.

'Highly unlikely. The police did not find anything of that nature. Your husband must have hidden them somewhere safe.'

'And Marsh is convinced I have them?'

'Or know where they are to be found.'

Horrified, Lucy mulled this over for moment then rose from her chair and walked around to him. 'I don't wish to end my days in that awful mortuary, Mr Stone.' He took her outstretched hand with a surprised look on his face. 'Would you be so good as to help me? Someone must convince this Mr Marsh I don't have his precious sapphires.'

He shook her hand. 'It would be my pleasure, Mrs Lawrence.'

Lucy awoke to the sound of the doorbell. She bolted upright, her pulse wild. At least it was daylight. There it was again. She crept across the room and peeped out. To her delight, her maid Mary was standing on the front steps looking up at her. Lucy gestured for her to wait and flew down the stairs.

'I'm so glad to see you, Mary,' she said, closing the door quickly and slipping the bolt back in place. 'How did you know I had returned?'

'Nuala—Nuala Cassidy, the maid next door—sent me a message first thing to say you were back. I've been staying with my sister since leaving your service. Anyway, I thought I'd chance it and see if you'd take me on again.'

'I'd love to, Mary, but the truth is I've very little money. That hasn't changed.'

Mary smiled. 'Pay me when you can; it don't bother me much. Once I have bed and board, I'll manage.'

Lucy wanted to hug her. 'Come in to the drawing room. There's something I need to tell you before you make any commitment.'

Mary's eyes widened, but she followed her in. 'Good Lord, what a mess! What happened in here, ma'am?' Mary asked, looking around the disordered room. She righted a small table and shook her head.

'That's what I wish to talk to you about. Take a seat.'

Her mouth open in amazement, Mary listened as Lucy recounted the events of the night before.

'Holy God, ma'am. That's awful, that is. Poor old Horace—I was very fond of 'im.' She paused as if suddenly struck by an awful idea. 'You're sure there's no one hiding out in the attics?'

'Yes. Mr Stone checked the house thoroughly before he left. There's no need to be nervous. Do you remember the gentleman? He called here shortly after Mr Lawrence died.'

'Yes, I do. Very insistent he was, but I was having none of it and sent him off. Bothering a widow like that ain't right. Are you sure he's up to scratch?'

'Yes,' Lucy replied, smiling to herself. If Stone could only hear Mary's comments, he would be horrified.

'He shouldn't have left you all alone last night, ma'am.'

'Mr Stone did offer to stay but I've enough scandal in my life as it is, Mary. Besides, he had secured the house; I was no longer in danger. I insisted he went home.'

Mary didn't look impressed. 'How did they get in?'

'Through the window in the washroom at the rear of the kitchen. We locked the internal door, and Mr Stone was able to drag the small dresser across it. Now you know the worst. Will you stay?' Lucy crossed her fingers.

Mary beamed at her. 'I'd like to, ma'am. Sure I love a bit of excitement, me.'

· · ·

Mary announced Mr Stone three hours later. Immaculate as ever, it was hard to believe he had only left her home at two in the morning. It was deflating to see him so dapper; Mary had done her best to help her disguise the dark circles under her eyes but she knew she was barely presentable.

'Good afternoon, Mrs Lawrence. I hope you managed to get some rest last night,' he said, removing his hat and taking a seat opposite. He looked towards the door. 'Where did she spring from?'

'Mary arrived mid-morning. Servants' grapevine.'

'Ah yes, highly efficient it is too. I have often remarked to my friend, Chief Inspector McQuillan, that the constabulary could do with a similar system. I hope you have briefed her on the situation.'

'Yes. I was totally honest with her and she still wanted to stay. I have employed her these last four years; she's always been loyal and hard-working.'

'Excellent. I was going to suggest you stay in a hotel or with a friend but the maid will suffice.' Lucy smarted but did not comment. 'As promised, I visited your brother's insurance company and told them of my suspicions regarding the whole affair. They have agreed to my plan.'

'I'm glad, though I'm sure they are always reluctant to pay out.'

Stone smiled. 'That's often the case.'

'It will be interesting to see how long it takes Richard to attempt to sell the pearls.'

'Best not to dwell on it for now,' Stone said. 'Speaking of the local constabulary, I'd like you to accompany me to Vine Street Station this afternoon.'

She stiffened. Why did he want her to go there? Was it a ruse to have her arrested again? 'I don't see why that's necessary,

Mr Stone. We both know who was responsible for what happened here.'

'Indeed. However, it is my hope that the Chief Inspector will be amenable to providing you with protection. Knowing him as I do, he will be more co-operative if he meets you in person. I'm sure you have realised Marsh must have you and your home under surveillance.'

'I did wonder...' Lucy said, her heart sinking.

'Then you can't object.' Stone had the gall to smile at her.

Vine Street Police Station

They found the chief inspector at his desk, his red hair peppered with grey just visible above stacks of folders and old newspapers. He glanced up and waved them to uncomfortable-looking wooden chairs.

'With you in a minute,' McQuillan said after greeting Lucy and Mr Stone. 'I must finish this report for Old Henley.'

'Take your time, my friend,' Stone replied with an amused glance at Lucy. 'I would hate for you to be on the wrong side of your superior through any fault of mine.'

A harrumph from behind the paper tower was the only reply. They waited patiently as McQuillan signed off a sheet and pushed it into a file.

'Now then, what can I do for you?' McQuillan asked, breaking into a smile.

'This is Mrs Charles Lawrence,' Stone said.

McQuillan quirked a brow, then leapt forward to shake her hand. 'I'm pleased to meet you, Mrs Lawrence.' He glanced at Stone. 'Should I order tea?'

'That won't be necessary, Oliver, we are here on business.'

'I see,' the chief inspector replied, looking very much as if he didn't, and returned to his desk.

Stone filled him in on the Somerville pearls case and Lucy's involvement in it.

The colour rose in McQuillan's face. 'I can't believe police officers could be so incompetent. You should make an official complaint, Mrs Lawrence.'

'I'd rather just forget about it,' Lucy said.

'Then I'll ensure those officers are reprimanded. I'm acquainted with a senior officer in that division. Let me take the opportunity to apologise on behalf of the force.'

Stone interjected: 'That's all well and good; unfortunately, there's more, Oliver. Have you failed to recognise the name Lawrence? *Charles* Lawrence?'

'Oh! Are you related?' the Chief Inspector asked her. He glanced at Stone then back to her, a frown darkening his features.

Lucy managed a weak smile. 'I am his widow.'

Stone took up the story of the previous evening. The chief inspector sat up when Stone told him about the dead cat.

McQuillan frowned. 'Nasty!' Then he smirked at Mr Stone. 'I would dearly like to have seen you getting your hands dirty.'

Lucy glanced at Stone to see how he would take the ribbing, but he ignored it. 'With no servants in the house, I could hardly expect Mrs Lawrence to dispose of the animal. Thankfully, it is not every day a lady encounters such a threat.'

'True. In all seriousness, this is a worrying development,' McQuillan replied.

'And a frightening one, Chief Inspector,' Lucy said.

'Of course. However, I do not know how I can help. The perpetrators are, as you said yourself, Stone, long gone.'

'Yes, but don't you see? Marsh's people must be watching Mrs Lawrence and her movements. I rather hoped I could persuade you to increase the police presence near her home. I have explained to Mrs Lawrence about the sapphires and the probable link to her late husband.'

'What would the Met do without you, Stone?' McQuillan shook his head. 'I'd love to help, but it's not my district. The best I can do is to put a word in for you.'

'Thank you, but it's in your interest too. The case must be re-opened, and you don't want a valuable witness to come to grief. How would that look to Old Henley, eh?'

McQuillan tried to look affronted and turned to Lucy. 'I'm not happy about certain aspects of this situation. Most of all, Mrs Lawrence, I fail to understand why you didn't report Mr Marsh and his threat to your local station.' He flicked a glance at Stone before he fixed her with a hard stare. 'You have nothing to hide I assume?'

'Oliver, be careful!' exclaimed Stone.

'No, Mr Stone, the Chief Inspector is right to question my motives. My inaction, in hindsight, must appear peculiar. I have regretted not reporting the original threat but at the time I was too frightened, and I had no idea what Mr Marsh wanted. That's the reason I fled to my family in Yorkshire.'

'And you knew nothing about your husband's involvement with Marsh's gang?' McQuillan asked.

'Nothing until Mr Stone gave me the details last night. The first time I saw Mr Marsh was at my husband's funeral.'

McQuillan sat back in his chair. 'I'll consider your request, Phineas. What is your plan? You're hardly going to use this good lady as bait?'

'Certainly not,' Stone replied.

'I'm glad to hear it!' Lucy exclaimed giving him a dirty look. The corner of Stone's mouth twitched.

'You're up to your old tricks, aren't you?' The chief inspector glared at Mr Stone. 'Always keeping me in the dark until you need the cavalry. Fine! Keep your counsel.'

Stone merely grinned back at him before looking around

the room. 'Oliver, were you demoted recently? It is the only explanation I can find for this ridiculous new office.'

'You know well I was *promoted*. You even forced open your wallet and bought me a drink.'

Stone gave him a pitying look. 'My dear friend, there's no need to be so defensive.'

'I don't know why I tolerate you,' McQuillan commented, tipping his chair. 'If you weren't so useful...'

'It's as well I am as you don't have the resources to keep on top of half of what goes on out there.' Stone looked out the window as another gust of wind, laden with sleet, rattled the panes. 'By the way, I have to say your old office had a better view.'

'Stone, are you going to tell me what you have planned or do I have to take you down to the cells and leave you to the ministrations of my sergeant?' McQuillan demanded.

'Good Lord! You do realise a serious crime has been committed,' Stone said, his eyes wide.

'What are you talking about now?' McQuillan snapped.

'It would appear someone has stolen your sense of humour, as well as your nice office.'

McQuillan glared at him, but ruined it by starting to laugh. By now, Lucy had realised they were old friends. They made an odd couple but she could see they had respect for each other, beyond the teasing.

'I assume you don't want me to wade in and take all the glory just yet then,' McQuillan said. 'Please humour me. How will you proceed?'

'Do my best to find the sapphires, of course. But at least I know they are not in St John's Wood.'

'How can you be sure?' McQuillan asked.

'Marsh's men were thorough. If the gems were in the house, they would have found them, and there would have been no need to leave the cat as a warning.'

'Agreed. Marsh was pinning all his hopes on finding them in Abbey Gardens. Now, what will he do?' asked McQuillan.

'Hard to know, but what worries me is he appears to believe Mrs Lawrence knows where they *are* hidden.'

'It worries me too, Chief Inspector,' Lucy piped up. 'I don't want to be a lure for this lunatic.'

'Yes, I can understand your concerns, Mrs Lawrence.' The policeman turned to Mr Stone. 'I agree Mrs Lawrence is in danger.'

'Hence, my request,' Stone said.

'Very well, I'll ensure you have protection,' McQuillan said to Lucy. She smiled her relief and thanks.

'If the sapphires are not in Mrs Lawrence's home, where could they be?' McQuillan asked Stone.

'A knotty problem—they could potentially be anywhere. The obvious place to start my investigation is to question your servants, Mrs Lawrence. They tend to be the best possible source of information, I find. If you know where they went on leaving your service, and can provide their direction, it would save me a great deal of time.'

'Yes, of course,' Lucy said. 'I have provided references for most of them.'

'Excellent. I need to build up a picture of your husband's habits, his friends and his haunts. Servants tend to be far more observant than wives in these matters. Then it will be on to his clubs. Charlie Lawrence didn't have the gems on him the day he was killed. Most likely, he wanted to negotiate a deal with the police before he produced them or perhaps he considered claiming the reward. Either way, he must have stashed them away in a safe place.'

'Or he gave them to someone he trusted,' McQuillan said eyeing Lucy. A blush rose in her cheeks as her heart filled with dismay. Despite her earlier assurances, the chief inspector thought she was involved. If he didn't believe her, there was a strong possibility Stone didn't either.

FIFTEEN

That night, Lucy lay awake staring into the darkness, only too aware of being alone, the bed cold and empty beside her. It was too easy to indulge dark thoughts as the night progressed with agonising slowness towards dawn. She relived each humiliating event of the past few months with absolute clarity. Her dreams, when she did sleep eventually, inhabited cold sinister places. She was in the woods at Somerville in the depths of the night, conscious of being followed and absolutely terrified. She came upon a clearing. In the centre, Charlie lay dead as he had on the mortuary slab with Horace lying on his chest. Shadowy figures closed in, gradually taking on the faces of her family, Marsh and Stone. It was a relief to wake.

But that relief didn't last. As she sat at the breakfast table, reality intruded once more, and it was worse than any night-mare. What a fool she had been, she thought, crumbling her toast to pieces. If only she had paid more attention to Charlie's day-to-day life, but all they had shared was a roof in the latter years of their marriage. Lucy had realised her marriage was struggling, but not the disastrous direction Charlie's life was taking nor what the consequences would be for her.

And the worrisome deficiency of funds had to be faced. Without word from the solicitor, she didn't know what her future financial position would be. However, she dared not approach Richard. The continued silence from Yorkshire didn't surprise her, and after all that had transpired, she welcomed it. Initially, Lucy feared Richard would follow her to town. But when she had voiced this concern to Stone, he had pointed out Richard would be too preoccupied with the state of his own affairs.

At least Stone appeared to be concerned for her safety and, so far, trustworthy even if he probably didn't trust her. From the intensity of questioning he had subjected her to the previous afternoon, she was convinced he was trying to trip her up. Proving her innocence was going to be a challenge. Despite that, he was the one bright light in the whole ruinous tangle of her life. She felt nothing but gratitude to him for rescuing her from a sticky situation. But he bothered her. There was something about him, some elusive aspect to his personality, which made her ill at ease. Lucy's instincts told her he was holding back, but whether it was on a personal or investigative level, she couldn't be sure. Saving face in front of him had become important, even though she wasn't sure why it mattered as he already knew her darkest secrets.

Lucy looked about the room, suddenly restless; she had to escape the house or she would go mad. Her duties at the hospital would take her mind off things, but Stone had commanded she stay at home with the doors locked. He had left strict instructions with Mary not to let anyone in other than him or the police. True to his word, McQuillan had organised an extra officer on duty, but the sight of him walking up and down Abbey Gardens only made Lucy feel more caged in. It was unbearable. What harm could there be in going out for a few hours?

As she suspected she was being watched as much as

protected, Lucy deliberately sneaked out to the rear laneway when escaping the house just after midday. But her bravery didn't last long, and the entire journey by cab was fraught. Danger lurked around every corner and in the glance of every stranger she encountered. Stone's assertion that Marsh had people everywhere was foremost in her mind.

The Royal Free Hospital

Lucy spent the afternoon sitting with an elderly lady who dozed on and off as she read to her from the newspaper. It wasn't stimulating company but at least she was being useful. When visiting time was over, she walked slowly down the main staircase of the hospital, dreading the return to Abbey Gardens.

'Hello there, stranger,' a female voice greeted her. Walking across the hall was Lady Sarah Strawbridge, magnificent in a green visiting ensemble. Petite and blond, the younger daughter of an earl and married to a rising Tory politician, Lady Sarah moved in high society and was acquainted with anyone of importance. Her vivaciousness had endeared her to Lucy immediately on first meeting her several years before. They had become firm friends.

'Sarah! I hoped you would be here today. Are you on your way home?' Lucy asked.

'Yes, I was just about to call for my carriage but I don't have to be home for another hour. I wasn't expecting to see you back here so soon. Shall we take tea?' Sarah asked, her eyes alight. 'Did Yorkshire not agree with you? Were the natives unfriendly?'

'You could say that; it was, in fact, a nightmare!'

'I must have all the details, my dear. Shall we visit our usual?' Sarah asked.

Lucy agreed, eager to escape any prying eyes and ears in the busy hospital hallway.

. . .

Once settled in a private booth in the tea shop around the corner from the hospital, Lucy poured out her adventures to Sarah. By the time Lucy was finished, her friend was staring at her in horror, her tea untouched.

'My dear Lucy, I'm astounded. This is ghastly. Whatever was your husband up to?'

'No good and on a very grand scale!'

'Indeed. But more importantly, you can't stay in that house alone—it isn't safe. You must come and stay with us.'

'Thank you, but if I leave the house unattended, I fear Richard will take possession, change the locks, and then I'll be homeless,' Lucy explained.

'Is he capable of such an act?'

'Sarah, have you not been listening? Of course he is. It didn't bother him in the least to accuse me in the wrong and leave me to my fate. He did his best to convince the police and the insurance company that I had stolen Mother's pearls. So yes, I do believe he's capable of making even more trouble, given half a chance.'

'That is shocking bad form,' Sarah said, 'You must cut him off!'

Sarah's indignation on her behalf warmed her heart, but her suggestion made her chuckle. 'But he... all of them, have cut *me*. Again!

'Seriously Lucy, you need to protect yourself,' Sarah replied with a frown.

'Only tell me how, my friend. I'm trapped. I have little or no money, a master criminal who is convinced I have his stolen gems and an insurance agent and the police thinking I was complicit in the original theft. It wouldn't surprise me if they are watching me too, waiting for me to abscond with the gems.

They are very clever, you see. It's all under the guise of giving me protection.'

'Nonsense, Lucy. Isn't that a trifle paranoid? Do you want Geoffrey to speak to the police? He will vouch for you.'

'No, Sarah. There's no need to involve you or your husband in this disaster.'

'On the contrary, I hope you realise Geoffrey and I would be only too happy to help you in any way, including a loan, if that's of any benefit to you.'

Lucy grasped her hand in gratitude. 'Thank you, but I'm not desperate enough to impose on my friends. My hope is Mr Stone finds the sapphires before this Marsh character decides it's time I join Charlie in Kensal Green Cemetery.'

'Don't speak so!' Sarah said with a shudder. Then she tilted her head and narrowed her eyes. 'Would the Mr Stone you refer to be *the* Phineas Stone?'

'The very same. Do you know him? I was hoping you could tell me something about him.'

Sarah sat back, looking pleased. 'Top up your tea, my dear, this may take a while. *Everyone* knows the lovely Phin. I can give you all the details. Do you want the whole family tree or the pertinent details?'

Lucy smiled. 'The abridged version, please.'

'Splendid! The family hail from Kent. Landowners for hundreds of years, no coronets in the old family tree but highly respected and all that. The father is still alive. If I remember rightly, Mrs Stone passed away about eight years ago. Phineas has two brothers. Andrew is the eldest and as dull as dishwater, not as clever or handsome as Phin and word is he's extremely jealous of his successful and popular brother. The other brother, whose name I can't recall, is in the army, stationed in India, I understand. Phin has two sisters, both married, one living abroad, the other lives in Devon somewhere with a promising and rather large family.' Sarah picked up her cup and regarded Lucy from above the rim.

'That's all?' Lucy asked.

'You want the interesting bits too? How greedy!'

'Of course! I wish to ascertain what kind of man I'm dealing with. He's wily; I need to stay one step ahead.'

Sarah took a deep breath, clearly enjoying her position of power. 'What exactly do you need to know?'

Lucy had to play along. 'How long have you known him?' she asked.

'Forever! We have moved in the same circles for years.'

'I didn't get the impression he was a man-about-town,' Lucy said.

'You're right, but he can be seen at the more select occasions and house parties, particularly since he took up his present occupation and been so successful. What mama would not want such a man adorning her drawing room?'

'And no doubt it is useful for him to have contacts in high places, he intimated as much to me.'

'I never really considered that, but I suppose you could be correct.'

'I would have assumed his profession would be frowned upon—that he would be excluded from the upper echelons?' Lucy remarked.

'There are those who might frown upon it, certainly, but his excellent manners and family connections are such that he has the entrée almost everywhere,' Sarah replied.

'How old is he?'

'About thirty-five.'

'Is he married?'

Sarah tilted her head. 'Oh—you're interested in him!' Lucy gave her a dirty look. 'No, my dear he isn't married... but he nearly was.'

'What do you mean?'

'He was jilted about nine months ago,' Sarah said.

'Good Lord!'

'It never ceases to amaze me, Lucy, that you have lived in London so long and know absolutely no one and the juiciest bits of news never fall on your tender ears.'

'Perhaps I'm above that sort of thing,' Lucy replied, trying to keep a straight face.

Sarah burst out laughing. 'Then why the questions now, my dear? You don't fool me.'

Lucy was impatient, dying to hear more. 'But you're my dearest friend, the font of all gossip when I need information.' Sarah bowed in acknowledgement. 'So who was she?' Lucy probed.

'Alice Muldoon. You have heard of the Muldoon family? Please tell me you have or I shall despair of you entirely.'

Lucy racked her brains. She had a vague memory of hearing of a Lady Muldoon. 'Sorry, I don't recall anything much about them.'

Sarah closed her eyes briefly. 'My dear Lucy, Lady Dot is one of the most important hostesses in Mayfair. She was a great friend of Phin's mother, and the families spent a lot of time together. Out of the blue, when we had all given up hope of seeing Phin trip down the aisle, the engagement was announced in *The Times*. Quite a coup for Phin, we all believed, as Alice will inherit the Muldoon fortune. Not that he's poor, my dear, quite the opposite. He's earned a fortune over the years in commission and rewards; another reason his brother Andrew dislikes him so.'

'But what happened about the wedding?'

'No one knows. She broke off the engagement and six months later married a trumped-up nobody by the name of Edward Vaughan. Phin disappeared for a few months, supposedly on a case over in France, but I believe he was tending a broken heart.'

'That might explain why he's such a cold fish.'

Sarah's eyebrows shot up. 'My dear, we can't be speaking of the same man. Of course, when it comes to business he may act differently. But he's generally considered a charming man, though I'll admit I have found him intimidating on occasion—he seems to know absolutely *everything*. However, Geoffrey thinks highly of him and has consulted him on many occasions regarding legal matters.'

Lucy wasn't sure she liked being referred to as *business* but thrust aside her irritation, her curiosity to the fore. 'It was odd her marrying someone else so soon after the break-up with Mr Stone.'

'Indeed, it was the talk of London. As it transpires, I saw them only last night at a supper party. Your Mr Stone was there too, reputedly the first time he has visited the Muldoon house since the debacle. Everyone was curious to see how they would react to each other.'

'Gosh, it must have been tense,' Lucy said.

Sarah's eyes lit up with mischief. 'Yes, lots of nervous laughter and darting eyes, with everyone pretending not to notice, but agog all the same. Lady Muldoon is fond of Phin, and they appeared to be on friendly terms. They chatted for a while in the drawing room, but on Phin entering the salon, Alice's husband turned surly. Mind you, he is most of the time. Not that he would stand up to Phin, far too mousey a creature and Phin has at least a foot on him. But the lovely Alice was a different matter. She laughed a little too loudly and flirted a little too wildly, for my liking. If her aim was to attract Phin's attention, it didn't work. He avoided her the entire evening, sitting with Martin Deville, one of his closest friends.'

Lucy was confused. 'Do you believe she regrets not marrying him?'

Sarah smiled. 'You wouldn't ask that question if you could see Edward Vaughan with his sullen expression and dreadful manners. There's no comparison.'

SIXTEEN

New Year's Eve

When Stone called the following afternoon, Lucy welcomed him as brightly as she could. Tucked under his arm was a large parcel tied with string. But his demeanour was grave as he shook her hand. With a sinking heart, she wondered how much more bad news she could deal with.

'Forgive me, but you're very pale. Are you quite well? I trust there have been no more incidents?' he asked, as he settled down in a chair opposite. He placed the parcel down on the carpet at his feet.

'Nothing, Mr Stone. I would let you know immediately if anything of that nature occurred. I'm fine, thank you. I have some trouble sleeping. Every sound in the house has taken on a new and sinister connotation.'

'I'm sorry to hear that, but it is understandable.' He reached into his coat pocket. 'I have brought something which may help assuage your fears.' To Lucy's surprise, he withdrew a small ivory-handled pistol. She stared at it in fascination.

'Do you know how to use a gun, Mrs Lawrence?'

'Yes, my father taught me to shoot. I'm quite a good shot, actually.'

'That eases my mind somewhat. If you're tempted to go out, please take it with you.' This was said with a knowing look. Had her visit to the hospital been observed after all? He handed the pistol over, along with a small box of ammunition. 'Keep it near you in the house, too. The chamber is full, so please be careful.'

Dismay swept over her as the implication of his gift sank in. 'You *do* think they will return?'

'It is wise to be prepared for all eventualities.'

She weighed the pistol in her hand, surprised at its lightness. 'Thank you.'

'I also have your escritoire,' he said, reaching down for the parcel at his feet. He handed it over with a smile. 'My man George has done a good job, I believe.'

Lucy pulled off the brown paper. The writing box had been repaired beautifully. 'Why this is marvellous! Please pass on my thanks.'

'I will.' Stone gave her a long searching look. 'I'm afraid that isn't the only reason for my visit today, Mrs Lawrence. I have something of a delicate nature to tell you. I have no wish to distress you further, but there are a couple of things you need to know about your husband.'

She swallowed hard. 'I have a feeling I'll regret this, but please, go on.'

'I met an old friend of mine at a supper party the other night. It transpires he's in the same club as your late husband.'

'The Marlborough?'

'Yes. Martin Deville is also in the insurance business and I was telling him about the Somerville pearls case and naturally your name came up. He knew your husband.'

'And?'

'He told me there were some interesting rumours circulating in the club. It would appear your husband approached some members to find out if they would be interested in—'

'A sapphire mine in Kashmir?' Lucy asked, dreading the answer.

'I'm afraid so. However, one member, John Bannon, is a banker. One of the investors sought his advice. When Bannon saw the share certificate, he challenged your husband as to its validity, right in the middle of the club. It would appear Mr Lawrence couldn't answer his questions and blustered. After a nasty shouting match he upped and left and wasn't seen again. This was a day or two before his death.'

'Could a disgruntled investor have murdered him?'

'Unlikely, Mrs Lawrence, my money is still on Marsh.'

Lucy was dismayed. 'It was unlikely I would be accepted back into society, but this makes it impossible. I'm only surprised so many of Charlie's fellow club members turned up to the funeral at Kensal Green. I suppose it was lurid curiosity.'

He cast her a worried look. 'I'm afraid that isn't all.'

Lucy let out a slow breath and eyed the decanter on the sideboard with sudden longing. 'Go on.'

'This morning I paid a call to the Bannon household. I believe you're acquainted with them?'

'Yes indeed, we dined at each other's houses occasionally. In fact, I told you about Mrs Bannon. She's the one who cut me on the street after Charlie died. Why did you go there? Was it to question John about the row at the club?'

'No, I'm afraid not. My friend claimed there was a connection between your husband and the lady.'

Lucy caught her breath, the image of Charlie and Florence Bannon together sickeningly real. The pit of her stomach plunged. 'Somehow I have the impression you don't mean she was involved in the mining scandal.'

'Correct.'

Lucy took a shaky breath. 'She was his mistress?'

'Yes, I'm sorry to say. I called on her once I was sure her husband had left for the bank. At first, she denied the affair and claimed the only connection was through her husband. But I was confident my information was correct. Eventually, when pressed, she admitted the whole thing.' He had the good grace to look uncomfortable. 'This must be painful for you, but you have a right to be told the truth.'

Lucy had the urge to laugh or perhaps it was to cry. It took her a few moments to compose herself. 'It would appear I was ignorant about many, if not all, of my husband's exploits,' she said. Stone's eyes were full of sympathy. 'Don't worry, Mr Stone,' Lucy continued. 'It is a shock, but compared to everything else I have learned lately, I can't say I'm surprised. I have been the blindest of fools. Charlie was a liar and a cheat. There it is! The rest of the world knew it, it seems. How dim-witted I must appear to you.'

'No!' he exclaimed.

She rose up and walked over to the fireplace, trying to order her swirling, miserable thoughts. Numbness enveloped her, as if her insides had turned to ice. This was a nightmare she would never wake up from. She had loved Charlie, and although she knew their marriage had been in trouble, she had never considered the possibility he would betray her. How could she have been so mistaken?

'It is demeaning,' she murmured, 'what he's done to me.'

'Yes, it is,' Stone answered, his voice firm. She spun around to find he was a few steps away, a crease of concern puckering his brow.

'Was their affair common knowledge in society? Was I a laughing stock?' Lucy asked, her voice breaking.

'Don't tease yourself with these questions. There's nothing to be achieved.'

'Except the truth!'

'For what it is worth, I believe he was a fool,' he said, stepping closer, his voice low, almost husky.

'Thank you, Mr Stone.' She barely got the words out, her throat was so tight.

His mien softened and for a moment she thought he was going to move even closer. It would be so easy to take comfort in the arms of such a man, but any more sympathy and she would be a howling heap on the floor. She had some shreds of pride left.

'Tell me, why did you visit that woman?' Lucy asked.

He blinked as if coming out of a trance. Was that a trace of disappointment in his gaze? 'I... I hoped she might be able to provide information about your husband's involvement with Marsh.'

'And was she?'

'She claimed no knowledge. All she knew was he was planning to go out of town for a few days, but he didn't reveal his destination. He would not let her accompany him. Seemingly, they argued about it.'

Lucy skirted around him to the safety of her seat. 'How distressing for her!' She saw a flicker of unease cross his features as she sat down and immediately regretted her sarcasm. Somehow she would have to find the courage to rise above the sordidness and avoid sinking to Charlie's level.

Stone remained standing, regarding her with concern.

'If she's telling the truth, then Charlie did leave London. I wonder where he went. It's unlikely to have been Edinburgh, as he told me,' she said.

'I agree. The timeline is too tight and the distance too great. Did you enquire of his family if he turned up there?'

'I never thought of it. His parents are elderly and too frail to travel. His only brother is in India. Only a cousin came down for the funeral. They weren't a particularly close family.'

'Did he have a valet?'

'Yes, but he rarely travelled with him,' she said. 'Charlie said he found him irksome.'

'That's peculiar, is it not?'

'Yes, and we argued about it, as it happens. I wondered why he did not dismiss him, particularly as our finances were so volatile, but Charlie wouldn't hear of it. It made no sense to me.'

'Could he have mentioned his destination to this man?'

'I doubt it. I can't imagine Charlie unburdening himself to him. Robinson was a peculiar fellow. When Charlie died, the household had no use for a valet. Robinson was one of the first servants I dismissed, but I've no idea where he went. There has been no approach for a reference.'

'Would your maid know where this Robinson fellow might be?' Stone asked.

'She may do.' Lucy stood up and tugged the bell pull. 'Let's ask her.'

'There is one other thing,' he said, sitting down.

'Yes?'

'Why didn't you mention your husband had an office?'

'He did? But I never knew—how extraordinary! I assumed he carried out his business at his club. How did you find out? Where is it?' she asked.

'Mrs Bannon mentioned it. They met there once or twice. It is on the Kennington Road in Lambeth, above a bookshop apparently.'

Before she could respond, Mary came into the room. 'You rang, ma'am?'

'Yes, Mary. Be so good as to answer some questions for Mr Stone. Don't be alarmed, you aren't in any trouble. He's looking for information.'

Mary gave them a timid smile. 'I'll do my best, ma'am.'

'Would you by chance know the present whereabouts of Robinson, the late Mr Lawrence's valet?' Stone asked.

Mary looked to her as if seeking permission. Lucy gave it with a nod. 'Last I heard, sir, he was gone to Brighton.'

'Would you have an address for him?'

'Sorry, sir, no. I'm afraid we didn't get along very well, me and him. Fierce nosey, he was. In fact, most of us didn't like him. He wasn't here long. We were glad to see him go.'

Stone looked across at Lucy and lifted an eyebrow.

'Thank you, Mary, that's all for now.'

'Sorry, ma'am,' Mary said, before bobbing and quitting the room.

'When did your husband take the man on?' Stone queried.

Lucy frowned, trying to remember. 'Last January, as far as I recall.'

Stone pursed his lips. 'I suspect he was placed in your husband's service by Marsh to keep an eye on him.'

Lucy gaped at him, appalled. 'You can't be serious?'

Stone shrugged. 'Your husband had been given thousands of pounds worth of gems; of course Marsh would want to keep him under surveillance.'

'And Robinson would have been familiar with the layout of the house, too. No doubt, he told Marsh's men the best way to gain entry.'

Stone nodded. 'There would be little point in wasting time trying to find the so-called valet; I'm sure he's long gone, back to the rookeries from which he no doubt came. However, I do know where Lambeth is. I shall go there directly and investigate this office.'

Lucy stood up. 'I'm coming too.'

'No, I don't think that would be a good idea, Mrs Lawrence. You would be far safer here.'

'Mr Stone, since you are neither my father nor my husband, I'll remind you I may do as I please. Would you be so good as to hail a cab while Mary fetches my coat?'

He looked as though he was going to object, then gave her a hint of a smile. 'I know better than to argue with a lady.'

'How sensible you are!' Lucy declared.

SEVENTEEN

The cab pulled up outside Russell's Book Shop on the Kennington Road. As Stone paid the cabbie, Lucy stood on the pavement trying to gauge the character of the area. It was a busy thoroughfare with a constant stream of carriages, hansoms and trams. The road was dominated by long red-bricked terraces with shops along the ground floor with two to three storeys above. White and cream awnings stretched out over the shops like sails on a becalmed sea. Wasn't it odd Charlie had chosen this locality? Why not somewhere nearer home? There could only be one reason, and it was a depressing one: it all pointed to clandestine meetings and underhand transactions.

The bookshop had a jaded quality to it. The paint was cracked and peeling with age and beneath 'Russell's Book Shop', the yellowed awning had a rip in the fabric. Lucy stared up at the windows, wondering which one might be Charlie's office. From what she could see, the windows were grimy and without curtains. *Vacant as the faces of the dead*. What on earth had put that thought in her head?

The bell of the bookshop sounded and drew her attention to the ground floor. A tall man in a black coat and bowler hat emerged, then stood in the doorway, sizing her up. Stone was chatting to the cabbie, asking him about the locality. She wished he would hurry up. The bookseller glanced towards the wooden table to his left and back to her again. A variety of books were piled upon it and just above 'Libraries Purchased' was written in white paint across the front window. Unhappily, this put her in mind of her father's books. She turned away.

'Shall we? This way, I believe,' Stone said, linking her arm and pointing with his cane towards a door to the side of the shop she had failed to notice. As Stone pushed it open, she was relieved to hear the bookshop bell jangle once again. The shop owner must have gone back inside.

They entered a long and narrow hallway. An odour of boiled cabbage and mouldering timber hung in the air. Much to her alarm, a scurrying sound suggested they had disturbed the building's four-legged inhabitants. When something cold touched her cheek, she brushed it away with a panicked swipe of her fingers. But it was only a cobweb. Nerves on edge, Lucy followed Stone to the bottom of the stairs. Looking up into the gloom, she could make out broken spindles and bare wooden treads.

'Normally, I would insist on ladies first, however...' Stone regarded her with a serious expression.

'Please,' she answered. 'Be my guest!'

Stone stopped halfway up and tilted his head as if listening for something. But even the mice were silent. She waited patiently for him to move on.

'Do you happen to know which floor, Mr Stone?' she whispered, when they reached the first landing. There were three doors, but no signage to indicate what lay behind.

Stone appeared lost in concentration, scrutinising the outside of each door in turn. 'A process of elimination, I would imagine,' he said.

'Could it be the red door at the end? There's post on the floor and sticking out of the letter box.'

'Perhaps. Stay here. I'd like to check the floor above first,' he replied quietly, before disappearing up the next flight.

Lucy breathed out slowly in frustration. Minutes dragged by, and there was no sign of him returning. She couldn't resist. After a quick glance up the stairs, Lucy stooped down and picked up a handful of letters. The second envelope was addressed to the Padar Mining Company. Her heart began to pound. *Padar*. That was the place in Kashmir Stone had spoken of, she was sure. This had to be Charlie's office. It was so disappointing. A little part of her had hoped it had all been a mistake, but most of the letters were similarly addressed. She crossed over the landing and was about to call up to Stone when the red door was wrenched open. A stocky and rather ugly man with greasy hair and patched clothes halted in the doorway, a look of surprise on his face. Lucy froze too. A livid scar ran down the side of his cheek, but it was his eyes that scared her most. Lucy had never seen such a malevolent glare.

The man looked down to her hands and then back to her face. Before she knew what was happening, he had advanced upon her with a swiftness she couldn't fathom for such a bulky man. Snatching the letters from her, he pushed her against the wall before making for the stairs.

For a second, she was winded.

'Mr Stone!' she yelled as soon as she caught her breath. Almost without thinking, she pulled the pistol out of her purse. When she reached the top of the stairs, she pulled back the safety catch and managed to fire off one shot before the escaping man hurtled out of the front door and on to the street. The bullet lodged in the door frame, splintering the wood.

Stone flew past her, careering down the stairs. She followed slowly, finding her limbs were suddenly trembling. What had possessed her? What if she had hit him? It would take some explaining to the police. When she reached the front door, Stone was already walking back up the street.

'He's gone,' he said breathlessly as he reached her. 'I couldn't catch him. He jumped onto a tram.' Gasping, he braced his palm against the wall and tried to catch his breath. 'Why did you shoot at him?'

'I wasn't aiming to injure him, just stop him. I'm sorry,' she said, pointing to the damaged door frame. 'I'm a little out of practice.'

'And you're unharmed?'

'Yes,' she assured him. 'I don't think he meant to injure me. He only pushed me out of the way to get to the stairs. Mind you, he grabbed the letters from me none too gently.'

Stone smiled and tapped his pocket. 'He dropped them as he jumped on to the tram. Now, I should put you in a cab and send you home,' he said, straightening up fully. 'You shouldn't be involved in this. It is far too dangerous.'

'Nonsense! I'm perfectly fine, Mr Stone. Let's finish what we came to do.' Lucy turned back inside and headed up the stairs before he could carry out his threat.

'Why did you let him close the door?' Stone asked her, after trying the handle. 'Now I shall have to break in.'

'I didn't—it closed over itself, and besides, I was too busy defending myself to be overly concerned about it,' she replied, thinking his irritation unreasonable. Then she realised it was probably a reaction to what had just happened. It would appear he didn't like to lose control of a situation. She watched as he pulled out a set of metal prongs from his inside pocket.

'Mr Stone! Are those what I think they are?'

'You never know when these will come in useful,' he said with a wink.

Seconds later, there was a click and the door swung open. It was immediately obvious what the man with the scar had been up to. The office of Padar Mining had been thoroughly searched. Papers were strewn everywhere. Lucy groaned. Even if there was anything left to find, it was chaos and would take hours to comb through it.

Stepping over the mess on the floor, they advanced in to the room. The rear window was missing a pane of glass, allowing an icy breeze to whistle through. Lucy took in the hideous wallpaper, damp-stained cornice and threadbare carpet. It was a fitting place for a sordid little affair. With an effort, she pushed the awful image of Charlie and his mistress out of her mind.

Stone placed his hat and cane on the desk. He wore a bleak expression as he righted the only chair which partially blocked a large filing cabinet. Its drawers had been pulled out and the contents scattered.

'I don't think much of Charlie's filing system,' Lucy muttered. Stone threw her an impatient look. 'What are we looking for?' she asked.

'Anything which might indicate where he hid the sapphires. It is highly unlikely your husband hid them here as his compatriots would have known about this place, but he may have left a clue.'

'I doubt it, Mr Stone. He wasn't a great person for puzzles.'

Stone shrugged. 'Look anyway, Mrs Lawrence. Something may strike you. It may be a reference to a place or a name you recognise.'

'But surely whoever has already searched here has taken anything of that nature away.'

Stone looked as though he was going to answer, then clamped his mouth shut with an impatient snap.

'And the man who was here,' she said. 'He can't have been one of Marsh's men, could he? They would hardly have waited this long to come here. I imagine this was the first place they searched immediately after Charlie's death.'

Mr Stone removed his gloves and placed them on top of his hat before picking up an envelope and blowing the dust off. 'Yes, I would have to agree; most of this mess was created months ago.'

'Who could he be then, my friend Scarface?' she asked.

Stone began rifling through some papers on the desk. 'His name is Coffin Mike.'

'Good Lord, you know him! What an extraordinary name. He was hardly christened so, Mr Stone.'

Stone smiled. 'No one knows his real name, but I'm sure you can guess how he picked up that particular moniker. Unfortunately, I believe he may be in the employ of another party who has an interest in all of this. Although, he's been involved with Marsh's gang from time to time. He's not famous for his loyalty; like most of his ilk, he would happily sell his soul.'

'And who might he be working for, Mr Stone?' Lucy asked.

He looked up at her in surprise. 'Why, the original owner of the sapphires, of course, and more importantly, his representative. Mr Khan paid me a visit only yesterday. The police informed him the case had been re-opened. He's under orders to stay in England until the sapphires are recovered. The other pieces of jewellery have now been completed, and he's anxious to return home. The maharajah's reward for the return of his gems has been increased, he informed me, in the hopes I will "get to it with greater speed".'

'How rude!' Lucy remarked. 'Is the reward substantial?'

'Twenty thousand pounds.'

Lucy stared at him. It was a small fortune. 'So that's why Mr Khan has sent Coffin Mike here. He hopes to find the sapphires himself and claim the reward.'

'No, that would be impossible as he's a servant in all but name. I'd surmise Khan wants to redeem himself in the eyes of his lord and master and save him having to pay out. He feels responsible for what has happened to the maharajah's property.'

'Well, this is wonderful news. I almost feel honoured. I have a master criminal *and* a disgruntled Kashmiri maharajah to fend off. How exciting my life has become! When all of this is over, and I'm hopefully not six foot under, my existence will become frightfully dull. No doubt I shall go into a decline.'

'Are you feeling sorry for yourself?' Stone asked. 'Best to keep busy.' He indicated the papers on the floor. He bent his head quickly, but she didn't fail to notice his lips twitch with amusement.

'Your advice is duly noted,' Lucy retorted, before picking up the papers and sifting through them.

Suddenly, Stone's head shot up. 'Someone's coming,' he said. 'Quickly, get behind me.'

Sure enough, Lucy could hear footsteps coming up the stairs. She moved behind the desk, half hiding behind Stone's broad back, her fingers resting on her bag. She could feel the outline of the pistol inside.

The door swung open and the bookseller entered, brandishing a cricket bat. He took in the state of the room before glaring at them. 'Who are you? What in heaven's name is going on? I could have sworn I heard a gunshot.'

'You did, sir. The lady was assaulted and attempted to defend herself,' Stone said.

Lucy smarted. The 'attempted' rankled a bit.

The bookseller waved the bat in agitation. 'This is outrageous! I shall summon a constable. Explain what you're doing here this instant, sir!' His angry eyes flicked between them.

'And you are?' Stone asked, sounding very unperturbed, Lucy had to admit.

'John Russell, if it's any of your business. I own this building. I demand to know, sir, what you're doing in this room without my permission.'

'My name is Phineas Stone, and I'm investigating a crime.' Stone handed over his card to the bewildered bookseller. 'If you have any concerns, I suggest you contact Chief Inspector McQuillan at Vine Street Station. He can vouch for me.'

'And the lady?' Russell asked. Lucy didn't like the emphasis he put on *lady* and glared at him.

'The lady is none of your concern,' Stone answered before she had a chance to let fly.

Mr Russell placed the bat on the table, his eyes fixed firmly on Stone's face. Then he glanced at the card and grunted. 'I would be interested to know what kind of crime you're investigating'—he referred to the card again—'Mr Stone. I would be very interested indeed.'

'Why so?' Stone asked.

'The tenant who rented this room owes me rent. I would very much like to speak to him. I can't let the room until all of this is disposed of and he settles his account. Do you know where I can find him?'

'I'm afraid he's beyond your reach now, Mr Russell. The gentleman is dead.'

'Dead! Confound it!' The bookseller's face flooded with angry colour. 'I beg your pardon, madam, but as I explained, he owed me rent.'

Lucy was sorry for the man as he stood in the middle of the room, almost rigid with impotent anger. She considered how empty her own purse was and smothered the impulse to offer him the money Charlie owed. Mr Faulkner the solicitor would have to deal with it.

'And now who will clean up this mess, I'd like to know,' Mr Russell demanded, 'if Mr Somerville is deceased?'

Lucy's bag slid unheeded from her hands and landed with a thump on the floor.

EIGHTEEN

As Stone closed the door after Mr Russell, Lucy sank down on the chair, trying to process what the man had said. Stunned by his revelation, she wasn't sure what to make of it. How on earth could her brother Richard have become involved? It didn't make any sense. She examined Stone's face as he turned towards her, certain he must be as shocked at the disclosure as she. However, he appeared to be his usual composed self.

'Whatever is the matter?' he asked, stepping closer.

'You heard what he said,' Lucy exclaimed. 'My brother must have been tangled up in this whole sorry affair as well.'

'I very much doubt it, Mrs Lawrence. Your husband would hardly have used his own name to secure this place. Most likely, your maiden name popped into his head. Spite against your brother may also have featured in his choice for I doubt he ever intended paying the rent.'

'I never considered that possibility. Of course, that makes sense,' Lucy said slowly.

Stone drew out his watch. 'It will be dark in half an hour. It's time we left. I'll have Chief Inspector McQuillan send someone here to remove all of this. It needs to be properly examined.'

'An excellent idea. I only wish you'd come up with it earlier. I've lost the feeling in my fingers. Look, they are quite blue with cold.'

'You would insist on coming,' Stone replied, with a quirked brow. Lucy gave him a withering look. He spread his hands in supplication, but a smile lurked behind his eyes. 'Forgive me, I couldn't resist.'

She sniffed. 'What about Mr Russell?'

'Once McQuillan is involved, it will become a crime scene and there will be little he can do about it.'

'I must admit, I'm sorry about his being out of pocket,' Lucy said, as she gathered up her things. 'He looks like he needs the money. I'll ask my solicitor to contact him.'

Stone chuckled. 'You're far too soft.' He opened the door and bowed as she passed through.

As soon as Mary closed the front door behind her, Lucy wriggled out of her coat and pulled off her hat.

'Don't just stand there, Mary, come up and help me get ready. I'm going out to dinner.' Lucy raced up the stairs to her bedroom.

'Yes, ma'am,' Mary said, sounding surprised, but she bounded up after her.

'Pull out the black velvet and see if it's fit to wear,' Lucy called over her shoulder. 'I don't have much time. Mr Stone is calling for me at seven.'

While she stripped off her day dress, she could hear Mary rummaging in the wardrobe.

'Sure it's grand, ma'am. All the creases have come out. I'll lay it on the bed for you. Can you manage while I fetch some hot water?'

'Yes, yes. Do be quick!' Lucy said.

Lucy sat down at her dressing table and unpinned her hair. Then halted, shocked by the image that confronted her in the mirror. *My God, I've aged a hundred years today,* she thought, taking in the pallor of her cheeks and the lines of fatigue around her eyes. A peculiar feeling in the pit of her stomach had been growing all day, ever since she had learned of Charlie's affair. Was it some kind of grief? The realisation her marriage had been a farce? Part of the reason she had accompanied Stone was so she wouldn't have to think about it. But she couldn't help herself now. Florence Bannon's face hovered in her mind. It almost made her ill to visualise them lying together. Had there been others before Florence? She rubbed her temples and was shocked to discover she wanted to cry. No, not just cry—howl.

She sifted through her memories, trying to recall occasions when they had socialised with the Bannons. But no suspicion had ever entered her mind. How that horrible little trollop must have been laughing at her. And Charlie too. He had betrayed her in every possible way and with such a woman.

Lucy groaned and dropped her head into her hands. It was as if trouble was stalking her and she was too stupid to avoid it. And now she had accepted Stone's dinner invitation. What had possessed her? Halfway back from Lambeth, he had turned to her. It was New Year's Eve after all, he had said, his voice coaxing. The city would be celebrating, and he hated to dine alone. The words were hardly out of his mouth when she accepted. Of course, she shouldn't have, only a few months into her mourning. Widows weren't supposed to enjoy themselves. But then a little voice had whispered, *Oh to hell with it! It wouldn't have stopped Charlie. Why should I shut myself away for a husband who played foul in every way?* Unfortunately, this little escapade, if she went through with it, could destroy any vestige of reputation she had left.

And Phineas Stone. Would he think ill of her for accepting? Of course, he must have felt sorry for her. Why else would he have asked? She groaned again. He felt bad because he was the one who had told her about Florence. Surely he must be regretting the impulse now and hoping she would send her regrets? Although... he had looked genuinely pleased when she accepted, and his gaze had held more than warmth that afternoon. She could have sworn he was on the point of embracing her when she had been upset. The heat rose in her face at the thought. What would it feel like? Quickly, she banished the thought: that was an even more dangerous path to venture down.

'You're in luck. I'd boiled the kettle for a cuppa just before you arrived,' Mary said, carrying in a jug of steaming water.

Lucy turned around and looked at her. Mary beamed back. For the last week the poor girl had been the household drudge. Here at last was an opportunity for her to perform her proper job of lady's maid. *There's enough misery hovering in this house as it is*, Lucy thought. *Besides, society has already condemned me*, she reasoned. It was about time she explored her more wicked side.

'Please fetch my black evening gloves, Mary.'

'Yes, ma'am.' Mary pulled open the top drawer of the chest of drawers and carefully pulled out a wine-coloured box. Lucy had forgotten the gloves had been a gift from Charlie and was on the point of telling the maid to put them back, but Mary's face was a picture of reverence. She removed the delicate tissue paper and gently laid the satin evening gloves on the dressing table. They both stared down at them. Mary appeared to be mesmerised by their satin loveliness. Lucy, however, succumbed to the treacherous notion her husband's lover might have helped him choose them.

Verrey's Restaurant, Regent Street

For the first time, Lucy realised how well known Phineas Stone
actually was. To be given a table at Verrey's at such short notice
on New Year's Eve was next to miraculous. The restaurant was
crammed full of the social elite. It was, after all, reputedly a
favourite haunt of the Prince of Wales. Lucy had often passed
the restaurant and knew of its reputation, but their finances had
never been sufficient to indulge in one of its famous dinners. On
entering the main dining room, all eyes fell upon them and
Lucy almost stumbled. Stone tightened his grip on her arm with
a reassuring squeeze. How dowdy she must look next to him, in
her dyed velvet dress, while he was the personification of taste
in his black dress suit, crisp white shirt with a cream bow tie and
waistcoat. He was a living, breathing advertisement for
Savile Row.

A waiter showed them to a table in a corner. With relief,
Lucy sat down, glad to be away from the curious stares. The
table had a pristine white cloth, highly polished silver cutlery
and sparkling crystal. A cathedral to food, she had once heard
the place described, and now she understood the reference. Her
eye was drawn upwards as soaring silver arches rose up to the
vaulted roof. The cosier atmosphere at table level had been
achieved through the clever manipulation of mirrors and dark
green panels. The overall effect was grandeur and elegance.
And intimacy.

Over the top of her menu she sneaked a look at Stone.
Compared to their first meal together at the Red Fox Inn in
Harrogate, this was a far more cosy setting. They could be
mistaken for any other couple out for the evening to enjoy each
other's company. How normal that would be and yet so far from
her reality. After the news she had received earlier in the day,
she wondered if she would ever feel normal again. Lucy stole

another glance at him. He caught her glance and smiled back. A devastating smile that triggered a physical response in her. All of a sudden, she was tongue-tied and lowered her eyes. If only he wasn't so attractive. Stupidly, it felt as though she was betraying Charlie. The words on the menu before her began to blur, and she had to swallow several times to ease the tightness in her throat.

A grey-haired gentleman came up to the table. 'Good evening, Mr Stone,' he said, with a hint of a German accent. They shook hands.

'Good evening, Albert,' Stone said with a smile. 'Let me introduce Mrs Lawrence. It is her first time here. Mrs Lawrence, this is Albert Krehl, one of the owners and a very good friend of mine.'

'Madam, it is my great pleasure to welcome you to Verrey's,' Albert said. 'If there's anything you need, please let the waiter know and I or my brother will come directly.' He turned to Mr Stone. 'My gratitude once again, Mr Stone, for the service you rendered. We are especially grateful for your discretion in the matter.'

Stone smiled. 'Not at all, Albert. It was my pleasure.'

Krehl bowed and was replaced almost immediately by a waiter. 'Madam, sir, Monsieur Krehl has instructed me to serve you the special *diner* tonight, as his most welcome guests.' He presented with a flourish a printed menu on stiff white card, heavily embellished with golden scrolls.

Caviar sur croûtes
Consommé à la Prince de Galles
Petits filets de bœuf à la Riga
Jambon à la broche aux epinards
Grouse
Choux de Bruxelles à la maître d'hotel

Salade à la Napolitaine
Biscuit glacé à la Verrey
Canndons de moka ou talmouses au citron

No wonder the place was famous; Lucy's mouth began to water. She was famished. A week of Mary's efforts in the kitchen had left a lot to be desired: cooking was not her maid's foremost talent.

'Would you prefer to order from the other menu?' Stone asked her.

'No, indeed, this looks wonderful,' she said. 'Am I allowed ask what it is you did for Mr Krehl?' she asked, as soon as the waiter had taken their order and was out of earshot.

'I'm sure you know better.'

The waiter reappeared moments later with a bottle of Perrier Jouët champagne and poured two glasses. 'Whatever you did, he is very appreciative, it would seem,' Lucy commented.

Stone merely smiled and took up his glass as if to toast.

Lucy forestalled him. 'To finding the sapphires,' she declared and clinked his glass.

He looked surprised. 'I was going to welcome in the New Year.'

'I don't believe it will be a good year unless those gems are found... for me at least,' Lucy admitted.

'You doubt I will find them?' Stone asked.

'Forgive me, but I do not see how you can possibly succeed.'

'Someone must know where your husband went before he died. Those missing days are vital,' he said. 'But I do not wish to talk about your late husband this evening. To your very good health.'

'Thank you,' she said, taking a slow sip of her champagne. How had she not noticed the golden flecks in his eyes?

'Why Phin, what a delight to see you here!' A woman's voice broke the spell.

Lucy turned to see one of the most beautiful women she had ever beheld approach their table.

NINETEEN

Stone rose to his feet looking none too pleased at the interruption. The raven-haired lady beamed at him, then treated Lucy to a haughty glance. Her expensive satin evening dress shimmered: a beautiful pink concoction with French lace flattering a low-cut bodice. Diamonds sparkled on her earlobes and around her slender neck. A tiny snake of envy slithered into Lucy's thoughts. The young woman was magnificent and evidently wealthy. But why was Stone so unsettled by her presence?

'Mrs Vaughan,' he said. 'How nice to see you.'

Lucy regarded the newcomer with renewed curiosity. This was the famous Alice. A young man with a long white face joined them, looking uncomfortable and sulky. Peering around nervously, he held back. Stone made the introductions. Lucy was treated to a cool green-eyed stare from the lady.

'Are your parents here tonight?' Stone asked.

'No. It's only Edward and I,' Mrs Vaughan replied. 'All alone.' She glanced at their champagne, and then threw Stone a sickly sweet smile.

Silence. Lucy watched Stone's face for a reaction. The

tension at the table was palpable, with Stone's shoulders stiff and his features blank. He flicked a glance towards Lucy. 'Isn't that wonderful,' he said at last, 'your first New Year's Eve together as a married couple. I do hope you enjoy your evening.'

Lucy allowed herself a tiny sigh of relief: he was dismissing them. But Mrs Vaughan took a step back and a flush of anger crossed her pretty face. *Not a lady who likes to be thwarted*, Lucy thought.

Mr Vaughan stepped forward and took his wife's arm. 'Thank you, Mr Stone, we fully intend to. Come along, Alice, our table is over at the far window.'

'Good evening, Phineas. Mrs Lawrence,' Mrs Vaughan said stiffly, before allowing her husband to pull her away.

'My apologies,' Stone said, taking his seat again.

'Mrs Vaughan appeared to expect an invitation to join us,' Lucy remarked.

Stone gave her an embarrassed smile. 'Lady Muldoon, her mother, is a dear friend of my family...' He trailed off, frowning heavily. 'We were engaged to be married earlier this year.'

'You and Mrs Vaughan's mother?' Lucy asked, widening her eyes as if she were thoroughly shocked.

'No!' he exclaimed. 'Ah, you're teasing me, I see.'

Lucy tilted her head and smiled at him. 'It is far too easy this evening. Mrs Vaughan is very beautiful. A high society lady, if I'm not mistaken.'

He coughed and shifted in his chair. '*Alice* and I were engaged for several months. Unfortunately, she demanded I give up my profession as she found it distasteful. I found I couldn't oblige.'

'Her family objected to what you do?'

'Not as such. Of course, they would have preferred me to be a gentleman of leisure, but I am one of the broken brigade—'

'And younger sons are used to making their way in the world without assistance,' she said.

'Yes. I see you understand.'

Lucy sighed. 'Charlie was in the same position. Unfortunately, unlike you, he didn't make good choices.'

'Or perhaps he was unlucky. Believe me, I did consider retiring. I could have given it up for I'm not without means at this stage and could support a wife. The problem is I love what I do.' He shrugged. 'I'd be chafing at the bit in a month and would be impossible to live with.'

'I understand. There's nothing worse than boredom. But you do realise if she gave you such an ultimatum she can't really have cared for you. Why is she acting this way now?'

He shrugged. 'Like many spoiled young ladies, she can't bear to be denied anything. Within a week of breaking off our engagement, she attached herself to Vaughan, but ever since her marriage'—Stone paused for a moment—'she's been acting strangely. Lady Muldoon is concerned, but there's little I can do. After all, she married another man. The rest is history, as they say.'

'The poor fellow! He doesn't look particularly happy,' Lucy remarked.

'No, though I'm sure at first he couldn't believe his luck. Alice was considered the catch of the season.'

'An heiress?'

'Yes.'

'But you escaped unscathed?'

'I like to think so,' he said, with a lopsided grin. 'In general, women are an enigma to me, Mrs Lawrence. I find dealing with villains much more straightforward.'

'Oh dear, what do you do if you come across a female villain?'

'Run!'

'And what about me?' she asked softly, leaning towards him.

'You are the greatest enigma of them all,' he said, his eyes brimming with laughter. Lucy found it a very satisfying answer.

Midnight, Victoria Embankment

Throughout dinner, Stone was attentive and eager to please. The forceful energy he usually displayed being absent, his conversation was light and easy. This was more like the man Sarah had described. Lucy couldn't deny it was wonderful to be on the receiving end of such flattering attention. They spoke of everything under the sun and the day's unfortunate revelations and adventure were ignored. Any concerns Lucy entertained about his motives were pushed to the back of her mind. The ordinariness of being out to dinner, especially with a handsome man, was to be savoured. Months of loneliness had left her craving contact and, despite being in a room full of people, it was almost as if they were alone. His gaze never left her face and as she relaxed she found herself wondering how he viewed her.

By mutual agreement, neither of them wanted to go home before midnight. Stone suggested a stroll by the river and the waiter called them a cab. They walked slowly along the embankment in companionable silence, their breath mingling in the frosty air. Lucy was content. The champagne had gone to her head a little, and she was able to relax for the first time in weeks. It was one of those pleasant, cold evenings which made you feel alive. For most of the winter a sulphurous fog had made it unpleasant to venture outdoors. But tonight the sky was a dark velvety blue with a sliver of a moon reflected in the water below. She could hear the lapping of the water against the embankment wall, a sound which wrapped her in contentment. Ahead, a curved ribbon of gaslights drew her eye towards the hands of Big Ben inching inexorably towards 1887.

As they walked along, they both encountered acquaintances who either acknowledged them or regarded them with curiosity. Lucy couldn't help but feel self-conscious and knew she would be the talk of some drawing rooms in the week to come. She wondered how Stone felt about it. Was he the kind of man who would care about gossip? Having had a tantalising glimpse into his personal life that evening, Lucy found she longed to know more, but was unsure how he would react to her curiosity. She didn't wish to break the spell.

'Are you superstitious about New Year's Eve?' he asked.

'Not at all, but my father was. Every grate was cleared of ashes before the hour struck, and he would fling open the front door on the stroke of midnight to welcome the New Year in. Rather foolish when we usually had a few feet of snow, and you were likely to get frostbite.'

He chuckled. 'My own family do the same, but Kent tends to be warmer than Yorkshire. I have heard your winters can be bitter.'

'Yes and thankfully a bad memory now. Somerville was always a cold house at the best of times. In the winter, we used to joke the ice house was warmer. One year there was a blizzard blowing, but it didn't deter my father. Much to his disgust, he had to perform the rite on his own, as we refused to move from the warmth of the drawing room. His favourite hunter died the next spring, and he always blamed it on our abandonment. It was silly, of course. Jasper was well past his prime and had been sickening for months.'

'Country traditions are often hard to understand,' Stone said. 'But they give people security in these rapidly moving modern times.'

'You could be right. Thankfully, Charlie thought it was a lot of humbug. It was New Year's Day we enjoyed the most. Everyone knew we had an open house and dropped in during the evening. I loved those informal parties,' Lucy said, feeling a little wistful. 'Charlie would be full of plans for the coming year. The more wine he took, the more outlandish they became. He was going to make his fortune, and we would travel the world. His friends would laugh at his hare-brained schemes and

often encouraged his foolishness. Charlie was an eternal opti-
mist, you see. I was usually the one who had to remind him of
reality, which did not make me popular.'

'Your husband was a dreamer?' Stone asked.

'Yes. Unfortunately it becomes tiresome when you're living
hand to mouth,' she said.

'But you must have prospered some of the time? Houses in
St John's Wood with armies of servants do not come cheap.'

'We were fortunate. Charlie's uncle had a great fondness for
him and left us the house in his will, but yes, we did prosper for
a time, and I won't deny I enjoyed the fruits of it. The problem
with Charlie, though, was not a lack of ideas, but an inability to
focus. He didn't have a head for business matters and grew disil-
lusioned quickly. To give him his due, life was never tedious.
His impetuosity was what drew me to him in the first place. He
was so different to anyone else I had ever met. The season of '76
was particularly lacklustre. I don't know if you recall?'

'I was pursuing my legal career at the time and socialised
little in those circles,' Stone explained.

'Such a shame we didn't meet at that time.'

'Indeed,' he replied, 'but even if we had, there's nothing to
say we would have liked each other.'

'You may have the right of it,' Lucy replied. But it was a
tantalising thought.

'You were saying?' he prompted.

'Oh yes. I met Charlie soon after my arrival in London. He
was a handsome and charming fellow, and initially my mother
was taken with him. However, it didn't take long for her to find
out the truth from the gossips. Aligning the house of
Somerville to an impoverished though ancient Scottish family
was not to be borne. I was forbidden to see him. But the more
Mother objected to him, the more drawn to him I became. Life
with him would be exciting for he wasn't staid and stuffy like
so many of the men I met. If only I had realised how uncom-

fortable exciting can be. I have paid a heavy price for my naivety.'

'You were unfortunate, certainly, but it is easy to be wise in hindsight,' he said.

She bowed. 'Granted, and you're kindness itself, but at least I should have listened to my father. After one disastrous meeting with Charlie, he knew he was wrong for me. With the stupidity and stubbornness of a first passion, I would not heed his advice; even when he told me, in no uncertain terms, what the consequences would be. Escape to London was my only consideration. I was suffocating in Yorkshire and London represented everything I wanted. It shone like a beacon and Charlie was offering it to me. I was blinded, of course. When you're young and in love, you consider yourself invincible.' Stone cast her a glance laced with sympathy. 'Don't worry, I'm not being maudlin. Despite everything that has happened, I don't give up easily.'

'But the days ahead will be difficult for you, particularly after what we have learned today,' he said, stopping just beyond a gaslight.

'A day of shocks, I'll admit. But it is for the best. I had been clinging to an illusion of love since Charlie's death, convincing myself the trouble in my marriage was only temporary. The truth, grim as it is, has to be faced. Life with Charlie was a sham, possibly from the very beginning.'

Stone grimaced into the darkness. 'Revealing your husband's transgressions has brought me no pleasure, I can assure you.'

'I promise not to hold it against you,' Lucy replied with a grin. 'Now, I have had such an enjoyable evening, Mr Stone. I'm grateful to you. It has been a lovely way to end a year which has been utterly dreadful. I hope the next few weeks will bring some answers, and I can begin to put my life back together.'

He stared out over the water towards Westminster Bridge.

Big Ben began to chime. As the last echo faded, he turned towards her. 'I'll do my best for you, Mrs Lawrence. It would give me great pleasure to see you free of all of this.'

'Thank you,' she said. His words were gracious but did they hint at something more? For a moment she thought he was going to make an advance, but then his expression closed. The moment had passed. Disappointed, she realised he still didn't trust her.

TWENTY

The Strawbridge Townhouse, Mayfair, London

'Tell me truthfully, Sarah, did you ever hear any rumours about Charlie and Florence Bannon?' Lucy asked. 'Was I the only fool in London who didn't know what he was up to?'

A telltale blush rose in Sarah's face. 'The Bannons are unknown to me; however, Geoffrey did mention something a few months' ago. But as it was an unsubstantiated rumour, Lucy, I didn't want to say anything without proof, particularly as you were newly widowed. The clubs are notorious for that kind of dangerous gossip.'

'I wish you had mentioned something, all the same. It was so demoralising to hear it from Mr Stone, of all people.'

'Yes, it must have been mortifying.'

Lucy regarded her friend a moment, unsure if she should voice her worries. 'Yes, and now I can't help thinking there may have been others, too. The idea is stuck in my head, festering away. Having one's life torn apart, practically in public, gives you great insight, even if it is so late in the day.'

'You had no idea?'

'Oh the signs were there, but I was in denial. The more frequent absences from home and his coldness towards me—it all makes sense now.' She gave a mirthless laugh. 'No doubt he felt trapped, much as I did.'

'However, the difference was you didn't run into the arms of someone else,' Sarah said.

'Yes I was faithful, but I thought—hoped—he would rekindle his feelings for me,' Lucy continued. 'Foolish of me, I know. He probably couldn't help himself, and I'm sure he had no difficulty finding willing partners. He was an attractive man.'

'And charming,' Sarah said.

'Lethally so,' Lucy replied with a sad smile. 'I can't really blame the women, for I fell for it too.'

'You're far too forgiving. Those women knew very well what they were about. Furthermore, he was a fool to risk losing you.'

Lucy almost laughed. 'Perhaps that was exactly what he was trying to do; that or at least forget my existence. I imagine once you find solace in the arms of someone else it becomes easier to justify it to yourself, to imagine your partner's faults have driven you to it.' Lucy frowned. 'Perhaps I did drive him away for I tend to be impulsive, and he used to complain I was headstrong.'

Sarah glared at her. 'Drive him away? Of course you didn't! Honestly Lucy, that's foolish talk. Charlie was a lying and deceitful cad. You did nothing wrong. The affairs were bad enough, but his criminal exploits have put your life in danger. Don't you realise the picture you paint is of a very shallow man who only ever thought of his own needs and desires?'

'I do now.' Lucy closed her eyes briefly, suddenly weary of it all. She knew Sarah was right; it was just difficult to accept the last ten years of her life had been based on falsehoods.

Sarah's expression softened. 'Sadly, infidelity isn't uncommon once the first flush of romance dies. Many wives are happy to look the other way once the requisite heir survives babyhood and familial duty is satisfied. The physical side of marriage isn't to every woman's taste.'

Lucy shook her head. 'Perhaps that's true for some, but I missed him. I loved him so desperately in the beginning. When I realised he no longer felt the same, it slowly broke my heart.'

'Why did he change, do you know? Sarah asked.

'Honestly? I believe my miscarriages triggered it. He began to change after the first one; he became distant and impatient about trifling matters. When I lost the second baby, months later, he actually disappeared for several days without explanation.'

'Charming!' Sarah's colour rose.

Lucy shrugged. 'Recently I have come to the unpalatable conclusion the real reason Charlie was upset was he assumed grandchildren would soften my father's heart and loosen the purse strings. Unfortunately, it would never have worked; Father was the least sentimental man I have ever known. When he passed away, all hope of financial aid died with him. And then Charlie's parents didn't help with their spiteful letters filling his head with poppycock. *No Lawrence before had failed to produce heirs*. He lapped up their nonsense and threw it in my face.'

Sarah scowled. 'And you had no family to support you, so he played on your vulnerability. He deserved a good thrashing, my friend.'

'You may be right, but I do not believe he set out to be heart-less; it was the circumstances we found ourselves in. Our expec-tations never truly aligned: I married for love, he married for the Somerville money. Maybe if it had materialised, things would have been different.'

'Was Charlie truly that mercenary?' Sarah asked.

'The sad thing is, I'll never be entirely sure.'

'I wish you had confided in me, Lucy.'

'But it would have felt as if I were betraying him to have spoken of such things at the time.'

'And you had no choice but to carry on. I don't know how you bore it,' Sarah said, her brow puckered.

'I had no alternative. Divorce or separation was out of the question; I had to make the best of it.'

'Hearing this makes me realise how incredibly lucky I have been,' said Sarah.

'Yes, and I'm happy for you. It is clear Geoffrey adores you, and little James is such a sweet child.'

'Yes, he's a delight,' Sarah replied, beaming. 'Fate has been kinder to me, it is true. I do not know what I would do if Geoffrey looked elsewhere.'

'Realistically, there's nothing a woman can do. Men have the power in these situations,' Lucy said.

'Except where a woman has wealth of her own. Then, at least, she can leave,' her friend replied.

'But she instantly becomes a social pariah, and probably has to live abroad, whereas the man never has to endure the same level of contempt,' Lucy countered. 'Even if I had had the funds, I'm not sure I would have been brave enough to take on the world. Of course, it is all academic now. Charlie is dead and his dirty secrets are spilling out from the grave. I have attained pariah status after all.'

'Do not let this defeat you, my dear. You must stay strong and move forward. Remember, your true friends will support you.'

Lucy had to fight back sudden tears. 'Thank you, but I have so few options, Sarah. Please don't tell me to remarry, as my mother suggested.' Then Lucy laughed. 'Not that any man of standing would contemplate associating with me now.'

'Poppycock! Besides, you're grieving and hurting far too much to even consider it for now,' Sarah said. 'In a few years' time you may feel differently.'

'Granted, however, at the moment I could contemplate nothing worse than to be under the control of a man again.'

Sarah's brows shot up. 'Please tell me you're not considering a nunnery; I'd miss you dreadfully.'

Lucy chuckled and shook her head. Sarah's lips twitched as she poured out another cup of tea. As she leaned over towards Lucy with the cup, she suddenly paused, her eyes narrowed. 'How was New Year's Eve? Did you find it very difficult on your own in that *awful* house?'

Was nothing missed by this woman and her network of spies? '*Who* told you?' Lucy demanded.

The cup was passed over and a satisfied smile settled on her friend's face. 'My dear, I can't reveal my sources. Was it delightful? Verrey's is so romantic, is it not? I hope you saw his more charming side.'

'He was excellent company.'

'And?'

'And the food was fabulous.'

'Lucy?'

'*Nothing* happened.'

Sarah cocked her head, her eyes brim full of laughter. 'What a pity. An affair might be the very thing to perk you up.'

Lucy gulped back her laughter. 'You are outrageous. Besides, I do not believe an affair with a man who is only waiting to pounce and put me in prison would be such a wonderful idea.'

Sarah's response was to splutter with laughter.

PART 2

Lucy Spreads Her Wings

TWENTY-ONE

Spring 1887

March announced its arrival with cloudbursts and brooding skies. Lucy fretted. Frustrated by a lack of progress in Charlie's affairs, she became despondent and prepared for the worst. Losing her home was inevitable with no hope of financial aid from any source. Early in February, Mr Faulkner had sent around one of his clerks to do an inventory of the furniture, so she dared not touch the larger pieces in the house. However, she scoured her home for portable items of value: all those little knick-knacks and souvenirs of their travels they had gathered over the years. Some brought back happy memories, while others, like the tiny music-box from Brighton, only reminded her of her husband's duplicity. No doubt Florence Bannon had received similar gifts.

The only piece of jewellery she had left was an opal pendant Charlie had given her on their first anniversary. She could never have imagined parting with it, but that was before she knew of his mistress. It was added without hesitation to the growing pile of items on Charlie's desk. When she could find nothing more, bit by bit the pieces were taken to various pawn-brokers across the city, sometimes by her, more often by Mary. The transactions were humiliating, but before long she had a small amount of money put by. Still aggrieved by Charlie's lies and philandering, she felt no remorse at her subterfuge, but rather saw it as a matter of survival. Lucy had every expectation of being reduced to near penury once probate was granted.

In the second week of March, the long-dreaded letter arrived: she was summoned to Mr Faulkner's office. Met by his stern demeanour and fusty manner, it wasn't long before her expectations were fully realised. It was obvious he hadn't forgotten the unfortunate incident the previous autumn when she had reacted so forthrightly to the first sight of Charlie's will. He opened the file with a look of distaste and droned on for several minutes about legal procedure before insisting the will be read again. Through the fog of legalese, she ascertained that once Charlie's debts were cleared, there would be only a small allowance to live on. Looking at her over his glasses, the crusty old solicitor complained about his client's lack of financial acumen and ill-fated decisions. Why he was lecturing her she couldn't fathom, but she had an inkling he blamed *her* for Charlie's misdemeanours.

But when he began to quiz her about Richard, she became increasingly irritated. Richard was ignoring his telegrams and letters. How was he to finalise probate if the executor didn't sign, he asked her in an aggrieved tone. Was she to be held responsible for Richard's foibles as well? It was verging on preposterous. Lucy had no great desire to divulge the state of her relationship with her brother, so she prevaricated as best she could. Faulkner wasn't pleased and muttered under his breath, while she was suddenly enthralled by the view out of his window. It was the only way to keep a rein on her temper.

As she left the solicitor's office, she succumbed to gloom. The tea room round the corner with its tantalising aromas almost lured her in. But on checking her purse, she had to forego that simple pleasure. Instead, she went into a small park across the road and found a bench in the sun. The pit of her stomach was like lead. A frisson of envy crept over her as she watched a group of ladies walk past. Most of the women appeared affluent and carefree. Not for them the prospect of poverty in the near future. More likely concerts, balls and all the trappings of the social life she had once enjoyed. How would she bear living in London without all of those things? However, one problem was clear and urgent: she would have to commence a search for a new home immediately. Mr Faulkner had told her the house was to be advertised that week. Being in such a good neighbourhood, he was certain of a quick sale. He made the comment with a blank expression, but from the tone used she knew he considered it her just comeuppance. For at least five minutes she indulged some less than kind thoughts about Charlie.

But as upsetting as it was, it might be for the best. The house in Abbey Gardens was far too big for her and Mary anyway. It also held some unpleasant memories now, not least Marsh and the threat he represented. Moving out to the suburbs and renting one of those newly built villas was a pleasant prospect. It would be a fresh start, and, above all, it would give her something to do. The situation couldn't be as bad as the grumpy solicitor made out. A little ingenuity and a smattering of luck would sort it all out.

Lucy's thoughts turned to Phineas. There had been no repeat of the intimacy of New Year's Eve, and his manner had reverted to one of formality. Was it lack of interest or acknowledgement of her mourning state dictating his behaviour? Even Sarah thought it odd. He had continued to be solicitous for her welfare and safety, but with no progress on either the theft of the pearls or tracing the sapphires, his calls to Abbey Gardens had become intermittent. In fact, she had not heard from him in

over a week. A telegram had informed her he was called away to
Norfolk on a case, and if she needed assistance of any kind, she
should contact Chief Inspector McQuillan. It made her uneasy
to know he was out of reach. She had to admit she missed him.
And if he abandoned any hope of solving either case, where
would it leave her? Inevitably, he would drift slowly out of her
life forever.

A gentleman not unlike Richard strolled past, and she
recalled Faulkner's complaints about him. She would dearly
like to know what was happening up in Yorkshire. Had Sibylla
discovered the true state of their financial affairs yet? She didn't
imagine she would take it lightly when she did. To Lucy's
surprise, her sympathies lay with Sibylla and she hoped she
gave Richard hell; it was what he deserved. And how would
Mother react? What would happen to her when the bubble
burst? Richard could hardly hold out indefinitely. Lucy had no
idea how long a bank would tolerate someone being in his position, but she didn't believe they would let the situation go on
much longer before they acted.

Richard's silence was both intriguing and annoying. Obviously, he had to wait until he thought it was safe before trying to
sell the necklace, but she wished he would hurry up. Until he
was caught, her reputation hung in the balance. Unfortunately,
it was in Richard's interests to keep the story of her guilt alive so
no one would suspect him. This, however, could be problem-
atic, for if the suspicions regarding her were to become common
knowledge, it could do her immeasurable harm. Any whisper of
wrongdoing would close every door against her as she strived to
rebuild her life.

Lucy didn't care about Sibylla, but Mother thinking her
capable of theft was a different matter, and it still hurt that she
had been so quick to believe Richard's lies. Hopefully, by now,
she would have recovered from the shock and seen how ludicrous the whole incident had been. It was ridiculous the way

her mother was so obsessive about those pearls. But Mother was deeply entrenched in the family traditions and the necklace symbolised the family's heritage and standing in society. All the same, Lucy regretted leaving Yorkshire without attempting to see her mother again. If only there was someone she trusted to ask about the state of affairs at Somerville. But there was—her old friend Judith! She decided to write to her at Blackheath Manor that very evening. She could disguise her curiosity with an invitation to London as she had promised at Christmas, and Judith might be willing to take a message to Mother as well.

But in the meantime, what was she to do? She closed her eyes, desperate for inspiration. How was she to support herself and keep Mary too? She was too proud to ask Mother or Charlie's family for even a small loan.

Then a tiny but compelling idea started to form in her mind. Stone's wealth was based on commission and rewards. She prided herself on her puzzle solving abilities. What if she were to find the sapphires before anyone else...

Discovering a new-found love of economy, Lucy decided to forego a cab ride home and walk instead. The afternoon was closing in as she dawdled along contemplating the prospect of another solitary and possibly inedible dinner. To her consternation as she rounded the corner, she saw every light on in her house. What was Mary thinking of? Surely she realised how costly it was to have the gas on in the whole house. She skipped up the steps ready to admonish her. But as Lucy turned the key, the door was pulled open. Mary's anxious face immediately put her on her guard.

'Whatever is the matter?' Lucy asked as she stepped inside. She quickly removed her hat and coat. 'And why on earth are all the lights on?'

Mary gnawed at her bottom lip and merely pointed down

the hallway before taking Lucy's things to hang up. The passageway was half blocked by trunks and boxes, stacked against the wall.

'Good heavens!' Lucy exclaimed, before bending down to examine the largest trunk. The initials 'CS', embossed in gold, brought her up short.

This was the last thing she had expected. No wonder Mary was befuddled. 'Where is she?'

The maid's eyes lifted slowly towards the ceiling.

'When did she arrive?'

'Not long after you left, ma'am. Sorry, ma'am, but I had to pay the cabbie.' She blinked as if on the verge of tears.

Lucy stared at her for a moment, but it wasn't uncommon for her visitor to have such an effect on household staff. She had once witnessed a housekeeper at Lady Ashton's reduced to tears because the chimney in the guest room assigned to her mother smoked. With a sigh, she pulled out her purse and handed it over. 'Take what you need, Mary, and don't fret.' Then she flew up the stairs, two at a time.

Lucy eventually found her mother sitting on a bed in one of the rear bedrooms. A small trunk lay at the foot of the bed and clothes were scattered across the counterpane.

'Mother?' Lucy stepped closer, concerned.

Her mother's mouth twitched and she swung around. 'Lucy!' she exclaimed, then gestured helplessly.

'Is everything all right?' Lucy asked. 'Why have you come to London?'

'Am I not welcome in my daughter's house?' her mother cried. But her indignation was somewhat belied by her look of nervous anxiety. Her face was pale, with deeply etched lines of misery around her mouth. Lucy was overcome with pity.

She sat down beside her on the bed and took her mother's hand. 'Of course, you are welcome. But why didn't you send a telegram and let me know you were on your way? I would have met you at King's Cross and accompanied you here.'

'I wasn't sure what to do for the best, and there was no time for telegrams. She threw me out!'

'Sibylla?' Her mother confirmed it with a sour look. 'I don't understand, Mother. Why would she do that? What did you do?'

'*I* did nothing!'

'But she must have had a reason and why would Richard allow it?'

Mother stiffened. 'Don't mention his name, Lucy. I'm too distraught.' Her chin trembled. 'Oh Lucy! It is the end of the House of Somerville. All is lost!'

TWENTY-TWO

With patience and the remains of a bottle of brandy, Lucy managed to soothe her mother before assisting Mary to unpack her belongings. While they bustled about, Mother sat at the dressing table watching them closely, her face forlorn. Every so often, a snuffle broke the silence. Mary cast Lucy a nervous glance. They hurried. When they were finished, Lucy gently coaxed her mother downstairs with the promise of refreshment. Having settled her beside the fire, she slipped down to the kitchen to Mary.

As they waited for the kettle to boil, she told Mary it was likely her mother would be staying for some time. Mary said with a somewhat dismayed expression she had guessed as much from the amount of luggage. Lucy turned away to hide a smile. Mary was the most pragmatic of maids. But Mother had to realise what the reality of life in Abbey Gardens was, particularly the lack of servants. The last thing Lucy needed was her mother making impossible demands, and Mary packing her bags and leaving as a result. Lucy picked up the tea tray, and Mary began to object.

'No, Mary, she needs to realise it's only the two of us here. She's used to a house full of servants to do her bidding.'

Mary blew out her cheeks. 'If you say so, ma'am. I do hope she recovers. She was in an awful state when she arrived.'

'Mother suffered a nasty shock but I'm sure she'll be fine. My mother has always been resilient. Thank you for looking after her, Mary. I do appreciate it very much,' Lucy said.

Charlotte Somerville appeared lost in contemplation as Lucy entered the room with the tea tray. The expected rebuke was not forthcoming, and Lucy realised just how upset she must be.

'Thank you,' her mother murmured, taking the offered cup and saucer. Her hand shook as she lifted the teacup to her lips. A hundred questions ran through Lucy's mind, but she needed to give her mother time to recover her equilibrium.

'This is a fine house, Lucy,' her mother commented at last, looking about the room. 'I'm pleasantly surprised.'

'What exactly did you expect?'

'There's no need to be so defensive. I'm merely... If I'm honest, I was astonished to discover your address. Richard had led me to understand your circumstances were somewhat limited.'

'He was correct, Mother. They happen to be very limited. Tell me, in all the years we have been apart, did you never feel the urge to write to me?'

Her mother sighed again. 'Of course, I often wondered about you, but as it transpired, I only found out where you lived a few days ago. When all the unpleasantness began, I made sure Edith retrieved your particulars for me in case I would need them. And it wasn't easy, let me tell you. She had to search Richard's desk when Sibylla was distracted.'

'I see,' Lucy said. Why had she bothered to ask the question? She might have known the answer would be unsettling.

Mother had not changed. 'Do you feel up to telling me what happened in Yorkshire?'

'I'd much prefer to forget about it, but I suppose I do owe you some explanation for my sudden and unannounced arrival.'

Lucy did not trust herself to reply, but waited.

'Last Monday, I had just returned to Somerville from visiting the Frobishers. As my carriage pulled up, I saw this fellow alight from a hired cab. Most odd, I thought. As it turned out, he was from the bank.'

'Ah!' Lucy said. Had Mr Stone had a hand in it, she wondered.

Mother frowned at her. 'What do you know of it?'

'Please continue. I'll tell you what I know when you have finished your tale.'

Her mother didn't look pleased and settled back deeper into her armchair. 'I happened to be passing the library and heard the raised voices. It transpires Richard is in financial difficulty and the bank is calling in all of his debts.'

'Did no one realise?' Lucy asked. 'Surely there were signs?'

Mother gazed at the fire, her face set. 'No, he did not indi-cate anything of that nature to me and Sibylla never spoke to me unless absolutely necessary.'

'She may have been in the dark too.'

'She's standing full square in the light now!' Her mother cast her an angry glance. 'Ungrateful creature! The next morning it was discovered Richard had disappeared during the night. She wasted no time in summoning her pet solicitor from Harrogate. After consulting with him, she swept through the house in a rage with the odious man trailing after her like a love-sick puppy telling her what to do and say. Poor Uncle Giles and I were told in no uncertain terms we would have to leave. Just like that! The shame of it is she didn't care one iota what became of us.'

'Wait a moment, Mother. Richard has vanished?'

'Yes, that's what I just said. Are you not listening? Absconded without a word to anyone. I was furious, as you can imagine.'

Lucy's heart began to pound. Richard had bolted. Matters must come to a head now.

Mrs Somerville continued. 'The banker fellow returned the next day and confirmed we would all have to leave as the house was to be sold. The servants were dismissed, and Sibylla packed her bags and left yesterday morning. Off she went back to Newcastle to her father. Somerville gone! Can you imagine it? And I'll never see the grandchildren again.' She began to weep.

'Try not to be distressed, Mother. It is all most unfortunate, but you're welcome to stay with me.' There was little point in telling her how temporary it would probably be. Time enough to break the bad news.

Her mother blew her nose and gave her a grateful look. 'I thought the worst was over, but today was even more humiliating. You see, I went straight to the house in Mayfair from King's Cross. My plan was to move in there, but imagine my shock to discover Richard had sold it last summer. The gentleman who owns it now was kind, but I'm sure he considered me deranged. I have never been so embarrassed.' She gave a tiny laugh, but her chin began to wobble again.

'Happily you remembered you have a daughter,' Lucy remarked, unable to help herself.

Her mother glared at her. 'Sarcasm is unbecoming, Lucy.'

'Forgive me, I have become cynical of late. By any chance do you have any idea where Richard has gone?'

'No! I do not care where he is. He has betrayed us all.'

The histrionics were beginning to grate on Lucy's nerves, but then Mother only ever viewed the world from one perspective: her own. Setting up home together would prove challenging to Lucy's sanity. If only Uncle Giles had come too. He might have diluted the situation. She was suddenly struck by an awful idea. 'Mother, what has happened to Uncle? Did he come to London with you?'

'Do not concern yourself. Giles went straight to Blackheath Manor as he's great friends with Myles Chancellor. They took him in, and he will be fine.'

'Does he have any means?' she asked, wondering how Judith must have viewed the prospect of having another elderly man to care for.

'Yes. A pension of some kind from the navy,' her mother said dismissively.

'And you, Mother, what about you?'

'It's good of you to be concerned, Lucy, but luckily Richard was unable to touch my funds. Your father left me a modest allowance. But what am I to do? I'm too old to be setting up an establishment on my own.'

A heavy hint indeed, but Lucy could hardly show her the door. Instead, she would buy some time. 'You may stay here until you decide what to do.'

'Thank you, you're so good, my dear. I won't be any bother, let me assure you.'

Somehow Lucy doubted this, but she nodded and poured out another cup of tea. 'Mother, you do realise Richard was the one who took your pearls?'

Mrs Somerville went very still. 'Is that so?'

'Yes! I did *not* take them. Do you recall the insurance investigator, Mr Stone? His enquiries uncovered the interesting fact that Richard was in serious debt. Possibly his actions were born out of desperation, but it doesn't excuse what he did to me.'

Still her mother wouldn't meet her eye. 'He should have come to me,' Mother said quietly.

'Too proud by far, and he thought he would get away with it and have everyone believe I was to blame. He gave a pearl to the police and told them it was found under my bed. The height of nastiness, don't you agree? Meanwhile he hid your pearls and made a claim on the insurance. When all the fuss had died down, he probably hoped to sell them discreetly and double his money. Immensely clever, but, of course, Mr Stone wasn't fooled for a minute.'

Her mother began to cough. 'Mr Stone has been busy indeed, but I find what you say difficult to credit. We were all convinced it was you. Best to forget about it, Lucy. What is done is done.'

'Don't you believe me? Do you not understand? I want my name cleared. If Richard has disappeared, he must intend to sell the pearls for he has no other assets. He will be caught and everyone will realise I'm innocent.'

'Sell them?' her mother exclaimed, the colour draining from her face. 'But he can't!'

'He has very little choice if he's gone on the run,' Lucy replied with some satisfaction.

TWENTY-THREE

Vine Street Police Station

Early the next morning, Lucy went straight to Vine Street to inform the chief inspector of Richard's flight. Several unsavoury-looking men stood waiting at the front desk. If only her mission had not been so urgent, she would have considered returning later.

''Ere, wot's your game?' a scrawny fellow complained as she made her way through to the front. The desk sergeant looked up from his ledger and his pen halted mid-air.

'Have you come to claim one of these vile specimens of humanity?' he asked, his weary gaze sweeping over the motley group waiting to be processed.

'Heavens, no!'

Giving him her sweetest smile, she informed him she needed to see the chief inspector straightaway.

'Is that so?' he said, sizing her up and down. 'And who shall I say?'

'Mrs Lawrence. The chief inspector is acquainted with me.'

Laying down his pen, the desk sergeant hollered, 'Rogers!'

A young constable appeared from the rear office. 'Yes, Sergeant?'

'Be so good as to escort this lady, Mrs Lawrence, up to the chief.'

After countless flights of stairs, they reached the upper floor of the building.

'Enter!' a voice replied to the constable's knock.

Rogers opened the door. 'Excuse me, sir, a Mrs Lawrence to see you.'

McQuillan jumped up from behind the desk and came forward to greet her. 'Mrs Lawrence, what can I do for you? Please, take a seat.'

'Mr Stone indicated I should come to you if anything urgent came up,' Lucy explained.

McQuillan remained standing. 'Of course. I'm only too glad to be of assistance. Stone is in Cromer on a case, I believe,' he said. Suddenly, his face darkened. 'You haven't had another visit from our East End friend?'

'No, no, it's my mother,' she said.

McQuillan bent towards her as if he hadn't heard her correctly. 'I'm not with you, Mrs Lawrence.'

'She arrived unexpectedly at my home yesterday. It would appear my brother has taken off and left all in disarray in Yorkshire. The bank decided to call in his debts. He left in the middle of the night and no one knows where he's gone.'

'Ah, ha! I detect Stone's hand in this. He must have tipped off the bank.' McQuillan sat down on the edge of his desk with a satisfied smile brightening up his features. 'Stone was right about the case.'

'Yes, undeniably so. I have the impression it is a common occurrence?'

McQuillan gave a chuckle. 'Tiresomely so, but I wouldn't tell him. He's far too sure of himself as it is.'

'I can't argue with that! But what about my brother

Richard?' she asked, anxious to return to the subject in hand.
'What if he gets away? He must have taken the necklace with
him.'

'Of course he has. We shall telegram York and Harrogate
immediately and see if we can trace his steps. Not much gets
past country folk, and with your brother being well known, it
should be easy to track him, at least for the first part of his flight.'
McQuillan strode over to the door. Poking his head out, he
called for one of his men. Once he had given his instructions, he
turned back to her.

'We will have a description sent to the ports as well, in case
he attempts to leave the country. Stone has already alerted the
jewellery trade to the likelihood of Mr Somerville trying to sell
the necklace. If he attempts it, we will be notified immediately.
Thank you for coming in with this information, Mrs Lawrence.
Rest assured, we will catch him. Men on the run tend to be
desperate and make foolish errors. Forgive me, but I was under
the impression from Stone that your brother and mother were
close. Does she have any idea where he might go?'

'She says not, and I believe her in this instance. Her only
thought is for her own woes. My sister-in-law took the opportunity to throw her out of the house. They never got on, you see.
As far as I know, the servants have departed and the house is
now standing empty. The bank intend to sell the entire estate.'

McQuillan made sympathetic noises, but was staring off
into the distance. 'Stone will be disappointed to miss all the fun.
Hopefully, we'll have Mr Somerville behind bars before he
returns from Cromer.'

Lucy stood and held out her hand. 'I couldn't agree more.
Please let me know when you catch up with Richard. I'd like to
give him a piece of my mind. The last chance I had to do so, Mr
Stone talked me out of it.'

. . .

On her return to Abbey Gardens, Lucy found her mother dozing in the drawing room, a tea tray on the table beside her.

She woke with a start when Lucy shut the door. 'There you are, Lucy. Where have you been?' She glanced at the clock and frowned. 'It's far too early to be making calls, is it not?'

Lucy smiled and sat down. 'It is and I wasn't.'

'How foolish of me! Of course you weren't visiting. You're still in mourning. Did you have a pleasant walk?' she asked.

'I had an errand to run,' Lucy replied. She had decided not to tell her mother what her intentions were regarding Richard. Setting the police on his trail might not do anything for mother–daughter relations. Lucy had a strong sense Mother would take his side again when she had overcome her current annoyance and distress. No matter what he had done as a child, he had always been forgiven. 'Where is Mary?'

'She went out to the butchers, at least that's what she told me, but you can't always trust these young women, particularly the lazy Irish.'

'I can assure you Mary is extremely reliable, loyal and hard-working.' Her mother's only response was a sniff. Lucy stared across at the tea tray wondering why there were two used cups. 'Have you been entertaining in my absence?' she asked, half joking.

'Why yes! He arrived shortly after Mary left, and I even made tea. Can you imagine that? I can't even remember the last time I did such a thing. Such a charming man. He was so very sorry to have missed you. So well-to-do, isn't he, and such a pleasant manner? Why you naughty thing, why did you not tell me you had an admirer?'

Stone could hardly have returned so soon. 'He is... Your assumption is incorrect. Mr Stone has been helping me with some of Charlie's affairs.'

'Mr Stone? Who is he? I'm talking about Mr Marsh.'

'Marsh?' Lucy gasped, stiffening with fright.

'You're as white as the antimacassar on your chair; whatever is the matter with you?' her mother asked. Lucy shook her head, as her mind raced. Mother's eyes narrowed. 'Mind you, you probably shouldn't be receiving male callers so soon and alone. It is highly improper, Lucy, but it can be our little secret, and I'm here now to act as chaperone. Isn't that fortunate?'

Lucy's heart was pounding so hard she was finding it difficult to breathe. 'What did he say, Mother?'

Mother frowned. 'Let me see. He apologised for intruding. Then he enquired after your health and said something about being sorry for neglecting you for so long. He was most put out about it and anxious the message be passed on.'

'Anything else?' Lucy squeaked.

'Now that you ask, he did say something odd. He asked about your cat. Wasn't that peculiar?'

'Yes,' Lucy said, as a cold sweat broke out all over her body.

'I wouldn't let it put you off, Lucy. You can't afford to be so pernickety. A wealthy man is a godsend to a woman in your circumstances. Keep him interested, and when sufficient time has lapsed, you can bring him up to scratch.'

Two hours later, a solemn Chief Inspector McQuillan was announced by Mary. Her mother regarded him as if he were an exhibit at the zoological gardens as he eased his bulk down on to the sofa. However, Lucy found his presence reassuring. While they had waited for him to respond to her urgent telegram, she had explained who Marsh actually was. Mrs Somerville's response had been a startled exclamation followed by a diatribe on Charlie's imperfections. Lucy had listened in silence. For once, she was in total agreement with her.

'This is a very serious development, Mrs Lawrence,' McQuillan said. 'It proves he's continued to have your house watched closely. These cat and mouse antics worry me greatly. I have brought along a constable who will remain outside, at least until we have decided on the best course of action.'

'Thank you. That's a comfort,' Lucy said.

'Marsh is fearless, I'm afraid, but I did not think he would dare to do such a thing. He must be aware that you're under police protection.'

'I'm not particularly impressed either, Chief Inspector. And what better method to frighten me than to wait until I'm out and use my mother in such a provocative way.'

'I don't understand it,' her mother interjected, 'he was such a nice fellow.'

'I can assure you, Mrs Somerville, he's the most unpleasant fellow it is possible to meet,' McQuillan said before turning to Lucy with a bewildered look. 'Have you not told Mrs Somerville about your previous encounters?'

'Yes! But only just now, as I didn't want to upset her when she arrived. I really didn't believe he would come back, despite Mr Stone's warnings.'

'Chief Inspector, if what you say is true then what are we to do?' her mother asked.

McQuillan glanced at Lucy with a sympathetic expression. 'My advice would be to remove to a hotel,' he replied. 'Increasing the patrols here has not deterred him.'

'Oh dear,' Mother sighed, 'I've only just unpacked. The Langham would hardly have rooms available at such short notice.' Lucy regarded her with disbelief. She doubted either of them had the funds to stay there.

McQuillan coughed gently. 'Might I suggest the Princess Hotel in Brook Street? My brother-in-law is one of the managers and would be only too delighted to help. It is also convenient for us as it's in our division, and we can keep a closer eye on things.'

'You are very kind, Chief Inspector,' Lucy replied, with a

grateful smile. 'The hotel sounds ideal.' From the corner of her eye, she saw an expression of distaste cross her mother's features, but she didn't care. Self-preservation took precedence over her mother's pretensions.

TWENTY-FOUR

The Princess Hotel, Brook Street, One Week Later

Lucy sat in the small salon to the front of the hotel. She was nervous as she waited for Mr Stone to arrive. Several weeks had passed since they had met, and Lucy had to admit she had missed him. Of course, his sojourn in Norfolk couldn't have been worse timing, leaving her feeling vulnerable when the danger had erupted again. Being the object of Marsh's attention was terrifying; his latest intrusion had been so daring. The implied threat had given her some sleepless nights, even after they removed to the hotel. Despite the chief inspector's claim that she was safe away from St John's Wood, she found it impossible to relax. Living cooped up with her mother wasn't helping matters. Her nerves were frayed. It had been a relief to receive Stone's request to meet.

A waiter came into view and hovered with an expectant look. Lucy gave her order and took up a copy of the *Daily News* to help pass the time. But within a few minutes, Stone appeared in the doorway and approached her. He didn't return her welcoming smile, his serious expression doing nothing for her composure.

'Good afternoon, Mr Stone,' she said. They shook hands. 'I've ordered tea.

'Perfect.' He took the seat opposite. 'Thank you for agreeing to see me so quickly. Marsh's troublemaking didn't upset you too much, I hope.'

'Not at all, I adore being the focus of his attention. If only he had waited for me to come home, he could have joined us for dinner.'

'You don't fool me, Mrs Lawrence, with attempts at humour. You must have been frightened.'

'It was... disturbing. Let us leave it at that. I hope you didn't mind me writing to you in Norfolk about it?'

'Not at all. I was pleased to receive your letter, though alarmed by what you told me about Marsh. However, I had every confidence Oliver McQuillan would deal with the situation satisfactorily.'

'Yes, well... my mother and I are here now and nothing has happened since.'

'I'm sure it was distressing to leave your home, but it is for the best. McQuillan was right. To stay in Abbey Gardens would have been foolish. Is the accommodation here to your liking?'

'Yes, however, I had not anticipated how difficult it would be to live under the same roof as my mother again. We are confined to a suite, which isn't large, and Mother has been demanding at times. This afternoon she's resting and won't be joining us. I hope you don't mind but the events of the last few weeks have taken their toll. It wasn't easy for her to swallow her pride and ask for my help. Richard's actions have distressed her, and Sibylla throwing her out was cruel beyond words. She misses Somerville. The family losing the estate is devastating, which is understandable, for she's lived there for most of her life.'

'I'm sure it has all been a great shock; however, it is for the best she's *not* joining us. Your mother is one of the reasons I asked to see you.'

Lucy was baffled. 'Why? Is there news? Has Richard been found at last?'

'Yes, he has and is now in custody at Vine Street. This morning I attended his interrogation. Most enlightening, it was, too.'

Lucy gasped. 'Where did they find him? Was the necklace in his possession?' She lowered her voice as the waiter approached. 'Do tell all!'

'Here is the tea,' Stone said, giving her a warning glance.

They sat contemplating each other while the waiter placed the tray on the table between them. Lucy thought she would burst with curiosity.

'Will there be anything else, madam?' the waiter asked.

'No, thank you,' she replied, rather more abruptly than she had intended.

As soon as the waiter left the room, she leaned towards Stone. 'What is it? I can tell something is wrong.'

'Let's take our tea first,' he said, reaching for the teapot, 'Why don't I pour?'

'Never mind the tea. I want to know what is happening. What about Richard?'

With a sigh, he put down the teapot. 'Three days ago, your brother was arrested at Queenstown Harbour in Cork.'

'Ireland! Did he have the pearls?'

'A set of pearls were in his possession.'

'Thank heavens! How clever of Richard. Was he headed for America?'

'Yes,' Stone said.

'And once he arrived there, he'd change his name and start a brand new life on the proceeds of the sale of the necklace!' Lucy exclaimed. 'How heartless of him to abandon his wife and children.'

'The act of a desperate man, I believe. Without doubt, it was his intention to sell the pearls when he reached New York,' Stone replied.

'I'm so relieved. No one can believe me guilty any longer— my reputation is restored,' Lucy said. 'It's as if a dark cloud has been casting a shadow over me since Christmas.'

'But your innocence was proven. There was no need to be dwelling on it. Besides, I was sure you trusted my judgement.'

'I do,' she said, 'but after all that has happened, I don't trust my own. I limp from one disastrous decision to another.' She gave him a wobbly smile. To her surprise, he reached across and squeezed her hand.

The contact made the colour rise in her cheeks. 'I'm sure of one thing, Mr Stone. I'm not sorry he was caught, after what he tried to do to me.' Stone released her hand, much to her disappointment, and he grimaced. 'There's more?' she asked, her voice barely above a whisper. 'Tell me everything.'

Stone sighed. 'I wish it were possible to spare you this.'

'I'm not a child.'

'Very well. McQuillan sent word to Norfolk to say Mr Somerville was in custody and that he wanted me to attend the interrogation. The insurance company were also anxious I be present. I returned to town last night. As you can imagine, I did not receive much of a welcome from your brother; in fact, he was extremely hostile. He was in a shocking state with travel-stained clothes and an ungroomed appearance. It was a far cry from the dapper country gentleman I encountered at Christmas.'

'It sounds as if he had a rough time of it. Serves him right!'

Stone gave her a wry smile. 'Perhaps. McQuillan got straight to the point and asked him what he had been doing in

Ireland, about to board a liner, with the pearls he had reported as stolen in his bag. And most pertinent of all, why he had not notified the authorities and the insurance company immediately if he had *found* them. Absconding with them was hardly the act of an innocent man.'

'He couldn't be further from innocent. What did Richard have to say to that?'

'Nothing at first. He shoved his hands into his pockets and stretched out his legs, for all the world as if he were in his club. But his defensiveness was to be expected in the circumstances. For all his nonchalance, he was extremely nervous.'

'Good!' Lucy exclaimed. 'I hope the chief inspector didn't give him an inch.'

'No indeed. McQuillan is well used to the vagaries of suspects. When McQuillan placed the pearls on the table your brother went white. I believe the gravity of the situation hit him at that point. Then he turned sullen and tried to stare him out. But he was no match for Oliver,' Stone chuckled and shook his head. 'Eventually, he caved in and admitted the bag was his and the pearls were your mother's.'

'Thank goodness! How did he manage to elude the police for so long?'

'Apparently, he crossed over from Scotland the same day he left Yorkshire and before any watch had been put on the ports. Then he travelled south by train and holed up in a hotel in Cork. It was sheer luck an RIC officer spotted him about to board, otherwise he would be well on his way to America as we speak.'

'You must be pleased, Mr Stone. You were correct all along. His insurance claim was fraudulent.'

Stone shrugged but looked gratified. 'The bank was closing in, he said, and he had no choice.'

'Did you have a hand in that?' she asked.

He cleared his throat. 'I may have. But I'm afraid matters are a little more complicated than we first thought.'

'In what way?' Lucy asked.

'While McQuillan was interrogating your hapless brother, I noticed something odd about the pearls. With the chief inspector's permission I examined them and discovered they were not what they seemed. In fact, they are a copy.'

'What?'

'No oyster produced those particular pearls. Your brother and McQuillan didn't believe me either, at first.'

'But they have been in the family for generations. Ever since I can remember, my mother wore them whenever she wanted to impress. Would we not have noticed they were fake? Are you absolutely sure?'

Stone sniffed. 'Positive! To the untrained eye they pass muster for it is an excellent copy, but the shape and colour of the pearls is too consistent. They are perfectly round with not even the slightest indentation, just like the one the good sergeant produced for us in Harrogate. Also the necklace is heavier than I would have expected, therefore I would hazard the pearls are glass with a mother-of-pearl coating. As for the emerald, it has no internal flaws whatsoever, which is highly suspect. Naturally enough, Sanderson & Irvine will have the necklace checked by a jeweller, but I can say with absolute certainty, they are *not* the Somerville pearls as described in the original insurance policy taken out by your grandfather.'

'Good Lord!' exclaimed Lucy. 'It doesn't make any sense. Why would Richard steal a fake necklace?'

'He didn't know it wasn't real. He's a country squire, not a jeweller,' Stone said. 'It never dawned on him to question their authenticity. No one would have found out if Sanderson & Irvine had paid up in the beginning. But his greed would have undone him. Eventually the temptation would have been too much, and he would have discovered the truth when he attempted to sell them.'

'I don't follow. Are you saying someone else has the real necklace?'

'No. I'd say several people own pieces of it and legitimately too. Your brother claims it must have been your mother's doing. At some stage, she had them copied when she found herself at *point non plus*. He claimed your father wasn't generous and kept everyone on a tight rein.'

'That's true. Oh dear, she's quite capable of doing such a thing. She's nothing if not resourceful. No wonder she didn't want Sibylla to get the pearls on her marriage. The game would have been up.'

'Only if Sibylla had noticed something amiss, but I suppose your mother didn't want to take the risk. They are a good copy and fooled most people. It hardly matters now when she did it or what her motivation was. The piece was most likely broken up once the copy was made, reset into other pieces and sold on by the jeweller.'

'Thank goodness you were clever enough to spot it. I have little sympathy for Richard being tricked by my mother. It is only what he deserves. Now, our tea is going cold.' She started to pour, then stopped mid-flow when she saw how tense Stone was. He hadn't finished.

Stone shifted in his chair and gave her a worried glance. 'It pains me to tell you, but it gets worse. Your brother told us your mother led him to believe the necklace was worth thousands... when *she* proposed the whole scheme.'

Lucy shook her head. 'Whatever do you mean, Mr Stone?'

'Mr Somerville claims the conspiracy to defraud the insurance company was your mother's idea, not his.'

Lucy gently placed the teapot down on the tray. 'My mother was behind it?'

'Yes, I'm sorry. Richard approached her when he realised the full extent of his financial problems with the bank. The estate has been in trouble for some time, his rental income barely covered the day-to-day costs of running the house and your sister-in-law had a taste for the finer things. Seemingly his own efforts to raise funds had failed. As he hoped, your mother would do anything to protect the family from scandal and offered up the pearls as a way of retrenching. She probably assumed they would disappear as part of the plan, which, of course, suited her. Over the years, she must have been in dread that her deceit would come to light. Unfortunately, she didn't reckon on Richard's desperation. Once I stopped the claim, she would have realised Richard would attempt to sell the pearls at some point, but clung to the hope the copy was good enough to fool most people—it had done for years.'

'And she couldn't reveal to him they were fake.'

'No. But it is worse than that, Mrs Lawrence. It was also her idea to use you as the decoy as soon as they learned you were coming to visit. They choose Christmas for the theft—'

'And I blundered in and was the perfect dupe.' Lucy struggled for a moment, remembering her mother's reaction to her on Christmas morning. 'Who would guess my own mother would conspire against me?' Slowly, her eyes welled up with angry tears. She was appalled. 'And I took her in when Sibylla threw her out... more fool I!'

'You couldn't have known any of this. You did what was right in the circumstances. How were you to know how deceitful your mother was?'

'I'm a fool. Her behaviour at Christmas was so uncharacter-istic. I should have been suspicious. She has no scruples, it would seem,' Lucy said. She mulled it over for a minute or two. 'But if my mother orchestrated it, that means she must have involved her maid. No wonder the girl was so upset the following morning. I have no doubt she was threatened with dismissal if she did not co-operate.'

'I'd say that's likely.'

'Was Sibylla involved too?' Lucy asked.

'Somerville said not, but reckoned she had her suspicions he was in difficulty. A solicitor friend of hers was sniffing around in his affairs which was another reason he decided he had to act at Christmas.'

The letter to John Ashby, the solicitor, and the glances he and Sibylla had exchanged across the dinner table on Christmas Eve, made sense now. But her mother's betrayal was incomprehensible. Lucy recalled the night of the party—her mother's plea for help to get to bed when she was ill. Mother had helped set the trap and had acted out her part beautifully. And Lucy had walked straight into it.

'Did you, at any stage, suspect my mother?' Lucy clenched her hands in her lap, her body rigid with anger.

'I realised she was formidable, as matriarchs often are. But criminal mastermind? No. I was sure it was all Somerville's doing.'

Lucy's anger bubbled up at last. 'I'm going to kill her!'

TWENTY-FIVE

Stone insisted on accompanying Lucy up to the suite, deep concern etched on his features. Lucy suspected he was afraid she would carry out her threat. She was certainly angry enough. As they entered, Mary emerged from her mother's bedroom. Stone closed the door and remained standing just inside. It was unlikely he wanted to be a witness to a scene but Lucy had had enough. He had lit the touchpaper with his revelations and would have to witness the consequences. Seething with anger, it was all Lucy could do not to charge in and drag her mother from her bed.

'Is my mother still asleep?' she asked Mary.

'Yes, ma'am. I was checking to see if she was awake and wanted her tea.'

'I need to speak to her, Mary. It's urgent.'

'You'd like me to wake her?' Mary asked, her eyes popping.

Lucy gave an impatient nod, and Mary gulped before slipping back in to the bedroom. Lucy paced the floor. The only sound was the clock ticking.

Stone advanced further in to the room. 'Might it not be

better to wait until you have calmed down? You may say something you later regret,' he said.

Lucy glared at him. 'I'm tired of being made a fool of, Mr Stone. If you don't have the stomach for this, I suggest you leave.'

He shook his head just as her mother appeared in the doorway. Charlotte Somerville looked half asleep. A lock of her hair was tumbling down on one side and her shawl was trailing down her back.

'What on earth could be so urgent, Lucy? I was taking a nap,' she said, stifling a yawn. Her face fell when she spotted Mr Stone. 'Oh! Why didn't that stupid girl tell me we had a guest? I'm not fit to be seen.' She began to retreat into the bedroom.

'No, Mother, please join us. I *insist*. Mr Stone does not mind in the least. Do you remember him, Mother? You met him at Christmas.'

Her mother's eyes widened and her lips compressed. She hesitated in the doorway. When she eventually stepped forward, she subjected Stone to a fierce scrutiny, her face rigid with hauteur. Slowly, she offered her hand to him. He shook it, his expression grim.

'Yes, you were that fellow who came about my pearls. Have you found them yet? They are worth a small fortune, and I want them back,' Charlotte said.

'Please sit down, Mother, we have important matters to discuss,' Lucy said before Stone could reply.

Her mother's gaunt cheeks flared red. 'Do not speak to me in such a way, Lucy, I will not tolerate it. What will Mr Stone think of your manners?'

'It's your behaviour that's questionable, Mother,' Lucy ground out. Her mother gasped.

'Mrs Somerville, it would be best if you were to sit down,'

Stone said, his placating tone irritating Lucy. She was ripe for a fight.

Her mother stood her ground, glaring at Lucy, but after a few moments she muttered, 'Oh, very well!' Once settled on the sofa, she pulled her shawl around her shoulders. 'I do not appreciate being treated in this manner. Say whatever it is you have to say. I wish to return to my room.'

'This won't take long, Mother. Firstly, you will be delighted to learn your favourite child has been found safe and well at last.'

'I told you already, Lucy, I do not wish to hear about him. He is dead to me!'

'Is that so? I can understand how it would be inconvenient for him to turn up,' Lucy responded. 'Very inconvenient, indeed. But he has. He was arrested a few days ago in Ireland about to embark for America.'

Her mother glanced at Stone. 'We shouldn't be discussing such matters in front of a stranger.'

'At this moment, I believe Mr Stone is the only person in all of England I can trust. He is staying. As he attended Richard's interrogation by the police this morning, he's privy to the whole wretched business, in any event.' Her mother scowled. Lucy plunged on. 'And you will never guess what Richard had in his belongings.'

'I do not care to know,' Mother said, but her voice shook slightly.

'But you *do* know! The Somerville pearls, of course. The same pearls *I* was accused of stealing.'

Her mother looked away.

'Unfortunately for you, Richard has been forthcoming about the entire escapade. What he has divulged is extremely interesting, isn't it, Mr Stone? Would you care to guess what Richard has told the police?' Mother shook her head. Lucy paused, her breathing rapid. 'Do you deny it was you and not Richard, who dreamed up the scheme to defraud your insurance company?' Charlotte remained silent, but her eyes shifted momentarily towards Stone then back to her.

Lucy stepped closer, fists clenched by her side. 'Richard claims it was your idea for me to take the blame? Can you deny it?'

'Obviously, your brother is lying to protect himself,' Mother said. 'This is foolish nonsense, nothing more.'

'Stop it!' Lucy cried, her voice breaking. 'How dare you lie to me, even now. And, by the way, the police have established the pearls are not the real Somerville pearls, but copies. What do you say to that?'

Her mother straightened up, rigid with anger. 'Who are you to judge me?' she spat. 'I have held the family together for a lifetime. Your father was a fool and your brother not much better. Neither knew how to manage an estate in the right way. And you, who abandoned your family as soon as a handsome face paid a little attention and whispered sweet nothings in your ear. Where was your family loyalty? You were supposed to marry money and save us. But you were always headstrong and foolish. Is it any wonder I had to sell the pearls? It was the only way I could save Somerville.'

'Don't try to put the blame on me! I never asked you to do it.' Her mother quirked a brow, a smile twisting on her lips. 'When did you have the pearls copied?' Lucy asked.

'A couple of months before your Season. It was a gamble, but I had to ensure you attracted the right sort and you weren't going to do that in rags. But what do you do but abscond with a good-for-nothing Scot. So I had to pin all hope on Richard, but then he fell for Sibylla, a woman with a father as tight-fisted as your own. The Metcalf dowry was laughable and spent within a year.'

'At least, we both married for love,' Lucy said.

'Love, was it?' Mrs Somerville laughed. 'After only a few years, the rumours about your husband reached me, even in Yorkshire. Yes, you may stare! With glee, my sister sent me the tidings. You forgot about your Aunt Beatrice tucked away in Wimbledon, I suppose. She was happy to pass on the gossip. What a fool you were! It is a simple thing to keep a man content, but you couldn't even manage to give him children. I heard about the string of fancy women and a—'

'My marriage wasn't perfect and Charlie proved false,' Lucy said, cutting her off. 'But my life was none of your business. You lost the right to interfere the day you turned your back. Don't imagine I'm surprised at your callousness for I always knew I was no more than an inconvenience. I should have been a second son, not a useless daughter—a mere pawn in your schemes, which is why, when Charlie offered me freedom, I grabbed it.'

'Don't be so naïve! It's a young girl's lot in life to make a good match. Marriage is the foundation stone of society. The right kind of marriage, of course,' Mrs Somerville scoffed. 'As for your dear husband's tomfoolery, it only confirmed our worst fears about him. Even though we had cut all ties, the gossips were having a field day. It was providential, that accident of his. But we needed to get you safely out of the way, and it almost worked, but for Mr Stone here. Sympathy would have swung to us, and we could have claimed you were deranged with grief, even had you committed, and the whole sorry affair would have petered out. But most importantly, the claim would have been settled and Somerville would have been saved.'

Lucy stared at her mother open-mouthed, her cruel words cutting into her.

'I don't regret a thing. If you had any decency, you would have taken the blame for the sake of the family,' Mother snarled.

'Are you quite finished?' Lucy demanded. A quick glance at

Stone revealed how shocked he was, staring at her mother as if she were mad.

But her mother continued as if she hadn't heard. 'I would advise you to grow up, Lucy. It's a man's world. Women have to do what it takes to survive. Do you think the likes of this fellow will always be there to come to the rescue? Do you? Let me tell you, as soon as your looks are gone, the beaux fade away. Romance dies, withers and dies, for it is but a meaningless illusion. There is always some pert little thing to take your place. I hope you learned that lesson with your precious Charlie. I know what I'm talking about. Your father's eye strayed constantly. I had to ignore it and keep every whiff of scandal out of the reach of the newspapers.'

'Stop! I do not wish to listen to you any more,' Lucy cried. 'I can't bear to look at you, and I certainly do not want to live under the same roof as you any longer. Mary will help you pack, but I want you to leave.' She turned to Mr Stone. 'You might care to accompany me on a walk, Mr Stone? I need to breathe some *fresh* air.' She looked back towards her mother with a mixture of disgust and sorrow. There was no sign of remorse.

'Certainly, Mrs Lawrence. I'll wait for you downstairs in the foyer,' he answered. At the door he turned for one brief moment and caught her eye, his expression full of sympathy. But she was furious and found no comfort in it. As the door closed behind him, her mother rose from the sofa, proud as ever and ramrod straight. She walked away, past Mary, who was standing wide-eyed and open-mouthed in the doorway to the bedroom.

'You girl! Come and help me pack,' her mother's voice came from the bedroom. Lucy waved Mary in, relieved her mother wasn't going to put up a fight about departing.

Foolishly, she had forgotten how unkind her mother had been when she was a child. Had she been that desperate for acceptance back in the family fold? With some bitterness, Lucy realised it was her own stupidity in thinking her family's concern was genuine that had made her such an easy target for them. The truth was, Mother hadn't changed one iota.

Suddenly her anger drained away. Lucy sat down, trembling. She should have been triumphant, but all she felt was a crushing sense of loss.

TWENTY-SIX

Wind-driven sleet was whistling down Brook Street as they emerged from the hotel. Lucy paused and turned to Mr Stone in dismay. The desire to get away from her mother was all-consuming. Stone murmured, 'Don't worry,' and before she knew it, he had hailed a cab and was bundling her up in to it. When he ordered the cabbie to take them to Westbourne Grove, it barely registered he was taking her to his flat. Under different circumstances, she would have been dying with curiosity to see where he lived. But she could hardly think straight. Head bent, she stared down at her gloved hands in her lap, lacing and unlacing her fingers, as the recent scene played out in her mind again. Stone tried to start a conversation, but Lucy could only glance at him in distress and shake her head. She needed to recover.

The cab swung out into the road, joining a stream of other vehicles. Traffic crawled. In an effort to calm down, she concentrated on her surroundings. The streets were busy as workers emerged from shops and businesses only to discover the weather had turned foul. Hyde Park was a gloomy blur, with a grey wet pall hanging over it, and only the occasional carriage lamp showing any sign of human activity within its boundary. On the pavement, poor souls were huddled in misery, waiting for trams caught up in the chaos. She wished them luck for the city was notorious for becoming gridlocked on an evening such as this. Londoners were as one, thinking of home, a hot meal and warm feet. With a shudder Lucy thought of the suite in the hotel and knew she couldn't face it again until she was sure her mother had left.

'We're here,' Stone said, almost ten minutes later.

Lucy glanced quickly up at the building as Stone ushered her into the entrance hall. His rooms were two flights up, and his man greeted them without a flicker of surprise, bowing to Lucy and helping her with her hat and coat.

Lucy greeted the servant with a smile. 'I'm delighted to meet you at last. George, isn't it?'

'Yes, ma'am.'

'I'm grateful to you for mending my escritoire. I assumed it was beyond repair. It is of great sentimental value.'

'It was my pleasure, ma'am, and no trouble at all,' George said, looking pleased. He turned to Mr Stone with an expectant look.

'Brandy, strong tea and something to eat, George, please.'

'Right away, sir,' George replied and slipped away.

'Come, you can warm yourself by the fire,' Stone said, taking her arm and leading her down the hall.

They entered a large room which Lucy liked instantly. It was part sitting room, library and dining room. Stone's taste was simple yet elegant with no ridiculous clutter. What struck her most was the collection of art, set off perfectly by the forest-green colour of the walls. Most were landscapes.

Lucy sat down. Stone appeared happy to let her compose herself, sitting across the room at his desk, sifting through his post.

'Are you an art collector?' Lucy asked, after a few minutes of taking in her surroundings.

Stone glanced up at her question. 'Only in a small way. At first, I bought purely as investments but found myself increasingly drawn to particular styles. Now I buy only what I like.'

'May I take a closer look?'

'Please do,' he said with a smile.

It was an eclectic collection but knowing nothing about art, Lucy was reluctant to make any comment. Many were quintessential English vistas but others, which she found more intriguing, were of foreign lands.

'Have you travelled much, Mr Stone?' she asked, standing before a large canvas depicting an Egyptian scene, the unmistakable Giza pyramids in the background.

'I have been lucky enough, in the course of my work, to visit many places.'

'I would love to travel.' Lucy pointed to the painting. 'The closest I've been to Egypt is the Egyptian Room in the British Museum. Have you been to Africa?'

'Once, but briefly. That particular painting is by a young man by the name of Franklin. He painted Abu Simbel and various other historic sites while touring the Nile a few years' ago. I came across his work in a gallery last year. There was something striking about his use of colour. I now have several pieces but my favourites are those miniature scenes on the far wall. They depict the colossi of Rameses II in astonishing detail.'

Lucy walked over. 'How beautiful,' she said, peering at the four images. Somehow even the image of the colossus with only its legs still intact was mesmerising. She sighed. 'It must be a wondrous sight to stand before them in person.'

When he didn't respond, she turned around. He had pulled the curtain back and was staring out the window, frowning.

'What is it?' she asked. Stone pointed down towards the

street. Pulling back the nearest curtain, Lucy scanned the road, wondering what was bothering him. Traffic was easing and only a few stragglers were still abroad. Then she spotted him. A solitary figure across the road, hands shoved into his pockets and hat pulled down over his eyes. For several seconds, she watched the man. He did not move. Worryingly, it was as if he wished to be observed. She dropped the curtain. 'Did he follow us?'

Stone drummed his fingers on the desk. 'He may have. One of Marsh's men, no doubt. It is likely they are watching me too.'

'In the hopes you will lead them to the gems?'

Stone flashed her a smile. 'Of course!'

He appeared unfazed by the fact and she supposed it was one of the hazards of his job, but before she could question him, George entered with a laden tray. Lucy watched him arrange their meal on the table.

'Will that be all, sir?' George asked.

'Yes, thank you,' Stone replied, 'I'll call you if needed.'

'Very good, sir,' George said, then hesitated. 'Might I draw your attention to the telegram? It arrived about an hour ago.'

Stone searched his desk, finding the telegram amongst his post. 'Thank you, George. Apologies, Mrs Lawrence, this may be urgent.' Sliding it open, he held it under the lamp. 'This is an interesting development. It's from McQuillan, informing me that Mr Khan has left for Kashmir.'

'But you told me he was trying to find the sapphires. That he wouldn't return home until he had them.'

'That was my understanding but I may have been mistaken, or he's been summoned to Kashmir to explain his lack of progress. Only this morning McQuillan was complaining about Khan, saying he was like a dog with a bone, constantly looking for updates on the case.'

'Was he under a lot of pressure from Kashmir?' she asked.

'There can be no doubt that was the case, and Mr Khan was happy to pass that pressure on, for all the good it did. No matter. He may be out of the picture but we still have Marsh to contend with.'

Lucy's heart sank, thinking of the man standing outside. Stone slipped the telegram into a drawer in his desk and waved her towards the table.

'Shall I pour?' she asked, on sitting down. He nodded.

Handing him his cup and saucer, she said. 'I apologise, Mr Stone. I'm poor company this evening. Thank you for helping me make my escape. But poor Mary. My mother will be fractious and disagreeable.'

'Your maid seems a sensible girl. I'm sure she's coping admirably.'

'She's a treasure, and I would struggle without her. How can I repay her for the trauma she's most certainly undergoing as we speak? I hope she's still talking to me when I return to the hotel.'

'I don't think you need worry. After all, she returned to your employ as soon as she could. She would hardly have done so if she was not loyal to you.'

'Mary is very kind-hearted. I was relieved to see her at the door that morning, I can assure you. Your man George seems to be equally indispensable.'

'He is.'

'And he makes excellent sandwiches,' she said. 'It would appear he's a man of many talents.'

'Life would be more challenging if he were not around. He often helps me with my cases too. In fact, it was during my first case we met. Recently widowed and discharged from the army, he was down on his luck. But I was so impressed by his wisdom and fortitude I acted on impulse and offered him the position of valet. The incumbent at the time had taken umbrage to my change of career and given his notice only the week before.'

'I have the impression you rarely give in to whims,' Lucy said.

'Correct. This exception, however, proved to be fortunate.'

They ate in silence for several minutes. But Lucy couldn't put the argument with her mother out of her mind. She put down her teacup before giving Stone a long searching look. 'Was I too hard on my mother? Was it cruel to turn her out?'

'No. You were completely justified in what you said and did. After all, she was barefaced enough to admit to her part in it all. Frankly, I was shocked by what she said,' Stone said.

'But I feel guilty. She's elderly and not very strong.'

'Strong of mind, however,' he replied. 'Don't waste your pity on her.'

'What will become of her? Will she be arrested?'

'You will have to ask McQuillan. It's up to him, and whether the insurance company want to press charges against her, as well as your brother.'

'She'll be worried about any hint of scandal,' Lucy said. 'Though Richard's actions have made it inevitable. The newspapers will eat us up.'

'Most assuredly. However, it may come down to her word against your brother's, in which case the prosecution may take her standing and age into account. But I can make you no promises.'

'I understand. I would not ask you to intervene. You already have done so much for me.'

'I only have a little influence. The insurance company will take my advice, but will come to their own decision.'

'Of course,' Lucy said.

'And what about you,' he asked. 'What will you do now?'

'I can no longer stay at the hotel, and it was only ever a temporary solution. We could just about afford it by combining our means. And now with my mother gone... hopefully... well, it doesn't make financial sense. As it happens, the solicitor has informed me he has received an offer for Abbey Gardens. It is my intention to go there tomorrow to retrieve the last of my belongings.'

'I'm sorry. It will be hard for you to give up your home,' he said.

'Actually, no, I don't think it will. It represents my old life and a myriad of bad memories. I must look to the future now. Last week while Mother was out visiting one of her cronies, Mary and I investigated a nice little property in Hampstead. The rent is reasonable and the area is attractive. It will do nicely.'

'You intend to stay in London,' Stone said, sounding pleased.

'Where else would I go? No, London has been my home for the last decade. I have friends and a life here, or at least, the threads of a life.'

'What about Yorkshire?'

'Somerville is gone. There's nothing to draw me up north now,' Lucy said with great firmness. 'The most important thing is that you find those sapphires and the delightful Mr Marsh loses interest in me.'

Stone scowled. 'I'm afraid I've made little progress. Despite my extensive enquiries, there's no trace of your husband from leaving Mrs Bannon to ending up in Dufour Place in Mr Hendrick's loving care. I have to say, this is the most frustrating case I've ever taken on. Someone must know where he travelled to, but how I am to pick up his trail at this late stage eludes me.'

Lucy shared his frustration. 'Near impossible, I'd say.'

'Marsh has covered his tracks well, and not one informant is willing to talk. As usual, he's put the fear of God into his people. But the fact he is still looking for the gems suggests he doesn't know where your husband went either.'

'If Charlie left London over those few crucial days, there's little hope of finding where he stayed. I would imagine too much time has passed for anyone to remember him,' Lucy said. 'But it doesn't make sense to me.'

'What do you mean?' Stone asked.

'Well, Charlie hardly hid the sapphires in some random place in the middle of nowhere. I reckon he gave them to someone for safekeeping.'

'I'm not so sure. They are worth a fortune. You would have to trust a person a great deal to hand them over and your husband doesn't appear to have had many close friends.'

'Except his mistress! Or me,' Lucy breathed.

Stone shook his head. 'I can't see you in such a role, Mrs Lawrence, now I know you better. Your financial situation is desperate. If you were his accomplice, you would have bolted before now and tried to sell the sapphires.'

Lucy swallowed hard, relief he believed her innocent flooding through her. But to her consternation, the urge to weep overtook her. She turned away in distress.

Seconds later, he had moved beside her. 'Please don't,' he said, taking one of her hands in his. She shook her head and tried to laugh, but it seemed once the floodgates had opened months' worth of distress was finally being released. He pulled her into his arms, and she rested her head on his shoulder, wretched to her core.

'You have had a long and emotional day. I suggest a nightcap, then I'll accompany you back to Brook Street.'

'How will I ever repay you for your kindness?' Lucy asked, drying her tears with the handkerchief he offered.

Stone didn't answer but the longing in his eyes triggered something deep inside her and long buried. Gently, he cupped her cheek, his thumb sweeping lightly across her face until he touched the corner of her mouth. She sucked in a shaky breath, transfixed by him. But when he caressed the nape of her neck, she closed her eyes, breathing in the citrus and spice scent she associated with him.

He pulled her closer, resting his forehead against hers. 'Lucy?' His voice was husky, the question one she did not have the strength to answer. When she felt the feather-light pressure of his lips against hers, her own desire flared. She clutched his upper arm, feeling the muscles tighten beneath her fingers in response. His kisses became more urgent, demanding. How had she ever considered him a cold man, was her last coherent thought.

When they finally pulled apart, he said in an unsteady voice: 'I'd better take you home.'

TWENTY-SEVEN

Abbey Gardens

It was mid-morning the next day when Lucy and Mary entered the house at Abbey Gardens. Lucy had almost put off the visit. The drama of the previous day had left her drained and depressed. She had always known how ruthless her mother was, but not the level of cruelty she was capable of. At least Phineas understood. It was akin to grief. Thankfully, he had made no ridiculous declarations, but had given her comfort in just the right way. The promise of a relationship was tantalising but until her own circumstances were straightened out, she would not let any man have control over her life. Although she trusted him, she was still too raw to take a risk. Besides, it was impossible until such time as her period of mourning was over.

Before the future was faced, however, the past had to be dealt with. Her mother's revelations the previous day had hurt her deeply, and she had lain awake for several hours after Phineas had left her back at the hotel. She had relived the awful confrontation, wishing her own responses had been less emotional and more pragmatic. There had been some difficult times over the years when she had wished for reconciliation with her family. She had even discussed it with Charlie. But he had always dissuaded her. He had seen what she had not. It was at least one thing she was grateful to Charlie for.

From Mary, she knew her mother had retreated to her sister Beatrice in Wimbledon. It was unlikely they would meet again in the near future, even by accident, as Aunt Bea moved in different circles to Lucy. Of course, she knew well the tale of woe Mother would pour into Aunt Bea's receptive ears. It hardly mattered. Her hurt was slowly turning to anger and a strong desire to act. For too long she had been the understudy in other people's dramas.

The house already had an abandoned air. Unheated for weeks, there was a damp smell emanating from some rooms and it was deadly cold. But it helped. She needed to detach herself from everything the place represented. She looked at Mary, guessing the maid was equally anxious to get on with the job and return to the comfort of the hotel.

'Look, ma'am, there's some post for you,' Mary said, picking up the letters from the hall floor and handing them over.

Lucy flicked through them. 'I'd better go through these. Can you make a start on your own?'

'Of course, ma'am.'

'The reception rooms are almost empty. Most of what is left is upstairs, if I remember correctly,' Lucy said.

Mary gave a nod of understanding before grabbing one of the suitcases they had brought with them. Lucy watched as the maid disappeared around the return before she made her way to Charlie's study. As she drew back the heavy velvet curtains, particles of dust rose up and pirouetted in a ray of weak sunshine. How melancholy they were, she thought as she stretched out her hand, splaying her fingers to catch the beam of light, desperate to feel some heat on her skin. But there was no comfort in it.

Sitting down, she placed the letters on the blotter and rested her hands on top. Her lethargy would have to be overcome; she must deal with this correspondence and then help Mary. Activity would help ease the hurt and the pain. Even so, her mind returned to the events of the day before.

After a few minutes of brooding her thoughts took a happier turn. Phineas. It had all happened so quickly, but she couldn't and wouldn't regret it. She had as much right to happiness as Charlie ever had. Strange, she hadn't realised how much she had missed the intimacy of a relationship. The early years of her marriage had been a blur of happiness, but slowly she had sensed Charlie's attention wane and Phineas had found the proof. But her mother had hinted at several liaisons. Were they also women she knew? It was humiliating. But it was just as well she had been unaware: the sympathy in people's gaze would have crushed her as much as Charlie's betrayal. She, however, had remained faithful—a fact she was proud of; but now she realised the years of Charlie's neglect had almost left her a hollow shell.

Lucy looked down at the post and tried to concentrate. Of all the letters, only three were of interest. One was postmarked York, one Harrogate and the other appeared to be from London. She opened the London letter first and scanned down the page. One of Charlie's creditors. Without hesitation, she redirected it to Mr Faulkner. Then she paused. The York letter was addressed to Charlie, which was strange. As far as she was aware he hadn't known anyone from there. She turned the envelope over again and again in her hands and a prickle of excitement shot through her. Had Charlie been to York? There was a hotel crest on the envelope. She tore it open.

Dear Mr Lawrence,

We refer to your visit to our hotel some months ago and thank you for the prompt settlement of your account. However, it has come to our attention that the article you left in our care is still in the hotel safe. We are, of course, delighted to be of continued service, but respectfully direct you to our terms. For the continued use of this service, we will require a further payment. We await your further instructions.

We hope this letter receives your earliest attention,

M Haywood,
Manager

This was extraordinary. This had to relate to those missing days. But why did Charlie go to York and what did he leave in that safe? Lucy dared not hope it was the missing sapphires. Surely, it couldn't turn out to be so simple? Drumming her fingers on the desk, she tried to calm down. She needed to think this through. Obviously, the police and Phineas would be very interested in this letter. Only, it might be nothing. What if she went to York to investigate? Whatever she found she could then share with them on her return. But a little voice in her head asked how realistic that was. If it was the sapphires in that safe, she would have a fortune at her fingertips. All her difficulties would be solved for she knew the reward was substantial. Lucy breathed out slowly in an attempt to reduce her rapid heart rate. Did she really trust Phineas, even now? Misplaced trust had resulted in her current predicament. But if she didn't tell him about it, she might lose him. Closing her eyes in exasperation, she thought about the evening before and how secure she had felt in his arms. Bother! She had to tell him.

Lucy pulled herself back to the present. The other letter was addressed in a female hand and was dated the previous week. It was a reply from Judith at Blackheath Manor. It was a sweet letter, telling her not to worry about Uncle Giles. He and her father were enjoying each other's company and, in fact, her father was now far more manageable and less demanding. The letter ended with Judith wondering if Lucy would care to pay them a visit. How opportune! A visit to Blackheath Manor would be the perfect excuse to leave London for Yorkshire without raising suspicion. Rooting around in a drawer, Lucy found some notepaper and immediately scribbled off an acceptance. Fortune at last was smiling on her. But there was still the knotty problem of Mr Marsh. Would he have her followed to Yorkshire? It seemed likely. She would have to consult with Phin on the best way to elude his men.

The door opened, and Mary popped her head in. 'Sorry to disturb you, ma'am, but I wondered what you wished to do about the master's clothes. I found some in the back bedroom.'

Lucy pushed the letters into her bag and stood up. 'Did Mrs Trevor not deal with all of that?'

'Not all, ma'am.'

It was only when she saw the brown paper parcel upon the bed, that Lucy realised what Mary was referring to. It was the parcel of Charlie's clothes from the mortuary. She recalled the night she returned from Yorkshire, finding the parcel and its contents scattered on the floor. Mary's apprehension was plain to see: she did not wish to open the parcel or touch the stained contents.

'Be a dear, and check the kitchen for anything useful we can take with us,' Lucy asked. She was reluctant to open it, too, but it was the least she could do since Mary had heroically endured the previous afternoon with her mother.

'Yes, ma'am, of course.' Mary almost ran out the door.

As Lucy unfolded the layers of paper, a faint metallic odour wafted up towards her from Charlie's blood-stained clothes. She recoiled for a moment as her last image of Charlie, of him lying in the mortuary, twisted and bloodied, came to mind. The clothes were stained brown now, not red as they had been on that awful day, but it was still a shock and a reminder she didn't want.

Wrinkling up her nose, she began to remove the items one by one. His linen shirt was on top, next his trousers, his jacket and at the bottom, his heavy wool greatcoat. His undergarments were missing, but she assumed those had been destroyed by the mortuary. She laid each piece out on the mattress. It seemed a shame to dispose of them. All were of the highest quality, something Charlie never stinted on, as Mr Faulkner had pointed out with asperity. Someone would be happy enough to receive them. Would a good soak get rid of the stains? It wasn't a subject she knew anything about. Mary might, however. It would be best to parcel them up again and decide what to do at a more convenient time.

Trying to avoid touching the blood stains, she carefully shook out each item before folding. But as she folded the trousers, something fluttered to the floor. It was a small piece of card. She bent down and picked it up. It had been soaked in Charlie's blood and was now brown and stiff. How had the police not found it? Then she realised that if it had been wet, it had probably stuck to the inside of the blood-drenched pocket. Wasn't blood sticky? Or perhaps the policeman involved hadn't wanted to reach inside, and she could hardly blame him. Recognising what it was, she stared down into her palm, her mind racing with possibilities. It was a punched train ticket. It was dated October, and it was a return to York.

Later, at the hotel, Lucy sat on the edge of her bed in the semi-darkness, the letter from York and the train ticket before her on her bedside table. What should she do? Someone would have to go to York to investigate, but once she told Phineas about this, she would lose all control. That still didn't sit easily with her. Here was a chance for her to shape her own destiny. But would

Phineas forgive her if she kept him in the dark? Whatever the
outcome, he would find out eventually she had deceived him.
He didn't deserve it, for he had treated her fairly since the
beginning. After all, she might be languishing in a mental
asylum but for him, if her mother was to be believed.

These thoughts swirled in her head until she could have
screamed in frustration but she couldn't justify deceiving
Phineas or even the chief inspector. On entering the hotel
earlier, a police constable had saluted her as he walked past. A
pang of guilt hit her. McQuillan was making sure she was
protected, even still. With a groan, she realised what she had
to do.

Out in the sitting room she found Mary sitting by the
window, sewing.

'Order me a cab, Mary, please,' she said from the doorway as
she drew on her gloves.

Mary laid down her sewing and rose to her feet. 'Certainly,
ma'am. Where to?'

'Westbourne Grove, Kensington. I need to consult Mr
Stone urgently.'

Mary's lips twitched with a smile. 'As you wish, ma'am.'

TWENTY-EIGHT

By the time her cab turned into Westbourne Grove, it was seven o'clock and darkness had fallen. Lucy was already regretting her impulse. To arrive unannounced was the height of bad manners. What if he had guests, a client, or he was out? Why hadn't she considered those possibilities and sent a note instead, inviting him to visit her the following morning? She was being impetuous, but a tingle of anticipation brought a smile to her lips. Lucy was sure he would not mind another opportunity to advance their blossoming relationship. Besides, she knew the ticket and letter in her bag were of vital importance and their significance beyond doubt.

The cabbie opened the hatch. 'What number?'

Glancing out, she realised they had passed Phineas's rooms. 'Here is fine, thank you.' Hopping down, she handed up the fare.

'Want me to wait?' he asked, with a quirk of one shaggy brow. 'It's a bit dark to be out and about on your own.'

'No, thank you. I'm visiting a friend.'

'Evenin' so,' the cabbie said.

Phineas's building was on the other side of the road. Gazing up, Lucy counted the storeys until she reached his floor and was relieved to see the lights were on in his rooms. Just as she was about to cross over, a man brushed past her. Lucy snapped to attention with a gasp. She recognised him. With a pounding heart, she watched his progress along the pavement. He stopped suddenly and seemed to be getting his bearings. When there was a break in the traffic, he strode across and, to Lucy's mounting horror, entered Phineas's building.

A rush of adrenalin coursed through her. She plunged after him, dodging a carriage by inches. She had to warn Phineas. The man must mean him harm. Heedless of the stares of passers-by, she raced along the pavement, barely drawing breath as she swung into the doorway of the building. Thankful there was no porter present to delay her, she dashed up the stairs as fast as her skirts would allow. As she reached the top of the flight of stairs leading to Phineas's landing, she paused, breathing hard. Slowly, she drew the pistol out from her bag. Her hand was shaking. As she was about to step out into the open, she heard a knock, then a door opening, followed by George's voice.

'Mr Stone is expecting you, come in.'

Lucy peeped around the corner, only to catch sight of Coffin Mike entering Phineas's flat.

In the first throes of her fury she almost followed Coffin Mike and banged on the door to demand an explanation, but sanity prevailed, and she retreated, shaking and on the verge of tears. For half an hour, Lucy stood in the freezing cold in a doorway opposite. Waiting. How could he do this to her? There could be no benign reason for what she had seen. It was clear Coffin Mike had been expected. Phineas Stone was going to betray her —like all the others.

As she waited, she remembered the incident at Charlie's

office in Lambeth. Had Phineas deliberately led her to believe Coffin Mike was in the employ of the maharajah, and if so, why? When he had taken off after him down the stairs, had he really tried to catch him or had he let him go? None of it added up... unless Phineas was working for Marsh.

At last the front door of the building opened and Coffin Mike slipped out. He pulled his cap down over his eyes and took off at speed towards Ladbrook Gardens. As she watched, he took a left and disappeared down Kensington Park Road. She looked upwards; a shadow moved across Phineas's window. Whatever was going on, she knew one thing for sure: Phineas Stone was no longer to be trusted.

The return journey to the hotel was miserable. What was she to do? Thank goodness she hadn't given away the clues. She would probably have met a similar fate to Charlie if she had. Clutching her bag tightly, Lucy groaned. What a fool she had been. Now she had no choice but to take matters into her own hands. That meant going to Yorkshire alone.

By the time the cab pulled up outside the hotel, she had made up her mind. Her only hope was Mary. The girl had proved loyal, and she had to trust someone. She would take her into her confidence. What she was about to attempt could be highly dangerous. *And foolish,* she could almost hear Phineas say. Ignoring the possibility her phantom Phineas might be correct, she made her way up to her suite.

Mary greeted her cheerfully and seemed surprised to see her so soon. Once settled before the fire, she called Mary over and bid her sit down. Giving her a confident smile, she launched into her prepared speech. Slowly, she explained about the stolen Kashmiri sapphires and Charlie's involvement with Marsh's gang. The colour drained from Mary's face and she gave a little shudder. After briefly outlining Charlie's move-

ments before he died, Lucy explained the significance of the
letter from the hotel in York. Mary's brows shot up and her
expression verged on priceless, but she made no comment.

'I'd perfectly understand if you don't want to be involved,'
Lucy told her. 'You have been wonderful and I admit I would
hate to lose you. But you must decide now if you are to stay with
me. I have to do this. I owe it to myself to try to make things
right. This will be a dangerous trip, and I have no idea what
awaits me, but if I can find the sapphires and return them to the
insurance company and the maharajah, it will in some small
way compensate for my husband's actions.'

'Surely, ma'am, the world can't blame you for what he did?
You weren't involved.'

'Unfortunately, society is always ready to judge. What a
husband or wife does affects their spouse, and they are considered guilty, purely by association. As it is, my brother may
shortly be on trial for fraud and I'll be a witness for the Crown.
My reputation, what is left of it, will be destroyed once the truth
about him comes out. It is only fair I warn you. Things will not
be pleasant for a while. I may have to leave London.'

'You have always been a kind mistress to me. And you took
me on even though I know you can barely afford it. I'd like to
stay, please.'

A lump rose in Lucy's throat. 'Thank you. You have no idea
what a comfort that is, Mary.'

'But it's hardly right, ma'am, what you say about reputation.'

'No, it isn't, but I don't intend to dwell on it, not now, at
least. I must go to York as soon as possible and find out what my
husband left in that hotel safe. The problem is how to get to the
station without being followed. We can hardly walk out of here
with bags and not raise suspicion. Marsh has people watching
me all the time.'

'Even here?'

'Yes, I believe so. Mr Stone warned me about it.'

'Could Mr Stone not go instead, ma'am?'

Lucy swallowed hard. 'No, unfortunately he's not to be trusted.'

Mary's face fell. 'I'm sorry to hear that for he seemed such a nice gentleman.' For several minutes she appeared to be deep in thought. 'If we need to disappear, could we not hop out the back, through the kitchens?'

'You can be certain someone is watching there, too,' Lucy replied. 'Some of the hotel staff may be in Marsh's pocket, and there's no doubt he knows I'm here. Mr Stone told me Marsh's network covers the entire city.'

Mary appeared daunted, but only for a brief moment, and soon her eyes lit up with an impish glint. 'But, ma'am, it will be easy. Sure, can't we go shopping?'

'We... could?'

'Oh yes, ma'am; I know you love your shopping. It would be like old times except I'd be going with you, like. But it does be very tiring, ma'am. I'm thinking you'd get thirsty too with all that walking.'

'I probably would—'

'And we would have to rest up at one of those nice tea rooms on Oxford Street or Regent Street.'

'I take it I'm buying?' Lucy asked, stifling a smile. Mary frowned at her. 'All right, I'm with you so far, Mary. Then what?'

'After a while—'

'Sorry to interrupt, Mary, but would we have cake with our tea?'

'I don't think you're taking this seriously,' Mary said with a scolding look. 'Cake is an absolute necessity.'

'And nothing to do with your sweet tooth?'

Mary's lips twitched. 'Indeed, no, ma'am. Now, as I was saying, we slip out the back way where there will be a cab waiting.'

'Ah! Pre-arranged?'

'Of course, ma'am, with my friend, Ned. He's a cabbie.'

'How resourceful of you, Mary, to have such a friend. But can he be trusted?'

'Absolutely! On my mother's life,' Mary exclaimed.

Mary's enthusiasm was infectious. Lucy began to hope.

'Then, ma'am, I was thinking it would be a grand idea to get him to take us to say, Paddington, and there we can switch cabs and go to King's Cross. Keep the blighters guessing in case they are on to us.' Her face fell. 'Sorry for the language, ma'am.'

Lucy tried not to smile while marvelling at her maid's aptitude for intrigue. Somehow it left her feeling inadequate, but grateful to have such a resourceful and enthusiastic accomplice. However, it was hardly surprising. Mary often left the cheap novels she read lying around, and when she had nothing better to do, Lucy had read one or two of them, purely on the grounds she was responsible for the girl's morals. The fact they were outrageously entertaining was irrelevant, she often told herself.

'That just leaves us with the problem of our baggage,' Lucy said.

'No, not at all. The hotel sends on bags and trunks for many of the guests. They all go in a cart, all mixed-up like. Who will know our bags are amongst them?'

'Clever girl! Fancy you knowing that.'

Mary beamed. 'Of course, you may need to slip the driver a coin to be sure he doesn't blab to anyone he shouldn't.'

Lucy wondered if she would have enough for their train fares. Still, there didn't appear to be any alternative. Mary's plan it would have to be.

'When can you arrange it? I'd like to go tomorrow, if possible,' Lucy said.

Mary glanced at the clock. 'Most days he's at his rank in about an hour. I'll go and see him this evening, if you wish.'

'Excellent! And Mary, don't be too late home,' Lucy said, with enough emphasis to make the young maid blush scarlet.

The acceptance to Judith's letter was already in the post, but there was a far trickier note to be written. She had to inform Phin she had received an invitation to visit Judith and, that out of concern for Uncle Giles, she should go. Hopefully, that would put him off the scent. It was unlikely he would be suspicious of her visiting an old friend, but her guilt nagged at her. Someone as clever as he was bound to be instantly on the alert. No, as he wasn't aware of the train ticket or the hotel in York, this was silly, Lucy told herself. She made the note brief and casual and after about five attempts had a version she was happy with. As she gave it to the receptionist for posting, she crossed her fingers behind her back.

TWENTY-NINE

There was a discreet knock at the door. Mary ushered in a young man, a hotel porter, who, she had earlier informed Lucy, was a fellow Dubliner and therefore a *regular brick*. Lucy tipped him generously, and he left with their two bags, labelled for King's Cross.

'Don't be worrying, ma'am, Sean knows what he's doing. They will be with the other luggage in the baggage room at the station. When we arrive at King's Cross, we just have to ask one of the porters to fetch them for us.'

'Let's hope there are no hitches along the way. I'm more worried about being followed than losing the bags, Mary.'

'Don't fret! Ned will take care of us.' Mary's face positively glowed. 'Oh, isn't this exciting, ma'am! An adventure to tell my children about one day.'

Lucy buttoned up her coat with unsteady fingers. She hoped it was a story that would have a happy ending. Sleep had been elusive the night before, but she had finally decided to forge ahead. No matter what the outcome, she couldn't bear inaction any longer.

As they entered the lobby, Sean appeared before them.

Lucy requested he call a cab. With a nod and a wink, which made Mary giggle, he went off to do her bidding. Lucy gave Mary a stern glance—conscious spying eyes could be anywhere.

Not long after, they were on Regent Street. Under different circumstances, Lucy would have enjoyed strolling along, looking at the lavish window displays. Many a time she had spent a pleasant morning or afternoon doing just that. But now the street had another association: this was where Charlie had died so horribly. She didn't know where exactly his *accident* had occurred and she didn't want to. But as Lucy stepped down from the cab, she realised how distracted she had been on New Year's Eve on Phineas's arm, for she had given little thought to the location that evening.

'What time are we to meet Ned?' she asked, banishing her ghosts.

'One o'clock, ma'am. He said he'll be waiting at the end of the laneway that runs behind the tea rooms. That will give us plenty of time to make the three o'clock train.'

Lucy consulted her watch. 'We have two hours. I have no doubt we were followed, so we must act the part.' Mary's eyes danced. Lucy envied her appetite for adventure; she found her mouth was dry, and she couldn't shake off a sense of foreboding. And guilt.

'Where shall we go first?' Mary asked, half distracted by a window display. 'Oh ma'am, do you see those beautiful blue shoes? I've never seen the like.'

It was a display with an Egyptian theme to the entire window. The shoes and boots had been placed in such a way as to form a pyramid. The shoes in question had crystals adorning the heels and tiny ribbons to the front.

'Yes, they are lovely, but not something a widow would wear,' Lucy said.

'Would they not have them in black, ma'am?'

'I'm sure they do, Mary, but if you look closely, you will see the price.'

Mary leaned closer. 'Oh dear, yes I see.'

'We shall go to Jay's and browse. Anywhere else might appear odd. Above all, this has to give the appearance of a normal shopping trip.'

'If you say so, ma'am,' Mary said, her eyes still on the display.

They made their way through the crowds to the corner of Oxford Circus. When they stopped before the London General Mourning Warehouse, Mary's mouth dropped and she turned to her with a puzzled expression. 'Why, it's not a warehouse at all. It's a proper shop with windows. I always thought it was a big shed, you know, like down on the docks.'

'Have you never been on this street?' Lucy asked.

'No, ma'am. Sure, it's not for the likes of me.'

The sombre atmosphere of the main salon sucked you in as soon as you crossed the threshold. Even the shop assistants were all attired in severest black. The walls were decorated in muted greys and greens with displays of mourning finery arranged at intervals to catch the eye. They were hardly inside when the bell jangled and a young woman entered the shop behind them. She was not in mourning, and Lucy was instantly on her guard. From behind one of the displays, she watched her, a prey to nerves. But the woman walked away and entered a side room and was soon lost to sight. Mary gave Lucy a questioning look. Lucy shook her head, realising this was going to be a nerve-wracking day.

A gentleman assistant materialised from the next room and glided up to them. After a profuse welcome, but no smiles, he insisted on escorting them to view what was on offer. As they toured the shop, he reeled off a mind-boggling range of goods. Lucy would have preferred to meander around unaccompanied. Now she would have to buy something she didn't even need to have any chance of getting rid of him.

'My condolences, madam, at this sad time. Was there anything in particular you wished to purchase?' he asked as his eyes swept over her clothes.

'Handkerchiefs,' she blurted out. It was the first thing that came into her head.

He reacted with a disappointed smile. 'Certainly, madam. This way, please. We do, of course, have the widest and finest range available in London if not the entire country. Only the best linen and silk and a choice of the plainest of borders or, if madam prefers, we have a fine selection with English lace.' He led them across the room and stopped before a large glass cabinet, and indeed, it was full of white handkerchiefs with black borders of various widths and materials. None of the borders were below the minimum of one and a half inches, he was eager to point out.

Lucy surveyed the gloomy selection. There were no prices on the dratted things, making her nervous. It was hard to tell if there was any difference, but which to pick? In the end, she chose one, the plainest in the cabinet, and prayed it was cheap.

'An excellent choice, if I might say, madam. Would you like them monogrammed? How many dozen does madam require?'

'No monogram and I only need one, thank you,' Lucy replied.

He turned to the sales assistant waiting eagerly behind the counter. 'Please parcel up one dozen of those for madam.'

'No,' Lucy interjected. 'I meant one handkerchief.'

The gentleman froze, then turned slowly. 'One?'

'Yes, thank you.' Lucy put up a valiant fight to maintain a straight face.

He coughed. 'I'll leave you in the capable hands of Miss Andrews.' He walked away, shoulders slumped.

Lucy noticed Mary's shoulders shaking with laughter so she stood on her toe.

'Lordy me! What about that fellow with the limp? He's a queer looking cove,' Mary commented. They were sitting a couple of tables from the front window of the tea room. A steady stream of shoppers passed by.

'It is pointless speculating; it could be anyone. Someone may even have followed us in here.'

Mary's swivelled round in her chair, eyes wide.

'Don't stare!'

Mary blushed. 'Sorry, ma'am.'

'Don't forget they are skilled and can blend in anywhere.'

Mary concentrated on her cake for several minutes but was soon on the alert again. 'Maybe it's him. See the man with the red scarf? I'm sure that's the second time he has passed by.'

Lucy wished Mary would stop for it was making her uncomfortable. With a sigh, she consulted her watch. Ten minutes to one. Her stomach rumbled, but she couldn't eat for nerves. She pushed her cake towards Mary.

'Oh, thank you, ma'am. Are you not hungry?'

'No, Mary. Please, be my guest. But be quick, we will have to move soon.' She drained her tea and sat watching her maid demolish the slice of lemon tart, marvelling at her appetite. 'Are you sure Ned will be there?'

'Course he will. Very reliable,' Mary said, wiping her mouth with her napkin.

Lucy called over the waitress and asked for the bill. The minutes crawled by. Mary stared down at the crumbs on her plate. Lucy fidgeted on her seat.

'What's keeping her?' she asked Mary, as she had her back to the counter.

'Serving. It's all right, she's coming now,' Mary said.

Once the bill was paid, they made their way to the rear of the premises where the ladies' cloakroom was situated. No one followed them. Mary grinned at her. 'All clear.' They scuttled down the corridor to the back door. With a good tug, Mary opened it and peeped outside.

She turned to Lucy with a smile. 'There he is, didn't I tell you?'

Relieved, Lucy followed her out into the gloomy laneway. At once her senses were overpowered by the smell of decaying food and something else quite unspeakable, which she had no desire to investigate. Lucy glanced up and down. At one end of the lane she saw a cab was waiting, the horse's head moving restlessly up and down. But to her dismay, at the other end, a man stood silhouetted under the archway and appeared to be watching them. He took a step towards them. Panic gripped her and she broke into a run towards the cab, past the rows of dustbins and boxes of rubbish, with the sound of Mary's boots echoing behind her.

The cabbie greeted Mary as they bundled into the hansom. Lucy sneaked a peek back into the lane as the cab began to move away from the kerb. The man had almost reached them. She started to pull down her veil, but it was too late. They locked eyes for a split second before her cab lurched out into the traffic.

It was Coffin Mike.

Lucy gasped and clutched Mary's arm in fright. Mary's eyes popped wide as saucers. 'We've been seen! We must warn your Ned.'

Lucy rapped the roof with the silver-tipped handle of her umbrella. The slot slid open and a grey-eyed and smiling Ned peered down at her. He was a handsome man, even with cheeks ruddy from the cold. Lucy could see why Mary liked him.

'Ned, I'm terribly pleased to meet you, but there's a great hulk of a man who has seen us and will probably follow in another cab. Can you watch out for him? Do you think you can lose him? He must not find out our destination.'

'Delighted to meet you, Mrs Lawrence. What does this cove look like then?'

'Ugly scar down his right cheek.'

'Right you are. Now don't you fret, ladies. I know these streets like the back of me hand.' The panel closed over with a snap. Mary looked at her in dismay.

The cab began to weave in and out of the other vehicles in an alarming manner, just making a gap between a carriage and an omnibus. Lucy hoped the heavy traffic on Regent Street would prevent Coffin Mike from catching up with them. Lucy rapped on the roof again.

'Yes?'

'Ned, whatever you do, don't go to King's Cross directly. Take us somewhere busy and we will hop out and change cab as fast as we can.' She thrust some coins at him up through the slot. 'This should cover the fare and any inconvenience.'

Ned took them with a smile and winked. 'Not to worry. 'Old tight. I'll let you know when it's safe to do it.'

The cab swung across a wagon on to Conduit Street, narrowly avoiding an elderly lady trying to cross the road. Mary crossed herself and squeezed her eyes tightly shut.

'Mary, what are you doing?' Lucy asked.

'Praying, ma'am.'

With less traffic, Ned urged the horse on to a spanking pace, then suddenly pulled up before turning down a laneway. The hansom barely fitted yet he whipped the horse and kept the pace up. Mary squeaked when they hit an obstacle, her hand flying up to her mouth.

Suddenly, they were back out on to a main street, the cab swinging precariously as they turned. Lucy frantically tried to get her bearings before realising they were on New Bond Street, heading roughly north.

Left again and on to Brook Street and into heavy traffic. Lucy longed to know if they had shaken off their pursuer, but she had to trust Ned was keeping ahead. Coffin Mike was bound to be following them, but the question was who was he spying for? Who should she fear the most, Phineas or Marsh? If they were in league, was Phineas using Marsh's men to keep tabs on her? It was a distressing idea.

Soon they were bowling along Grosvenor Square, then Brook Street Upper. Up ahead, Lucy spotted the railings of Hyde Park. At the junction, Ned had to stop, waiting for a gap in the traffic. The panel slid open.

'Across the way is a cab stand, ladies. I'll get you as close as I can and I'll stop long enough for you to get out, then I'll keep going. Be ready!'

Lucy suspected Ned was enjoying himself very much. Really, he and Mary were well matched.

Traffic around the park was heavy. A horse and cart pulled across their cab just as they drew parallel with the cab stand. Ned had to stop. Lucy and Mary jumped down quickly, squeezed between a couple of cabs, and walked briskly away towards the top of the stand.

Mary nudged her. 'There he goes,' she whispered. Lucy spotted Ned's cab continuing northwards. Hopefully anyone in pursuit would keep following him. They clambered into their new cab.

'Where to, then?' a hearty voice enquired.

'King's Cross, please,' Lucy said. 'And hurry!'

The rest of their flight was uneventful and although Lucy experienced a moment or two of doubt along the way, on seeing the entrance to King's Cross her resolve hardened. Mary went to fetch a porter to find their bags while she made her way to the ticket office.

They regrouped in the Ladies' Waiting Room and sat down, exchanging knowing smiles. All they had to do now was wait, for it would be another twenty minutes before the train would depart. At least, in here they were out of sight of most of the passengers coming and going. Lucy only hoped Marsh or Phineas weren't clever enough to have people watching the stations.

Having exhausted her book as entertainment, Lucy decided to stretch her legs and leave Mary in their first-class compartment. Lucy made for the dining car. Once settled at a table and her order taken, she kept her gaze fixed on the passing landscape, hoping no one would intrude. In the few short months since her last trip north, spring had started to take hold. Soon the trees and hedges would green up with the promise of new life. She sat back to enjoy the scenery and gradually began to relax.

The conductor came through the carriage calling for the Retford stop. As the train pulled into the station, Lucy watched the passengers disembark and a few people get on. Now at least, the worst of the journey was over. Feeling more cheerful she finished her tea and decided to return to Mary.

But when she reached her compartment, she found the door was closed and the blind pulled fully down. Lucy tugged the handle but it would not budge. Tapping lightly on the door, she called softly to Mary. A corner of the blind lifted to reveal a frightened face. On recognising her, Mary quickly unlocked the door.

'Whatever is the matter?' Lucy asked as soon as she got inside.

'Oh ma'am, I woke and I didn't know where you were and then I saw this man staring in at me. He frightened me so.'

'Can you describe him? Did he have a scar?'

'No, no scar. He was in uniform, army, I think... silver hair...' Mary started to weep. 'I'm sorry, I can't remember. I got such a fierce shock. I wish we'd stayed in London.'

Relieved it wasn't Coffin Mike, Lucy sat down beside her and gave her a quick hug. But her mind was racing. Why would a stranger be looking into their compartment? It wasn't who she feared, but could it be someone else who intended them harm? Perhaps it was only Mary's overactive imagination.

'Dry your tears,' she told the young girl. Mary pulled out a cotton handkerchief and wiped her eyes. 'We will take the precaution of getting off before York. We can wait at Selby until the next north-bound train comes through.'

'You think he was looking for us... for you?'

Lucy shrugged. 'I don't know, but best we assume it's a possibility. It will be late getting into York but at least our room is booked for tonight and our bags will be waiting for us at the station. We have come too far to abandon our adventure. Let's hope it was merely a coincidence.'

Mary didn't appear convinced and, if Lucy were honest, she wasn't either.

THIRTY

York Train Station, Later that Evening

The last train of the day crawled into the station. After waiting two hours at Selby, Lucy was tired and anxious but hopeful they had shaken off any pursuit. She hustled Mary off the train, sympathetic to the maid's weariness but reluctant to linger. Lucy would not feel safe until they were inside the hotel. A porter approached, and Mary instructed him to fetch their small bags, telling him they would collect the bigger pieces of luggage the following day. He scurried off. A few minutes later, he reappeared and gave each of them their overnight bag. He gestured towards the entrance and the waiting cabs but Lucy shook her head and kept walking to the exit. As they passed the unlit waiting room, she swore she saw movement in the shadows. Rattled, she linked Mary's arm and marched her out of the station.

The gaslit street was almost empty but their hotel wasn't far. Lucy was thankful she had had the foresight to book their room in advance. She kept up a brisk pace until they reached the hotel entrance. As she went in the door, she stole a glance back towards the station. A figure stood about halfway down, avoiding the pools of light under the street lights. It looked like a man but she couldn't be sure. While she watched, the person turned and walked away in the opposite direction. Was she paranoid? With a shake of her head, she followed Mary inside.

The following morning, after an early breakfast and a council of war, Lucy and Mary left the hotel. Again, Lucy paused on the steps and studied the area. But all appeared to be well with only an elderly gentleman walking down the street. As they approached, he went into a tobacconist shop. It was ridiculous: she was seeing danger in the most innocent of passers-by.

They halted at the station entrance. 'I'll be as quick as I can, Mary. The hotel is on the other side of the city and I don't know how long it will take to retrieve whatever Charlie left in that safe. Please stay in the waiting room and I'll find you on my return. Do you have your book?'

Mary patted the pocket of her coat. 'Don't worry, this will keep me busy.' But then she frowned. 'What if you don't come back?'

'Don't fret so. But if I don't return in a couple of hours, head out to Blackheath and give my friend Judith the message, as agreed. She'll take care of you.'

Mary bobbed her head. 'Yes, ma'am, I will for sure. Best of luck.'

A porter sidled up and took their bags. Mary gave her a little wave and followed him inside.

Taking a deep breath, Lucy consulted the letter from the Haywood Hotel. From her memory the location wasn't in a nice part of town. Determined she would not fail in her mission, she hailed a cab.

The Haywood Hotel, York

The hotel was tucked away in a narrow street, its exterior unprepossessing with a tarnished nameplate and unswept steps. A gloomy foyer led to an unattended reception desk. Undeterred, Lucy headed straight for it. Striking the call-bell with force, she listened as the sound reverberated then dissipated into the ether. Then silence: the place appeared to be empty of staff and guests. This wasn't a promising start. Lucy tapped her foot impatiently. After all the trouble to get here, to be hindered in her plan now was almost unbearable. As she waited, she looked about with distaste at the marked wood-panelled walls and the unfortunate tartan carpet of brown and yellow. Lucy found it difficult to imagine fastidious Charlie choosing such a place to stay.

After a surreptitious glance around the lobby, she lifted her veil a smidgen and leaned over to sneak a peek behind the desk. The hotel register lay tantalisingly close.

'Can I help you?' a voice said, making her jump just as she contemplated reaching out for it.

Pulling back, she took in the over-sized suit, spikey hair and nervous disposition of a young man barely out of his teens. 'Good morning, I wish to see the manager, Mr Haywood, please.'

The young lad slid behind the desk. 'Have you an appointment, madam? He may be... indisposed. May I be of assistance instead? If you would like to reserve a room, I believe there is one available.'

'No, thank you. I do not require accommodation. I'm here to see Mr Haywood on business.'

Blowing out his cheeks, the youth gave her a sceptical look. 'If you insist. Take a seat and I'll see if I can find him.' He indicated a chair beside the empty fireplace before disappearing off down a corridor. In the silence that followed, Lucy's apprehension rose. This could be a bad idea. What if this Mr Haywood was an associate of Marsh? Might it be a trap? She hadn't considered that possibility.

She tried to quell the unease which lay solid and unhelpful in the pit of her stomach. *I'm not cut out for this*, she thought, *I should leave this sort of business to a professional*. But, of course, she couldn't afford to hire anyone. Exhaustion was not helping her state of mind. It had been almost midnight when they had finally gone to bed and the lumpy mattress and Mary's snores had made sleep difficult.

Opening her bag, she took out Mr Haywood's letter, read it quickly, then folded it and put it away again. Still no one came. Staring up at an unpleasant stain on the ceiling, it struck her this was the kind of place men brought their mistresses. Would Charlie have brought a woman here? *Now* the register was singing to her with sirenlike allure, but if caught at the desk again, she knew her credibility would be questioned and they might refuse to give her Charlie's property. Would Phineas take the chance if he were here? Something told her he would, in double-quick time.

Too late. The young man returned and asked her to follow.

The whisky fumes were the first thing she noticed when the door to the manager's office opened. A large, florid-faced man sat behind a desk in the tiny office.

'Thank you, son,' he said, slurring his words ever so slightly as he rose unsteadily to his feet. 'Please,' he said to Lucy, waving towards the only other chair. This was an unlucky gesture as he had to grip the desk to steady himself. Sweeping a shaking hand across his forehead, he sat down abruptly.

Not an auspicious start, Lucy thought, trying not to examine the fabric of the chair too closely before sitting down. But it might work to her advantage if the man wasn't sober. The desk was cluttered with papers and the general appearance of the man and the office was one of disorder and a shortage of money.

'Please forgive me, Mrs... I'm sorry. I did not catch your name?'

'Mrs Lawrence.' She offered him her visiting card, which he glanced at and dropped to the desk.

'Delighted.' He drew out a handkerchief and blew his nose. 'Terrible cold, so sorry.'

Nodding in sympathy, Lucy was quite sure it was a very different kind of affliction. The room was chilly, yet his forehead shone with perspiration.

'What can I do for you, madam?'

Pulling out his letter to Charlie, she handed it across. He coughed, then smiled apologetically. 'Glasses,' he muttered, before scrambling around through the papers on the desk. The spectacles found, he plonked them on his red-tipped nose. After scanning the letter he frowned at her.

Lucy pointedly pulled away her black net veil and glanced down at her widow's weeds. 'As soon as I read your letter, Mr Haywood, I knew I would have to come all the way from London to relieve you of this burden. Anything of my husband's is so precious to me now he's deceased. I hope you can understand, sir? It has been a most distressing time.'

'Oh! Yes, of course. I'm sorry to hear of your husband's demise, but I'm not sure...'

Looking down at the letter in his hand, she continued. 'Your letter states my dear Charlie left something in your safekeeping. He can't reclaim it, poor soul, so I hoped—' At this point, she began to weep.

Mr Haywood took on a sickly hue and stared at her with a gaping mouth. Aware she might be laying it on too strong, she reduced the flow to more dignified snuffles.

At last, he found his voice. 'My dear lady, please do not be distressed. I do recall now... such a nice young man. Tragic, tragic!'

Clutching her handkerchief to her bosom, she asked, 'My poor dear husband, Mr Haywood, did he enjoy a pleasant stay here with his friends?'

Haywood's brow crinkled. 'I do believe he was alone, ma'am.'

'How terribly sad! Poor Charlie hated to be without company.' She shook her head and sighed deeply. 'It sounds most unlike him.'

'Why don't I check the register for you? My memory sometimes lets me down and it is some time ago.'

Lucy gave him a watery smile of thanks. Tottering slightly, he managed to negotiate the desk and left the office.

A quick sweep of the room and Lucy spotted the safe jutting out from under a table in the corner. A quiver of excitement coursed through her. She was very close now—she just had to hold her nerve.

A few minutes later, Mr Haywood appeared with the register under his arm. 'Now, let me see.' Having placed it on the desk, he gingerly lowered himself into his seat and put his glasses on again. 'Would you happen to know the date your husband was here?'

'Yes,' she sniffed. 'Around the fourteenth of October. A few days before he died, in fact.'

Mr Haywood threw her an anguished look, then proceeded to leaf through the register. Muttering to himself, he ran his finger slowly down the lists of names, then shook his head and moved on to the next page. Lucy had to restrain the impulse to push him out of the way and do it herself.

'Ah! Here we are. Yes, he arrived on the fifteenth and he took a single room for two nights. One of our nicest rooms, as it happens.'

'And his belongings, Mr Haywood,' Lucy prompted when he sat staring at her blankly.

Half-turning in his chair, the man glanced at the safe. 'Your husband asked to use the safe as he didn't want to leave his belongings unattended in his room while he was out. He returned briefly later that day and reclaimed the bag. But he left it back to me soon after, saying he would retrieve it before catching his train to London. He was most insistent about it, if my memory serves. But he never did. Most peculiar, if you don't mind me saying.'

'Indeed. Have you any idea what his destination was that day? Did he say who he was calling upon?'

'I'm sorry, I don't recall. But my son Frank may remember. He generally attends the front desk.'

'You have been so kind, sir. To have taken such good care of his things—'

Taking the hint, Mr Haywood moved over to the safe, slowly bending down. After a few grunts, he dropped to his knees. Lucy prayed she would not have to help him up again for she doubted she'd manage it. He began to fiddle around with the dial. After a couple of clicks, the metal door swung open. To her immense relief, Mr Haywood gradually rose up to his feet, looking the worse for the experience, but with a small leather satchel in his grasp. She did not recognise it.

Regaining his seat, he gave her a long considered look, no doubt weighing her up. Would her dowdy clothes be enough to stop him demanding money to hand it over? She contemplated whether to play the grieving widow card again. There wasn't much in her purse if he insisted on payment. He tapped his fingers on the leather as a cunning glint came into his bloodshot eyes.

'We normally charge for the service, Mrs Lawrence,' he said at last. 'And it is at least five months since your late husband was here. I'm sure we could come to some mutually beneficial arrangement.' His gaze drifted slowly down her body.

Lucy squirmed and her heart sank, but she couldn't walk away now. Knowing how uncomfortable the earlier tears had made him, she let her eyes rest on the bag then back up to his face with as forlorn an expression as she dared. Then she wobbled her chin ever so slightly as one solitary tear rolled down her cheek. Mr Haywood broke eye contact first and hurriedly pushed the satchel across the table.

'However, in the circumstances, it would be unseemly to take your money, you being recently widowed.'

Surprised and pleased at how easy it had been to persuade him, she picked up the bag before he might change his mind, giving him a kindly look. 'How sweet of you, sir!'

'It's nothing, ma'am, nothing.' He kept staring at the satchel even as she rose up to depart.

As she closed over the door, she heard a deep sigh followed by the clink of a bottle being pulled from a drawer.

The young man was still at the desk as she went through the reception area. 'Frank, isn't it?'

'Yes, ma'am. Is there anything I can do for you?'

'I wonder if you can recall my husband staying here. It was last October. Mr Charles Lawrence?'

'Sorry, ma'am, we have lots of guests. I don't remember them all.'

Leaving the satchel down on the desk, Lucy opened her bag and pulled out her wedding photograph. She pointed to Charlie. 'Here he is.'

Frank took the photograph from her and squinted at it. 'Yes, I do recall your husband,' he drawled. 'He tipped well.'

She smiled her encouragement. 'Would you remember, by any chance, where it was he was travelling on to? Did he leave York during his stay?'

Frank scratched the side of his head and scrunched up his

eyes. 'I can't say for sure, ma'am, but I do recollect something about hiring a gig. I would have directed him to Mr Cassidy. He might know.'

'And where would I find his establishment?'

Frank gave her the directions and she bade him farewell.

Holding the satchel close as she walked along, she wondered if it were possible the Haywoods hadn't tampered with the contents. Her only hope was the state of their business. If they had found the sapphires, they'd hardly still be in York running a seedy hotel.

THIRTY-ONE

Lucy entered the train station in a despondent mood. Following Frank's directions, she had found Cassidy's Livery Stables easily enough a few streets away from the hotel. But Mr Cassidy and his employees had no memory of Charlie. After some gentle persuasion, Mr Cassidy had agreed to check his records. It turned out Charlie had hired a gig for a day, but the entry gave no details as to where he was going. The gig had been returned on time and in good order.

She found Mary sitting patiently in the station waiting room, her nose in her book. With a sigh, Lucy took the seat beside her. Mary snapped her book closed and glanced up expectantly. Lucy showed her the satchel.

'Oh, well done, ma'am,' Mary said with a delighted smile. 'Are they in there?' she whispered.

'I haven't looked inside yet.' It wasn't an ideal place to investigate the satchel's contents, but there was only an elderly gentleman in the waiting room, and he was buried in his newspaper. With trepidation, Lucy undid the buckle and opened the flap of the bag. Inside, there were three sheets of paper and a small red velvet drawstring bag. She glanced at Mary who gave her an encouraging nod. Lucy pulled the little bag out and probed it with urgent fingers. It was empty. No sapphires, not even tiny ones.

'Oh!' Mary exclaimed, mirroring Lucy's own disappointment. 'What a shame. Maybe those papers are important?'

Lucy flicked through the sheets. Each one bore the Padar Mining Company name at the top. 'These appear to be lists of shareholders' names, addresses and how much each invested in the mine.'

'Nothing about the gems?'

'No. What a waste of a day. I have learned nothing new.'

'What happened at the hotel?' Mary asked.

'It's a horrible place, owned by an unsavoury man who is pickled in whisky. He confirmed Charlie took a room for two nights, then disappeared off somewhere on the second day. I would imagine he was meeting someone near to York. He left this,' Lucy ran her hand over the satchel, 'in the hotel safe. But he did not return to retrieve it as he told the manager he would, and I have no idea why. He hired a gig which suggests he may have left York, but where on earth would he have gone?' She glanced down at the list. 'Unless he was visiting someone on this list, someone who lives within a reasonable distance.' Reading down the list of names and addresses on the first two pages, she recognised some names, but they were London-based. The rest were unknown to her and from various parts of the country and most definitely not within striking distance of York. With an impatient shuffle, she turned to the third page. As she moved it, she realised there was something scrawled on the other side. A series of letters.

STAL. Was it a name? How bizarre. She checked the other sheets.

LGH was on the next one.

ANM on the last, along with a rough sketch of a hunting horn.

It had probably been Charlie. He had often absently doodled on his newspaper, a habit she had detested and remonstrated with him about. With an impatient sigh, Lucy went back to the third sheet and started to read down the printed side of the page. What she saw brought her up short. 'Good Lord!'

Mary clutched her arm. 'What is it, ma'am? Have you found something?'

Lucy shoved the papers into the satchel, her heart pounding. 'Most definitely. My brother Richard is on this list! He was an investor in the mine... which must mean Charlie visited Somerville Hall!'

Blackheath Manor Estate

It was almost ten o'clock in the evening when they reached Judith's home. Lucy had been in eager anticipation of seeing the beautiful old house again since leaving London. Her happy memories of days spent playing with Judith and her sisters in the shadow of its mullioned windows and towering chimneys had come flooding back. The house was far older than Somerville, with the central core reputedly Elizabethan. But it was pitch-dark as the hired coach pulled up, with only the entrance porch lit up. Judith's welcome, however, made up for any disappointment. Judith embraced Lucy before linking her arm through to the drawing room. The familiar surroundings were a cheering sight after a day of travelling and her maiden dive into the world of investigation.

'It's good to be here, Judith,' Lucy said, sitting down on the sofa. 'It has been a long day.'

'I had almost given up on you. I expected you much earlier and was beginning to worry. Father and your uncle retired a short while ago, but they are looking forward to seeing you tomorrow.'

Lucy felt a rush of affection for her old friend. 'And I them. I'm sorry, but things did not turn out as I had planned today. It's a long story.'

'You know I love stories, particularly yours. But first, you must have some refreshment,' Judith insisted.

'Thank you, but no. We ate at the station; part of the reason we are late. My poor maid would not have lasted until we arrived here.'

'Is she poorly?'

'No, no, quite the opposite. I've never seen a girl put away so much food, but I don't mind, for she works hard. You just have to provide plenty of fuel.'

Judith laughed. 'You always said the funniest things. You haven't changed at all.'

Lucy pursed her lips. 'I wish that were true, but life has taught me some valuable lessons of late. But let's not be mawkish. How are your father and my uncle? Tell me all your news.'

After breakfast the following morning, Judith suggested taking the opportunity provided by a clear blue sky to venture out for a walk. Spring had arrived at last with swathes of daffodils nodding in a light breeze beneath the ancient horse chestnuts and oaks. As they walked along the woodland paths, their old playground, the tension gradually eased from Lucy's bones. She watched as Judith picked some daffodils, explaining they were her father's favourite, and he loved to have them in his room. It struck Lucy how different her relationship with her family was.

As they meandered through the woods, they chatted about inconsequential nothings. But when Judith turned to the local gossip, Lucy began to feel uncomfortable again. The main topic was the fall of the house of Somerville, with her brother's arrest making tantalising fodder for the wagging tongues of the neighbourhood. The house being repossessed by the bank had also caused quite a stir and much anger as most of the servants had been local. Not surprisingly, Judith was dying to know the details and eventually Lucy found herself regaling the whole sorry tale of the theft of the pearls, the trap which had been laid for her, and the awful revelation that her mother had been the master conspirator.

When she had finished, Judith paused on the path and clutched her arm. 'How awful for you, Lucy! To be arrested and taken to jail like a common criminal. You must have been terrified.'

'I was.'

'There were some odd rumours flying around,' Judith explained, 'but no one knew what was going on. And who would believe your mother could do such a thing? It is so shocking.'

'I won't deny it was unpleasant, but thankfully Mr Stone came to my rescue. Otherwise, I don't know what would have become of me.'

'You should have sent a message to us here. I would have come or engaged a solicitor for you.'

'I doubt they would have let me send any messages. The sergeant was in Richard's pocket. If it wasn't for the insurance company sending Phin... Mr Stone...'

Judith quirked a brow. 'I must say, I thought Mr Stone such a pleasant gentleman,' she said.

'You met him? When?'

'Yes, he called here and spoke to Father and then to me. Rather dashing, isn't he?'

'He has his moments. Hmm. He never mentioned to me that he had visited here. How odd.'

'I believe he visited all the local families who attended the party on Christmas Eve,' Judith said.

It made sense. He was being thorough. However, Lucy was left with the uncomfortable feeling he had been checking up on her as much as Richard. From the very beginning he hadn't trusted her. And now here she was going behind his back for her own ends. It didn't sit easy, but it served him right for being deceitful. For all she knew, he meant her real harm. After all, he must be in league with Marsh. It was the only explanation for Coffin Mike visiting his home.

When she noticed Judith was looking at her with a curious expression, she pushed the unpleasant thought away.

Hurriedly, she manoeuvred the conversation back to Richard. 'It turned out Mr Stone's suspicions about Richard were correct in the end, and now he faces the consequences of his actions,' she said. 'Mother also may face a trial and even prison.'

'Your brother deserves it, but how could they inflict such a thing on an elderly woman.'

'Mr Stone said it was up to the police and the Crown prosecution. Mind you, I wouldn't waste your sympathy on her. I have no doubt she'll wriggle out of it and scapegoat Richard. Isn't that what she tried to do to me?'

Judith shook her head. 'I would never have believed her capable of such infamy. It is distressing to hear, though I suspected for some time all was not as it should be at Somerville. It was common knowledge the estate was going through some difficulties. A year or two ago, while Father was still in good health, he approached Richard and offered him some advice. Richard didn't take it well and after that our invitations all but dried up, bar the annual invitation for Christmas Eve, of course.'

'Richard was a pompous fool.'

'Perhaps, but Sibylla never liked me and made it quite clear she considered us beneath her from the beginning.'

'Which is thoroughly ridiculous!'

'It didn't matter, Lucy. As father's illness became worse, there was little time for socialising. Besides, Somerville was never the same once you left, at least for me.'

Lucy linked her arm. 'What an inconsiderate fool I was. All I dreamed of was escape. I was so wrapped up in my great romance with Charlie I rarely thought about life back in Yorkshire or how my dear friend was faring. You must forgive me. We shouldn't have lost touch over the years.'

'There's nothing to forgive and I neglected you too. Besides, we had little in common. I'm unmarried and have no experience of life in London. What would we have talked of?'

Lucy shook her head. 'No, you will not excuse my inattention. I'm guilty. But tell me, Judith, have you ever been tempted to abandon it all and escape Blackheath?'

'Where would I go and what would I do? I have no independent means. Besides, Father needs me here. Dr Smyth says he only has a few months left.'

'Oh, my dear, I'm so sorry to hear that,' Lucy said, feeling terrible. 'Forgive me. It was a foolish question.'

As they walked on, Lucy wondered how her friend could bear it. Effectively, she was a prisoner at Blackheath Manor. A fate many spinsters faced. But it was such a waste. Judith was intelligent and warm-hearted, and Lucy didn't doubt for a moment she would thrive in the right environment. She decided then and there that she would take Judith under her wing as soon as Myles Chancellor passed away.

'Do you remember this spot?' Judith asked, interrupting her thoughts.

They had reached the boundary with Somerville. 'The stile is still here. Do you recall the time I snagged my dress on it and your dear mother repaired it for me so I wouldn't get into trouble?' Lucy asked.

'Yes, but you were always in a scrape of some description,' Judith replied with a smile.

Lucy could only smile back. 'That, at least, has not changed!'

THIRTY-TWO

Lucy was shocked on finally meeting Myles Chancellor before dinner. Two footmen carried him in to the drawing room and Judith stood by with a concerned look as he was gently lowered into a chair by the fire. A decade had ravaged the once tall and regal frame, now bent with arthritis. The progress of his illness was etched on his kindly features. They had last met the evening prior to her brief Season in London. It was difficult to believe it was the same man. Every breath rattled in his chest and spots of high colour marked his sunken cheeks. Dismayed, she exchanged a sympathetic smile with Judith before coming forward to greet him.

Myles turned to her with a gracious smile. 'Lucy, I'm so glad you arrived safely. Another pretty face is such a welcome sight.' Then he snorted with laughter. 'Not that I'm referring to your rogue of an uncle.' Taking hold of both her hands, he said with a look of concern, 'But where are my manners? My deepest condolences on the loss of your husband. Such a tragedy and so young, poor man. You must have been devastated. We were shocked and saddened to hear of it, my dear.'

'Thank you, sir, you are most kind. It was difficult at first but the worst is over. Judith's invitation couldn't have come at a better time for me. I'm happy to be here amongst old friends. How are you, sir?'

With a self-effacing smile, the old man shrugged. 'As you see, my dear, this old body has all but given up on me. But I have the best of care, and I couldn't ask for a more attentive daughter.' He glanced over to Judith, his eyes shining with affection. 'This is all very pleasant, isn't it, Judith?' he said. 'I do so love company. It's just like the old days.'

The door opened and Uncle Giles strolled into the room. With an exclamation of pleasure, he walked straight up to Lucy and put his arm around her shoulders. 'How wonderful to see you again, my dear,' he said, kissing her cheek. 'You must tell me all the family news. Since Somerville has been closed up, we have only the newspapers and the gossips to rely on. Did your mother materialise in London?'

'Yes, she did, sir.'

'Poor Charlotte,' Uncle Giles chuckled. 'She always was a brazen one.'

Myles laughed and shook his head at him. 'At least *you* are free of her machinations now, my friend.'

Lucy was taken aback. Gone was the blundering, forgetful Uncle Giles. He must have picked up on her confusion for he winked before taking his seat. 'Come and sit down beside me,' he said. 'Tell me how my naughty sister fares.'

Before she had a chance to reply, the butler came in and announced, 'Mr Thorn, sir.'

Lucy almost missed the expression of distaste which passed over Judith's face for her friend quickly set her features and looked away. The vicar crossed the room and shook Mr Chancellor warmly by the hand. Acknowledging Uncle Giles with a bow, he turned his gaze expectantly towards Judith. Her friend would not meet his eye but gave him a curt nod. What was behind Judith's strange behaviour? Thorn recovered his composure quickly and came over to her, standing a little too close for comfort.

'Mrs Lawrence, so delightful to meet you again,' he drawled before taking the seat beside her. The sofa was large, but somehow he managed to sit extremely close to her. 'I understand you have come from London?' The emphasis placed on London made it abundantly clear what he thought of it and anyone who hailed from its environs.

'Yes, I arrived last night,' Lucy said.

Judith sprang up, and muttering about an extra place for dinner, escaped the room.

'I have never visited,' Mr Thorn continued, his eyes following Judith. 'The reports I hear distress me greatly. It is a steaming cesspit of immorality. I don't imagine I would like it.'

'London's loss, I'm sure, sir.'

Thorn sniffed, but thankfully Myles called over to him, requesting an update on the repairs to the church roof. Thorn moved back across the room to sit nearer to Myles.

Lucy and her uncle shared an amused glance.

'I'm jolly glad to see you, Lucy,' her uncle said.

'And I you, sir. I trust you're well?' she asked.

'Indeed I am, and never better in fact. Things have worked out well for me, my dear. Here I can potter about and no one minds me. Myles and I were at Harrow, did you know?'

'No, I didn't.'

'When he's feeling well enough, we play chess or reminisce about the old days. It gives Judith a chance to have some time alone. Frankly, her life is wearisome stuck here with us old gentlemen.'

'Oh come, I'm sure you're no trouble at all. But I suspect you may be right about Judith. I understand her sisters rarely visit or take any of the burden.'

'Aye, that's true.'

'But is it not strange to be living here, Uncle? Do you not miss the family and Somerville?' she asked.

Uncle lowered his voice with a warning glance towards the cleric. 'Much happier here by far, my dear.' Lucy saw the truth of this in his relaxed manner. 'It is only temporary, of course, for Myles is very ill.'

'Yes, so Judith informed me earlier. When Mother told me about Richard leaving, I was worried about you. It can't have been a pleasant few days after Richard's disappearing act.'

Uncle Giles chuckled softly. 'It was pure pandemonium and almost entertaining except we were caught up in it. Sibylla ran around the house screaming banshee-like at everyone. The servants downed tools as soon as they got wind of the true state of affairs, and your mother took to her bed in her typically helpful manner. Luckily, into the midst of all this chaos, Judith happened to call. When she saw my plight she came home, consulted her father and within the hour had sent a message inviting me to move here. Needless to say, no one at Somerville cared one way or the other. I bade Charlotte farewell, packed my bag and left the same afternoon.'

'I'm sorry you were treated so badly. Please remember you would always be welcome in my home. Unfortunately, I'm not quite sure where that is at the moment.' She quickly filled him in on her financial situation.

He smiled. 'Thank you for the offer, Lucy. That's most kind of you. But there's nothing for you to be sorry about. It has all turned out for the best. I was well aware I was barely tolerated at Somerville. They always made it plain what they thought of me. I was thankful to get away in the end.'

Lucy couldn't help but smile. 'Funnily enough, I felt the same the day I eloped. Forgive me, but was your absent-minded-ness some form of protection you employed?'

'I won't deny I'm becoming a little forgetful, but one

couldn't survive long at Somerville without employing strategies of some kind.'

'Was it because of Sibylla?'

'No, my dear, your mother.' He leaned closer and lowered his voice. 'Let me explain. I was the youngest of the Bradshaws, but even at the age of fourteen, I had been quite shocked by your mother's behaviour. I'm sad to say she was shrewd and manipulative even then. Old Dick Somerville, your father, was supposed to marry Gertrude, the eldest, but once Charlotte clapped eyes on him she made sure she got her claws into him first. Gertrude was deeply in love with your father and was heartbroken when he announced his engagement to Charlotte.'

'Didn't Aunt Gertrude die young?'

'Far too young. It was all hushed up at the time, but she walked out into the river which ran through our estate and kept on walking. I was the one who found her the following day. It almost broke my parents, your grandmother in particular.'

'I wasn't aware of any of this,' Lucy exclaimed, truly shocked.

'Hardly surprising, my dear. It's not something your mother should be proud of. "All's fair in love and war," was her response in a letter to our sister Beatrice on hearing the news. Your parents were on honeymoon when it happened.'

'Good God! How callous!'

With a shrug her uncle continued. 'Not long after, I joined the navy and did not set foot on English soil very often. On retiring, I was surprised to receive a letter from your mother. I can only imagine she was afraid of what I might say once back in the country and considered it safer to have me under the same roof.' He sighed. 'Perhaps I'm being too harsh, but I could never quite trust her. But my means were limited and, on the face of it, it appeared to be a godsend. However, I soon realised how things were in the house and quickly assumed the persona I did, purely to avoid trouble. Between the bickering and the strained silences, I dearly wished I was back at sea, I can tell you. Most days I hid in the library.'

'Uncle, I'm of the opinion we have both had lucky escapes.'

'Ah, the pearls. That was a nasty business,' he said, a fierce frown marring his brow.

'Did you guess what Richard and Mother were up to?' Lucy asked. When he shook his head, she revealed exactly what they had planned.

Uncle Giles gave a silent whistle. 'I suspected something was afoot but nothing as daring as that. Charlotte and Richard were always whispering in corners, but I put it down to other reasons. There was always tension in the house, and I avoided it as best I could. Then when I was told about the theft and you were carted off by the police, I did have my suspicions. But I wasn't in a position to help you, my dear, as I had no proof.'

'And, of course, they knew how difficult it would be for you to speak out being under such an obligation to them. What a pair! But please don't distress yourself about it. If you had expressed your concern, it would have made little difference for Richard had the police doing his bidding. I was fortunate, Uncle. Mr Stone realised something wasn't right about it and secured my release.'

Uncle Giles looked thoughtful. 'A clever gentleman, from what I saw of him. He interviewed me briefly the morning he arrived, though Richard tried to prevent it.' Giles chuckled. 'I may have dropped a few hints to him that all was not what it seemed at Somerville.'

'Then I have you to thank!' Lucy exclaimed. 'Mr Stone claimed he suspected Richard through his superior powers of detection.' She sniffed. 'And I was so impressed.'

'I'm delighted if my little contribution helped you. However, it is my belief you make your own luck in this life,' her uncle said. 'Most of all, you need to know who to turn to when you encounter trouble.'

For some reason, Phin's face popped into Lucy's head. 'But what if you're too scared to trust?'

'Then you must evaluate the risk,' he replied, taking her hand and squeezing it gently. 'Isolating yourself might make you feel safe, but I can't think of a quicker path to loneliness and despair.'

THIRTY-THREE

Next morning Mary was putting the final touches to Lucy's hair when there was a tap at the bedroom door. They had been discussing what to do next about the sapphires, but couldn't agree. After cutting down most of Mary's wilder ideas, Lucy was still unsure how to proceed. Judith's appearance was a welcome diversion.

'Only me,' Judith said, advancing into the room.

'Thank you, Mary,' Lucy said pointedly, smothering a smile at the maid's mulish expression.

'Come in, come in,' she said, turning around in the chair and watching Mary stomp from the room. 'Now, I'm so glad to have an opportunity for a chat, Judith. For I suspect after what I observed last night, you need to unburden yourself, my friend.'

Judith's eyes fluttered and her cheeks turned pink. 'Excuse me!'

'The *Thorn* in your side, is all I'm going to say.'

A nauseous expression flitted across Judith's face. Collapsing down on the edge of the bed, she gave a helpless gesture. 'What am I to do? Such a disagreeable man.'

'How do you tolerate him? The way he watches you is

unnerving. All through dinner last night, I wanted to slap his arrogant face and tell him off for being so insolent.'

'But I have no choice but to accept him as a guest. Father enjoys his company, and they share a love of poetry.'

'Good grief! That's one mark in his favour, but hardly sufficient reason to tolerate his ways.'

'That's easy to say, but you don't understand. Until your Uncle Giles came to stay we had few visitors. Mr Thorn's predecessor, Mr Quake, do you remember him?'

'Yes. A bit stuffy but a pleasant enough man.'

'Mr Thorn came to the parish as his curate and accompanied him on his visits to Father. When Mr Quake died a couple of years ago, Mr Thorn was promoted and has haunted us with his presence ever since. He's a nuisance. Several times a week he turns up for dinner. Father is too kind-hearted to say anything; he feels sorry for him.'

'Is he not received elsewhere? You should hint he's neglecting his duties by ignoring other families and risks upsetting them. He strikes me as the kind of man who likes to be seen to do the right thing.'

'On the contrary, Lucy, he's popular in the neighbourhood,' Judith said. 'The general opinion is that he's a man of high morals and surprisingly rousing in the pulpit.'

Lucy recoiled at the image. 'Now I'll have nightmares tonight, thank you very much.'

Judith giggled. 'Lucy! I must own, he speaks well. You will see for yourself on Sunday.'

Lucy blew out her cheeks. 'If you say so.'

'It wouldn't be so bad if we only saw him in church,' Judith said with a frown.

'But, there has to be a "but".'

'The man is trying to wear me down.'

Lucy stared at her friend. 'Thorn had the audacity to propose to you?'

'Yes, and I have made it clear I'm not interested.'

'Surely your father has put him in his place? Why he's far beneath you in every way.'

'Unfortunately, Father gave his blessing initially when Mr Thorn approached him. I refused him, of course, but it put Father in a difficult position. He knows he doesn't have many months left and fears for my future when he's gone.'

'Who will inherit the estate?' Lucy asked.

'My eldest nephew.'

'Please say you won't give in to that beastly man. You can come and throw your lot in with me.'

Judith's eyes welled up. 'Thank you. But don't worry. Although I do not have either your charm or beauty and I have had few suitors over the years, I have no intention of accepting Mr Thorn.'

'Good! Would you like me to mark his card? Trust me, I would be only too happy. I have nothing to lose and it was quite clear last night he considers me beyond salvation. Those snide remarks about my family, though perfectly correct, were hardly appropriate. And you shouldn't have to put up with his unctuous ways.'

Judith walked over to her and placed a hand on her shoulder. 'You're kind to offer, but it will not be necessary. I'm made of sterner stuff than you think.'

'It's just I would hate to see you throw yourself away on such a nincompoop.'

Judith sighed. 'I have missed you all these years. You could always put into words what I feared to.'

Lucy laughed. 'And always in trouble because of it.'

'When you eloped I wasn't surprised,' Judith said. 'Even as a child you were restless. Always dreaming. Is that your wedding photograph? May I see?' She picked up the frame from the dressing table and looked at it closely.

'What is it?' Lucy asked. Judith was frowning and staring intently at the photograph.

Judith tapped the picture. 'This is your Charlie?'

'Yes.'

'But I met him some months ago!'

A tingle of excitement ran through Lucy. 'Where?' she demanded.

'On the road from the village. I was out for a walk when a gig pulled up beside me. The gentleman asked the way to Somerville Hall. Yes, it was definitely him.' Judith turned to her with a frown. 'But you were both estranged from the family. Why on earth would he be going there?'

'I have my suspicions. You had better sit down again, Judith. You will not believe what I'm about to tell you.'

By the time she had finished her story, Judith was staring at her, aghast.

'Are you not terrified?' Judith asked. 'All of these unsavoury characters are watching your every move. Your life has been threatened, your home ransacked.'

'I'll admit it has been rather unsettling. But don't worry, we weren't followed. I would not put you in danger like that. By now Marsh must have realised I have left London, but he can't know where I have gone. You are quite safe.'

'It's not my safety I'm concerned about, but yours,' Judith said.

'Yes, and I do appreciate your concern for my welfare... but the problem is I may need your assistance. My best guess is the sapphires are hidden somewhere in Somerville Hall.'

'But the house is closed up now. You can't get in.'

'I'll have to find a way, Judith. The gems have to be there. I'm convinced Charlie had them when he arrived in York but he returned to London without them. They weren't in the safe at the hotel so he must have hidden them on his visit to Somerville.

Most likely, he considered it was the last place anyone would look. Don't forget, he was desperate and if he hadn't revealed to Marsh his familial link to Richard, it would make sense. Besides, Marsh can't have made the connection, or even known about Charlie's visit to Yorkshire, if he's still watching me. His men would have ransacked Somerville Hall months ago if he had the least suspicion the sapphires were there.'

'But would Richard not have used them to free himself from debt once he knew Charlie was dead?'

'Charlie wouldn't have confided in him. Remember, Charlie must have brought Richard into the scheme. Richard invested a lot of money and lost it all. He even sold the town-house in London to raise more funds to invest in the Padar mine. Their last meeting can't have been pleasant for either of them. I doubt they trusted one another. Perhaps Charlie's conscience got the better of him, and he came here to warn Richard. We'll never know for sure. No, Richard couldn't have known Charlie had the sapphires and left them behind. If he had known they were within reach, he would hardly have bothered staging the theft of Mother's pearls.'

'I suppose so. What will you do?'

Lucy glanced out the window. 'Look, it's a fine day and I hate to be cooped up. A stroll would be just the thing. Would you care to accompany me later?'

Judith's alarm showed in her face. 'Would this stroll take us anywhere near Somerville?'

Lucy jumped up and embraced her. 'What a jolly idea, Judith! I knew I could rely on you.'

Once Judith had left, Lucy paced the room, trying to think clearly. If she was to have any chance of recovering those gems, she would have to use logic. But no inspiration was forthcoming and eventually she sat down on the window seat, cursing her stupidity. Her eye fell on the satchel where it lay on the bedside table. It had to be important, but why? What had she missed? But staring at it wasn't going to help. Her gut feeling was Charlie had deliberately left it in the safe hoping it would be found or handed over to her when Haywood wanted payment. Lucy walked over and picked it up, feeling the old leather with her fingers. Then she emptied the contents out on to the bed. She had to be methodical, for surely that was how any investigator would work. Firstly, she probed the inside of the satchel to see if there were any hidden pockets or flaps. Nothing, so she put it aside. She picked up the drawstring velvet bag and examined it closely. She turned it inside out. But there was nothing to even suggest the sapphires had ever been in the bag.

Frustrated, she sat down on the bed and turned her attention to the documents. Slowly, she read down the lists of names, hoping one of them would trigger an idea or a clue. But again, she was left confused for it looked like a genuine list of shareholder names and addresses, nothing more. As she was folding the papers over, she once again was confronted by the strange doodle and the blocks of letters. Her heart began to race as she wondered if they had significance and weren't mere absent-minded squiggles. Charlie must have realised his life was in danger and the possibility of ever returning for the gems was faint. Faced with that knowledge, had he decided to trust her, knowing the satchel would most likely end up in her possession? Had Charlie left some kind of clue? Lucy laid the three sheets with the printed sides face down on the bed and read across the blocks of letters.

STAL, LGH, ANM

She rearranged them but they still made no word she recognised. Staring at them brought no insight, but they had to mean something. Was it a word or phrase in a foreign language? It made no sense, just a stupid senseless puzzle... but then it slowly dawned on her. Snatching up the sheets, she brought them over to the dressing table. From her escritoire she pulled out a blank sheet of writing paper and a pen. It had to be an anagram of some kind. She worked furiously, with a thumping heart. It didn't take long, and when Lucy was finished, she stared down at the page in disbelief.

After luncheon, while she was waiting for Judith to change into more suitable outdoor clothes for their walk, Lucy tracked down Uncle Giles. Her hope was he might remember seeing Charlie at Somerville Hall.

She found him snoozing in the small parlour, a book open on his knee.

With a delicate cough, she managed to wake him from his slumber.

'Ah, my dear, there you are,' he said as he straightened up. 'Nothing like forty winks. How are you today?'

Lucy drew up a chair beside him. 'I'm well, thank you, Uncle. I'm sorry to disturb you, but I wondered if you would be able to help me?' Lucy showed him her wedding photograph. 'This is Charlie, my late husband. Do you recall ever seeing him at Somerville? I'm fairly certain he visited Richard in October last year.'

Uncle Giles peered at it for a few moments. He then regarded her with a serious expression. 'Why do you want to know?'

Something about his tone made Lucy's skin prickle with excitement. 'It's very important for I believe there's some connection between you and my Charlie. He left this clue for me.' She pulled out the sheet of paper and showed him the solution to the anagram: *HMS Gallant.*

Uncle Giles smiled. 'I was beginning to despair you would ever figure it out.'

Lucy exhaled slowly, watching his face closely. 'Did he speak to you that day?'

'Aye, he did. It was a brief meeting, you understand. He was in a tearing hurry to get to York to catch a train to London.'

'How long did he stay at Somerville?'

Uncle Giles rubbed his beard. 'He was closeted with Richard in the library for several hours. We crossed paths as he was leaving, as I said. I was returning from a walk around the park. Somerville is always glorious in the autumn.' Lucy nodded impatiently. 'Yes, well, he approached me and asked who I was. When he learned of my connection to you and my profession, he asked me if I could be trusted with a dangerous secret. I was taken aback, of course, but assured him I could. Do you remember the old summerhouse down at the far end of the lake?'

'Yes, of course.'

'I brought him there as I knew it was out of sight of the house and any prying eyes. He was a deeply troubled young man, and I was honoured he took me into his confidence. We didn't have much time to come up with a plan. He divulged little, only that his life was in danger, and it was vital that you receive some documents and interpret them correctly.'

'Why was he going back to London? Was he going to the police?'

'I don't know, my dear, he didn't say.' He stood up. 'You must excuse me, I need to fetch the note he left for you.'

'A note? Why did you not give it to me at Christmas?'

He paused at the door. 'Ah! He was very particular. Told me I had to wait for you to come to *me* and ask about him or that,' he said, pointing to the sheet of paper. 'I made sure to mention *Gallant* at Christmas. Do you not remember? I hoped it might trigger something for you. But I didn't know if you had received the documents yet. My understanding was that it was imperative you received everything in the right order or it wouldn't make any sense.'

'I see!' Lucy exclaimed. She could never have imagined Charlie to be so cunning.

'I'll be as quick as I can,' he said.

As she watched Uncle Giles quit the room, she thanked heaven Charlie had known who to trust in the end. Sitting with her hands tightly clenched, her anger at Charlie's machinations soon softened to exasperation. Of course, if her uncle had given her the note at Christmas, she would not have known what it related to. It was unlikely Charlie told him about the sapphires, so Uncle Giles would not have been in a position to enlighten her anyway. Most likely she would have discarded the note or ignored it. The idea made her blood run cold.

Moments later, Giles reappeared. With a concerned look, he gave her a folded piece of paper. 'I didn't read it, my dear. I gave him my word.'

'Of course. Thank you, Uncle,' she said.

'I'll leave you in peace to read it then.'

On hearing the door close, Lucy unfolded the scrap of paper. It was Charlie's writing. From the look of it, it had been scrawled in a hurry. It was dated the sixteenth of October.

Dear Lucy,

If you're reading this, my worst fears have been realised. Try not to be too angry with me. I intend to do the right thing, but there are certain people who are anxious I do not. It has all become such a muddle. Hopefully, you're looking for what I have hidden. I know you will leave no stone unturned for me. You were always a great one for puzzles. Put that skill to work, my dearest.

I'm sorry. Too late, I have realised how much I have thrown away: your love, your respect and our happiness. I could fill three sheets of paper, begging your forgiveness, but I would not blame you for turning your back. Try to remember me with kindness.

Charlie

'Damnation, Charlie!' she whispered. 'It *is* too late and I can't forgive.'

There was no new insight in the note. She already had the three sheets of paper and had found the anagram. Was she missing something obvious? She read the note again several times, but it just made her temper rise. She groaned in frustration as she crushed the piece of paper. Of all the times to be cryptic, Charlie, Lucy thought with a savage shake of her head, it wasn't now. The note was no help at all.

THIRTY-FOUR

Somerville Hall

'It has always struck me as particularly foolish for heroines in novels to insist on having their adventures at night. I can only suppose it is for dramatic effect, for it must be far more sensible to do these things in daylight,' Lucy remarked as they crossed over the stile and on to Somerville land.

'And I believe it is particularly stupid to have adventures at all when one could be comfortably by the fire, reading something of higher literary value than those low-brow books,' Judith countered.

'Oh come, are you trying to tell me you have never read any of those remarkable adventures? Mary adores them and always leaves them lying about. I enjoy them immensely for they are some of the funniest books I have ever read. They are so wonderfully bad and utterly predictable.'

'Mary is a maid and knows no better,' Judith replied. 'You, however, should.'

'Do I detect the influence of the good pastor on your morals?'

'Don't be nasty!'

Lucy laughed and linked her friend's arm. 'You're far too sensitive, my dear, and you weren't so craven when we were children. I recall many an adventure in your company. Remember the day we had to run for our lives when Farmer Tomkins's cow charged at us? It was your idea to go into that field.'

'Yes, it was, but I'm sure you somehow put the idea in my head. The only time I was ever in trouble was with you.'

Trudging through the undergrowth, they headed towards a path that circled Somerville Hall beneath the trees. Mary, who was proving unsurpassed in spying, had ascertained from the Blackheath Manor servants what was happening at Somerville. It was reported to be swarming with men, employed by the bank to catalogue and remove all items of value. The wagons had been seen on the road to Harrogate. An auction house there was said to be the destination of the Somerville Hall contents. On hearing this, Lucy panicked and decided they had to gain access to the house as quickly as possible. The sapphires could be hidden anywhere or in anything. It would be too cruel for them to be removed and lost forever or fall into the wrong hands now she was so close to finding them.

Judith asked. 'How do we explain our presence?'

'I have no intention of being seen. Shh, look!' From the edge of the trees they had a good view of the front of the house. A group of labourers were wrestling with a large sideboard, trying to load it on to a wagon. 'Bother! I hope we are not too late,' Lucy muttered.

'This is a fool's errand. Somerville is huge. It may take weeks to go through it.'

Lucy turned impatiently. 'Charlie was only in there for a couple of hours, so there are a limited number of places he could have hidden the gems.'

'That's assuming he hid them there at all.'

Only too conscious of the possible truth of this, Lucy shrugged. 'Come along, the rear of the house may be quieter.'

But to her dismay, there was as much activity at the back of the kitchens as the front carriageway.

'Perhaps the novel writers have it right,' Judith remarked. 'We will have to return when it's dark.'

Eight hours later, they viewed the edifice of Somerville Hall with some trepidation. An easterly wind had picked up and, despite warm winter coats, they shivered beneath the trees. What had seemed a lark in daylight now bore the coldness of reality. After dinner, both Judith and Lucy had made their excuses, proclaiming the need for an early night. They had met up with Mary as pre-arranged at the back of the stables.

'Keep the lantern covered, Mary,' Lucy whispered. 'There might be someone standing guard. Wait here, you two. I'll skirt around the house and see if I can spot anyone.'

'Be careful,' whispered Judith.

'Don't worry, I can find my way around these grounds even in the darkness.'

Lucy slipped away, keeping behind the trees. With only a sliver of a moon, she had to pick her way along the path, terrified she would make a noise and alert a watchman. Every sound was amplified. A crack when she stepped on a twig almost gave her heart failure. Her spirit of adventure was being seriously challenged. *If only Phin were here.* The treacherous thought was unwelcome, and she pushed it to the back of her mind. Hadn't reliance on men been her downfall?

It was almost ten minutes later when she rejoined her fellow conspirators. 'I can't see anyone at all,' she told them breathlessly. 'They must be relying on good locks. Isn't that lucky?'

'How so?' Judith asked.

'No one to hinder us or cause... difficulties,' Lucy said. The seriousness of what she was proposing could easily spook Judith, and she knew her friend was looking for an excuse to abandon the scheme.

'How do you propose we gain entry?' Judith asked at last. 'Are you going to ask the bank for permission?'

'Eh, no, Judith, I don't think so. There's no time to lose, and they would not give it anyway. We have to break in tonight.'

Judith gasped. '*Break in!* You can't be serious, Lucy. How can you even contemplate such a lawless act?'

'Easily, Judith. In a few more days there will be nothing left inside the house. There's no alternative. We must act now.'

'Ma'am, might I suggest I try the kitchen door?' Mary said, her voice brimming with excitement. 'They are often left unlocked.'

'Good idea.' Lucy squeezed her maid's arm in gratitude and watched as she scooted along the path before breaking out into the open. Soon she had disappeared behind the kitchen garden wall.

An owl hooted somewhere above them and Judith jumped. 'I must be mad,' she muttered. Lucy ignored her, her eyes straining to see and her ears cocked for the slightest sound. Minutes later, Mary came racing towards them.

'No one around, ma'am, as you said. But there's a padlock on the kitchen door. I tried the windows, but they are all locked too.'

'This is hopeless,' Judith whispered.

Lucy shot her a stern look. 'Not at all. Either we break the lock on the door...'

'But with what, ma'am?' Mary interjected.

'...good point, Mary. We didn't bring anything suitable in the way of tools. Very well, it will have to be breaking a window. It will make a noise, but as there's no one about—' Lucy continued.

'They will realise in the morning someone has broken in, ma'am. We will have to find the sapphires tonight,' Mary said.

'Agreed. They will definitely post a watchman tomorrow night once our activities are discovered. Ladies, are you ready?'

Mary was almost jumping up and down with excitement. Judith, however, wore an anguished expression.

'Would you prefer to stay here and keep watch, Judith? I don't want you to do anything you'd rather not. After all, it would ruin your chances with Mr Thorn if he were to learn of your clandestine activities.'

Judith pursed her lips as if to take offence, but ruined it by starting to smile. 'I wonder what he would say if he saw me now? Give me the lantern, Mary. I'll keep watch.'

'Thank you,' Lucy said, then turned to Mary. 'Do you have the candles?'

Mary patted her pocket. 'Yes, and the matches.'

'Good girl. Let's go!'

They started off down the path. 'Wait!' Judith called. 'How will I warn you if someone comes?'

'Can you hoot like an owl or whistle?'

'Whoo, whoo,' Judith attempted. It was barely audible.

'Perfect,' Lucy said, pushing a sniggering Mary ahead of her.

For a few heart-stopping seconds, Lucy and Mary clung to each other in the kitchen. But no one came charging in to discover them, despite the loud crack as the stone had hit the window pane and the mild swearing as Mary had caught her skirt on a shard as she had passed through the frame. Lucy fingered the cold metal of the pistol where it lay snugly in her pocket. It gave her some reassurance though she hoped she would not have to use it.

'Careful, don't walk on the broken glass,' Lucy whispered.

She tried to remember the layout of the kitchen. 'The lamps used to be kept over on the far dresser. See if you can find one, Mary.'

She heard the rasp of the striking match and a minute later, Mary handed her a lantern with a lit candle inside. Holding it up, she surveyed the room by the weak light. There were boxes everywhere: some were half filled, others were nailed closed. 'Good Lord!' she exclaimed. 'They must be going to auction everything. We need not bother with the kitchen. Charlie would not have been down here. Follow me.'

They headed up the servants' stairs and came out into the hall through the green baize door. It was eerily quiet and dark. Lucy swung the lantern up. Again, large boxes, crates and heaps of straw lay scattered about. The fireplace held the remains of a fire, the unclean grate confirming her uncle's tale of the servants abandoning the house. Suddenly, her heart dropped. They were probably too late. But determined to at least try, she made straight for the library. If Uncle Giles was to be relied upon, this was the place Charlie spent most of his time during his visit to Somerville Hall and the most likely location of the hidden sapphires.

Setting her lantern down on the desk, she took stock. Someone was cataloguing the collection of books, as a hand-written list of titles lay on the desk. The upper shelves were already bare.

'I hope we are not too late. It looks as though some books have been crated already,' Lucy said to Mary.

'Most of these boxes are shut tight, ma'am,' Mary said from the other side of the room. 'They have been nailed down. What do you want to do? Should we open them?'

Lucy was flummoxed. It would take too long to go through all the boxes. She tried to put herself in Charlie's shoes. Where would he have hidden them? Hardly on the top shelves as he probably only had a few minutes alone at most. Logic suggested

he might have stuffed them behind some books lower down or
into a piece of furniture. Somewhere accessible.

'Only if we have to, Mary. Leave them for now. Check all
the shelves with books still to be packed. I'll examine the
furniture.'

They worked in silence. Lucy swept her fingers under the
desk and pulled out every drawer, checking the underside of
each one. Nothing. Moving around the room, she prodded and
poked the upholstery of the remaining chairs. Again, nothing.
From Mary's muttering, she knew she wasn't faring any better.

'Look, ma'am!' Mary exclaimed, suddenly. Lucy rushed
over to her. Mary was pointing to a safe, which had been hidden
behind some books. With trembling fingers, Lucy pulled on the
door. It swung open. Both sighed with disappointment. It was
empty.

'I've checked all of these,' Mary said, waving to encompass
the shelves. Lucy sat down at the desk.

'Oh ma'am, what about the curtains?' Mary flew over to the
windows and started to feel along the hems of the heavy drapes.
'There is something here.'

'Most likely the weights. Unless you can find a hole in the
hem where he might have made an opening?'

Lucy watched her search. Eventually, Mary rose up,
shaking her head.

Lucy thumped the desk in frustration, all her hopes dashed.
This was a complete waste of time.

THIRTY-FIVE

Mary sat down on a crate, her expression glum, while Lucy racked her brains. 'It must be this room. What am I missing? Come on, Mary, do you have any ideas?'

Mary shook her head. 'Sorry, ma'am. I don't think we are going to find them. We have looked everywhere. Perhaps Mr Lawrence didn't hide them here after all. Might he have hidden them in his hotel room in York?'

'Good God, don't say that, Mary! No. He would not have risked leaving them in so public a location. This is the only logical place.'

As Lucy's gaze passed across the fireplace, something glittered high up on the chimney breast. Intrigued, she stood up and held the lantern aloft. The stag's eyes loomed out of the darkness, cold and ghastly. As if mocking her.

Lucy shivered. 'Oh, that vile old thing,' she complained, pointing it out to Mary. 'I'm not surprised it hasn't been taken down. I can't imagine anyone would want to buy it and have it in their home. It would give you nightmares.'

Mary looked up and grimaced. 'I hate those animal heads, ma'am. Something ghoulish about 'em, isn't there? Why people want them, I don't know. Not natural. Now pets that are alive, they're useful. Like poor old Horace. A great ratter, was Horace... ma'am, what's the matter? Are you all right?'

Lucy stood stock-still, staring up at the stag's head. Her heart began to pound, her mind galloping as the most fantastic idea had just popped into her head. The sketch of the horn; she could see it in her mind's eye. Had Charlie left a better clue after all? A hunting reference: a stag's head! It was certainly tenuous, but he did say he was leaving her a puzzle. How did he reach up so high? Desperately, she tried to recall the few times she had been in the room at Christmas. Yes, she was sure there had been chairs placed either side of the fireplace and Charlie had been over six feet tall. The possibility was real if he had had enough time.

'Hold this for me,' she said, hurriedly pushing the lantern towards Mary. Frantically, she looked for something on which to stand, cursing her own lack of height. One of the wooden crates nearby was half full and she was able to drag it over to the fireplace. Mary regarded her as though she were mad, but Lucy had the strangest feeling her luck was about to turn. Placing a lid on top, she hitched her skirts up and by levering herself off Mary's shoulder she could stand on the lid of the crate.

'Oh, do be careful,' Mary exclaimed as Lucy reached up. The lid twisted slightly under her feet but she was just about able to reach the stag's head. It was revolting to touch. The animal's hair was matted and slick with years' worth of grime. She had to swallow her disgust. Offering up a little prayer, Lucy continued to probe the head. Eventually, she found a slit behind one of the ears, but it was too high up for her fingers to reach inside. Tugging at the head, she grew increasingly frustrated as she could get no purchase on it. Whoever had placed it there had never meant for it to come down again.

'Can you find me something to use as a lever?' Lucy asked.

She watched as Mary ran down the room with the lantern, searching amongst the crates.

Seconds later Mary returned, a wide grin on her face. 'How about this?' she asked, handing Lucy up a wicked-looking crowbar.

'You're worth your weight in gold, Mary O'Reilly,' Lucy said, grasping it. 'Remind me to increase your wages.' Mary giggled.

With some tinkering Lucy was able to wedge the crowbar under the base of the head. 'Here goes!' She pushed the crowbar upwards with all her might. There was a loud crack and the stag's head, along with a quantity of plaster and dirt, came hurtling towards her. Banging against her shoulder, it crashed to the floor. Unbalanced and in pain, Lucy followed, landing in an undignified heap on the ground. Winded, she could only stare up at the ceiling.

Mary squealed and rushed to her side. 'Are you badly hurt, ma'am? Oh, speak to me!'

Lucy sucked in her breath. Her shoulder was on fire and her vision was momentarily blurred. Mary helped her up to a sitting position. 'I'll live,' she said through clenched teeth, leaning back against the crate. 'Quick, check the side of it. I found a hole behind the right ear.'

Mary scrambled across the floor on her knees. With a grunt, she pushed the heavy stag's head over on to its side, its ugly snout resting on the floor. She rummaged around for a few moments then froze.

'What is it?' Lucy called out. 'Have you found something? Quick, tell me!'

Mary slowly drew her fingers out. Dangling between them was a velvet drawstring bag, identical to the one they had found in the satchel.

Lucy caught her breath. 'Well?' Hardly daring to hope, she watched as Mary gently fingered the bag. Slowly a huge grin spread across the maid's features. She loosened the string and tipped the bag. Three dark blue stones slid out onto her palm. Mary stared down at them, transfixed.

Relief flooded through Lucy as she stared at the sapphires. She might easily have missed the stag's head and gone home with nothing.

Gingerly, she got to her feet and joined Mary as the maid placed the stones on the desk and pulled the lantern close.

'They're not terribly pretty, ma'am, are they?' Mary said. 'Feel how rough they are. Are these really sapphires?'

'This is their natural state. These are what come out of the mine,' Lucy said, turning one over, marvelling at the depth of colour as she held it to the light. 'A jeweller has to cut and polish them, before setting them in a necklace or a ring. Once finished, these would be magnificent.'

Mary didn't look convinced. 'I thought they'd be more sparkly. Like the lovely diamond bracelet you used to have.'

'They are still worth a king's ransom, even in this uncut state.' Lucy scooped them up. She wrapped them in the handkerchief she had bought in Jay's.

'Fetch me some clinkers from the grate, Mary.'

Mary did as she bid, then stood beside her and watched as she put some small clinkers in the velvet drawstring bag.

'Why are you doing that, ma'am?'

'This is a precaution, in case we are intercepted; it might give us some time,' she said. Then she shoved the handkerchief containing the gems down the front of her bodice and the little bag in her coat pocket. Mary's eyes popped. 'They should be safe there. Now we had better get back to Judith and tell her the good news. I only hope she hasn't frozen to death on the spot.'

Once they had safely negotiated the kitchen window with its jagged shards of glass, they cautiously made their way through the walled kitchen garden. When they reached the gate, Lucy stopped, squinting towards the trees. 'I don't see her lantern, do you?'

'No, but it may have gone out on her and she doesn't have any spare candles or matches.'

'You may be right. It should be safe but let's be quick. On the count of three, run for the cover of the woods.'

Lucy sprinted across the grass with Mary close behind. It was only a short distance but was like a lifetime to Lucy. When she stopped, her shoulder throbbed horribly, and she had to suck in her breath to relieve the pain. Once it had eased, she scanned the area for Judith but in vain. 'Where is she? I'm sure this is where we left her,' she muttered.

'Perhaps she's moving around to keep warm?' Mary suggested.

Lucy didn't want to alarm Mary, but she suddenly felt vulnerable. What if someone *had* followed them and hurt Judith? She should never have involved her.

'I'm not sure, but we can't stay here. Follow the path; she must have returned to the house,' she whispered.

As they moved forward, there was a pull on Lucy's skirt. Frustrated, she tugged it and heard a ripping sound as the fabric tore. Something was clinging to it. 'Mary, I'm caught in a bramble. Be a dear and go ahead. See if you can find Miss Chancellor. I'll catch up in a minute.'

Mary took off, softly calling out for Miss Chancellor. It took a few minutes for Lucy to untangle herself from the bramble and when she looked up, she was alone in the darkness. Blast! Mary had taken the lantern with her. A prickle of fear went down her spine. Beneath the trees it was almost impossible to see the path so she would have to trust to memory. A sudden gust of wind shook the branches above her head. They creaked and groaned in response. Her heart struck up a drum tattoo.

Then there was a rustle in the undergrowth to her left. She froze. Now I'm being silly. *It's only a rabbit*, she thought, *stay calm.*

Crack!

Somehow, she managed to pull the pistol from her pocket. Pulling back the safety catch, she aimed and fired in the direction of the noise. There was a yelp of pain and something crashed down. Maybe it was a some*one*? Lucy didn't wait to find out who or what it was. She took off in a panic-stricken run.

Some minutes later she stumbled out in to a clearing near the boundary with Blackheath, to find the two women, clinging to each other, trying unsuccessfully to hide behind some bushes near the stile. She was overwhelmed with relief.

'Where did you two get to?' Lucy asked, as she stood trying to catch her breath.

Judith stepped forward. 'I'm sorry, Lucy, I was sure someone was coming through the trees. I tried to hoot, but I was so afraid, my throat seized up. I decided to go to Blackheath for help, but Mary caught up with me. Then we heard what sounded like a gunshot. Did you hear it?'

'Yes, that was me,' Lucy replied calmly, holding up the pistol.

'Lucy!' Judith exclaimed, taking a step back and staring at the gun in horror. 'This is outrageous! You never told me you had a gun.'

'Wasn't it lucky I had? Whoever was spying on us is discommoded now.'

'You can't go around shooting people!'

'You can if they mean you harm,' Lucy retorted. 'Come on, let's return to Blackheath. I have no idea how many of them there are. They may be following me even as we speak.'

Lucy made for the stile, the others close behind. But she was angry and halted halfway over the wall. 'Do you know,' she said turning around. 'I'm tired of running. I want to know who is spying on me. You two return to the house. I'm going back to investigate.'

THIRTY-SIX

With her pistol drawn, Lucy crept along the path, her heart thumping. For several minutes she heard nothing but the creaking of the branches above her head and the distant cries of nocturnal creatures. She stopped every so often, straining to hear. There! That wasn't the wind, it was more like whispering. Terrified she would give herself away, she advanced inch by inch, praying her luck would hold.

'I'm sorry, George. This is most unfortunate,' she heard a voice remarkably similar to Stone's say. 'Here, let me help you sit up. Where were you hit?'

Lucy froze and almost squeaked. It *was* Phin!

'Right arm, sir,' she heard George respond.

The voices were coming from behind some nearby trees. She crept closer and dropped down in to the undergrowth, squinting into the darkness. Suddenly a match flared and a lantern was lit. Now she could see the two men. Phineas was on his knees next to George, who was sitting up against a tree. Phineas was holding up the lantern and examining George's arm. If she hadn't heard Phineas's voice she would not have recognised either man. What a fool she had been and how dare

he! They had followed her from London, both in disguise.
George was in an army uniform; he must have been the man
Mary saw peering into their carriage. And Phineas was dressed
as an elderly man, with glasses and a grey beard and wig,
looking much like the fellow at the station in the waiting room
reading his newspaper. How could she have been so careless?
She groaned; he would have heard everything she said to Mary
on opening the satchel.

She had never felt so close to despair. The game was up,
for he must know she had a good reason for breaking into an
empty house late at night. Could they have seen their exploits
in the library? The curtains had been open. Of course
they had.

'Let me take a closer look,' Phineas said, holding the lantern
up again. 'Damn it! That's a lot of blood.'

'Is it bad, sir?' George asked. A pang of guilt hit her. Poor
George!

'You may have been lucky. It's a deep graze, but the bullet
doesn't appear to have lodged. We need to stem the bleeding
though.' Phineas put the lantern down, took a handkerchief
from his pocket, then pulled off his necktie and used it to bind
up the wound.

'Sir! Not the new Ascot tie!'

'Do be quiet!' Phin exclaimed as he made a knot in the tie.
'Can you make it to the gig if I help you? We can't stay here.
We'll freeze to death and there's a distinct possibility the ladies
will raise the alarm. It's not too far to the inn at Blackheath
village.'

'I'll do my best, sir, if you think it safe to move?'

'I do. My apologies, George, this is my fault. I shall be more
careful in future about arming young ladies.'

Lucy flinched at his words and watched as he heaved
George to his feet.

'Not at all, sir. It was entirely *my* fault for standing on that stick. I'm sure the lady was frightened. It was a natural reaction in the circumstances.'

'Sometimes, George...'

'Sir?'

'Oh, never mind.' Phineas put George's arm around his shoulders, supporting him. Lucy crouched down in the undergrowth, holding her breath, thankful she had worn dark clothing. They passed close to her, moving off towards the boundary. She counted to ten before tailing them through the trees.

From the beginning Lucy had known Phineas suspected her of being involved in Charlie's tomfoolery, but had hoped she had laid his fears to rest. Unless he had let her think that to gain her trust? She remembered that evening at his rooms when he had comforted her. Had that interlude been false?

Of course, haring off to Yorkshire and following clues meant she was now deceiving *him*, but only because he had not been honest with her. She still couldn't come up with a benign reason for him to be on terms with Coffin Mike and that scoundrel was the only possible source of information that she had made a suspicious-looking exit from London. But Coffin Mike couldn't have figured out she was fleeing to Yorkshire, so how had Phin traced her to York?

Oh bother, she thought, why did it all have to be so complicated? The only reason he could be here was the sapphires and now he knew she had them. What chance of success did she have pitting her meagre skills against his? But was he working for Marsh, the maharajah or himself? Twenty thousand pounds was, of course, extremely motivating. And, with such a large reward for their safe return, what was he capable of to achieve his goal? For all his suave and sophisticated manner, he couldn't be as successful as everyone claimed without being utterly ruthless too. It was galling; she had underestimated him.

There was nothing to be achieved by following them

further. She stood and watched the pair melt into the darkness. All the way to Blackheath, Lucy mulled over her next move.

Just after dawn the following morning, the three women were in the Chancellor carriage heading for York. After tossing and turning most of the night, swinging between guilt at hurting George and anger at Phineas, Lucy had eventually come up with a plan. Now her mind was in turmoil and her stomach was twisting. What she was about to attempt was verging on suicidal, but she had little choice with Phineas closing in. She glanced across at Mary, kitted out in her widow's clothes, which had been hastily adjusted to fit. Mary was slightly smaller, but Lucy hoped it would be enough to fool anyone following them.

The carriage took a sharp bend and swerved. She briefly glimpsed a solitary figure muffled up in a cape, driving a gig in the opposite direction. She was certain it was Phineas.

'Bother!' she exclaimed.

'What is it?' Judith asked clutching her arm.

'Mr Stone has seen us—he was driving the gig that just passed us.'

'Don't worry, he'll never catch us.'

'No. But he will see our bags and work out our destination,' Lucy said crossly.

'Just as well we have a plan then, isn't it?' Judith answered with a smile.

Half an hour later the carriage swept along Queen Street towards the station, then slowed down as pre-arranged. Lucy pulled her borrowed hat down low on her forehead and wrapped Judith's scarf around her neck.

'Wish me luck, ladies. I think I'll need it,' Lucy said.

'Are you sure about this, Lucy?' Judith asked, grabbing her

hand and squeezing it. 'Perhaps we should go to the police instead.'

'What? They would not believe us. This is my best chance. Play your parts and I'll have enough time to get away.' Judith tried to smile but still looked worried. Lucy turned to Mary. 'You're a good sport to do this, Mary. I won't forget it. When you get back to London, go stay with your sister, and I'll contact you when all is well.'

Mary's eyes filled with tears. 'The best of luck, ma'am!'

'Please be careful, Lucy,' Judith urged.

'I will, Judith, and thank you for everything. Some day we will laugh about this,' Lucy said, hoping she wasn't tempting fate.

As soon as the carriage came to a stop as pre-arranged with the coachman, Lucy alighted and walked away from the station. After a few yards, she paused and looked back. The carriage was at the station entrance. Lucy waited to see the two women go inside before she moved off in the opposite direction. Hopefully, the ladies would be seen getting their tickets. As she reached the top of the road, Lucy saw Phineas driving his gig at full speed down towards the station. So far so good.

Half an hour later, Lucy snuck into the train station through a side entrance, and, head down, made for the Ladies' Waiting Room. From here she could keep an eye on the ticket office and the platforms. She soon spotted Phineas and his servant in the queue for tickets. George's arm was in a sling, but she was happy to see he appeared to be fine. The fact he was here confirmed her suspicion that Phineas would have had him posted at the station to keep watch for her. Very clever of him, she thought, but not quite clever enough.

Having consulted Bradshaw's the night before, their plan was for Mary, disguised as her, and Judith to board the

Newcastle train hoping Phineas would follow, leaving her free to catch the London train due to leave half an hour later. By the time he would discover his mistake, she would be well on her way, and he would be too far behind to catch her.

She waited impatiently to see which platform the men would make for. Hearing the call to board for the Newcastle train, Lucy crossed her fingers, her body tensing up. So much hinged on this. They were at the top of the queue. The clerk handed Phineas his tickets and the men raced towards the platform.

She let out a slow breath as she saw them entering the third-class carriage of the Newcastle train. Now all Lucy had to do was wait and pray her plan would work.

THIRTY-SEVEN

Lucy had never travelled third class before. She had managed to obtain a seat on the bench beside the window, but her travelling companions were less than fragrant and the wooden bench extremely uncomfortable. A lady beside her had brought a cushion to sit on. She was obviously a frequent traveller. A dishevelled young man sitting opposite was giving her strange looks, which she did her best to ignore. At least no one who might recognise her would be travelling in this class. Lucy had borrowed an old dress and coat of Judith's and had pulled her hair back tightly under a bonnet to try to hide the colour. A gauzy veil further boosted her confidence of remaining incognito. But would it be enough to fool Marsh's men if they were lying in wait at King's Cross?

After breakfast, she had sought out Uncle Giles and consulted him. Although astonished by her revelations, he had congratulated her on her cool head and urged her to return to London as quickly as possible. He told her there had been rumblings of poacher activity on the vacant Somerville estate in recent times. Hopefully that would put the local police off the scent if anyone made a fuss about hearing the gunshot the night before. Lucy had half expected to be greeted that morning by the police. It would have been the perfect way for Phineas to scupper her or make her bargain for her freedom with the gems. Perhaps that was why he had been on the road to Blackheath so early in the morning. And, no doubt, Sergeant Wilson would have been only too delighted to have cause to arrest her again.

As she watched the landscape slip past, she relaxed. She had beaten Phineas and Marsh to it and found the sapphires. Thank goodness Charlie had left the satchel at the hotel, otherwise they might have been lost forever. She thought of the gems tucked into her corset and her heart pounded. So much furore over such small stones. As Mary said, they were like insignificant pebbles. But it wasn't over yet. The jaws of danger were open wide and waiting for her. It was important to stay focused and not let down her guard. A few more hours and she would be back in town. With a bit of luck the insurance company offices would still be open. At least she had had the foresight before leaving London to look up the company's details. Bradford's was located on Fleet Street.

Unfortunately, she would be arriving at King's Cross late afternoon and the traffic would be heavy. It might even be quicker to walk rather than take a cab. That wasn't a pleasant prospect. No respectable woman would brave the dirt of the streets or the jostling of the predominantly male pedestrians in that part of town. Still, all that mattered was reaching Bradford's before they closed. She would not feel safe until the sapphires were handed over.

Shifting to get into a more comfortable position, she jerked her shoulder and winced. That morning as she had dressed, she had discovered a large purple bruise from where the stag had hit her. A war wound, she reckoned with a wry smile. She'd been lucky though—it might have been far worse. Lucy's stomach rumbled, and she wished she'd had the foresight to bring some food with her for the journey. Consulting her watch, she was disappointed to see there were still about two hours to go.

At last. With a jolt, Lucy emerged from a dreamless doze to realise the train had stopped. A glance out of the window confirmed she was at King's Cross. The other passengers were getting to their feet, pulling on coats and hats and retrieving their bags from under the benches. Aware of being under scrutiny, Lucy looked up to see the young man gazing at her intently.

'First time in London?' he drawled.

Lucy shook her head before standing and turning away from him.

''Cos if it is, you want to be careful. Lot of folk who prey on young women like you. Why not let me show you around? I'll see you come to no harm.'

His tone and words made her flinch. God help any young girl who might fall into the hands of such a man. Best to get away as quickly as possible, she thought.

'Thank you,' she said, 'but my husband is meeting me here.' Hoping this would be enough to fend him off, she pushed past him and made for the carriage door, not daring to look back.

The train had been full and the passengers were streaming towards the ticket collector at the barrier ahead. Lucy had no choice but to follow. She guessed Marsh or Phineas would have people posted at the station entrances watching out for her. Alone, she stood out. A family group was a few feet ahead of her. She slipped in behind them, hoping she would be taken for a family member or servant. The ticket collector barely looked at her, and she passed through and followed the family closely as they made their way to the ticket hall. When they stopped suddenly and one of the party turned around and frowned at her, she was momentarily flustered. Before any awkward questions were asked, she took off at a brisk pace towards the main entrance, every sense on high alert.

Then she spotted him. Wearing a check flat cap, he was leaning against a pillar just inside the door, reading a newspaper. There was something familiar about that cap. She had definitely seen the man before. Yes. Outside the Princess Hotel in Brook Street. She was certain.

Their eyes met.

The newspaper was folded and tucked under his arm, and he took a step towards her. Panicking, Lucy turned back and tried to lose herself in the crowds. Desperately, she tried to remember if there was another exit from the station. She glanced over her shoulder. The man was no longer at the pillar. Where was he? Frantic, she pushed her way through to the far end of the hall, trying to think calmly. She would have to double back. Hopefully, she would lose him. Lucy searched for the pistol in her pocket, the cold metal giving her a tiny boost of confidence, but she felt the dampness of perspiration forming on her body. This was foolish. Pulling out a gun in a crowded public space was not feasible. With regret, she removed her fingers from the handle of the gun, pulled down her veil and, with her head down, forged her way towards the main entrance.

Outside, the queue for cabs snaked down the pavement. Could she risk waiting? She glanced up at the clock tower. It was five minutes past four. She didn't have much time. It would take at least half an hour on foot but Lucy wasn't sure which end of Fleet Street Bradford's was located. It would have to be a cab. With luck, the queue might move quickly. But then she caught sight of two men standing near the entrance, deep in conversation, and one was the man with the flat cap she had seen inside. The other man was older with grey hair and a pockmarked face. They both turned in her direction. From the corner of her eye she saw them start to move towards her. Lucy made a dash down the narrow gap between the people and the cabs, hoping the cab queue would shield her enough to allow her escape.

'Here! You can't skip the queue,' a man shouted, grabbing at her arm as she passed. Terrified, she pulled herself away. But she had lost vital seconds. When she heard footsteps close behind, she broke into a run, not waiting to see who it might be.

The distinctive metal arch of the underground station came into view. Why hadn't she considered that option? The Metropolitan Line would take her close to Fleet Street if she went as far as the Farringdon Street stop. She halted, unsure if she should chance it. Might she be trapped down below on the platform?

The next thing she knew, her arm was grabbed and held in a vice-like grip. It was the flat cap man she had seen inside the station.

'Now, then, girlie, you wouldn't be thinkin' of giving us the slip again?'

The second older man took her other arm. 'Not friendly, at all, Joe, I say. And us only tryin' to be 'elpful.'

Terrified, Lucy began to struggle. 'Play nice, now. We're going on a little trip,' the first man hissed into her ear, his breath making her recoil.

They started to pull her away from the station towards a carriage with drawn blinds which was standing at the kerb. The blind was pulled up and a face she recognised stared out at her.

Marsh.

Lucy knew if they got her into that carriage she was finished. She had nothing to lose. She began to scream. 'Help! I'm being robbed!'

The first man let go, looking alarmed, as the second man cursed roundly and tried to drag her towards the carriage. Lucy resisted with all her might, hitting out at him with her bag and continuing to shout for help. Within seconds an angry group of people had surrounded them, cutting off his route.

'What's going on?' an irate gentleman demanded. 'Unhand that lady this instant!'

'Blackguards!' a lady shouted before thumping the first of Lucy's assailants with her umbrella. 'Someone call for a policeman.'

Marsh's men exchanged anguished looks. From the corner of her eye, Lucy saw the carriage move off from the kerb and out into the traffic.

'Please help me!' she cried, continuing to struggle. 'They mean me harm.'

'Don't mind her, missus. She's me sister. Not feeling well, we're taking her home for a little rest,' her captor said.

'Nonsense!' the lady with the umbrella exclaimed before walloping him. 'Let her go!'

Raising one arm to fend off the umbrella, he loosened his grip long enough for Lucy to break free. She lunged forward and pushed through the crowd, who then closed in around the two men. Unable to believe her luck, she ran towards the underground entrance. She took a quick look behind. The men were still caught up in the melée and, much to her relief, there was no sign of Marsh's carriage.

As she reached the top of the steps at the entrance, a policeman walked up from the other direction, craning his neck to see what was all the fuss behind her.

'Constable, you must be quick. They have detained a couple of thieves,' Lucy informed him.

'Have they now! Thank you, madam,' he said, pulling out his truncheon before running towards what was developing into a fracas.

As she started her descent into the underground, Lucy heard the policeman's whistle blow several times. That should keep Marsh's men occupied for a while, she thought grimly. But she had to make the most of the opportunity to escape. With her heart in her mouth, she picked up her skirts and careered

down the steps, almost knocking over a woman who shouted
after her.

Skidding out onto the platform, she saw a train, a steady
plume of smoke billowing from the funnel. It was about to pull
away. Glancing upwards towards the glass roof, she spotted the
ticket office perched above the platforms, but it was busy. No
matter—she couldn't afford the delay of buying a ticket, anyway.
She wrenched open the door of the last carriage, almost falling
inside.

'That was a close call, miss,' a young man said, firmly
closing the door after her. *You have no idea*, she thought, but she
smiled in gratitude and quickly took a seat. She was worried her
heart would burst it was racing so hard. As the train pulled
away, Lucy wondered what had happened her pursuers. But it
didn't really matter. Even if they had managed to free themselves from the angry mob, they were too far behind to catch
her now.

Farringdon Street Station was only a short distance, but the
sense of relief Lucy experienced during the four-minute
journey was profound. She straightened her hat and smoothed
down the skirts of her coat. It was unlikely anyone would be
watching for her at Farringdon Street, but a ruffled appearance
might draw attention if there was. Once she had paid her fare,
employing a plausible tale to convince the ticket collector she
wasn't a fare evader, she emerged onto Cowcross Street in a
daze of euphoria. The area was unfamiliar, but the sight of a
free cab and no queue delighted her. Her luck seemed to be
changing.

'Where to, missus?' the cabbie asked as she drew near.

'Do you know the premises of Bradford's, the insurance
company on Fleet Street?'

The cabbie scratched under his hat before breaking into a gap-toothed smile. 'Reckon I do. 'Op in, lassie.'

The trouble began almost as soon as the cab swung around into Fleet Street. Traffic was at a standstill. Lucy tapped on the roof and the panel slid open.

'What's the problem?' she asked. 'I'm in an awful hurry.'

'Usual, missus, 'orse gone down.'

'Can't they get the creature up? Will it take long?' she asked.

'Don't know for sure. Takin' off the 'arness now.' The panel slid across.

Lucy glanced at her watch. Forty minutes past four. The pavements were a swarming mass of black-suited, top-hatted men of business. Progress on foot would be slow, but at least she would be moving. There was no sign of any movement in the traffic ahead. Raising her umbrella, she tapped the roof again.

The cabbie peered in at her. 'So sorry, but I'll have to walk. Is it far to Bradfords?' she asked.

'No missus, right-hand side, just past 'ancock's chemist. You can't miss 'ancock's 'cos it's got a red and white awning; flash as anything, it is.'

'Thank you,' Lucy said. Stepping down onto the pavement she looked up at him, holding out the fare.

The cabbie reached down to retrieve the coin and winked. 'Hope he's worth it!'

Not having time or the inclination to disabuse him of his notion, she turned into the tide of men. This must be how the salmon feels going upstream, she thought, as she battled her way along. This was the face of London she hated. Everyone walked with purpose, their minds singularly focused on their business; there was no apology when you were jostled or clipped by a cane or umbrella. Added to the danger of injury by everyday objects was the slipperiness of the pavements due to the mud and other unspeakable substances which stuck like glue. Rain always made it worse and a recent shower had left the pavement slippery as ice and smelling foul.

Holding her skirts up, Lucy walked as quickly as she dared past the unfortunate horse which was half under its cart. The flustered carter was desperately trying to undo the harness, amid jeers from a group of bare-footed urchins and a flurry of instructions from various members of the public taking pleasure in his plight. A little further on, she spotted Hancock's chemist shop with its distinctive striped awning. Just as her nerves settled, she came up short. How could she have been so stupid? Marsh would know she had to go to the insurance company offices if she had the sapphires. He would have people on the lookout. Almost panicking, she turned in towards the window of the chemist shop. Using the reflection of the street, she scanned up and down the adjacent buildings and along the street. No one looked suspicious, but she couldn't just walk into the building. They would be sure to nab her.

And she didn't know which building it was. She would have to walk down and hope to spot a sign. Waiting until a group of gentlemen strode past, she fell into step, keeping close to the shops. Two doors down, she found the building she wanted. The ground floor was a draper's shop, but beside the entrance to the upper floors was an array of brass plaques displayed on the wall, one above the other. Amongst the solicitors was the one she was looking for: 'Bradford & Co'. Did she dare dart in the open doorway? Too risky no matter how tempting it was.

Walking away, Lucy fixed her gaze on a laneway coming up at the end of the row. Praying no one had spotted her, she slipped down the lane, then turned right at the junction. A quick scan up and down reassured her there was no one unsavoury hanging around. A few small boys were playing at the far end of the laneway but paid her no heed. Now to find the rear entrance of the right building. She counted down the row and fixed her sights on what must be the rear door of the Bradford building. But she hesitated. A closed carriage was waiting outside, the horse snorting impatiently. It was a different shape and colour to Marsh's carriage and the coachman was ignoring her. She had to chance it. After a nervous glance over her shoulder, Lucy walked along the lane up to the door. She couldn't believe she had made it. Her elation was short-lived, however, when an elderly man barged into her, coming out the door.

'Really, madam, do you have to block the door,' he said, glaring at her from under snowy-white brows, as though it were her fault. Then he stalked over to the carriage and wrenched the door open. 'Kensington, John,' she heard him say as he climbed in.

'It *would* be three flights up,' Lucy muttered, stopping to catch her breath when at last she saw the company name. The landing was brightly lit with four offices leading off the hallway, two of which were in darkness. It was now ten minutes to five. She followed the sound of voices and knocked on the door marked 'Office'.

A sandy-haired young man opened the door. 'Yes, madam?'

'Good evening. I would like to see the most senior person, please. It is most urgent.'

The clerk looked her up and down. 'There are no more appointments today. We are closing at five o'clock.' He regarded her with a scowl.

'Please. I wouldn't ask, but I have travelled a great distance. From Yorkshire, in fact. It is a matter of life and death,' she said, hoping to persuade him.

With an impatient sigh, he glanced into the room before slowly opening the door further. 'Come in.' He took out a pocket watch and then shoved it into an inside pocket with a disgruntled twist of his mouth. 'Are you a client? I don't believe I know you, madam.' With a flick of his wrist, he pointed to a chair. Another clerk was pulling on his overcoat and gave her a curious stare.

Lucy sat down with a grateful sigh. 'My name is Mrs Lawrence and I'm not a client of your firm. But—'

'That's unfortunate for Mr Thompson, who looks after new business, is on holiday at the moment. If you care to make an appointment for next week—'

'No! You don't understand. I have... that is, I wish to speak to the most senior person in the firm.'

'Perhaps you could tell me what it is about?' he asked, sounding impatient. 'Mr Bradford is an extremely busy man. Only our most important clients deal directly with him.'

'Is he here?' Lucy asked as a wave of fatigue swept over her.

A hint of annoyance crossed the man's face. 'No, he's left the office. You will have to come back tomorrow... If he agrees to see you.' Turning towards the desk, he picked up a large appointment book and scanned the page. 'Mr Bradford might be able to fit you in, but only for a few minutes, mind, about four tomorrow. That is if you can convince me that the matter warrants intruding on his valuable time.' He raised a brow and stared at her.

'He's not here?' Lucy's stomach was leaden; to be so close and now this.

'That's correct. I have just told you.' The clerk began to write her name into the book.

'I'm sorry, but four o'clock tomorrow will not do,' she protested, jumping up. 'I must see him as soon as he arrives in the morning.'

'Madam, that's impossible.'

'Mr Stone can vouch for me,' she blurted out. 'It is to do

with one of his cases and is most important.' It was a risk she had to take.

From his face, she knew the man had recognised the name. He exchanged a glance with the other clerk who raised a brow before jamming on his hat. The book was slammed shut and dropped to the desk. He regarded her intently. 'Which case, Mrs Lawrence? You need to be more specific.'

'I'd rather not say.'

'Madam—'

'Maybe she should wait, Tattersall. Mr Bradford said he was coming back later to pick up some papers,' the other clerk butted in.

Lucy gave him a grateful smile before turning to his less helpful colleague. 'Please, I won't be any bother, but it really is very important I see him today. It won't take long.'

Lucy held her breath as Tattersall considered her request. What on earth was she to do if he refused? Wait out in the laneway? She couldn't go back to the hotel for it was definitely being watched. Marsh knew she was in London. Nowhere was safe. She shivered as she recalled the look he had given her from the carriage window less than an hour before. She had no desire to renew their acquaintance.

'Oh, very well then,' the clerk said as he eyed his colleague slipping out the door. 'I have to stay, anyway.'

Lucy almost cried with relief.

THIRTY-EIGHT

Offices of Bradford & Co., Fleet Street

It was the longest hour and a half of Lucy's life. She fidgeted and fretted and kept looking at the clock on the wall above the clerk's head. What if Mr Bradford decided not to return but went home instead? Or decided to go to his club? It was hard not to take a pessimistic view: her luck tended to be of the fickle variety of late.

Out on the window ledge, a couple of pigeons were sitting surveying their world. Not for them a life on the run, she thought gloomily. Of course, it was her own fault. A sensible woman would have given over the clues to the police, done her civic duty as it were, and not undertaken a hair-raising escapade with death within touching distance. She almost laughed aloud. Who was she fooling? She knew she would do exactly the same again. Charlie's death had set her on this path, and she had to see it through to the bitter end.

The door swung open and the elderly gentleman who had bumped into her outside in the lane entered the office. When he saw her, he threw a questioning glance at the clerk who was hastily rising to his feet.

'Good evening, Mr Bradford,' the clerk said.

'What's going on, Tattersall?' the man asked, glancing again at her. 'Office should have closed an hour ago.'

'The lady insisted on seeing you. She refused to tell me what it was about, only saying it is in relation to one of Mr Stone's cases and can't wait until tomorrow, Mr Bradford,' Tattersall said.

Bradford's craggy brows drew together. 'Is this so, madam? Might I enquire who you are? You do look familiar. Haven't we met before?'

'Yes, we bumped into each other in the lane earlier,' Lucy answered.

Bradford's colour rose and he coughed. 'Yes, well—'

'My name is Lucy Lawrence, widow of Charles Lawrence,' she said, rising from her seat.

Bradford was still frowning. 'Name means nothing to me!' He glanced at the clerk, one eyebrow raised.

'Not clients, sir,' Tattersall said.

'I don't see—' Bradford said, looking increasingly perplexed.

'Sir, I know this is highly irregular, but I have risked my life to come here,' Lucy explained. 'If we can't conclude our business this evening there may not be another opportunity.' She watched as Mr Bradford mulled it over.

With a grunt he waved her towards the door of an inner office. 'Very well, madam. You may go, Tattersall. I'll lock up when we are done.'

'Take a seat, Mrs Lawrence,' Bradford said, following her in and closing over the door.

Sitting down, he frowned at her over the top of his glasses. 'Perhaps you would care to explain what is going on? I'm a busy man and don't have time for any missish nonsense.'

Before Lucy could reply, she heard the outer door of the

office burst open. Much to her astonishment, Chief Inspector McQuillan almost tumbled into the room.

Bradford jumped to his feet. 'What the devil, sir?'

McQuillan ignored him and came up to Lucy. 'Are you all right, Mrs Lawrence? We've been extremely worried. Half the force is looking for you.'

'I'm fine, Chief Inspector. But I don't understand—why are you here?' she asked, though there was something comforting about the policeman's presence. At least, she trusted him.

'Police, eh? Dashed impertinent entering a place of business like that!' exclaimed Bradford.

'My apologies, sir. I'm Chief Inspector McQuillan from Vine Street. Mr Stone sent a telegram from York before he boarded a London train. He suspected Mrs Lawrence might turn up here and asked me to confirm it.' He turned to Lucy. 'You have not come to any harm? We searched King's Cross hoping to find you. Phin is beside himself with worry.'

Lucy baulked. 'Is he indeed? So worried he's been spying on me!'

McQuillan blinked. 'You have misunderstood, surely, Mrs Lawrence; he's been trying to *protect* you.'

'Excuse me!' Bradford interrupted, now very red in the face. 'Would either of you care to tell me what is going on? I do not take kindly to my office being invaded.'

'My apologies, sir. This is Charlie Lawrence's widow,' McQuillan said. 'I believe you will find her an interesting woman.'

'The lady has already told me her husband's name—it means nothing to me, sir.'

McQuillan sat down beside Lucy. 'It is to do with the maharajah's stolen sapphires,' he said.

Bradford's eyes popped. '*That* Charlie Lawrence! I see. But we closed the file on Stone's say-so months ago, and despite all the damn fuss that Khan chappie kicked up.' Bradford's stern gaze settled on Lucy. 'Were you in cahoots with your husband?' he asked.

'Certainly not,' Lucy snapped, wondering if she had fallen into some strange nightmare world.

'Chief Inspector, I'm at a loss. Would you care to clarify?' Bradford said.

'It would be best if Mrs Lawrence explains it,' McQuillan replied, giving her an encouraging smile. 'Though perhaps we should wait for Mr Stone? He is on his way.'

'No!' she cried. 'He's not to be trusted.'

Both men protested, McQuillan aghast. She turned to Bradford. 'Sir, I'd like to proceed as quickly as possible, please.' Bradford blew out his cheeks and shrugged.

It was then she remembered the bag was down the front of her corset. 'I just need a moment,' she said, jumping up and going out to the clerk's office. 'Turn around, pigeons,' she said, as she searched for the string of the bag. Pulling it out, she stared down at it, almost losing her nerve. She eyed the open doorway, but she knew it would be foolish—she would never be free. Stone would find her. They had to be handed over. Lucy placed the drawstring bag in her handbag and returned to Bradford's office.

'Sir, I understand your company were the insurers of a certain jewellery firm in Hatton Garden, from where the Maharajah of Kashmir's property was stolen,' she said on regaining her seat.

Bradford cleared his throat. 'That's correct, madam. The theft occurred early last year.'

'May I ask what exactly was taken?' Lucy asked.

Bradford flicked a glance at McQuillan. The policeman nodded. 'Three uncut sapphires of the finest quality. Do I understand you have information about their whereabouts?'

Lucy took a deep breath and opened her bag. Out came the drawstring pouch of red velvet.

McQuillan stood. 'May I, Mrs Lawrence?'

Lucy gave him a shaky smile and handed over the bag. He tipped out the contents into his palm and caught his breath. Bradford jumped up and stared, then came around the desk, his eyes on stalks.

'Well, I'll be damned!' he exclaimed.

'Sir!' McQuillan said, tilting his head towards Lucy.

'Oh, yes, apologies for swearing, Mrs Lawrence, but I never thought these would see the light of day again. The maharajah will be delighted, I can tell you,' Bradford said.

McQuillan rolled the stones around in his hand. 'The jewellers will need to confirm, sir, but I believe these are the Kashmiri sapphires.' He turned to Lucy. 'Gosh! How clever of you.' She tried to smile.

'Excellent, excellent!' exclaimed Bradford. With a look of reverence, he took the gems from McQuillan and popped them into the bag. Then he came over to Lucy and shook her hand. 'Now, would you care to tell us how these came into your possession?'

Haltingly at first, Lucy told them about finding the train ticket stub, the letter from the hotel in York, and Charlie's clues, culminating in her flight from Marsh's men at King's Cross.

'Well, I never! Extraordinary!' exclaimed Bradford shaking his head. He glanced at Lucy as if sizing her up, then he turned to McQuillan. 'Might we have a quick word in private, Chief Inspector?'

McQuillan agreed. They excused themselves and went out to the outer office. But the door was ajar, and she heard their muttered conversation.

'Well, is this all believable, McQuillan? Could she have been involved in the theft and had them all along? That's some tale she has just recited.'

'No, sir. She's telling the truth. Stone saw her retrieve them as she described.'

'Most unusual.'

'Yes, she is.'

'You must understand; I need to be sure she's legitimate. It's a lot of money,' Bradford said.

'Mr Stone and I are happy to vouch for her.'

'Very well,' Bradford grunted.

They came back in and sat down.

'I assume you're aware that Bradford's offered a reward for the return of these stones? Indeed, the maharajah has also offered one, a substantial one, in fact,' Bradford said.

'Yes, sir, and I wish to claim them, but I would like to explain why, if I may?'

'Please do,' Bradford said.

'When Mr Stone informed me of my husband's involvement in the Padar Mining swindle, I was horrified. I knew nothing about it, but my husband's behaviour in the last few months of his life had worried me, though I had never imagined for a moment he was involved in anything of a criminal nature. Sadly, that was actually the case. My husband was a fool, and he paid dearly for it. As you know, he met an unfortunate death, most likely at the hands of Nathaniel Marsh's men.'

'Yes, most dreadful, Mrs Lawrence. Mr Stone gave me all the details at the time.'

'Finding those clues to the whereabouts of the stones made up my mind. I hoped by returning them, I would in some way make up for my husband's wrongdoings.'

'No one holds you responsible, madam.'

'That may be so, but it was important to *me*,' she said. 'It is my intention to use some of the reward to pay back a percentage of what each investor was swindled. I wish I could reimburse them fully but my own circumstances prohibit it.' She pulled Charlie's sheets of paper from her bag. 'I have the list of names and how much they invested. At least, Charlie was thorough in his accounts,' she said, her voice catching. 'I was hoping Bradford's might facilitate this?'

Bradford was staring at her open-mouthed.

'I'm sure that won't present any difficulty,' McQuillan replied. 'Might I suggest the gems go into your safe now, Mr Bradford. It makes me nervous to see them on your desk.'

'Yes, a good idea, Chief Inspector. And I'm happy to do as you ask, Mrs Lawrence. If you leave details of your bank for Mr Tattersall, my clerk, we will arrange everything.'

'Thank you, sir,' Lucy said, watching as Bradford opened a wall safe and placed the bag inside. A wave of relief hit her—it was over.

Bradford turned to McQuillan. 'I'd rather not keep these on the premises longer than I have to. If you would be good enough, Chief Inspector, a police escort would be appreciated. I'd like to return these to Hatton Garden tomorrow.'

'I'll arrange it first thing in the morning, sir. It might also be a good idea to issue a press release to the effect that the stones have been recovered. Until such is done, Mrs Lawrence remains in danger from a certain party.'

'Yes, of course. I'll have Tattersall do so in the morning.'

Lucy stood up, suddenly anxious to leave. McQuillan rose too and put a hand on her arm. 'If you wouldn't mind, Mrs Lawrence, I'd like you to come to Vine Street with me.'

'Why?' Lucy asked.

'To close the case, I'll need to take your statement. Nothing too onerous, but best to do it this evening while it's all still fresh in your memory.'

Lucy was on the point of refusing as all she wanted was food and bed, but he was right. It would be a relief to get it over with. 'Certainly.'

'Well done, Mrs Lawrence. You're a most unique young woman,' Bradford said, coming around the desk before clasping her hand and shaking it enthusiastically.

Just then the outer door of the main office banged against the wall as it was flung open. The familiar figure of Phineas Stone charged in to the office, out of breath as if he had run up the stairs. His colour was high and his clothes dishevelled. He froze inside the door and stared at them. Alarmed, Lucy shrank back against the Chief Inspector, for she sensed Mr Stone was not in a good mood. In fact, he was furious, his eyes sparking dangerously.

'A woman beating you to it—one in the eye for you, Stone, eh?' Bradford chuckled.

THIRTY-NINE

Vine Street Police Station

The interview room was stark, with a barred window high up in the wall. A table dominated the centre of the room, its scarred surface vandalised by many of the room's inhabitants over the years. Initials and dates had been roughly carved, showing white against the patina of the wood. Lucy wondered briefly if this was where Richard was interrogated. But she wasn't in the mood for the history of Vine Street and its 'guests'. She craved rest and solitude, the bliss of a hot cup of tea and the comfort of her bed. Instead, she was sitting with a sergeant, a pleasant enough man, who kept asking her questions. To ensure a full statement was available for the chief inspector, he said. It felt like some form of torture to Lucy.

Whatever relief she had experienced on handing over the sapphires soon evaporated as she found herself in a police carriage, with McQuillan and Stone sitting opposite. McQuillan's attempts at conversation died as even he couldn't compete with the silent rage emanating from Phineas Stone. The carriage ride to Vine Street was completed in silence. Stone's attention was fixed on the passing streets, as if he couldn't bear to look at her. Dismayed, Lucy realised the hollow sensation in her stomach was not only due to hunger. Their relationship was probably beyond repair if McQuillan's assertions were to be believed.

But her irritation grew. Phineas had lost and wasn't taking it well. But it might do him good, she thought. It might even take him down a peg or two and make him more human. She was a little disappointed to discover he was a poor loser; she had believed he had a more generous nature than that.

In the hallway at Vine Street, they parted company.

'Thank you, Mrs Lawrence,' the police sergeant said as she signed her statement. 'I'll let the chief inspector know we are finished. If you would be good enough to wait here?'

'Yes, certainly,' she said.

Sitting back in her chair, Lucy watched the sergeant leave and sighed. Recounting the entire story had made her realise what a fickle thing fate was. A wrong decision, a careless word, and the whole adventure could have come crashing down around her. Marsh's face, looking out from his carriage window, came too readily to mind. What would have happened if she had been dragged into that carriage? She'd be lying in the same plot as Charlie, that's what! That's if they ever found her body, she realised with a shudder. Would Marsh still want to harm her? For surely he would be as angry as Stone appeared to be, perhaps more so? She only hoped Marsh would not want revenge.

When McQuillan entered the room a short time later, she immediately voiced her concerns.

'Don't you worry about him, my dear lady. His second-in-command has turned informant. Coffin Mike—'

'Coffin Mike! But he's in league with Phineas Stone, Chief Inspector.'

McQuillan laughed. 'No, no, you're mistaken, Mrs Lawrence, but best Phin explain it to you. Coffin Mike has been co-operative once we struck a deal, and, all going well, we have a raid planned for tomorrow night. Marsh will be in one of his opium dens, and we will catch him red-handed. In the meantime, we will have police officers at the hotel to ensure your safety.'

'Thank you! And I feel much safer knowing Marsh will soon be behind bars.'

McQuillan ran a hand through his already wild hair. 'I've been after that bast— I won't deny I'll be glad to rid London of him for good. You have had a bad time of it, Mrs Lawrence, but your statement will ensure we get a conviction. I'm indebted to you. Now, I'll bid you goodnight.'

'Goodnight, Chief Inspector,' Lucy said, rising up and buttoning her coat.

McQuillan paused at the door. 'Don't concern yourself, we will protect you, but if you should get the urge to go off on another adventure in the near future, please curb it.'

Lucy laughed. 'Yes, Chief Inspector. I promise to be good from now on.'

'Excellent! Phin will be along shortly and will take you to your hotel,' he said, and disappeared out the door before she could utter a protest.

Lucy waited for Stone with growing anxiety, wishing McQuillan had stayed. His cryptic references to Stone and Coffin Mike played on her mind. Was it possible she had misinterpreted what she had seen? It seemed unlikely, and yet McQuillan had been adamant. She was so tired she could barely think. It would be best not to confront Stone about any of it until she was more herself. Surely there wouldn't be any need to go over it all with him tonight. McQuillan was bound to have told him what occurred already.

But it was a grim-faced Stone who entered the room minutes later. 'If you're ready, Mrs Lawrence, I'll escort you back to your hotel.' His tone left nothing to the imagination: he was still livid.

Lucy gripped her bag, fighting a sudden fear to be alone with him. 'There's no need, Mr Stone. I'm quite capable of finding my way. I would not like to inconvenience you.'

A muscle in his cheek twitched. 'I am well aware of your resourcefulness. I have been the victim of it for some time.'

Lucy gasped. 'Victim! You!' She took a step towards him. 'What right have you to be angry with me? You were ready to betray me to Marsh. I don't understand why McQuillan hasn't arrested you.'

'What nonsense is this?' he asked, his eyes glinting dangerously.

But she was angry too. 'Don't deny it. I saw Coffin Mike go to your rooms. Explain that, if you can,' she demanded.

He stared at her as if she were mad. 'I have nothing to explain.'

'It's true then—you were going to hand me over to Marsh.'

The colour drained from his face. 'Is that why you bolted? You believed I was working for *him*?'

She nodded.

He was breathing hard and looked like he wanted to throttle her. 'Of all the idiotic notions! You misconstrued what you saw,' he snapped.

'I don't think so!'

'If anyone should be angry, it should be me,' Stone exclaimed. 'When you found those clues in Abbey Gardens, you should have come straight to me.'

'I did! That was the evening I saw Coffin Mike in Westbourne Grove—entering your flat. What was I to think? What other explanation could there be?'

'A very simple one,' he told her. 'He was working for *me*. Do you know what a double-agent is?' She stared at him in disbelief. Stone briefly closed his eyes then fixed her with a stare so cold she wondered if her insides might freeze. 'I can only imagine it is tiredness making you so dim-witted.'

'I beg your pardon!'

'You're far too impetuous. If you had applied logic to the situation, you would have realised you were mistaken.' Lucy glared at him but he continued. 'Do I have to explain?'

'You most certainly do!'

'On coming across Coffin Mike in Lambeth at your husband's office, I guessed he was working for Khan. This was astonishing as he was Marsh's second-in-command and to double-cross Marsh was an incredibly risky venture. It pointed to a desire to go out on his own, no matter how dangerous it might be. I knew I could take advantage of this and made some discreet enquiries. When I discovered Coffin Mike had designs on taking over Marsh's gang, I sent an emissary to him with a proposal. One, which you will be glad to know, had Chief Inspector McQuillan's approval. Coffin Mike accepted if it meant Marsh was taken down.' Stone crossed his arms, his demeanour stern. 'As luck would have it, he had been given the task of co-ordinating the watch over you and was happy enough to feed false information to Marsh at my bequest. By manipulating what information reached him, I was able to shield you, particularly when you made the unexpected dash up north.'

'Oh!' Lucy said.

'Yes, Mrs Lawrence. Coffin Mike was keeping watch over you for me. After that absurd escapade on Regent Street, he lost you and came to me straight away. He was not pleased as he's rather proud of his tracking abilities.'

'Well, I'll apologise next time I see him,' Lucy snapped.

'You owe apologies to several people, for a more foolish and risky thing to do I couldn't imagine.'

She glared across at him. 'I had no choice. I didn't want Marsh's men following me to Yorkshire.'

'There's always a choice.'

'Is that so, Mr Stone? Let me tell you, I did what I considered best in a difficult situation. I was distressed to discover the one man I thought I *could* trust was consorting with the enemy.' He rolled his eyes. 'I decided it was time to take control of my life.'

'By getting yourself killed?' he asked.

'By using my brain and not waiting around like some damsel in distress,' she replied. 'Even if the misunderstanding regarding Coffin Mike had not occurred, I would have insisted on accompanying you to York. I couldn't have borne staying behind in London.'

'I don't doubt you would have tried!' he said. 'But let me assure you, madam, you would have stayed in London even if it meant having you locked up in the cells in this very building.'

'You would not dare!' His answer was a quirked brow. Trembling with rage, Lucy stared him down. 'When you learned I had left London you assumed I had been lying all along, didn't you? And that I was off to retrieve the sapphires from their hiding place.'

'Or they had been in your possession from the outset, and you had bolted. And who would blame me? Your actions were highly suspicious. I couldn't understand it. Foolishly, I assumed we had gained a level of understanding.'

'Perhaps if you had lowered yourself enough to inform me about your little scheme with Coffin Mike, I might not have drawn the incorrect conclusion and taken matters into my own hands. I'd say it was you who didn't trust *me*.'

He recoiled at that, his mouth a thin line of displeasure.

'Then to cap it all, you decided to follow me to Yorkshire and spy on me,' Lucy said.

'I followed you because I wished to stop you doing something foolish, and I was concerned for your safety,' he said.

'Or you hoped I'd lead you to the sapphires so you could swoop in,' Lucy snapped.

He froze, and she instantly regretted the words. 'Is that what you truly believe?' he asked so quietly she shivered. The question hung in the air between them. Her growing regard for him had been buried when she thought he was going to betray her to Marsh. The realisation she had been mistaken about his motives now ignited a tiny ray of hope. But was it too late? Their future hinged on how she answered. 'No,' she whispered.

Stone's knuckles were white where he clutched the back of a chair. 'I was left with no choice but to follow you on your madcap flight. How else was I to protect you, for God's sake?'

She almost groaned aloud as the significance of his words hit her.

'You had already indicated Yorkshire was your destination, feeding me some tale about visiting your friend. I prayed you hadn't lied about that, and we went straight to King's Cross just in time to see you board the York train with your maid. My greatest fear was Marsh had others watching you. Trust me, if Marsh had known about your little excursion to Yorkshire, he would have done something about it. You know what he's capable of. When he did eventually discover your escape from London, he put his agents at every railway station with strict instructions to bring you in for he knew you would have to come back to claim the reward. You were extremely lucky you evaded capture.'

'I admit it was a close-run thing. But it doesn't alter the fact you weren't entirely honest with me,' she said, too late realising she was poking a nest of vipers.

He recoiled and something that might have been hurt flickered in his eyes.

'Without trust…' she trailed off, dismayed to see the effect of her words. She was making things worse. 'I'm sorry. I can't think clearly. I need to go home now. Alone.'

'As you wish, Mrs Lawrence,' he said, his tone cold and formal. He stood back.

Choking down her tears, Lucy quit the room.

And cried all the way to Brook Street in the privacy of a cab.

FORTY

Mid-afternoon Lucy was delighted to receive Sarah Strawbridge and lost no time in telling her of her Yorkshire exploits and subsequent disastrous confrontation with Stone. It still made her squirm. 'Sarah, I could not have made more of a mess of it. My only excuse is I was exhausted. There can be no hope of reconciliation for he must despise me,' Lucy said, finishing her tale.

'Don't be so glum, my dear; I'm sure you're wrong,' Sarah replied. 'I take it you do have feelings for him?'

'Of the confused variety,' Lucy admitted.

Sarah frowned. 'Phineas is a reserved man who is always in control. For him to show such emotion indicates how upset he was. He was cross because you frightened him so. Haring off with no notion of the danger you were in; he must have been frantic with worry. It's no wonder he was furious with you.'

'But it was his own fault for not telling me the truth. *I* suspect he's angry because I found the sapphires first and claimed both rewards. It may even be because he was beaten to it by a woman and is afraid his reputation will be damaged.'

'If you really believe that, Lucy, you do not know the man at all!'

'Perhaps I don't,' Lucy said, feeling rather despondent.

'Poor Phin!' Sarah laughed.

'Pooh! You should be on my side.'

'I am, but you must remember male pride can be a delicate thing, Lucy,' Sarah said, shaking her head. 'Geoffrey can't bear to be in the wrong. Phineas is probably the same; he needs time to lick his wounds.'

'You may be right for there has been no communication since,' Lucy said. 'But I don't see why *I* should apologise.'

'Of course, but it is such a shame, Lucy. I'd rather hoped the two of you...'

Lucy huffed. 'Don't be foolish. Besides, the last thing I need in my life now is a meddlesome man. And you can't get more interfering than the insufferable Phineas Stone!'

'But such a man! Those eyes. Admit it—he's divinely handsome.'

'You are welcome to him!'

'But I'm happily married,' Sarah said with a snort of laughter.

'Stop, Sarah, it isn't funny. He's far too dangerous, and I'm never *comfortable* with him.'

'Only because he challenges you,' Sarah said.

'Entanglements of any kind are out of the question. You forget I am in mourning.'

'For Charlie—after all he did? Come, Lucy, I know you have to go through the motions of being the grieving widow for a few more months, but are you honestly telling me your heart still yearns for that deceitful and unfaithful good-for-nothing?'

'Not exactly, but I loved him once and, despite all, I owe

him some respect. Only for him I might never have escaped Somerville all those years ago.'

'You paid a high price for that particular favour, my dear. Which reminds me, how fares your mother?'

'The chief inspector has informed me the Crown has decided not to prosecute her. I'm not quite sure how I feel about that.'

'I suspect she has friends in high places.'

'Of course she has. She's always been the queen of manipulation. Every favour has been called in, you can be sure. However, I do not see how her part in it all won't come out. Richard may well expose her in the witness box. He will hardly be willing to take all the blame. If he doesn't, it may be up to me to reveal what she did when I take the stand,' Lucy said.

'Be careful, my dear. Are you certain you could live with it? You're angry now and hurt, which is understandable, but a few weeks' reflection may temper those feelings. Remember Fleet Street loves a scandal. If you throw her to the lions, they will hound you just as much. Charlie's misdeeds will emerge into the light, including his liaison with Mrs Bannon and any other nuggets of scandal they can unearth. They are relentless once they get a whiff of wrongdoing. I would hate to see you go through that.'

'I suspect you're right,' Lucy said.

'Will you stay here or leave town?'

'I'll stay until Richard's trial is over,' Lucy replied. 'I want to see justice done and, as a witness for the prosecution, I'll have an opportunity to clear my name.' She held up her hand when Sarah protested. 'Yes, but Richard's rumours about me did percolate throughout Yorkshire society, Judith admitted as much. Some damage was done. Though whether I'm considered a thief or merely the sister of a fraudster, there's probably little difference in the eyes of most people. Somehow, I doubt

I'll be invited to the palace for afternoon tea in the near future,' she said with a grin.

'Trust me, nothing more stuffy! You should be thankful.'

'You are a dear,' Lucy said. 'But you won't desert me, will you? Geoffrey may not like you to associate with me now. Consider his career.'

Sarah reached across and patted her hand. 'Just let him try to stop me.' Lucy's throat tightened, and she took a shaky breath.

'Will the sapphire affair come out in court?' Sarah asked, skillfully changing the subject.

'I doubt it, as it isn't directly connected to the fraud concerning the pearls. When Marsh faces trial, it will be for murder. It is unlikely the theft of the sapphires will ever be pursued, according to the chief inspector.'

'But wasn't it the catalyst for what Richard did? Will it not come out during his trial?'

'The chief inspector said it was improbable. The maharajah would not like for it to become public knowledge, and he has a great deal of power.'

'Even more than your mother?' Sarah asked with a glint in her eye.

'A tad more.'

Sarah smiled and finished her tea. 'As a matter of interest, has your brother revealed what his dealings with Charlie were? What brought them together?'

'Richard was in town last summer trying to raise funds and a mutual friend introduced them, not knowing the connection. Richard said Charlie was keen to ingratiate himself, saying he was willing to let him in on a marvellous scheme that would make him a fortune. Being in financial difficulty, Richard took the bait. Some time later, Charlie asked Richard to become his executor. Richard had the impression it was for my sake, and that Charlie wanted me to be on good terms with the family if anything ever happened to him.'

'I imagine your husband was feeling guilty... about many things. Why did he visit Somerville in October?'

'Richard said he came to warn him and ask for help, but of course it was too late for both of them. Charlie's actions had already set it all in train.'

'What a tangle it turned into,' Sarah commented. 'And what about that criminal chap?'

'Marsh? Thankfully, he has been arrested and his organisation exposed. It is a great coup for Chief Inspector McQuillan as he's been trying to catch Marsh for many years.'

'Is there any evidence to link Marsh to Charlie's death?' Sarah asked.

'Not only Charlie's, but many others. The informant, Coffin Mike, has been *very* co-operative, I'm told.'

'Are they sure he will testify and will a jury listen to the testimony of a criminal? I'd hate to see that fellow Marsh get off.'

'As would I!' Lucy exclaimed. 'But the chief inspector thinks others will talk now as well, in the hope of saving their own skins. One voice might not be enough, but a whole chorus of turncoats should do the trick.'

'What loyal fellows they are!'

'It's not loyalty but fear that governs the gangs, Sarah. Marsh has dispensed his own form of justice over the years. You would not believe the stories the chief inspector told me. That's how Marsh built his organisation. His reputation for cruelty and violence helped him hold sway over those men up to now, but Coffin Mike turning informer has upset the balance.'

'But is it not likely that someone else will step into Marsh's shoes as soon as he's safely behind bars?' Sarah asked.

'Marsh won't just go to prison—he will hang, Sarah, and Coffin Mike fully intends to take up the reins. The only saving grace is the organisation he will take over will be a much weaker one.'

'One hears of these gangs but it quite gives one the shivers to learn of them first-hand. Geoffrey is fascinated by it all and is dying to hear more about it from you. He's involved in some committee or other.'

Lucy was saved from answering by the entrance of Mary to clear away the tea things.

'Have you recovered from your exploits?' Sarah asked Mary.

'Oh, yes, ma'am, thank you,' Mary said. 'Ever so exciting, it was.'

Lucy and Sarah exchanged a smile.

'Mary was a useful companion for she showed quite a talent for intrigue. I would not have succeeded without her,' Lucy said.

Mary beamed back at her and left the room with a bounce in her step.

'You never told me what happened to your lady accomplices once you left York for London.'

'They played out their roles perfectly. Mr Stone and his servant George followed them onto the Newcastle train.'

Sarah frowned. 'George—wasn't that the chap you shot?'

'Oh yes'—Lucy grimaced in embarrassment—the night before in the grounds of Somerville... I feel dreadful about it, particularly since he had been so helpful, fixing my escritoire. I sent him a note of apology, and he was kind enough to reply. He was a gentleman about it.'

'Lucy, you're incorrigible.'

Lucy grinned and continued. 'By the time their train reached Darlington, Phineas began to suspect all was not right and decided to confront me.'

'Except it wasn't you—it was Mary dressed as you, and Judith Chancellor.'

'Correct. Mary told me he was furious and demanded to

know where I was. Judith refused to tell him, but Mary eventually caved in and explained it all, though I'm sure he had already guessed.'

'I'd like to have seen his face on hearing you had tricked him,' Sarah said.

'I'm not so sure. I've seen him in a temper; it's rather frightening. Anyway, he insisted they all got off the train at the next stop and catch a train back to York. Judith would have nothing more to do with it, and once they reached York station, she left for home. Mary travelled to London with Mr Stone and his servant.'

'Phineas must have been frantic. Don't look at me like that, Lucy. Obviously, he was afraid you would fall into the wrong hands when you arrived at King's Cross and he was a couple of hours behind and couldn't intervene.'

'Perhaps, and I nearly did end up meeting Marsh again. I still have nightmares about that aspect of the day. Phineas did try his best, though. Before he left York, he sent a telegram to Chief Inspector McQuillan to warn him about what had happened. The police arrived at King's Cross looking for me, but it was too late. I was already in Fleet Street at that stage, waiting for Mr Bradford. The chief inspector caught up with me there. Phineas insisted Mary go back to his rooms with his servant as it would be safer while he dashed off to try to find me.'

'Ah yes, the cavalry!'

'I doubt Phineas would deign to crease his clothes by getting up on a horse!'

They both burst out laughing.

'On the contrary, I've ridden to hounds in his company. He's a fine horseman. But that's by the by,' Sarah said. 'In the end, it has all turned out for the best, Lucy. You returned the sapphires and tried your best to make up for Charlie's actions. Your generosity in reimbursing those men is humbling. It is unlikely I would do the same. Fools every last one of them. They should have investigated the scheme a little closer before handing over their money so easily. Some basic research would have shown it could only have been a fraud.'

'That's as maybe, but I have sympathy for them. Some, like Richard, may face financial ruin because of it. I can't help thinking of their innocent families. Charlie was complicit in a terrible crime,' Lucy said.

'Yes, you're right. And it is your decision, and I admire you for it,' Sarah said.

'Thank you.'

'What are your immediate plans?' Sarah asked.

'Once the trial is over, I'll travel for a while. London will be a circus with the Jubilee celebrations going on this summer. I'd rather be out of town.'

'And when you return will you settle in London? I do hope you will,' Sarah said.

'At the moment, escaping London is the only plan I have.'

FORTY-ONE

June 1887

Queen Victoria's Golden Jubilee would be memorable to most Londoners for its pomp and celebration, but Lucy spent the days leading up to it in the Old Bailey while an elderly judge passed judgment on her brother. She was the only family member present as neither her mother nor Sibylla had shown their faces for the entire trial. The sentence pronounced—five years' penal servitude—was harsh, sending a ripple of astonishment around the courtroom. Time had softened her anger, and Lucy had nothing but pity for Richard. Stoic though he had been throughout the trial, the mask suddenly slipped to be replaced by a wild look in his eyes. He scanned the court, no doubt looking for a sympathetic face. Swallowing hard, with her eyes welling up, she tried to convey her compassion from across the courtroom.

As she was one of the first witnesses called, it was possible for her to be present in court for Stone's testimony on the second day of the trial. He carried it off with his usual crisp delivery and authority, even managing to make the defence barrister stumble over his questions. How he managed to portray her part in it all without making her look foolish, she couldn't explain, but he did. When his time on the stand came to an end, he happened to glance up at her. She smiled tentatively, hoping it would communicate her gratitude, but she was too far away to judge his reaction. The following day, he arrived in court early, but took a seat at the furthest end of the public gallery. As there was a vacant seat beside her, she was disappointed and could only conclude he had not forgiven her.

Whatever her expectations had been regarding newspaper interest in the case, she was totally unprepared for the ferocious appetite the press had for scandal. Despite the worldwide frenzy the Queen's Jubilee had ignited, Fleet Street journalists were in their element with Richard's trial. They loved nothing better than the gentry falling off their pedestals. As a witness and sister to the star player in the sordid case of the Crown v Somerville, Lucy struggled to cope with the constant intrusion into her life. Mary, stalwart as ever, ensured no journalist infiltrated beyond the second-floor hallway where their suite was located, but as soon as she left the hotel, Lucy was ambushed without mercy. The hotel staff, at first sympathetic, grew increasingly irritated about it to the point the manager was obliged to 'have a quiet word' with Lucy. Hopefully, now the trial was over they would lose interest and turn their attention to Her Majesty's celebrations.

The Princess Hotel

It was the day of the Queen's procession to Westminster Abbey. Lucy closed the book which lay in her lap—she hadn't read one single page. She could settle to nothing, it seemed. Moments later, she heard the door open and Mary cough discreetly behind her.

'Ma'am, are you sure I can go? I'll stay if you need me here.'

Lucy smiled at the maid's expression, hovering between anxiety and excitement. She was dressed in her best coat and hat and looked very smart. 'No, Mary, there's no need. Please go and enjoy yourself.'

Mary's face lit up. 'Oh, I will, thank you. Have you seen the flags and the lovely pictures of her? It's all so grand. If I leave now, I may find a good spot and see her up close. Ned says he knows just the right place.'

'I wish you luck, Mary. It will be quite a crush out there. Everyone wants to catch a glimpse of her. The whole world has descended on the city.'

'Won't you come, ma'am? It would be a distraction,' Mary said, her eyes full of sympathy.

Lucy swallowed. 'Thank you, no. I don't have the stomach for the crowds. Besides, I have some letters to write before we leave for France tomorrow. Don't be late, we will have an early start. The train leaves Charing Cross at ten.'

An hour later as Lucy passed reception, the young man behind the desk called her name.

'There's a gentleman who wishes to see you. He's waiting in the small salon beside the restaurant,' the man said.

'It's not one of those annoying journalists?' Lucy asked. 'I do not wish to speak to them.'

'Definitely not, madam,' the receptionist said, looking put out. He turned away to deal with another guest. Wondering if it was McQuillan, she made her way down the corridor, humming softly under her breath.

But on entering the salon she was brought up short. It was Phineas. She stood rooted to the spot staring at him as if he were a ghost—the very last person she had expected to see. He was standing by the fireplace looking far too good to be real. Lucy opened her mouth to greet him but nothing happened. Her composure fled.

'Good morning, Mrs Lawrence,' he said, looking amused.

'Why are you here?' she blurted out after a few moments. *What was wrong with her*, she thought frantically, *and why had she asked such a stupid and ill-mannered question?*

'Forgive my intrusion, but I met Lady Sarah yesterday evening, and she informed me you're planning to go abroad.'

Lucy closed over the door and leaned against it. 'Yes, that's correct. Now the trial is over, I thought it best. We leave for France in the morning.'

He regarded her for several moments before he spoke. 'We parted on bad terms some months' ago, much to my regret. I'm anxious to rectify the situation.'

Lucy's heart lifted. 'We were both angry, Mr Stone; best forgotten,' she said, hoping he wasn't going to rake it all up again.

'Nonetheless, I recognise now I had no right to be quite so harsh. My only excuse is that I had come to care for you. What you did shook me to my core. As we followed you back to London, I feared the next time I would see you would be in Superintendent Henrick's care in Dufour Place.' He gave her a self-effacing smile which almost undid her. She wasn't sure how to respond as her stomach had just done an extraordinary somersault. 'I would like to offer my sincerest apologies,' he said, his voice low.

Lucy exhaled slowly. 'As do I, Phineas. I should have trusted you.'

'And I should have realised what a vulnerable state you were in. You had to endure shock after shock, and I was the harbinger of doom on far too many occasions. How you must have hated the sight of me.'

'No! I never felt that way.'

'That's a relief,' he said.

'In fact, I have missed our...' she trailed off, struggling for a suitable word.

'Business arrangement?' he supplied, with a quick smile.

'Yes, indeed. We made a bargain, didn't we? That night in Abbey Gardens? I asked you to keep me out of that mortuary and you succeeded.'

'Despite *your* best efforts, Mrs Lawrence,' he said.

'Can't you resist teasing me, Phineas? I'm trying to be serious,' Lucy admonished him.

He bowed. 'My apologies, again.'

But she couldn't refrain from a little bit of mischief. 'I hope my sleuthing success hasn't damaged your reputation?'

He laughed. 'It is in tatters, obviously. I doubt I will ever work again.'

Lucy tried to keep a straight face. 'You need not fear I'll try to usurp you in your chosen profession. I don't have enough courage for it. Mary, my maid, on the other hand...'

Phineas smiled. 'An intrepid young woman, certainly. You made a formidable team. However, you underestimate yourself. You have a sharp mind, when you choose to apply it. If you should ever decide to take it up, let me know. I may have use for a deputy.'

'You would rue the day! Though I'll admit, despite the danger and the terrifying moments, I enjoyed working out Charlie's puzzle and tracking down those jewels in the end. Have I honed my skills sufficiently?'

He spluttered. 'Except for the use of firearms.'

'Why so? I'm an excellent shot.'

'So you claimed before, yet your record is abysmal. Do I need to remind you of Lambeth or your attempt to deprive me of my valet?'

She pouted. 'Moving targets are particularly troublesome, you have to admit. But I almost winged Coffin Mike, and I did manage to hit poor George, although I couldn't even see him it was so dark.'

Stone raised his eyes to heaven. 'I rest my case.'

'Will George ever forgive me? I do hope there's no permanent damage.'

'Only to his pride.'

'I'm relieved to hear it. He was very good about it,' she said.

'George always is,' Stone said.

Lucy blushed, suddenly shy. Which was absurd.

To her dismay, Phineas picked up his cane and hat from the table. 'I'm sure you're busy with your preparations for travel, so I won't detain you, Mrs Lawrence,' he said.

Lucy was alarmed by his formality. She stood back from the door, but she was reluctant to let him go. 'I'll return in the spring,' she said in a flurry as he drew closer.

He paused, a hint of humour in his dark eyes. 'Bon voyage, Lucy,' he said sotto voce, leaning down and kissing her cheek. The door closed behind him with a click.

Lucy made it to the nearest chair and sat down rather quickly. He was giving her time, she realised, and hope of something at the end of it. She wasn't sure if it was professional or personal but that didn't matter for now.

It was then she spotted the parcel on the table. He must have forgotten it, she thought. But when she picked it up, she discovered it was addressed to her with the message: *A peace offering – Phin.*

What could it be? With frantic hands, she ripped the brown paper off and gasped. It was one of the miniature Abu Simbel paintings from his sitting room. One of his favourite Egyptian paintings.

'Well, I never!' she exclaimed, her eyes welling up with happy tears. Perhaps my adventures are not over after all, she thought with a grin.

A LETTER FROM THE AUTHOR

Dear reader,

Many thanks for reading *No Stone Unturned*, Book 1 in The Lucy Lawrence Mystery series. I hope you enjoyed Lucy's first sleuthing adventure. If you would like to hear more about new books, you can sign up here:

www.stormpublishing.co/pam-lecky

For news about my writing, upcoming deals and recommendations, you can check out my author newsletter:

subscribepage.io/jf9sWM

If you enjoyed this book and could spare a few moments to leave a review that would be hugely appreciated. Even a short review can make all the difference in encouraging a reader to discover my books for the first time. Thank you so much!

So, how did Lucy's story come about? I have always loved historical fiction, whether it be romance, crime or mystery, so I wanted to create a series combining all these elements. The initial idea for *No Stone Unturned* was the prodigal daughter returning home only to become embroiled in a crime by her less than loving family.

As a backdrop to the mystery and murder, I wanted to explore how a relatively young Victorian woman, with a strong personality and high intellect, would cope within the confines of a troubled marriage. Would she accept her lot or chafe at the bit? But, in Lucy's case, with no money and estranged from her family, she could not walk away. To do so would mean social ruin. However, when circumstances finally release her (her husband's sudden and suspicious death), she struggles to cope. Pretty much every man in her life so far has betrayed her on some level for their own ends. Her dilemma and her reaction to her circumstances gave me great scope to put poor Lucy through the mill, but there is the hint of a happier future ahead. I hope you will accompany me on Lucy's journey in *Footprints in the Sand* and *The Art of Deception,* for, as poor beleaguered Phin puts it – Lucy is always a magnet for trouble!

Thanks again for being part of my writing journey.

Pam Lecky

Linktr.ee/PamLecky
www.pamlecky.com

 x.com/pamlecky

 instagram.com/pamleckybooks

 linkedin.com/in/pam-lecky-b0b646109

ACKNOWLEDGEMENTS

Without the support of family and friends, this book, and indeed my entire writing journey, would not have been possible. My heartfelt thanks to you all, especially my husband, Conor, and my children, Stephen, Hazel and Adam. I am very grateful to my chief beta readers, Lorna and Terry O'Callaghan, who have read every draft and given me invaluable feedback.

Special gratitude is owed to my agent, Thérèse Coen, at Susanna Lea & Associates, London, whose belief in me, along with her sage advice, helped to bring Lucy Lawrence to life.

Producing a novel is a collaborative process, and I have been fortunate to have wonderful editors, copyeditors, proof-readers, and graphic designers working on this series. To Kathryn Taussig, my editor, and all the team at Storm Publishing, thanks for believing in this series and taking it to the next level. A massive thank you to Bernadette Kearns, my original editor – all the books in the Lucy Lawrence series benefited hugely from your input. Thanks are also due to Hilary Johnson for her initial assessment and advice on this book.

When it came to research, I received help from many quarters. But I would especially like to thank author Lee Jackson, who saved me hours of research by cleverly knowing that Dufour Place Mortuary (no longer in existence) was in the Vine Street Police District. His non-fiction books have pride of place on my research shelf.

The London Transport Museum provided information on the steam locomotives operating on the London Underground and even sent me the relevant timetables. Thanks so much for your invaluable help.

I am extremely grateful to have such loyal readers. For those of you who take the time to leave reviews, please know that I appreciate them beyond words. To the amazing book bloggers, book tour hosts and reviewers who have hosted me and my books over the years – thank you.

Last, but certainly not least, I am incredibly lucky to have a network of writer friends who keep me motivated (and grounded), especially Valerie Keogh, Jenny O'Brien, Fiona Cooke, Brook Allen and Tonya Murphy Mitchell. Special thanks to the members of the Historical Novel Society, RNA and Society of Authors Irish Chapters, and all the gang at the Coffee Pot Book Club.

Go raibh míle maith agat!

Pam Lecky
July 2024

Printed in Great Britain
by Amazon